MEANT FOR EACH OTHER

Electricity began to fill the small room. Neither could move. Neither could speak. They could only feel the current growing stronger between them.

Time seemed to stand still.

Then another flash of lightning brightened the sky outside. Another clap of thunder reverberated throughout the cottage. Suddenly, they moved toward each other.

Like a drowning man grasping for a lifeline, Payne reached for Chloe, hauling her close to him.

She could do nothing more than give herself to the sensations he ignited. Her life, her mind, her body, it seemed, were no longer her own. . . .

Also by Carol Jerina

Tropic Gold
The Tall Dark Alibi
Sweet Jeopardy
*A Golden Dream

*Available from
HarperPaperbacks

The BRIDEGROOM

CAROL JERINA

HarperPaperbacks
A Division of HarperCollinsPublishers

HarperPaperbacks *A Division of* HarperCollins*Publishers*
10 East 53rd Street, New York, N.Y. 10022

Copyright © 1993 by Carol Jerina
All rights reserved. No part of this book may be used or reproduced in any manner whatsoever without written permission of the publisher, except in the case of brief quotations embodied in critical articles and reviews. For information address HarperCollins*Publishers*,
10 East 53rd Street, New York, N.Y. 10022.

Cover illustration by Aleta Jenks

First printing: June 1993

Printed in the United States of America

HarperPaperbacks, HarperMonogram, and colophon are trademarks of HarperCollins*Publishers*

❖ 10 9 8 7 6 5 4 3 2 1

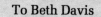

To Beth Davis

1

April, 1890

Sheltered by tall grasses, a patch of blue bonnets, and low-growing mesquite trees, two observers lay on their bellies at the top of a slight hill, watching the large group of merrymakers below them. They heard strains of music carried up the hill by a gentle breeze—a primitive-sounding combination of squeeze-box, harmonica, banjo, and guitar. People mingled in the yard of the sprawling one-story house, some dancing, some conversing with friends, others partaking of the wide array of food laid out on two long tables. A whole cow and pig roasted on spits over open fires.

Blodgett, who surpassed his companion by at least a score of years, seemed to wear with inherent pride the foul stench and grime of his recent lodgings, the livery stable in town. He coughed and wiped from his bewhiskered chin what his tongue couldn't reach with a stubby, dirt-covered finger. A stream of brown tobacco juice and spittle trickled down from the corner of his mouth.

"Which one be him, Cap'n?" Blodgett asked, squinting. He often boasted, when plied with spirits, that his raspy voice was the result of one of his close brushes with a British hangman's noose. A grave, nearly deadly case of mistaken identity, as he told it. "Me old eyes don't see so good these days. Least, not at this distance."

The younger and far cleaner of the two observers remained silent as he continued to look through his spyglass. He couldn't tear his gaze away from the scene below, especially one couple in particular. The longer he looked, the more bile he felt rise up in his throat, produced by long-suppressed feelings of need, of envy, of self-pity, of deprivation, and of outright hatred. They churned into a sour mixture in his belly.

The man he observed below had taken everything that had rightfully belonged to him—first his father, then his mother, but most painful of all, his very birthright. The man had no right to look so happy, so at ease, so prosperous. Furthermore, he had no right to look so damn much like him. Blast the blackguard straight to hell.

With a jerky movement of his hand, he shifted the spyglass slightly and focused on the tall, voluptuous young beauty who stood beside the object of his rage. With one look at her, despite the anger that seemed to surge through him unabated, he felt a hard jolt of awareness. Creamy, almost translucent skin covered her face and throat. Though he couldn't see the color of her eyes, he was willing to wager that they were blue—so clear a blue that they probably vied with the cloudless sky above him. And her lips, wide and succulent, sent tremors of recognizable lust through his body.

His fingers itched to sift through the blond hair that cascaded in loose curls down to her shoulders and the modestly dipping neckline of her gingham-checked dress. Her waist was so small beneath her full, ripe bosom that he felt certain he could span it with both hands. She was a decidedly delectable piece.

When she turned her head and smiled up at the man beside her, his twin, he saw a deep dimple appear in her cheek. Without warning, his momentary captivation with her loveliness vanished, and his rage returned tenfold.

He snapped the spyglass shut and turned his dark gaze on Blodgett. In a voice that could on the right occasion be as smooth as velvet and on the wrong occasion as sharp as the blade of a British cutlass, he said, "The tall one is my brother."

"Which tall one is that, Cap'n? They're all as big as giants down there."

"The tall one next to the girl in pink."

"Girl?" With a hungry gleam in his eye, Blodgett grabbed the spyglass, pulled it open, and began searching the crowd. "Aye, I see her. She's right comely, ain't she, Cap'n? Your brother's done right well for himself."

"It appears that way." Remembering the expression of adoration on the young woman's face as she had looked at his brother, he rose with quick stealthiness and started down the hill to the tree where they had tethered their horses earlier.

Blodgett followed reluctantly. "What you reckon's going on?"

"I wouldn't know." Nor did he care.

"But all them people down there—they be your kin, or somethin'?"

"No, they're not all my kin. Just the one who looks like me. He's all the family I have left, now that my father's dead."

"Aye, aye. But the rest of them, who are they?"

"Neighbors, I suspect. Friends, business acquaintances, the usual lot." He extracted a folded piece of paper from his coat pocket. "When you get back to town, take this to the telegraph office. Send it under your name, not mine."

"This goin' to that bloke up in Dallas?"

"Yes. He needs to know that I've met my family and that our plan is running smoothly."

Without reading it, Blodgett stuffed the note in his trousers pocket. Then he untied his horse's reins from a low-hanging tree limb and let out a raspy cackle. "They're in for a right surprise, that lot down there at the house."

"How is that?"

"They see you ridin' up, they're all likely to fall dead of fright."

"I doubt that," said the younger man as he mounted his horse. "They're so used to my brother's face, seeing mine shouldn't be so startling to them. As to the purpose of such a large gathering, I imagine they're celebrating some local event or other, or some sort of Texas holiday."

"No, I think not. When I was in town, going about your business, I didn't hear no one speak of such a thing. And I heard a good deal, as you recall."

"Well, the reason doesn't matter. But since they've gone to so much trouble to prepare a fatted calf, I may as well go down and help them partake of it."

Blodgett cackled again. "Partake of the calf, Cap'n? Or that high-spirited filly in pink we saw?"

The young man smiled. "I believe you told me that my brother was currently courting a young woman named Patience?"

"Aye. Patience Chloe. Or was it Chloe Patience? A right odd name, whichever it was."

"Blodgett, if the woman in pink is linked in some way with my brother, and her name is indeed Patience, I doubt very much that she's spirited. On the whole, she looked quite docile to me. And even if she isn't as submissive as she appears, I'm sure I can handle her."

Recalling his young companion's many past exploits with the women in London—women from all walks of life, from the lowest shop girl to the highest ladies of nobility—Blodgett nodded. "Aye, I'll wager you can."

Chloe stood next to Prescott, smiling as she exchanged small pleasantries with her guests. The warm weight of Prescott's hand on her waist as he leaned close to whisper a comment in her ear felt more comforting than she cared to admit. Under ordinary circumstances she liked being with people— talking with them, listening to what they had to say— but today was different. There were far too many guests present for her to feel comfortable, let alone be able to tolerate them all at one time.

The women seemed intent on gabbing about the most frivolous of topics, while the men had done nothing all evening but offer looks of condolence to Prescott. For heaven's sake, he was only marrying her. He wasn't being sent to prison for horse theft.

Chloe decided not to dwell on her present uneasiness. The evening wouldn't last forever. In a few hours the guests would all be gone, either returning to their own ranches a short distance away or making the one-hour ride back to their homes in Waco.

In a few hours, she and Prescott could bid them all a safe journey and then resume their normal, happy, uneventful way of life. She wouldn't have to smile and pretend that she enjoyed listening to all the women's chatter, the constant exchange of pickling or pie recipes, or the latest fashions from Godey's or Worth they had seen at the dressmaker's shop in town. Best of all, once they were gone, she could take off the blasted corset that was about to choke her to death and relegate it to the bottom of her clothes cupboard, where it rightfully belonged. Dressing and acting like a lady, she decided, were very painful bores.

Inhaling as deeply as her constrictive undergarment would allow, Chloe willed herself to relax. Tonight she would not let anything or anyone alter her present good mood. She was going to marry the man she had always wanted, had always loved, and that was all that mattered.

Looking away from the guests around her and focusing her gaze on the gently rolling hillside that lay to the east, she saw a rider appear. Even at such a distance, she could tell that he was a tall man, one who sat very erect in his saddle. Then she noticed that he wore no hat, which struck her as very odd. All Texans wore hats—ranch-owners, ranch hands, doctors, lawyers, politicians down in Austin, even businessmen and shopkeepers in town. No one in his right mind would be caught outdoors in Texas without the proper head covering.

As he rode closer, she found herself admiring the way he handled his horse, guiding it with a steady hand down the inclined road toward the house. It was not an easy feat, considering that just two days ago they'd had a rain so hard, with hail and driving winds, that it had left the road full of holes. There were times when she had trouble staying mounted on her own horse after a rain such as that, and she'd been riding for almost all of her eighteen years.

When she noticed the newcomer's clothes, she realized just why he seemed so odd, so out of place. During her brief stint a year ago at Miss Ponsonby's School for Young Ladies in Austin, she had learned a thing or two about foreign fashions. Of course, she had also learned how to walk and talk and behave properly in society, how to serve tea, how to plan menus and large dinner parties, and how to run a household, but the lessons on foreign people and their customs had been the most interesting to her. And this man was definitely a foreigner. Even at a distance, she could tell that his clothes were more European in cut and design than Western American.

If his clothes weren't proof enough of that, his lack of facial hair was. Unlike Prescott and most of the other men present, who sported mustaches, beards, and muttonchop sideburns, the stranger's face was smoothly shaven. The stranger's face was . . .

Chloe inhaled sharply as the newcomer reined his horse to a stop near the far edge of the front porch.

Prescott heard her gasp and turned to look at her with a trio of lines marring his brow. "What's the matter, sugar? Your corset stays so tight you can't catch your breath?"

Embarrassed by Prescott's audacious and most ungentlemanly remark, Chloe jabbed an elbow into the arm that circled her waist, making him loosen his hold on her. "Keep your voice down. There's nothing wrong with my corset stays. It's him." Then, in a very unladylike fashion, she pointed a finger in the direction of the porch and the stranger who was climbing down from his horse.

"Who?" Prescott looked over her head and followed the direction of her gaze. When he caught sight of the newcomer he, too, inhaled a deep breath. "Jesus Christ. Payne!"

Chloe stared up at Prescott in confusion. "Payne?"

Prescott didn't bother to explain, nor did he bother to apologize as he began to push his way through the crowd that surrounded them. As soon as he cleared the throng, he broke into a run, a loud yell erupting from the depths of his lungs.

All conversation ceased, and the music stopped as every head in the front yard turned to see what had caused their host to shout.

"Good God Almighty," Prescott said, standing with his hands on his brother's shoulders, staring at him, studying each minute detail about him, especially his prosperous-looking appearance. "I'd know that face of yours anywhere. Damned if it ain't just like looking in a mirror."

"Not quite," Payne said. "I shaved this morning."

With a grin, Prescott rubbed his bewhiskered cheek. "Yeah, well, usually I've got more important things on my mind than shaving. Like running this ranch. Jesus, it's good to see you."

Without preamble, Prescott grabbed his brother again, this time enveloping him in a hug so tight that Payne felt his air supply constrict in his chest.

A hushed wave of comments from the guests began to roll through the late afternoon air as Chloe approached Prescott and the newcomer he embraced. She knew from experience that her fiancé could be affectionate under the right circumstances, but that he, like most men, drew the line at public displays of affection with members of his own gender. And of course the stranger had to be more than a mere acquaintance. He looked just like him!

Hostility surged through Payne as he withstood his brother's unexpected welcome and the stares of all the onlookers. How could one man greet another with such warmth when he knew so little about him? Probably quite easily, he decided, if that man were a fraud. And if Prescott was a fraud, then they had more in common than their looks, for he was a fraud, too. After all, he had come to America, to this ranch in Texas, under fraudulent circumstances. He was here to defraud his own brother.

Realizing that he couldn't just stand there without showing some sign of happiness at a reunion with his long-estranged brother, Payne hugged Prescott in return. Not to do so might arouse Prescott's suspicions and make him wonder why Payne had come. There could be none of that. Suspicion from anyone at this stage could prove disastrous. But hugging his much brawnier brother proved to be a difficult task.

Finally Prescott released him, stepping back to study Payne again. Shaking his head, he said, "All this time, I knew I had a twin who might look something like me, but I didn't know how much alike we were until now."

Only on the surface, dear brother, Payne thought. *Only on the surface.*

"How long have you been here?" Prescott asked.

"Not long." In truth, he'd been in Texas for almost a month; first in Galveston, where his ship had landed, then in Dallas, where he'd met with a certain Mr. Wyngate, and more recently, in a lonely hotel room in Waco, where, with the help of Blodgett, he'd put his and Wyngate's plan into action. "The voyage from London was quite tiring."

"Yeah, I bet it was."

"I needed to spend a few days recuperating before I began the final leg of my journey here."

Prescott continued to grin. "Well, you're home now, that's all that matters."

"Yes, home." Payne looked past Prescott to the house behind them.

Built of wood and native stone, it spanned a good seventy feet or more across the front and easily that much along the side. Curtains fluttered through the tall open windows that marched eight abreast across the wide porch. A pair of mismatched, weathered rocking chairs graced either side of the double-wide entryway. Trees, newly budding, soared high overhead, promising a cool shade in the hot summer months.

In spite of the fact that it looked inviting and comfortable, a place that any man would gladly call home, Payne hated it. This place, the house and the very land on which it stood, had meant more to his father than he or his mother had. Knowing that, he could feel nothing but animosity toward it.

Mistaking the expression on Payne's face for one

of deep admiration, Prescott slapped a hand across his shoulder. "It's something, isn't it?"

Payne cleared his throat, hoping to sound calm rather than enraged. "Yes, it is."

"You know it's been in the family for over fifty years, don't you?"

"No, I didn't."

"Well, it has. Our grandpappy, Camden Trefarrow, built it for his wife, Mary Frances. A real man, our grandpappy was. That's not to say that Grandma wasn't a real woman, 'cause she was. She could really hold her own. Why, I could spend hours telling you stories about those two and still not tell 'em all. They were something, those two. Raised a house full of kids and a herd of the finest cows this side of the Mississippi." Prescott shook his head sadly. "Now they're resting next to each other in the cemetery in town."

What about our father? Payne wondered angrily. *What about the bastard who stole my life and our mother's?* He could only hope that the man burned in hell.

"Enough about them," Prescott said. "Enough about the house, too. I'll take you inside and show you around the old place after a while. Right now, though, I'd better introduce you to all the folks. They're a right nice bunch of people." He leaned closer and added, "Just try to keep that in mind if they start getting too nosy."

With one hand resting on his brother's shoulder, he turned around and yelled. "Everybody! I want y'all to meet my brother, Payne. He's come here all the way from London, England. Y'all be sure and make him feel real welcome now, y'hear?"

The curious crowd who had been standing at a polite distance, muttering hushed speculations among themselves, began to move forward. At the forefront of the human tide marched Chloe.

"Prescott?" she said, smiling sweetly. "Don't you think you should introduce me first?"

"You're right, sugar, I should. Come on over here." His grin grew boyish as he stepped away from Payne and wrapped a possessive arm around her waist.

Though Chloe smiled she stiffened inwardly. She would have to inform Prescott later, when they were alone, that a gentleman did not fondle a lady in such a manner when they were in public. The privacy of one's home was the only appropriate place for such displays. Nor did gentlemen call their womenfolk endearments like "sugar." "Darling" or "my dear," but never "sugar"; it was far too common.

"Chloe, my brother, Payne. Payne, my little bride-to-be, Chloe."

Little? Payne wondered. How sweet, but how totally wrong. She wasn't little, she couldn't be. Even without shoes, she was almost as tall as Prescott.

"Chloe?" Payne extended his hand to take hers, bending at the waist to kiss her fingers. He felt her cool hand tighten momentarily around his and then stiffen as she pulled it away. He gazed into her eyes and saw a startled look in them.

"Chloe Patience Bliss," Prescott said. " 'Course, she'll be changing the Bliss to Trefarrow come June. That's when she'll have officially hog-tied and branded me."

Chloe jerked her head around and gave her fiancé a direct look. "Prescott, you must learn to mind your tongue."

Payne took note of how her voice changed from one that dripped with honey to one with a hint of tartness. Obviously, the lady wasn't pleased.

"Ladies," she went on, "do not brand their men, as you well know. They certainly don't hog-tie them either."

Prescott lowered his head, his face suffused with color. Whether the color came from embarrassment or irritation, Payne couldn't say. He only knew that it was a good thing his brother's fiancé answered to the name of Chloe and not Patience, because the latter didn't suit her at all.

"I was just joshing, sugar," Prescott said. "I didn't mean no disrespect."

"I know, Prescott," Chloe said. "But you must try and curb the use of such colorful metaphors. It isn't fitting, especially when we're in public."

"Next time, I'll watch myself."

"See that you do."

Chloe's attitude toward his brother, Payne realized, was more like a mother scolding her recalcitrant child than a young woman correcting her intended. An intended, furthermore, who surpassed her by at least a dozen years.

"Chloe," Payne said, recapturing her full attention. "What a very unusual name, if you don't mind my saying so. I don't believe I've ever actually met a woman named Chloe before."

"If you had," Prescott said, pulling his bride-to-be closer to his side, "it's a safe bet she wouldn't have been anything like this little lady here. No sirree, my Chloe's one in a million."

"No, I'm not," Chloe said, a blush tinting her pale cheeks.

"Yes, you are. I don't know of any other girl in these parts who'd take her own self off to school the way you did."

No wonder she behaved the way she did, Payne thought. Too much education would turn any woman into a bloody bluestocking. He knew that much from past experience. "You sent yourself to school?" he asked.

"Darn tootin', she did," Prescott said, answering for Chloe. "She went down to one of the most high-falutin' schools in Austin and spent a whole year learning to become a lady. Ain't that something?"

"Ah, a finishing school," Payne said. "I thought perhaps you had gone away to a university."

"Actually, the only reason I went at all was that I wanted you to be proud of me, Prescott."

Proud or daunted, Payne wondered. In his opinion, a termagant was still a termagant, no matter how pretty she was. But he'd learned through experience that termagants were just as susceptible to flattery as any other woman. Perhaps a bit more difficult to seduce, but attainable nonetheless.

"I am," Prescott said. "I'm very proud of you."

"You must not have had to study very hard," Payne said, smiling as he looked into Chloe's eyes. They weren't the clear sky-blue that he had presumed earlier, but a stormy blue-gray, the irises ringed in a dark charcoal color. If a man weren't careful, he might find himself drowning in them.

Chloe accepted the compliment with a lowered gaze. "You're too kind, Mr. Trefarrow."

"Payne," he said. "If we're to be brother and sister soon, as Prescott says, you must call me Payne."

"Thank you . . . Payne."

"And where do you live, Chloe?"

"Here."

"You mean, in the Waco area?"

"No, I live here at the ranch."

"Yeah," Prescott said, "she's been one of the family ever since her ma and pa died. How long ago was that, sugar? Eight, nine years?"

"Ten," she said. "I was eight at the time, remember?"

Prescott nodded. "That's right. You were the tallest, skinniest eight-year-old around these parts. Always getting in the way. My way, more than anyone else's it seemed."

"Prescott, I doubt your brother is in any mood to listen to stories of my innocent youthful exuberances," she said.

"I don't mind," Payne said. "I don't mind at all."

"Well, I do," she said. "As much as I know you two would like to stand here and catch up on old times, we've got a lot of guests who are anxious to meet Payne. Where are your bags? I'll have one of the hands take them inside."

"Don't bother. I'll get them later," Payne said.

"All right. Prescott, why don't you take your brother over and introduce him to the mayor? I believe I saw him over by the cooking pit with John Mittelkopf."

"John's the banker," Prescott said to Payne. "A good man to get to know these days, especially if you're a rancher. The mayor's name is Tom Whaylon. Henry Johnson's the family lawyer, another man you'll want to get to know." He began to escort Payne away but then stopped and looked back at Chloe. "You coming with us?"

"No, I thought I'd go in the house and check up on

Aunt Emmaline. She's been in there quite a while, missing all the fun out here. She might need some help."

Chloe waited until Prescott and his newly found brother had wandered off into the chattering crowd and then slowly climbed the front porch steps. Once inside the house, she closed the door behind her and leaned against the wood panel, her heart hammering in her chest.

Something about Payne unsettled her, but she didn't know what. He hadn't said or done anything improper. In the short time they had conversed, he'd behaved like a complete gentleman. But the look in his eyes and the warm touch of his fingers as they encircled her hand hadn't felt gentlemanly at all. In fact, they had filled her with distinct unease.

She knew she couldn't explain the reason for her impressions but she had felt them all too clearly. He'd acted far too familiar, gazed at her far too aggressively, too intimately, as though he knew her, when he really didn't at all. How could he? They had just met. But her instincts led her to assume that he was up to something—something no good.

A moment later, after composing herself, Chloe walked the length of the house to the kitchen at the rear. There she found Aunt Emmaline standing at the worktable, humming to herself as she put the finishing touches on a large cake.

"How's the party going, sugar? Everybody getting enough to eat?"

"At the rate everyone's eating, they'll probably never be hungry again. You fixed too much food, Aunt Em."

"Better to fix too much than not enough, that's what I always say."

"This cake is beautiful." Chloe moved across to the middle-aged woman and wrapped her arms around her stout waist. "It's a shame we have to eat it."

"Well, of course you have to eat it, child. That's what an engagement cake is for. Lands agoshen, it'd go to waste if you just stood around and looked at it. After a while, it wouldn't be fit to feed the hogs."

"But to go to so much trouble to make something so pretty, and then destroy it by cutting it all to bits."

"It wasn't any trouble. A cake's a cake; nothing more. Besides, I was happy to do it. Hell's bells, it's not every day two of my young'uns decide to get themselves married to each other."

Emmaline McCardie considered almost everyone younger than herself her 'young'uns,' and she wasn't alone in this belief. Most of the ranch hands loved her maternal brand of pampering. Chloe was no different. When her own mother had died, Emmaline had stepped in and filled the position with little or no effort at all.

She'd done the same with Prescott, too. Then again, Prescott had never had a real mother so he'd never known the heartbreak of losing one. He'd only had his father.

Chloe stepped away from Emmaline, dipped her finger into the bowl of sweet icing, and licked it off. "Payne's here."

"What's that, dear?"

"I said Payne's here. He rode up a few minutes ago."

"Who's Pay—" Emmaline broke off abruptly and gasped. The broad-bladed icing knife slipped from her fingers and clattered on the edge of the china cake plate. "Lord have mercy! Prescott's brother Payne? His twin?"

Chloe nodded.

Emmaline touched her chest with one hand and groped behind her for a chair with the other. "My sweet Lord."

Concerned that she might be ill, Chloe rushed to her side. "Are you all right?"

"Who, me? Lord, yes! I'm just fine. Or I will be, as soon as I catch my breath."

"Are you sure?"

"Sure, I'm sure. There's nothing wrong with me. Just a little startled is all, hearing that Garrett's boy has come home. Been cooking all day, too. That's bound to have something to do with it. It gets mighty hot in here, and it must've finally got to me."

"First thing tomorrow morning, I'll tell Prescott to put some more windows in here."

"You'll do no such thing. You put in too many windows in this room and I'll be freezing myself to death come next wintertime. You just leave my kitchen the way it is." Emmaline shook her gray head. "Payne's home. I can't believe it."

"I can't believe it, either," Chloe said. "I saw him riding up before anyone else did."

"Does he look anything like Prescott? Garrett always said he could never tell them apart. But that was way back, when they were just babies. Everybody knows twins often grow up to look different."

"Well, they're not babies now. They're both grown men, Aunt Em. I suppose if Prescott didn't have a beard and that broken nose of his, they'd be as alike as two peas in a pod."

"Lord a-mercy."

"Their hair color is about the same, too. Prescott's is just a shade or two lighter. They've got the same eyes, the same chin . . . I tell you, it's amazing."

"Is he still sickly?"

"Who, Payne?"

Emmaline nodded.

"I don't know," Chloe said. "He certainly looked healthy enough to me."

"Oh, I hope he is. You know, that's why Garrett left him behind in England."

"No, I didn't." Chloe knew very little of Prescott's father, Garrett Trefarrow. He'd been a good, decent man, and had always treated her lovingly, as he would have treated a daughter or a favorite niece, but he'd never once shared his past with her. His reasons for leaving his wife and other son in England had always been a mystery to her.

"Well, that's the reason, all right," Emmaline said. "He would have brought both of those babies home with him, where they belonged, leaving only that wife of his behind with her folks, but he was afraid Payne wouldn't survive the ocean voyage."

"What was his problem? Payne's, I mean."

"I don't rightly know, to tell you the truth," Emmaline said, standing up. "All I know is what Garrett told me when he got here with Prescott. I'll never forget that day as long as I live. He walked up to me—we were all standing on the porch when he rode up. He put Prescott in my arms and told me to take care of him, and that he could only pray that his other boy fared as well. I tell you, it nearly broke my heart. He had tears in his eyes when he said it. It's one of the few times I ever saw my brother cry."

Chloe had never seen Garrett Trefarrow cry

either, but she had heard him, late at night, when the rest of the house was asleep. She could remember lying in her bed and hearing the muffled sobs that came from Garrett's room across the hall.

Once, she'd even crawled out of bed and gone to him, wanting to comfort him as he'd comforted her so many times after her parents had died. She'd only made it as far as his door, though. Even at the age of eight, she'd somehow sensed that to intrude on his private misery would cause him embarrassment, and she loved him too much to do that.

Aunt Em and Prescott had found her there the next morning, curled up on the floor, fast asleep. They had never asked her why she'd left her bed, and she had never offered to explain.

"Enough about the past, it's dead and buried," Emmaline said, wiping her hands on her apron. "We've got a herd of guests waiting outside for us to feed them. Come on, dear. You bring that extra pitcher of lemonade and I'll carry the cake."

2

The sounds of early evening began to descend on the laughter and music. Crickets chirped in the tall grasses nearby, and cicadas buzzed loudly overhead in the trees. Off in the distance, Payne heard the faint cooing of a dove, a very calming sound, he thought.

As he stood off by himself, secluded under a tall tree, he watched the sun slowly set in the west. One minute the sky was a lovely blue, streaked with vibrant shades of pink and magenta, and the next, darkness began to fall. He'd never seen anything like it—not in England, where the tall buildings of London or the bad weather in the country shielded such a sight. Nor at sea, where he'd spent most of his evenings in the gambling salon with other men.

"Julio, get some of the boys to light these lanterns, would you please?"

"Si, señora."

Hearing the interchange above the sounds of the

crowd, Payne turned and saw a bowlegged man in a wide sombrero dash across the yard toward a large building near the barn. The woman who had given the order to him was descending the front porch steps. In the meager light of dusk, Payne could see that she was stout of build, somewhat stern of feature, and yet oddly maternal as well.

Following the woman and bearing a heavy-looking glass pitcher was his brother's fiancée, Chloe. How presumptuous he had been to assume that he could easily handle the likes of her. In the few minutes they had spoken, he'd gotten the distinct impression that Chloe was one young woman who knew her own mind well enough not to let anything or anyone deter her from the course she had set for herself. Her plans obviously involved his brother, a man she took such great delight in dominating, a man she supposedly loved.

For his part, Payne didn't believe love really existed. It was merely an illusion, a temporary aberration that disguised truer motives like lust and greed. Great families and empires had fallen and men of rank and stature had been transformed into blithering dolts, all because of the silly notion of love. Well, Prescott and his "little bride-to-be," as he had called her, could have all the love they wanted, and with his blessing. Love would never touch Payne, and in the end he would be a better man for it.

"Never," he said aloud.

"What was that?"

Turning sharply, Payne saw Prescott coming up behind him.

"The sunset," he said. "I've never seen anything like it."

"Yeah, real pretty, wasn't it?"

"Yes, it was."

"You ought to see some of the sunsets out around Abilene, about three hundred miles west of here. I tell you, seeing a sunset out there will send chills up your spine." Prescott shook his head. "Say, have you had anything to eat yet? I got so busy introducing you around and talking to folks, I plumb forgot to offer you any food. Aunt Em would skin me alive if she found out. She's almost as bad as Chloe about making sure a man minds his manners."

"Then your skin is safe. I've eaten."

"Good, good. Did you try some of that beef?"

Thinking of the whole cow roasting over an open fiery pit, Payne nearly cringed. "Yes, I did. I don't think I've ever eaten anything quite like it before."

"Coming from England, you couldn't have. That's honest-to-God Texas beef, raised right here on the Triple T."

"Triple T?"

"Yeah, the ranch," Prescott said. "This ranch. You mean, you didn't know the name?"

"No, I'm afraid I didn't."

"Hmm. I'm surprised the lawyer didn't tell you."

"What lawyer?"

"The one who told you about Papa dying and all."

"Oh, yes, him." In truth, Payne had never been contacted by a lawyer. Wyngate had informed him of his father's untimely demise. To avoid the matter, he needed to change the subject. "Now that I think about it, I don't know why I should have thought it odd that you Texans should choose to name your properties. We name ours in England. We have done so for centuries."

"You got much land back there? I mean, a prosperous-looking man like yourself is bound to have a couple of thousand acres or so."

"Then my looks, I'm sorry to inform you, are quite deceiving. I have no acreage. I have no estate, no country house, no hunting lodge—nothing at all of that nature."

"Nothing?" Prescott couldn't ignore his disappointment. If his brother had no land, then there was a good chance he had no money, either. And if Payne had no money, then he would be no help at all.

Prescott needed cash badly, and the sooner he got it the better. He had loans coming due the first of July, big loans. His brother showing up this way, out of the blue, looking like an affluent banker from Dallas, had seemed like a godsend. But if he had no land, well, that shed a whole different light on the matter.

"All I have is a small house in London," Payne said.

Prescott forced himself to relax. Aunt Em had always told him to not jump to conclusions so quickly, but to go on his first impressions. After all, the English were supposed to be a very understated bunch of folks who didn't like to boast or brag about their possessions or accomplishments. Keeping that in mind, he figured there was a better than even chance that Payne's "small house" was probably the size of Buckingham Palace. Which all boiled down to the fact that Payne had to have money, and lots of it, he hoped.

But Prescott knew he couldn't discuss finances, or his own lack of them, right away. It wouldn't be fitting, since Payne had just arrived. He would have to wait until the time was right to broach the subject with him and reveal his own predicament. Surely Payne wouldn't deny aid to his own flesh and blood.

Suddenly, a thought occurred to him. "I was talking to Henry earlier," he said.

"Henry? Oh, the family lawyer?"

Prescott nodded.

"Yes, I met him," Payne said. "He seemed an amiable enough fellow."

"He is. You won't find a nicer, more honest man than Henry Johnson. 'Sides which, he's a damn good lawyer, too. Been handling the Triple T's legal matters for the last twenty years. He said something about the two of us meeting him in town one day so we can tend to Papa's will."

Payne was surprised that Prescott had brought up the matter of their joint inheritance instead of waiting for Payne to mention it. "Tend to it?"

"Yeah. Now that you're here, Henry can finally read it. It was Papa's wish that both of us be present for the reading. We were his only heirs, you know."

"I had assumed that, of course, but I wasn't certain."

"Papa didn't have anyone else to leave anything to. Outside of giving Aunt Em a home here at the ranch for the rest of her life, and a few minor bequests that don't really add up to a hill of beans, he left the bulk of his estate to the two of us."

"He never remarried?"

"No, he never did." Prescott gazed down at the toe of his boot and dragged it in the dirt. Though he hated to give voice to the question that ran through his mind, he was far too curious to keep silent. He had to find out. "What about Mother? Did she ever get married again?"

Payne felt an unwanted surge of regret and remorse at the thought of the beautiful woman who had been their mother. With so many unmarried women to chose from, no decent man in England would have wanted someone so frail and unstable who would further complicate things by being divorced.

"No," Payne said, "she never remarried, either."

"I always wondered."

"She couldn't," Payne said. "I'm not sure how you Americans feel about it, but in England, a divorced woman of any social rank is treated like a leper. And a divorced woman who does flaunt convention and remarries becomes an outright whore in the eyes of society."

"Same here. Seems to me they get a much better deal if their husbands just up and die. That ain't right either, is it? I mean, a marriage goes bad, and both parties have to suffer for it. But if one just ups and dies, you can pretty much do what you like and nobody raises an eyebrow." Prescott broke off, feeling uneasy discussing the subject of divorce when his own marriage to Chloe was so close at hand. "What do you say you and me get back to the party? They're fixing to start dancing again, and there's somebody special over yonder I think you ought to meet before we wear out our legs."

"Another banker or lawyer or man of equal influence?"

Prescott laughed. "No, she's not a banker or a lawyer, but she is influential. Around here, leastways."

"She?"

"Our Aunt Emmaline. Papa's older sister."

Payne couldn't hide his surprise. He had an aunt?

"She calls herself a housekeeper," Prescott said, "but I ought to warn you that she's a hell of lot more than that. Truth is, she's been the undisputed ruler of this ranch and everybody on it ever since Grandma died. Nothing happens around here that she doesn't know about or approve of. And if she doesn't approve, it doesn't happen. It's as simple as that."

"She sounds a good deal like our Queen Victoria."

"Queen Emmaline?" Prescott laughed. "Now that's a thought. I don't reckon she'd cotton to the title, though. She'd think it was too uppity."

They found Aunt Em overseeing the placement of the lanterns around the darkening yard. Many ranch hands were scurrying about, some climbing trees to hang the coal-oil lamps on bare branches while others held the ladders on which they stood.

"A little higher," she told one black man. "Get it away from those new leaves. We don't want to burn the tree down, just light the yard a bit."

"Like this, Miss Emmaline?"

"That's perfect, George. Just perfect. Now climb on down from there and go get you a piece of my cake."

"I'm more partial to pie than cake, ma'am," the man said, grinning deviously as he descended the ladder.

"Well then, have a piece of that, too." She gave a dismissive wave of her hand. "In fact, eat all you want—you and the rest of the men. I'd say you've earned it. Besides, it looks like everybody else has just about stuffed themselves silly, and I don't like fooling with what's left over."

"Yes, ma'am."

"Aunt Em?"

Hearing her name, Emmaline turned. She caught sight of Prescott first, then she noticed the man who stepped up behind him. For a moment, she could do nothing but let her gaze dart back and forth between the two of them. Then slowly, tears began to well up in her eyes.

"Payne." She opened her arms wide and engulfed him in a warm hug.

Though at first reluctant, Payne soon found himself returning her embrace. He knew he would curse himself later for being so weak, but he couldn't control his emotions now. This must be how it felt to be part of a family, a real family, one that he'd wanted so badly as a child. To be welcomed without reservation or hesitation, to be treated as an equal, as someone of importance in the familial circle. It was almost more than he could bear.

"Aunt Em," he said, honest emotion thick in his voice.

"You're so much like your daddy," she said. "Both of you boys are. It's like having him back again, seeing the two of you side by side this way."

Her words, spoken so innocently, sent an icy curtain of mistrust over Payne's heart. To be compared to the man who had fathered him was the ultimate insult to him.

"But he's not with us anymore," Emmaline said, wiping a hand across her damp cheeks. "He hasn't been for nearly a year now, but I do still miss him so."

"So do we, Aunt Em," Prescott said, winding an arm around her shoulder. "All of us miss him."

Payne kept silent. To speak ill of his deceased father now would not only be insensitive, it would jeopardize his plan. The day would come, though, when he could reveal to the world how he truly felt about his father, his bastard of a sire.

The makeshift orchestra, composed of ranch hands

who could pick out a semblance of a tune on their musical instruments, began to play a waltz. Prescott dropped his arm from his aunt's shoulder and craned his neck to search the crowd.

"Where's Chloe?" he asked. "She made me promise to dance with her after sundown."

"She's around here someplace," Emmaline said. "You might check over near the porch. I saw her standing with the Campbell girls a minute ago."

Prescott released an audible groan. "Oh no, not them."

"Now, don't go on that way. They're nice girls."

"Nice? The three of them are nothing but a bunch of jabbering flibbertigibbets."

"Maybe so, but they're Chloe's friends, so you'd best be nice to them while they're here, or she'll be upset. And you don't want that, do you?"

One corner of Prescott's mouth curled in a sneer. "'Course not. I wouldn't dream of it."

"Run on, then," Emmaline said. "You, too, Payne. Grab yourself a girl and dance a lick or two. Have some fun."

"Come on, son," Prescott said, grabbing Payne's arm. "We may as well get you baptized right and proper."

"Baptized?"

"Yeah, like the preacher says—baptized in flames. At least, that's what our preacher says. I wouldn't know about anyone else's." He leaned close to Payne and lowered his voice. "See, I can't dance worth a damn. Neither can any other man here, but if me and the rest have to suffer through it 'cause it's what our womenfolk want, I don't see why you should be spared."

Baptized in flames? It all sounded too religious to him.

They found Chloe with the three sisters who, save for a slight variance in heights, could have passed for identical triplets. They all wore yellow calico dresses with sashes around the waist, bows in the back, and an inordinate amount of ruffles around the hem. They even had wilting flowers pinned in the same spot in their mousy brown hair. Looking as they did, they would never be accepted by London's so-called polite society, Payne thought. Even the street tarts in Whitechapel would laugh at these three.

With her back turned to the front yard as she spoke to the Campbell sisters, Chloe didn't see Payne and Prescott approaching. But when she noted the bright looks of expectation in her friends' eyes and the dimples that appeared in their freckled cheeks, she knew who was behind her. The Campbell sisters had never been shy about displaying their obvious fondness for Prescott, or any unmarried man within a five-hundred mile radius of Waco, for that matter. When she had told them of her engagement to him, the girls had all but broken into tears.

She turned with a smile, expecting to find Prescott behind her, but her smile faded at the sight of Payne, and a distinct uneasiness came over her.

Realizing she had to be polite and introduce the newcomer to the sisters, or else raise their suspicions, she managed to hide her disquietude.

"Ladies," she said, "I'd like you to meet Payne Trefarrow, Prescott's brother. Payne—Ivy, Rose, and Daisy Campbell."

Ivy, the oldest, stepped forward and extended her gloved hand. "How nice to meet you, Mr. Trefarrow."

Payne accepted it with a slight bow. "I assure you the pleasure is all mine, Miss Campbell."

"Do call me Ivy. Miss Campbell sounds so much like a spinster."

"You are a spinster," muttered Daisy, the youngest, drawing a scornful look from her sister.

"If you're going to call her Ivy, then you must call me Rose," said Ivy's sister.

"Rose."

"And I'm Daisy," said the youngest, fluttering her pale lashes.

As he had done with Ivy and Rose, Payne bent his head over Daisy's hand. Stepping back, he noticed that all three women's faces were flushed. It obviously took very little to impress these country girls; a kind word, a thoughtful gesture, and they would become putty in any man's hands. Too bad he wasn't interested. They might make for pleasant diversions.

"We were just discussing your upcoming wedding, Prescott," Rose said.

"Oh, it all sounds so exciting," said Daisy.

"Yeah, exciting," Prescott mumbled. Wanting to get away from the three gushing sisters, he flashed a quick, uncomfortable look at Chloe. "Wanna dance?"

Before Chloe could accept, Daisy giggled. "Why, Prescott, how unexpected of you to ask me. Thank you, I'd love to. I've been waiting all night for someone to ask me to dance."

Prescott sent Chloe a shocked look. "But I—"

"Don't dance very well," Chloe interrupted. "So you be sure and watch out for your feet, Daisy. He'll step all over them if you're not careful."

With another giggle, Daisy pulled the still stunned

Prescott out into the yard, where other couples twirled arm-in-arm beneath the glowing lanterns.

"If Papa ever gets wind of this," Rose said, "he'll have Daisy's hide for sure. She won't be able to sit down for a week."

"Surely he won't mind her dancing just this one time," Chloe said. "After all, it is my engagement party. She's just helping me celebrate."

"You don't know Papa like we do," Ivy said.

"According to him," Rose said, "the unspoken eleventh commandment in our house is, 'Thou shalt not dance.'"

"That's ridiculous," Chloe said. "There's nothing sinful in dancing."

"There is in Papa's way of thinking," Ivy said. "He's a Baptist preacher, remember? Baptists don't believe in dancing."

"I'm Baptist, and I believe in it," Chloe said.

"You're not his daughter, either," Rose said.

"Lucky you," Ivy said. "Tonight, though, the way I see it, what Papa doesn't know won't hurt him."

"It won't hurt us, either," Rose said, giving her sister a conspiratorial nod.

"That's right," Ivy said. "Now if we can only get someone to ask us to dance."

Payne ignored the female banter, choosing instead to watch his brother. Soon the urge to laugh at Prescott's feeble attempt at the terpsichorean art grew so intense that he had to redirect his gaze or else make a spectacle of himself. Glancing back at the two remaining Campbell sisters, he noted that both wore looks of anticipation, as if they expected him to rescue them from their wallflower status. Any other time, he would have been happy to oblige them, but not tonight. He had a more pressing matter to attend to, to try to ingratiate himself with his sister-in-law-to-be.

"Chloe, would you care to do me the honor of being my partner for this dance?"

She shook her head. "I don't—"

"Aunt Emmaline," Payne interrupted quickly, "said that you were most anxious to join in the frivolities."

"Yes, but I don't—"

"Oh, do dance with him, Chloe," Ivy urged.

"Yes, do," echoed Rose. "It's not like Payne's a total stranger. He's family."

Chloe didn't want to dance with Payne, but she realized that if she continued to hesitate, Ivy and Rose would question it. At the moment, getting into a lengthy discussion with them about her reservations would be worse than dancing with a man she didn't trust.

"All right," she said. "Thank you, Payne."

Leaving Ivy and Rose with an insincere smile, she took Payne's extended hand and followed him out into the yard. No sooner did his fingers encircle hers and their palms touch than she felt a hot jolt surge up her arm, causing her skin to tingle.

The sensation had to be revulsion, Chloe decided. It certainly couldn't be attraction. Prescott, her future husband, was the only man to whom she was attracted. Having just met Payne, she knew next to nothing about him. What little she did know of him, what little she had been able to sense, convinced her that he was as different from his brother as night was from day. Prescott was like a big, affectionate puppy—always getting underfoot, always getting into scrapes, but always there when she or anyone else had need of him. Payne, on the other hand, seemed more closed, more difficult to read, more mysterious— even dangerous.

Blocking out all the activity going on around her, she began to study her dance partner closely. Earlier, she would have attested to the fact that Payne and Prescott were very nearly identical. They were the same height and had the same basic coloring and the same facial bone structure.

But up close, she could easily see some notable differences. Where Payne wore his hair neatly combed from a side part, Prescott's grew long and thick, curling around the collar of his shirt. Where Payne's upper lip was smoothly shaven, Prescott sported a bushy mustache. Where Payne possessed a thin, regal-looking nose, Prescott's bore a lump across the bridge as a result of being broken years earlier. Where Payne was whipcord lean, Prescott was heavier, more muscular in the arms and thighs, a result of, she decided, years of hard work on the ranch. Obviously, Payne hadn't done much heavy labor.

Still, as Payne twirled her around and around to the music, she had to admit that the sensations of his touch did stir strange feelings within her—strange and mildly exciting sensations that she had never experienced with Prescott. Her heart had never fluttered so wildly, nor had she ever felt so lightheaded, as if she might faint at any moment.

But she wouldn't faint, she decided, reclaiming her composure. She had never fainted in her life and wasn't about to do so now. She was merely sharing a dance with Prescott's brother and nothing more.

3

Payne didn't have to look down at Chloe's upturned face to know that she was studying him and no doubt forming her own conclusions about him already. Good, he thought, let her keep guessing about him, let her keep wondering. When the time was right, when *he* was ready, she would know everything, as would Prescott.

Hiding a smile, he continued to dance farther and farther away from the crowd, his feet purposefully leading them into the enveloping shadows of early evening. Though the temptation to lead her off into the darkness of a nearby barn was great, to instigate a scandal right here and now, with his brother so close at hand, he knew he dared not.

Texas might be a world apart from his native England in decorum and culture, but he knew the two were quite alike where basic morality was concerned. To malign the virtue of a young lady like Chloe would do a lot more than raise a few eyebrows and cause gossip; it might well cost him his neck. With that in mind, he knew he had to remain civil, behave like the proper gentleman, and not draw too much attention to himself.

But the more he danced with Chloe, holding her at a close yet respectable distance, the more uncontrolled his thoughts became. A light breeze sprang up, carrying the faint scent of her perfume to his nostrils. Without warning, undefinable emotions suddenly surged through him. He began to feel giddy, strong, and highly aroused, all at the same time. No other woman had ever had the effect on him that Chloe had.

Giving his newfound feelings free reign for a moment, he began to fantasize what it would be like to compromise her. To slowly seduce her, baring every inch of her lovely lean body to his gaze. To touch her, tantalize her, then finally make love to her until she begged him for more. To let her assuage all the hungers that gnawed within him. Heaven, Payne thought. Making love to her, *with* her, would be like ascending into heaven.

And it would most certainly enrage the hell out of his brother.

The unexpected image of an angry Prescott vanquished his burgeoning fantasy in a flash and soon gave life to a second, more realistic thought. Making love to Chloe might prove to be more of a chore than a pleasure if she were a virgin, not that he held virgins in any sort of contempt. In his youth, he'd had the dubious honor of deflowering one or two, but he hadn't enjoyed the act very much. The young ladies he'd bedded had been too eager, in too great a hurry, and they had ended up in tears afterwards. The separate occasions had never afforded him much satisfaction, save the most obvious one. But having reached the age of thirty, the prospects of initiating another amateur held little appeal for him.

No, compromising Chloe now, so early in the game, just wasn't worth all the risks a lengthy seduction would entail. He couldn't at this point alienate Prescott. Later, perhaps, but not now.

"Are all Englishmen as quiet as you?"

Chloe's inquiry caught Payne by surprise. "Some are, some aren't. Does my silence disturb you?"

In truth, his very presence disturbed her. "Not particularly. I just wondered. I've never met an Englishman before."

"If you prefer, we could talk instead of dance."

"You may find this hard to believe, but in Texas, some of us can do both."

Payne caught the sarcasm in her tone and stopped dancing, letting one hand rest on her waist as the other maintained a loose grip on her fingers. "That may be, but I find it easier, less taxing, to do only one thing at a time. What do you wish to talk about?"

"How about you?"

"Me?"

"Yes."

"What about me?"

"I don't understand you."

He smiled. "A little mystery is a good thing, don't you think?"

"Not where you're concerned. You're Prescott's brother, his identical twin, for mercy's sake, yet you show up here tonight, out of the blue, without so much as a letter or a telegram to let us know you were coming."

"My coming to Texas was something of a spur-of-the-moment decision. I really didn't have time to write."

"Ever?" she asked.

"What do you mean?"

"You never wrote, Payne. Not to your father while he was alive, or to Prescott, or anyone else in the family, for that matter."

"My father, mother, brother, and I were estranged many years ago, but I'm sure you're already aware of that. As for the rest of my relatives—I didn't know they even existed until I arrived. However, if my being here has put any of you at an inconvenience, I—"

"That's not what I mean. I just want to know where you've been all these years."

"In England. That's where I've been."

"That's a problem, too."

"How is it that?"

"You should have been here. This is your home."

"No, England is my home. Outside of a few brief visits to the Continent, England is the only country I've ever known. Until now."

"Should I assume that now that you're here, you intend to stay a while?"

"A while, yes. That would be a safe assumption."

"But not forever?"

"I can't answer that."

"Can't, or won't?"

"Can't," he said, thinking that for a young woman, she was a persistent little devil. She was curious, too, almost to the point of being rude. "You see, I'm not unlike a lot of other people in that I can only take each day as it comes. I've never made it a practice of planning too far ahead. That way I'm never disappointed when my schedule is disrupted by unexpected events. I'm here, for the present. Other than that, I just can't say. I hope you don't find that too hard to comprehend."

"No, I suppose I don't." How could she? Too many times in the past she had made plans, only to have them dashed by unforeseen interruptions.

"Do you mind if I ask a question now?"

"Of course not."

He studied her a moment in the darkness, admiring the way the moonlight overhead turned her pale golden hair into a halo of silver, her stormy blue eyes into deep, dark, fathomless pools. "What have I done to displease you, to make you so suspicious of me?"

"Don't be silly. I'm not displeased with you." She just didn't think she liked him very much, but she wouldn't say this. "I'm not suspicious of you, either."

"You're certainly behaving as if you are."

"Well, I'm not."

"Then why not allow me to enjoy the pleasure of your company for this one dance? We've only just met, and I would like to get to know you better. I'd hate for us to continue to be strangers. After all, as soon as you marry my brother, we're going to be part of the same family."

"Yes, family."

Payne didn't have to be a mindreader to know that the notion irritated her. While her marriage to Prescott would make them relatives, he doubted she would ever accept him as a friend. But if the truth were known, he didn't much like the idea of having her as a friend, either. He'd never had a woman friend, and never wanted or needed one. From what he had already sensed, Chloe was made for a lot more than just friendship.

"When we are related," he continued, "can I look forward to a change?"

"What kind of change?"

"Will you become softer, warmer, and more welcoming? Or will you only grow harder toward me as time goes on?"

"Harder? I'm not hard now. I'm just being cautious. It's like you said before. We are strangers."

"You're right, my mistake. That was a bad choice of words. You're very soft and feminine, Chloe. You're just not very welcoming. Why?"

"I don't know," she said. "I guess that would all depend on a number of things."

"One will be sufficient."

"Oh, it's just too soon to say. I need to be with you a while, see how you behave while you're here."

"I'll be no different than I am now," he said, his voice dropping to a husky timbre. "I'll be friendly and loving toward my new sister."

Chloe bristled at his intimate tone. "I'm not your sister yet."

"No, but you will be in June. I believe that's when Prescott said that you and he were scheduled to be married."

"Not just scheduled," she said, mimicking his British pronunciation of the word. "That's when we *will* be married."

"Of course."

She detected a note of doubt in his voice and stopped dancing abruptly. "We *will* be married, Payne. Make no mistake about that."

"I didn't say you wouldn't be, did I?"

"No, but—"

"And a lovelier bride Texas will never again see. My brother's a lucky fellow."

Chloe hesitated a moment. "Thank you."

"You sound doubtful. Are you questioning the sincerity of my compliment? You shouldn't, you know. I'm quite sincere. You are lovely." In spite of her skepticism of him, she was probably the loveliest thing he'd ever had the good fortune to meet, and he had met quite a few lovely women in his day.

"I'm happy to think of myself as just ordinary."

Payne laughed. "If you were just ordinary, I doubt my brother would want to marry you. He has much better taste in women than that."

"How do you know? You know nothing about him."

"I *don't* know, really. I was just making a broad assumption. After all, he's a man, as I am. With that in mind, I think it's safe for me to presuppose that we have more in common than just our physical resemblance and our father's name. And if we do share more, so much the better. But even if we don't, it pleases me to know that my brother has chosen well for himself."

Chloe thought Prescott had made a wise choice as well, but she wasn't so conceited as to admit such a thing to Payne. After all the years she had spent growing up in Prescott's shadow, idolizing the ground he walked on one minute and hating him the next, all the while waiting for the moment when he finally woke up and realized she was a woman worth marrying, she couldn't be conceited on that subject.

"He's chosen quite well, in fact," Payne said, itching to touch the soft curve of her jaw and the slender line of her throat, feel the texture of her silky hair. "You'll give him beautiful children, Chloe."

"You think so?"

"I know so." The thought suddenly occurred to

him that her children with Prescott would look like
him as well. Since he was Prescott's identical twin,
how could they not? Come to think of it, he could
easily be mistaken for the father.

He felt oddly angered by this notion. But he was
no father—he'd always made certain of that fact.
Furthermore, he had no desire to be one, at least not
yet. Prescott, however, was another matter. If the
rumors he'd heard in town about his brother's frequent
dalliances with the fairer sex proved only half right,
then there was a good chance Prescott had already
entered the paternal state many times over.

Suddenly he glanced down at Chloe.

"Is it possible that you're breeding already?"

"Breeding?" she asked, frowning. She *had* breeding, certainly. Her year-long stint in Miss Ponsonby's
School for Young Ladies assured her of that. But was
she breeding? What did that mean?

"You know, in the family way."

Stunned by the blunt question, Chloe stepped out
of his arms, putting an end to their dance. "I'm not
that. How dare you even suggest such a thing!"

"Don't be so indignant, my dear. You're a very
healthy, very delectable young woman. You're going
to be married to Prescott soon, and if he isn't the man
I think he is, he's a fool for not having at least tried to
bed you."

"Bed me?" She could only stare at him in outrage. "Let me put your mind at rest about a couple
of things, mister. Your brother is very much a man,
but more than that, he's a gentleman. Something
I'm beginning to suspect you're not. Prescott
respects me. He holds me in the highest regard. The
idea that he—Well, I assure you, he's never . . ."

She broke off, too angry to complete the thought.

"Never?" Payne didn't know why he felt so compelled to continue goading her on the particular subject of intimacy. He only knew that he couldn't stop, that he had to find out everything about her, even the degree of her relationship with his brother.

"No, never. I don't know how you people do things over in England, but I'll tell you something, here in Texas, we wait until it's legal and moral before we do things like . . . bed and breed."

"How little you know. Many affianced couples the world over enjoy the act of bedding and breeding prior to marriage."

"Don't talk like that," she whispered, blushing.

"Why not?"

"It's not proper."

"Where love is concerned, Chloe my dear, propriety isn't very important. Basic human needs and desires are."

"Well, being proper is important to me. I'm a lady, not some kind of low-heeled hussy."

"The word you're looking for is wanton, not hussy. And most of the ladies that I've known, be they highborn or low, become the most wanton creatures on earth when they're making love to the right man."

Chloe chuckled and shook her head. "I'll bet your Queen Victoria doesn't."

"I'll bet she does."

She gasped in amazement. "The Queen of England . . . ?"

"Of course. She may be of royal blood, but she's no different from any other woman. Stop and think about it a moment. She's the mother of many children. *Many,* Chloe. I'd be willing to wager that she

and her consort, Albert, didn't produce all their offspring for the realm merely out of a sense of duty to
the crown. Love was involved at one time or another.
It had to be, or there wouldn't be so many princes
and princesses cluttering up the English countryside,
waiting in line for the throne."

"Well, I wouldn't know anything about that. All
I know is that Prescott and I won't be producing
any princes or princesses now or later. We'll be satisfied just to have a half a dozen or more ordinary
Trefarrows. And they won't be cluttering up the
Texas countryside, either. They'll be honest, hardworking, God-fearing men and women when they
grow up."

It was Payne's turn to gasp. "You intend to have a
half-dozen children?"

"If we're meant to, yes."

"My dear, that's the most ghastly, the most absurd
thing I've ever heard."

"There's nothing ghastly or absurd about it. Having children is as natural as getting up in the morning
and going to sleep at night. It's what we were put on
this earth for, to be fruitful and multiply."

"Ah, but some loving couples lie in bed 'til noon.
And they don't always sleep all night."

"That's awful!"

"No, it isn't. It's quite pleasant, as a matter of fact.
But back to the subject of your having so many
children. What about your own self-fulfillment?"

"What do you mean?"

Payne shook his head in dismay. "You're actually
saying that you'll be happy being my brother's brood
mare? That you'll enjoy watching your lovely figure
turn into a grossly misshapen mass of wrinkles and

scars and fat? That's obscene, Chloe. You're made
for far better things."

The note of disgust she heard in his voice made
her feel defensive. "Better things? What could be
better than being a mother, giving life to my husband's
children, loving them as much as I love their father?
That's the greatest achievement a woman can strive
for."

"No, it's not."

"In my opinion, it is."

"You're so innocent, my dear. So charmingly
unsophisticated and naive. It's a good thing you're
stuck here in these provincial backwoods of yours.
You wouldn't last a minute in London, or the rest of
the real world, for that matter."

"Backwoods? You think Texas is the backwoods?"

"Compared to London, Paris, and Rome it is. Over
there, little girls like you lose their innocence very
early in life." *Little boys, too,* he thought, recalling
his own arduous initiation and intense struggle to
survive in England's greatest cosmopolitan city.
"They see how hard life really is, how mean, and they
either adapt or perish."

"It's not exactly easy to live here, either, but then
you wouldn't know about that, would you? While
you've been living in comfort in London, do you
know what we've done here? Out of necessity? We
fought spring floods and summer droughts so bad
that there was very little water for us to drink much
less to give our cattle. We've fought diseases that
threatened to wipe out entire families and herds,
Comanche Indians, Mexican soldiers, and rampaging
Yankees. We may not be as sophisticated as you, Mr.

Payne Trefarrow, but we're tough. Put one of our backwoods Texans against your foppish Londoners any day, in any situation, and I can tell you who'd come out the winner. We would. Now, if you'll excuse me, I think I'd better go find Prescott. He's probably wondering what's happened to me."

"No, wait!" Payne grabbed her arm as she began to stalk away. "If I've in any way offended you, Chloe—"

"Offended me? The word you're looking for is insulted, Payne. You insulted me. And not just me, but every Texan who ever lived, who ever died for this great state of mine."

"I'm sorry. Truly, I am."

"Let go of my arm, please."

"I will, as soon as you accept my apology."

She looked him straight in the eye without blinking. "I'll do that when hell freezes over. Now, let go of me."

Still he refused to release her.

Chloe's full lips narrowed into a thin angry line. "I said, let go."

"Not until—" Payne broke off, realizing that there was only one way to convince her of his sincerity, and that he could no longer stand there with her so close and not take advantage of her nearness. He hauled her roughly against him, and his mouth descended to capture hers.

Payne had intended the kiss to be one of chastisement, solely to put Chloe in her place. But the moment their lips touched, the taste and feel of her overpowered him, and the simple kiss was transformed into a lethal dose of undeniable passion. Holding her in his arms with her full breasts crushed against his chest, he realized that he wanted her more than he'd ever wanted any woman in his life. Unwilling and unable to deny himself this need, he let his tongue slip past the barrier of her teeth. As it explored the hidden recesses of her honeyed interior, he felt his control dissolve even further. Desire flared in his veins, sending its flames of need through his body.

Though his kiss had taken her by surprise, Chloe found herself withstanding his gentle assault, actually finding enjoyment in it. Prescott had never kissed her this way, with his tongue, with his whole body. He'd only given her quick pecks on the cheek or forehead when he'd known she expected him to—

Her thoughts ended abruptly at the feel of Payne's masculine bulge against her belly. Good Lord! Even though she was a virgin, she knew what was happening to him. Worse still, she knew what could happen to her if she let this continue.

Wrenching herself free from his embrace, she drew back her foot and delivered a hard kick to his shin.

With a look of shock and pain contorting his features, Payne reached down and grabbed his leg. "What did you do that for?"

"When I say let go," she said with a defiant tilt of her chin, "I mean let go. Don't ever forget it."

As she turned smartly on her heel and advanced toward the crowd of guests, Payne hopped around on his uninjured leg in the darkness. Forget? Hell, how could he? He would remember this night for as long as he lived. She packed a powerful punch in that foot of hers, one that he would wear most likely for days to come.

But despite the throbbing pain in his shin, he knew he had learned a valuable lesson from their encounter. Miss Chloe Patience Bliss was not the kind of lady that a man should easily take for granted.

4

The moment Payne stepped across the threshold into the house he felt an overwhelming sense of comfort, as if he had truly, finally come home. Why he should feel that way, he didn't know. It looked nothing like the houses, either the grand ones or the small ones, that he had been accustomed to visiting in England. Save for a small rug in front of the door, the floors were bare, as were the walls. He found no paintings of his ancestors in the drawing room, which were a familiar sight in England, or pastoral scenes in the dining room. Yet despite the absence of such adornments and the austerity of the furnishings, he still felt welcomed.

"Land sakes, child," Emmaline said as she preceded Payne down the hallway, "you mean to tell me that you came all the way from England with just this one little bag?"

"No. I left the rest of my things at the hotel in town."

"At the hotel? Why on earth didn't you bring them

out with you when you came? It'd save you from having to go back to get them in the morning."

"I thought it would be more prudent of me to wait."

"Wait for what?" she asked, looking back over her shoulder and seeing Chloe enter the house with a large empty platter in her hands.

Payne looked back as well, an ache shooting up his wounded shin as he caught the angry gleam in Chloe's eyes. "I wasn't sure how my sudden arrival would be taken. For all I knew, you might not have wanted me here."

"Not want you?" Emmaline snorted. "That's about the silliest thing I believe I've ever heard. You're family, child. Family is always welcomed here at the Triple T."

"Always?" he asked, watching Chloe's expression as she drew nearer. If he didn't know better, he would say that the look in her eye definitely spelled trouble. Her kicking his shin had been painful and somewhat embarrassing, and if he didn't watch his step, she might decide to break the platter she carried over his head. That would surely be agonizing.

"Yes, always," Emmaline said, watching as Payne gave Chloe a wide berth. "Family is family. Always will be, no matter how you look at it."

"Even if they're black sheep?" Chloe asked softly as she brushed past them.

Emmaline chuckled. "Black sheep, white sheep . . . we've tolerated just about all kinds of folks here at one time or another. But it's too late to start telling past tales now." She beckoned to Payne. "Come on this way, child. I'll show you to your room. Chloe, just leave those dirty dishes in the kitchen. I'll get to them first thing in the morning."

"I don't mind doing them tonight," Chloe said.

"No, tomorrow will be soon enough. You run on to bed."

Giving Payne another withering look, Chloe headed down the hall and disappeared out of sight.

"I don't think my brother's bride-to-be likes me very much," Payne said, following Aunt Emmaline along the same route Chloe had taken, but turning left instead of right down another hallway.

"Well, she never has been one to cotton to strangers right off. Not even when she was a little girl. I recollect when she first came to live with us here at the Triple T, right after her mama and daddy died, she was as timid as a mouse. And she'd known us all of her life. Just give her some time. Once she gets used to having you around, you'll never find a sweeter girl. Make friends with Chloe, and you've got a friend for life. Here we are."

Emmaline opened a door that squeaked slightly and led the way into a darkened room. "Coming from England and all, I imagine you're probably used to much fancier places than this," she said, striking a match and lighting the coal-oil lamp that sat on a table beside the big brass bed.

Fancier places? In one respect, he had slept in much fancier places—grand town houses in London, small *pied-à-terres* in Paris, even a palace or two on the Continent. On the other side of the coin, however, he'd slept in places not nearly as nice—cold, empty rooms, where bitter English winds whipped through cracks in the walls and chilled him to the bone. Once, many years ago, he'd found lodging behind a mound of rubbish in a dark, damp alleyway. But the one thing even the elegant places had lacked was the warmth that he sensed was inherent in this rambling Western-style house.

"The sheets are clean, though," Emmaline said, bringing Payne back to the present. "Changed them myself just the other day. I had a feeling we'd be needing this room tonight for somebody. I just never suspected it would be you. I've been told the bed sleeps real good."

Payne sensed the woman's embarrassment and tried to put her at ease. "I'm sure it does, Aunt Em. From the looks of it alone, that bed is probably more comfortable than the one I've been sleeping on at the hotel in Waco. Far too many lumps in that one."

"That's because old man Snodgrass who owns the hotel doesn't make his girls fluff the ticking often enough. A good feather bed always needs a regular fluffing up." She turned back the large handmade quilt and top sheet and patted the pillows a bit. "Well now, you have a good night's sleep, and I'll see you in the morning."

"How early in the morning?"

"Oh, about five or so, I guess. Prescott's always been one to get up with the chickens. Just like his daddy. Your daddy, too," she added with a smile. "Lots of work to do here at the ranch. Chloe's the same way. Up before the crack of dawn. And I'm always up when they are. When you've got hungry mouths to feed, it's sinful to lay in bed 'til the sun comes up. 'Course, this being your first time here and all, if you want to sleep in later, that would be fine with me."

"No, five is fine."

Five? Payne thought as he watched Emmaline

close the door behind her, leaving him alone in the room. He couldn't recall ever getting up that early. He'd come home and gone to bed at five in the morning many times, but he'd never gotten up that early—not deliberately, at least.

"Ah, well, when in Rome . . ." he muttered, opening his valise.

In her bedroom down the hall, Chloe slipped into a simple white cotton nightgown and sat down at the dressing table to run a brush through the tangles in her hair. In the dim illumination from the lamplight she caught sight of her reflection, a look that filled her with embarrassment and self loathing. Her eyes were far too bright, her cheeks too flushed, her lips a bit too rosy, as though they had recently been kissed, and kissed hard.

Narrowing her mouth angrily, she tossed the brush down and jumped to her feet. How dare that man touch her as he had, she fumed as she climbed into bed. How dare he! Granted, he might be Prescott's long-lost brother and her future brother-in-law, but that didn't give him the right to manhandle her as he had done. No lady should have to stand for that sort of treatment, not from would-be relatives or total strangers. There were laws, weren't there? And if there weren't, there sure as shooting should be.

With a frustrated grunt, she turned onto her side, punching the pillow beneath her head for good measure and wishing it was Payne Trefarrow's face. She wished she had slapped him hard instead of merely kicking his shin like some sort of petulant child. A slap would have left a mark on his face, a mark that would have been more difficult to explain to Prescott and Aunt Em than a slight limp.

The longer she thought about what had happened—about what she had done and what Payne had done to her—the clearer his image became in her mind. She recalled the reckless, almost defiant gleam she'd seen dart across his dark green eyes a moment before his head had dipped down and his lips had claimed hers. She could almost taste the tobacco and whiskey that she'd tasted from his mouth then, and feel the roughness of his fingertips as they crept up her neck to the back of her head, where they had held her in place as he'd taken his pleasure. And she could certainly remember the mind-numbing gentleness of his kiss.

How could Payne have done that to her and make her feel this way? She loved Prescott. . . . Didn't she?

Of course she did. For heaven's sake, she was going to marry him, have his children, and spend the rest of her life with him. Just because Payne looked like Prescott on the outside, that didn't make them the same on the inside. Far from it, because they weren't the same. Though she had only met him a few hours ago, she could attest with certainty that Payne was the complete opposite of Prescott.

And just because Payne had flattered her with his attention and kissed her, and Prescott had never done anything more than give her a brotherly peck now and then, it didn't mean that she was lost altogether. She was a lady, not a woman of loose morals and easy virtue who would let an attentive man sway her.

But if women of loose morals and easy virtue always felt as she had when a virtual stranger kissed her, then maybe she was lost.

She rolled onto her back, heaved a sigh, and stared at the ceiling. Why did Payne have to come to Texas now? Why couldn't he have waited a few more months to be reunited with his brother? In a few months she would be safely married to Prescott and well beyond any form of temptation.

No, she already was. All she had done was let Payne kiss her. She hadn't asked for it. To her best recollection, she hadn't intimated in her behavior or speech that she'd wanted it. Payne had done it all on his own. Surely she couldn't be held responsible for his actions.

She was only responsible for her own actions, for her own behavior. With that in mind, she knew that from now on, she would have to be doubly cautious. Especially where Payne Trefarrow was concerned.

Prescott yawned widely and folded his arms beneath his pillowed head. What a day, he thought. Who would have imagined it would turn out the way it had? Only that morning he'd been worried about entertaining half the town at his and Chloe's engagement party. Did he have the money for all the gee-gaws and fripperies that Aunt Emmaline had said they needed? Could he invite all the important townspeople he and his father before him had done business with for years, and entertain them in the style they would expect? Food had always been in plentiful supply at the Triple T, but a hundred or more extra mouths to feed did cost money—money he didn't have.

As his father had often told him, necessities had to come before frivolities. Not that he considered his engagement to Chloe frivolous by any means, but the extra cash he'd spent on tonight's festivities was enough to make him realize just how tight his present circumstances were. He had ranch hands and loans from the bank and storekeepers in town to pay.

Until tonight, he'd been certain that one of them would have to go unpaid until the next big cattle sale—not that he expected a huge amount of cash to fall into his pocket from that endeavor. The past winter had been a rough one, and he'd lost over a hundred head of cattle in one ice storm alone, most of them his prime breeding stock. That, coupled with the falling prices for beef, made his dilemma even worse.

But all that had changed now. All those worries were behind him. His brother, Payne—his very affluent-looking brother—had arrived to help ease his financial burdens.

Though tired, Prescott found it impossible to sleep. Too many thoughts and plans occupied his mind. Getting money meant more than just paying off his creditors; it meant expansion. He wanted to increase his herd by at least a thousand head. He wanted to build a new stable for the horses, and the bunkhouse needed a new roof. But why stop with just the roof? Why not build a whole new bunkhouse? With a new, larger one, he could hire on more hands. After all, he'd be needing them to see after the increased herd.

Life was beginning to look pretty good—better than ever, in fact. So good that bright and early the next morning he intended to take Payne into Waco so they could hear the reading of their father's will. Of course, he already knew what was in it—he'd been with his father when the lawyer had drawn it up—but hearing it again would only confirm the situation.

Once his brother took possession of his share of the ranch, legal and binding, Prescott was sure Payne wouldn't refuse to give him the money that the Triple T badly needed. After all, it was going to be his ranch, too. In a week or two, or however long it took for Payne to get his money from England, they'd pay off all the old loans, all the old debts, and start expanding. By the time they finished, the Triple T would be the biggest dang ranch in all of North Central Texas.

Life sure was looking good all right, Prescott decided, grinning at the darkened ceiling. His brother was home where he rightly belonged, his financial worries were all but a thing of the past, and before too long, he'd have a sweet little bride to fill the empty side of his bed.

Sweet? Chloe? Prescott gave a second thought to this cogitation. Chloe was nice and all, but he couldn't in good conscience call her sweet exactly. She was too strong-willed and stubborn for that, too danged independent. She liked doing things her own way and had a nasty habit of going deaf when somebody else had an idea that differed from hers.

No, Chloe wasn't sweet. He wouldn't admit it to another living, breathing human being, but there were times when Prescott felt slightly intimidated by her. Sometimes even a little afraid of her, despite the fact that she was a mere woman.

But one thing he couldn't deny was the fact that she was good, strong, and decent, too. Why, there wasn't a dishonest bone in the girl's whole body. Never had been in all the years he'd known her. She was as upstanding and forthright a woman as he'd ever known.

A man needed a good, strong, decent, honest woman by his side, not some simpering little flibbertigibbet who'd run off with the first smooth-talking snake-oil salesman that came down the pike. Not somebody who'd pack her bags and take off for parts unknown when the going got a little rough. He needed somebody who would stand by him through good years and bad.

Yes, Chloe Patience Bliss would make him a good wife. And when the time was right, after a decent interval—say, nine or ten months after they were married—they would start having kids. She'd make a damn good mother, too; he was certain of it. She'd be stern yet loving, and gentle, too, though she probably wouldn't be averse to giving the kids a good tongue-lashing when one was needed.

They'd have a boy first, of course. Prescott wanted—no, actually needed—a male to carry on the Trefarrow line. Somebody would have to take over the running of the ranch when he and Payne got too old. Maybe two or three boys, or four, he thought. And then a girl or two. Yeah, two girls ought to be enough. Chloe would want them to help her around the house.

Prescott yawned again, feeling his eyes begin to close. Life wasn't looking just good, for a change. It was actually sweet. In fact, it couldn't be sweeter.

When sleep finally overtook him, he began to dream, a comforting, familiar dream that made him smile. He didn't know her name, and he'd never met her, but even as a child he'd often dreamt of her. As she had done so many times in the past, she seemed to float in front of him, suspended in air just out of his reach. Her long dark hair tangling around her shoulders, her wide black eyes flashing, she opened her mouth and called his name. She reached out for him with slender arms and graceful fingers, and he started toward her, wanting to be held, and wanting to hold her. But just as he reached her and started to embrace her, a look of sadness crossed her face, and she slowly evaporated into the mist that surrounded them.

Ah, well, Prescott thought. Maybe next time.

5

"*If you'll just sign here,* Payne, that'll be the last of the papers." Henry Johnson, the Trefarrows' lawyer, pushed the document across the shiny surface of his desk, at the same time holding his ink pen out to Payne. As Payne penned his signature in the appropriate spot, Henry pulled out his pocket watch and checked the time. "I think we're going to be able to get this over to the courthouse before everybody leaves for lunch. Once they get it filed, you two will be home free. Not that you aren't already. The ranch has been legally yours since the day your daddy died. All this is a mere technicality, you understand, but it's a good thing y'all decided to come in early this morning instead of waiting 'til this afternoon. I'm fixing to head out for Austin on the noon train."

"Early?" Prescott laughed and slapped a hand across Payne's shoulder. "Hell, Payne here was up before the crack of dawn."

"Thanks to that cursed rooster outside my window," Payne said.

"Yeah, old Charlie does like to crow loud, don't he?" Prescott said with a grin.

Crow wasn't the term Payne would have chosen. Shriek was more like it. He'd been roused from a sound sleep by the raucous sound just outside his bedroom window at four that morning, which scared the wits out of him. Until he realized it was merely a rooster heralding the break of a new day, he'd thought the world was coming to an end.

Prescott turned his attention back to the lawyer. "What's happening down in the capital? Anything I'd be interested in knowing?"

"Naw, just the usual political bullshit," Johnson said. "I swear, if I'd known being a state senator was going to take up so much of my time, I never would have let y'all talk me into running for the vacancy poor old Ed Bennett left when he passed on. I'd rather spend my time here in Waco, handling wills and probates, not wasting it wrangling with all those big-mouthed, long-winded mugwumps."

"Mugwumps?" Payne asked some time later as they left Johnson's office. "What are they? Some new breed of Westerner that I've never heard of?"

"Y'all got politicians in England, don't you?"

"Of course."

"Then y'all've got mugwumps. They're the one's who never can give you a straight answer on an issue. They straddle the fence every dang time, with their mug on one side and—"

"And their wump on the other," Payne finished with a nod. "Yes, I understand now. Unfortunately, we do have a number of them in England. Many more than we need, I'm sure."

Prescott glanced away, looking at the saloon across the street and thinking that now would be the perfect time, and Carrigan's would be the perfect place, to hit his brother up for a loan. But the sight of an odd-looking man staring in his direction caught his attention. Knowing he'd never seen him before, Prescott wondered why he nodded at him and quickly hurried away.

"Who was that?" he asked Payne.

"Who was who?"

"That man across the street—didn't you see him?"

Payne shrugged and shook his head.

"Never mind then. Maybe it was just my imagination. What were we talking about?"

"Mugwumps."

"Yeah, those critters. It's a shame we don't have mugwump season like we do rattlesnake and rabbit."

"In England, we hunt our own brand of vermin—fox," Payne said, understanding his brother's somewhat erratic line of thought. "Riding to the hounds, we call it."

"I've seen pictures in books about y'all doing that kind of thing. People get all dressed up in funny-looking coats and pants and jump hedges a lot, don't they?"

"Some of the better riders do. A lot merely attempt to jump only to end up on their wumps in the mud."

"Yeah, make it open season and we'd get rid of a lot of pesky politicians. Maybe elect somebody to office who'd do something."

"Right you are," Payne said heading for the horse

Prescott had loaned him, which was tied to a nearby hitching post.

"Hold up a minute," Prescott said. "How's about you and me having a drink to celebrate?"

"This early in the day?"

"It ain't that early. Didn't you just hear Henry? It's nigh on to noontime."

"Well, I don't suppose a small brandy would hurt," Payne said, turning away from the horse and following his brother out into the dusty street.

"Brandy? Son, if you want to hold on to your cherished Trefarrow manhood, you'll be wise not to order a brandy in Carrigan's."

"It's a civilized drink, isn't it?"

"That's just it. I can't recollect nobody ever saying that Carrigan's was civilized. It's one of the rowdiest places you're likely to find here in Waco. Or in this part of Texas, for that matter."

"Rowdy?" Payne asked. He would have to become familiar with the local vernacular if he stayed for any length of time in this sprawling wide-open country they called America.

"Let's just say that it gets right lively here on Saturday nights. Fact is, all hell breaks loose every hour. You can almost set your clock by the fracases. Daytime's different, sometimes. Usually the fist fights don't start 'til after sundown, and there's not as many shootouts or wounds for the doc to see to."

"I see," Payne said, understanding his brother all too clearly. A local ruffian well into his cups might mistake Payne's somewhat more refined manners and speech for a sign that he was something of a dandy, when of course he was anything but a man of that bent. He would have to follow his brother's lead closely, to avoid any kind of confrontation, violent or otherwise.

"All right, Prescott, I won't request a snifter of brandy. What libation would one usually request at an establishment of this sort?"

"Bourbon," Prescott said. "Smooth Kentucky sour mash." He let Payne precede him through the swinging doors into the dusty, dimly lighted saloon, adding in a lowered voice, "If you're in something of a reckless mood, you might want to try a shot of rye. But I gotta warn you, Carrigan's Rye has been known to take the varnish off of furniture."

"That strong, eh?" Payne asked, catching a strong whiff of rotgut, stale tobacco, and cheap perfume.

"Son, you don't know the meaning of the word strong 'til you've downed a shot of the stuff." Prescott shook his head and shuddered. "I had me one of the worst hangovers off all time after drinking Carrigan's Rye. It does things to your insides. Your mind, too, I reckon."

"Then I'll stick to the bourbon."

They found an empty table close to the long bar at the end of the room. Payne watched the portly man standing behind it, ruffled garters holding up his sleeves as he wiped glasses with a dirty towel and turned them upside down in a neat row atop the counter. He wondered if the bartender had recently washed the glasses, and if so, had he used clean water for washing or dirty? But in an establishment like Carrigan's, asking the nature of their sanitary habits would be tantamount to an insult, and insults, he imagined, would only lead to trouble.

A well-endowed young woman with brassy red hair approached their table. Her dress, which might have looked modest on another, appeared decidedly immodest with the amount of cleavage its dipping neckline exposed. Payne watched his brother smile broadly as she stopped beside his chair.

"There she is," Prescott said. "How're you doing this morning, Sally girl?"

"Just fine, now that you're here," she said in a high-pitched, girlish voice as she wound her arm around his neck. Bending low over Prescott to plant a kiss on his cheek, she gave Payne an excellent view of her charms—charms that nearly spilled out of the top of her dress. "What are you doing in town today? I wasn't expecting you to come around again until next Saturday."

"Business, sugar," Prescott said. "Family business."

Sally straightened, a look of mock horror crossing her features. "Lordy, Prescott, don't tell me you've up and married that Bliss girl already. If you have, sure as shooting, Jolene and Myra are going to be as heartbroken as I am."

"Aw, now, you're hearts are safe for a while. I haven't married her yet. I will in a couple more months, though."

A slow, tempting smile touched her rouged lips. "Then we'd better make use of what little free time you have left, hadn't we?"

"Uh, not today, sugar," Prescott said with a wink as he gave her a pat on her well-rounded backside. "Like I said, I came to town on family business. With family. I'd like you to meet my brother, Payne."

"Brother?" Sally slowly turned to look at Payne. "You never told me you had a—" She broke off abruptly, her brown eyes growing as round as saucers. "Good Lord Almighty, Prescott! Y'all look enough alike to be twins."

"We are twins," Prescott said.

Her eyes darted between the two for some time, her mouth unable to close from her astonishment. "I don't believe it. I plumb do not believe it. I've heard tell about identical twins before, but I ain't never met none. Until now. Y'all pardon me a minute, would you, gents? I've just got to go round up Jolene and Myra. They're going to be as flabbergasted as I am."

She hurried off in a swish of taffeta petticoats.

"You come here quite often, I take it," Payne said.

"I guess you could say I'm one of their regular customers, yeah." Clearing his throat, Prescott leaned forward to rest his forearms on the table. "Chloe and Aunt Emmaline—"

"Don't know about your secret predilections, do they?" Payne interrupted.

"Predilections?" Prescott shrugged his broad shoulders. "I've never heard it called that before. All I know is, this is a man's place. We come here and, I don't know, blow off a lot of steam we let build up. But ladies—decent women, that is—well, some of them don't take kindly to hearing that their menfolk might have activities outside of hearth and home. If you know what I mean."

"I do."

"Not that I'm active here. I'm not. Not very often, that is. It's just that Sally and the other girls . . . well, they're nice ladies, in their own way. They know how to listen to a man, how to treat him when he's got worries and he's lonely. Believe it or not, they get lonely, and sometimes they need a man to talk to, someone to give them advice, you know?"

"I understand perfectly." Advice and money for services rendered, Payne thought. Those belonging to the world's oldest profession were the same all over—eager and friendly when one had coins in one's pocket and indifferent when one did not.

"If it's all the same to you, I'd kind of like to keep my association with them just between the two of us."

"I wouldn't have it any other way," Payne said with, he hoped, an honest ring in his tone. He did, however, make a mental note of this bit of interesting information. He could cause a lot of friction between his brother and the feisty Miss Bliss if he mentioned Prescott's close association with the buxom Sally. So much friction, in fact, that it might cause a permanent rift in their relationship.

In a matter of moments, Sally led the equally buxom Jolene and Myra to the table where the brothers sat. Immediately they began ogling Payne, vocalizing almost in unison his close likeness to Prescott. But whereas Prescott enjoyed the attention and was openly charming to the ladies, joking and flirting with them, Payne remained cool and detached.

For all their erotic charm, he couldn't work up an attraction to any of them. Perhaps another time he might have been willing to accompany them upstairs to their private quarters and share an enjoyable hour or two. As Prescott had said, they were very friendly girls—somewhat dimwitted, but friendly nonetheless. For reasons he couldn't explain, Payne found them too coarse, too worldly, and, oddly enough, repulsive.

In a short time, the newness of Payne's presence wore thin. When other patrons began to fill the saloon, the trio of ladies wandered off to welcome them, leaving the brothers alone with a bottle of Carrigan's finest bourbon. Payne decided he liked the taste of it. It was very smooth and palatable.

"So, how does it feel to own part of Texas?"

Were he to tell his brother the truth, Payne would have said that he felt no different from the way he had before he left England. But he knew that Prescott wouldn't want to hear the truth, not yet. There would be plenty of time for that later.

"I'm not sure I've had the time yet to take it all in," he said. "How many acres did you say we owned?"

"Nigh on to half a million."

Payne shook his head in disbelief, a lock of light brown hair falling across his forehead. "I don't think there's that much land in all of England."

"Yeah, well Texas is a little bigger."

"Obviously. Such an enormous responsibility, seeing to all that vast amount of property."

"You don't know the half of it." Prescott poured himself a fresh glass of bourbon and topped off Payne's glass. Now was the time, he decided, feeling more bolstered by his intake of liquid courage. "You know, it ain't been easy since Papa died."

"No, I imagine not." The mention of his father set Payne's teeth on edge, reminding him why he had come to Texas.

"We may have land and cattle and water, but we've got problems, too. You know, it takes a lot of money to keep a spread as big as the Triple T a-going."

"Creditors?"

Prescott nodded. "Storekeepers here in town and the bankers. The storekeepers are good people; they understand that we ranchers have good years and years that are kinda lean. Most of them are willing to

give us time when the market's soft like it is now, but
the bankers, well, let's just say they make life real
hard when they don't get their money on time. And
then there's that bastard Wyngate."

"Who?"

"Wyngate," Prescott repeated. "Sam Wyngate. The
man takes great delight in breathing down our necks.
A time or two I've thought we'd be better off cutting
our losses here and starting up fresh again someplace
else where Wyngate can't get to us." He lowered his
glass to stare at Payne. "Just thought about it, you
understand. Nothing else. I could no more sell the
Triple T than I could stop breathing. It's been in the
family too dang long for me to do something so
dishonorable as that."

"You've never thought of selling off some of the
livestock to pay your debts?"

"If I sell any more, I'll be out of business."

"What about Chloe? Does she have any money?"

"Aw, I reckon her folks left her some when they
passed on, but it ain't nearly enough for what the
Triple T needs. I tell you, Payne, this last winter was
so bad it nearly wiped us out. Why, we had ice on the
ground for dang near three weeks. That's almost
unheard of here in Texas. We lost I don't know how
many head of steers. If that wasn't bad enough, Julio
came across two of my prize seed bulls frozen stiff
down by the Brazos. Stupid critters had wandered
into the mud just as the cold spell hit, got themselves
stuck, and just stayed there 'til they were froze solid.
Then the early spring rains came, flooded the Brazos,
and killed a few hundred more head."

Prescott paused and shook his head. "But do you
think the bankers give a damn about that? All they

can see is dollars and cents and the loans you've got coming due."

Payne downed the remainder of his bourbon and set the glass on the table. "And this Sam Wyngate person—what role does he play in all of this? Am I safe in assuming that he's one of the bankers?"

Pouring himself a fresh glass of whiskey, Prescott said under his breath, "That sneaky son of a bitch ain't no banker. He's just rich enough to own half of Texas is all."

"Then he's not one of your creditors, too?"

"No, he's some big high-rolling bastard from up Dallas way. Been after us to sell the Triple T to him for the past ten years or so. I swear, if I didn't know better I'd say he's the one who sent Papa to an early grave."

Payne deliberately narrowed his features and stiffened his spine. "Wyngate killed our father?"

"Not with a gun. With his infernal mouth. He just didn't know how to take no for an answer. Kept coming around every so often, mostly when times were rough, making Papa all kinds of offers. Making Papa sicker than he already was." Prescott leaned forward. "You ever hear of a man in control of his faculties selling off land that's been in his family for generations for fifty thousand dollars? Fifty thousand *measly* dollars for over a half a million acres of prime grazing pasture and good water? Only an outright fool would do something as stupid as that, and Papa was no fool."

No, their father was no fool, Payne thought. He was just an evil, uncaring bastard. He kept this thought to himself. "Fifty thousand is all Wyngate offered you?"

"At the beginning, yeah. Once he realized we weren't interested in his charitable handout, he upped the offer to a hundred thousand. Then a hundred and a quarter." Prescott shook his head. "Papa said no to two hundred thousand with his last breath. But do you think Wyngate let Papa's passing stop him? Hell, no. Now the bastard's stopped playing civil and started playing dirty. Real dirty. I found out the other day that he's trying to buy the Triple T right out from under us."

"How can he do that when he knows you're not interested in selling to him?"

"Easy," Prescott said. "And it's all legal, too. He's gone behind my back and started buying up all the outstanding loans I've got against the ranch. Now, instead of owing the bankers, I owe him. It's just a matter of time before he decides to call in those loans. When he does, I'm finished, and Triple T is history. There's no way I can raise the cash to pay him."

Payne focused his attention on the half-empty glass in front of him, forcing himself to show no outward response. Inside, however, he felt strangely ambivalent, though he was at a loss to explain why. He knew he should be pleased that his father's land, which the old bastard had held dearest above all else, would be taken from him posthumously. Instead, he felt an inexplicable sense of loss, as if something he cherished was going to be taken from him.

"I tell you," Prescott said, "if I can't come up with the cash soon, Wyngate'll be evicting all of us from the Triple T, lock, stock, and barrel." Taking a deep breath, he stared his brother straight in the eye, his uneasiness clearly obvious. "Which, I guess, is where you come in."

"Me?"

"Yeah. You're part owner now. Along with inheriting half a million acres of ranch land, the water rights, the house, and the herd, you're also responsible for the debts. You feel like helping us out?"

"Feel like it?" Payne released an unamused chuckle. "Of course I feel like it. Unfortunately, circumstances won't allow me to do so." Circumstances and a certain bargain he'd struck that he couldn't get out of, even if he wanted to.

"Aw hell, I'm next to useless where discussing foreign currency and the value of property are concerned, but if it's like it is here, it shouldn't take too long to sell your place in England, should it?"

"My place? You mean the house I have in London?"

"Yeah."

Payne could only laugh. "You have an exalted opinion of me, brother. My house isn't worth the amount you need. Not even a fraction, believe me."

"At this point, anything's better than nothing."

"You don't understand, Prescott. My house is nothing more than a few rooms above a converted stable in a mews. An alleyway," he added, seeing the confused look that crossed Prescott's face. "I have some nice pieces of furniture, a painting or two that might be worth more than I paid for them, but that's about all, other than the necessary amenities—gaslights and running water. There are no gardens, no drawing rooms, no old masters hanging on my walls. Hell, I don't even have servants' quarters, because I don't have servants. Just a lady who comes in when I can afford to pay her."

"But your clothes."

"What about them?"

"I may not know much about what men are wearing in London these days, but even I know you didn't buy them off a shelf in a dry goods store. They look tailor-made."

"They are," Payne said, realizing that his brother had a good eye. "But I need to dress this way to make a living. You see my, er, clients, for lack of a better word, wouldn't associate with me if I dressed any other way. They're rather fastidious in that sense. But as fashionably expensive as my clothes might be, they're only for show, to attract the customers. To put it in a nutshell, I suppose you could say they're the ill-gotten gains of my somewhat unsavory profession."

"How unsavory?" Prescott asked, minutely fearful of how Payne would reply.

"I imagine that would all depend on how one looks at it. Personally, I think of my profession as an honorable one. Others . . ." He completed the sentence with an eloquent shrug. "Well, you'll have to judge for yourself. I'm a gambler."

"A gambler? You mean you play cards for a living? Poker, five card stud, shit like that?" Good Lord Almighty, Prescott thought, finding the notion unbelievably absurd. He'd come across cardsharps a time or two, had even sat in on a few games with them, but his own twin brother, a gambler? He couldn't believe it.

"More than just cards," Payne said. "I'm rather adept at roulette and dice as well. Though I must admit, cards are my strong suit. Sometimes I play the games very well. Other times I'm lucky to walk away from the tables still wearing the shirt on my back. Recently, though, lady luck has been very generous to me. If she hadn't been, I doubt I'd have been able to afford to sail to America."

"Well, damn," Prescott said, unable to hold back his groan of disappointment. "What you're saying is, you're just as broke as the rest of us, is that it?"

"I'm afraid so."

"I don't suppose there's a chance in hell of you holding some big IOUs either, is there?"

"No. I managed to collect all of them before I sailed. I was short of working capital and needed it during the trip across."

"Yeah, working capital—I'm always short of that." Especially now, Prescott thought. And if he didn't find some soon, he didn't know what he'd do. The Triple T was everything to him, and if he lost it to a no-good son of a bitch like Wyngate, his father would rise up out of the grave and haunt him for the rest of his living days.

"Is there no chance that this Wyngate character would consider giving you an extension on your loans?"

"You mean go up to Dallas and ask him face to face?" Prescott shook his head. "You don't know the bastard like I do. He hasn't got a sympathetic bone in his whole body. He wants the ranch, and by God, he'll do anything to get it. Hell, he's already *done* that, hasn't he?" Suddenly a thought struck him. "But there may be a way."

"How?"

Prescott eyed his brother. "Not rob, but borrow from Peter to pay Paul, how else?"

Payne and Prescott went their separate ways when they finished celebrating at the saloon. Prescott returned to the ranch, but Payne stayed on in town, having made the excuse that he wanted to settle his bill at the hotel before moving permanently out to the Triple T. The moment he arrived at the hotel, however, he hurried briskly past the front desk and headed straight for the stairs and his room.

Just as he had hoped, Payne found Blodgett lying in bed, a bleary look on his face, as if he'd found a night's companionship with a bottle rather than a willing woman.

"Didn't think you'd be coming back so soon, Cap'n," Blodgett said, rousing himself. "Thought you'd be staying a while longer out at them new posh digs of yours."

The Triple T, posh? If Blodgett only knew, Payne thought as he sat down at the room's rickety desk and pulled writing materials out of the top drawer. The accommodations were comfortable, yes, but far from posh.

"I'm only staying a while, Chauncey. They're expecting me back before nightfall."

"Ah, your new kin. You likes 'em, do you?"

"Well enough, I suppose," Payne said with a frown. He found it difficult to concentrate on the words he was writing and talk at the same time.

"And that Patience girl? What about her? You like her well enough, too?"

With a sigh of impatience, Payne stopped writing for a moment. "She goes by the name of Chloe, not Patience. And as you know, I've yet to meet a lady that I've disliked."

Blodgett gave him a slow, gap-toothed grin. "Aye, that's my Cap'n. Always was one with an eye for a well-turned ankle, you were. Wish I had your luck."

If Blodgett would bathe more often and stay away from the demon rum, Payne knew the man could improve his standings with the fairer sex. "A well-turned ankle, as you put it, is the last thing on my mind at the moment."

"Wasn't before we got to this heathenish land."

"Well, things have changed. We've business to attend to."

"We? But I already been to the banks like you told me," Blodgett said defensively. "Spent nearly all that money you gave me, too. Barely had enough left to buy me a meal last night."

His meal obviously came in liquid form, Payne thought. "Yes, I know, and as I told you before, you did a good job. No one here suspects what we're up to. Well, they may suspect something, but they can't prove that I'm connected with you or your recent transactions."

"That's right. I never once mentioned your name. Wyngate's either, for that matter."

"Quite right. Now I've got another errand for you to run."

Realizing that Trefarrow wasn't chastising him for doing his job halfway, Blodgett relaxed. He rose from the bed, puffing out his chest as he pulled his soiled vest down over his portly stomach. "Aye, that's what I'm here for. Whatcha want me to do now?"

"I need you to catch the next train to Dallas."

"Dallas?" Blodgett asked, a frown crossing his shallow forehead.

"Yes. I believe there's one leaving within the hour. You'll have to hurry." Pushing away from the desk, Payne stuffed the note he'd been writing into an envelope. "You're to deliver this personally to our friend Mr. Wyngate. No one else, you understand? Hand it directly to Wyngate himself."

"But I thought Wyngate was in Houston."

"He was, when we first arrived. By now, though, he should be at his home in Dallas. I think he should be appraised of the latest financial developments."

Blodgett took the envelope and stuck it inside his vest. "Should I tell him how much of his money we had to spend?"

"If he asks, of course."

"He's not likely to get mad, is he?"

"No, why should he?"

"I don't know. It just seems to me that them bankers were far too jolly when I handed them all that cash. They weren't respectful at all when I walked in their fancy offices. Looked at me like I had two heads or something, they did. But were they beaming when I left. I say they were. Evil-like, you know? Like they couldn't wait to get their greedy hands on it. You think maybe they cheated us, Cap'n?"

"One can never be certain with a banker, Chauncey, but I seriously doubt it. More likely than not, they were overcome with delight at the notion of having one less outstanding account to foreclose. Now, you hurry and catch that train. The sooner you get to Dallas, the better."

Blodgett nodded and headed for the door, slipping on his wrinkled coat. "One more thing," he said, turning back to face Payne.

"Yes, what is it?"

"You'll be all right here alone, will you? I mean, I won't come back and find you missing your scalp or nothing, will I?"

Payne pulled a large valise out from under the bed.

"I'll be fine, Chauncey. I've got the protection of a family now, remember?"

"Aye, that you do."

"And as for the security of my scalp—I wouldn't worry, if I were you. I don't believe there have been any native insurrections in these parts in quite some time. Years, in fact."

6

Chloe had a strong, uncontrollable urge to scalp Payne, though. Gazing through the dressmaker's front window, she watched him in front of Atwell's Haberdashery for Men, apparently looking at the array of goods Mr. Atwell had on display. Even from a distance, and with his back to her, she felt certain he had a smirk of disdain on his face.

The nerve of the man, she thought. In the few days he'd been at the Triple T, he'd made a thorough nuisance of himself. He was always getting in the way, in hers especially, and he'd made a point of letting them all know just how much Texas differed from his precious England. What did he think they all were, backward clods, people with no sense of self-pride, let alone state pride? Well, they weren't. They were darn proud of who they were and where they lived. And he'd better get used to it or catch the next boat back to where he came from.

He wasn't in London, for heaven's sake. He was in

Waco, almost the heart of Texas. And if he didn't watch his step, somebody—she, if she had the chance—would take him down a notch or two.

What the dickens was he looking at so intensely, anyway? Chloe wondered. Lordy mercy! If she didn't know better, she would swear he was looking at a hat. No, it couldn't be that. The high and mighty Payne Trefarrow lower himself to don a Stetson? Ha! She'd like to see that.

Waiting for Verlene Buchholtz to finish with another customer so she could have her last bridal gown fitting, Chloe continued to move slowly about the front of the small shop, feigning interest in the dressmaker's notions and samples of fabric, but always staying close to the large window with its unimpeded view. Then suddenly she froze, her fingers curling tightly around a swatch of lace as she saw her future brother-in-law leave his post in front of Atwell's to enter the store. He was actually going in to buy something, she realized. Poor Prescott was having a devil of a time keeping the ranch running, yet there his brother was, fixing to spend good money on new clothes.

"Lovely, isn't it, dear?"

Startled by the unexpected voice behind her, Chloe jumped. Flushing with embarrassment, she turned sharply and saw Mrs. Buchholtz standing close by, the cheerfulness leaving her round face for a moment as a look of surprise took its place.

"The lace," Mrs. Buchholtz said. "It's lovely, isn't it?"

"Oh, yes. It's beautiful, Mrs. Buchholtz."

"I just got it in yesterday. I sent away all the way to Belgium for it."

The dressmaker had taken note of Chloe's distracted expression. "What were you staring at?"

"Me? Oh, nothing."

"It didn't look like nothing to me. My goodness, you looked as though you wanted to skin somebody alive."

"Gracious, no," Chloe said with an uneasy laugh, realizing that for propriety's sake, she had better move away from the window. It wouldn't do to have anyone in town suspect just how adversely Prescott's brother affected her. People would talk, and she couldn't afford to risk a scandal, not even one based on groundless innuendo.

"I just had something on my mind, that's all," she said. "You know, it's only a few more weeks until the wedding, and I've still got so many things to do."

The dressmaker smiled and patted her hand. "I understand."

"Are you ready for me to try on my dress?"

"As ready as I'll ever be. Why don't we go take a look at it. Tell me what you think." Mrs. Buchholtz led Chloe through the small shop to the fitting room at the rear.

Having been in the shop many times before, and knowing how Mrs. Buchholtz had her work room arranged, Chloe's eyes bypassed all the clutter, going immediately to the dress-form that stood against the wall. The moment she saw the dress hanging on it— her very own wedding dress—she gasped.

"It's beautiful," she said as she moved toward the garment. "I can't believe it's actually mine, that I'm finally going to get to wear it." That after all the years she'd waited for Prescott to realize she was a woman and not a child, that he loved her and wanted her to be his wife, her dream was actually going to come true.

Mrs. Buchholtz ran a hand over the garment's flowing skirt of white satin, touching it with almost reverent pride. "You really like it?"

"Like it? No, I love it. You've done a wonderful job. No one could have done better. Not even the finest dressmaker in all of London."

"London?" Mrs. Buchholtz frowned in confusion. "I would have thought that Paris was better known for its fashion styles than London, but what do I know?"

Chloe laughed uneasily, feeling the heat of embarrassment rush to her cheeks again. "That's what I meant to say—Paris, not London. My gracious, I don't know where my mind is half the time these days."

"It's on that handsome bridegroom of yours, where it ought to be," the dressmaker said as she unfastened the lovely dress and removed it from the form. "Once he sees you in this gown, he'll never be able to take his eyes off you throughout the whole ceremony. And he'll always remember how you looked as you walked down the aisle. Why don't you go ahead and step on into the next room and change? We'll have this fitting over and done with in a jiffy, and you can get back to that scallywag Prescott. If he's anything like all the other bridegrooms I've met in my day, I imagine he's getting right tired of waiting for you to finish in here. Men just don't seem to have the patience that we women do."

"Oh, Prescott didn't come into town with me this time," Chloe said, unbuttoning the topmost button of her blouse as she went into the changing room.

"He didn't?"

"No, he's real busy around the ranch these days."

"Of course he is. Probably tying up a lot of loose ends so the two of you can spend some time together, uninterrupted, on your wedding trip."

Chloe made no immediate reply. In truth, she couldn't say what Prescott had been doing. She only knew that he spent many long hours in the study, poring over lots of dusty old ledgers, and only coming out when it was time to eat or go to bed. The few times she'd been alone with him, he'd been so distracted that he hadn't done more than give her a quick peck on the cheek.

"I'm not sure we're going to get to have a wedding trip," Chloe said when Mrs. Buchholtz handed the wedding dress to her through a crack in the changing room curtain.

"No wedding trip? Why, that's awful, child. Every newly married couple should have at least a few days off to themselves. They need some time alone, to get to know one another. To get used to being man and wife."

"Oh, we'll have some time together. I've made certain of it." Chloe smiled to herself, envisioning their beautiful little hideaway, where no one with a lick of sense would dare bother them.

Months ago, while Prescott had been busy with his usual dawn-to-dusk chores around the ranch, she had occupied her time fixing up her parents' old house, the house in which she had been born eighteen years ago. She'd gotten some of the ranch hands to paint it inside and out, then she'd scrubbed it top to bottom, put new curtains on all the windows, and even managed to plant flowers in the beds around the front porch. Once finished, the house reminded her of a fairy tale cottage, a magical place where a prince and princess from warring families might have a secret, forbidden tryst.

Stop thinking such childish thoughts, she told herself chidingly. She was no princess, and Prescott, despite his few virtues, was far from being a prince. He rode a buckskin mare, not a white charger. He wore Levi's, scuffed boots, and a faded workshirt most of the time, not a shiny suit of armor. And he had never saved her from a fire-breathing dragon. Shoot, the closest thing she'd ever seen around these parts that even came close to resembling a dragon was a six-inch-long horny toad behind the outhouse, and it sure hadn't been breathing fire.

Instead of retreating to the back of Chloe's mind, the fairy tale image of herself and Prescott only grew stronger when she stepped out of the changing room and stared at herself in Mrs. Buchholtz's full-length mirror. Tears of joy suddenly stung her eyes. Why, with her hair worn up instead of down and tucked beneath her bridal veil, she *would* look like a princess. And once Prescott got dressed in his best Sunday suit, he'd surely look like a prince.

"It's still a little snug-fitting around the waist," Mrs. Buchholtz said, "but a tighter corset ought to take care of that. You do have one, don't you?"

"Yes, ma'am, I sure do!"

With an approving nod, Mrs. Buchholtz patted her hand. "You're a good girl, Chloe Bliss. One of the best in town. You've got a level head on your shoulders. You know what's right and what's wrong, and I've never known a time when you've ever done anything indecent. I don't know what I was thinking—you going without a corset. It was silly of me, wasn't it?"

"Not all that silly. There are times when I do go out without a corset. I have to. I can't really wear one when I ride Whicker. The stays poke me in all sorts of odd places."

"Well, all that matters is that you wear one on your wedding day. Besides, you're so small in the waist anyway, I imagine no one notices when you're on a horse. Now then, from the looks of you in this dress, I'd say I've only got a nip here and a tuck there, and it'll all be finished. Why don't you slip on out of it. We certainly wouldn't want it to get all tainted, now would we?"

"Tainted?"

Mrs. Buchholtz smiled. "Don't tell me you haven't heard that old wives' tale."

"I'm afraid I haven't."

"Heaven's above, child, it's been around longer than I have. And that's quite a while, let me tell you."

"What is the old wives' tale? Tell me."

"Well, I always heard that it was bad luck for a bride to wear her wedding dress for too long before her wedding. Just a few minutes at a time, until it's completely finished, but no more."

"Is that an old German tale?"

The dressmaker thought for a moment. "You know, I can't rightly say. It's just something I remember my mama always said to us girls when we were growing up. There were six of us, you know. Six girls and one boy. Poor little thing. Brother didn't stand a chance around all us women. Papa neither, for that matter." She shook her head. "Well, never you mind about old wives' tales or what country they came from. You just think about that handsome young man of yours."

Chloe needed no second urging to do that. She was thinking about Prescott. . . . Until she walked out of the dressmaker's shop and bumped into Payne. Then all thoughts of her future husband fled her mind as she took in the appearance of her brother-in-law-to-be.

Gone were the tailored pants and coat, the immaculate white shirt, and polished shoes that he'd been wearing that morning. In their place were a pair of Levi's that hugged his slim hips and muscular thighs in an almost unseemly fashion, a blue-and-white checked shirt that caressed the contours of his broad shoulders, and a pair of new boots, their pointed toes shining in the bright sunlight. To top it all off, a spotless black Stetson covered his thick blond hair.

For the life of her, Chloe couldn't take her eyes off the hat, or off of the face beneath it. Payne looked so rugged, so . . . handsome. And so unlike Prescott, even though she knew that if Payne had a day's growth of beard, a mustache, and muttonchop sideburns, she wouldn't be able to tell the brothers apart.

"Should I take your silence to be one of approval or disapproval?" Payne asked.

"What?"

"You're staring at me. I can't help but wonder if I've made the sort of impression that I intended. Or perhaps I merely look ridiculous."

Realizing that she had been gaping at Payne, Chloe snapped her jaw shut and swallowed. She turned away and stepped off the sidewalk into the street. "You look okay," she said.

"So then you approve?"

"I guess so, yes."

"You don't think the hat's too much, do you?" he

asked, adjusting the brim. It was so wide, he felt as though he was wearing an umbrella on his head—a rather large umbrella that not only blocked out the sunlight beaming down on them but, with the brim pulled down low, impeded most of his vision.

She chanced another quick look at him, making certain her gaze went nowhere near his face. She suddenly felt an impish surge. "Not if you're fixing to get yourself into a gunfight."

Her response surprised Payne. "A gunfight? Why would I want to do that? I'm not a gunfighter. I don't even own a weapon."

"Then it might have been better if you'd bought a white hat, instead of that black one."

"Why white?"

"This is Texas, Payne. The Wild West, like they say in all those dime novels. You *have* read a dime novel before, haven't you?"

"I've had a passing acquaintance with one or two, yes. But in case you don't already know, Chloe, a novel is a piece of fiction. Fiction means the body of work isn't true."

"Maybe not all of it's true, but sometimes a good part of it can be based on fact. A lot of those writers do a real convincing job of twisting the truth to suit their purposes. They exaggerate what really happened to make it more interesting reading. You'd better watch yourself. Around these parts, only scallywags and no-accounts and men hankering to get even with someone who's done 'em wrong would dare wear black on Main Street at high noon."

At that moment, Payne saw a mischievous grin twitch the outer corner of her mouth, and he realized that she'd been teasing him. Well, if she could tease, so could he. "That being the case, then I imagine I'd better ask Prescott for the loan of one of his revolvers. A man should be able to protect himself if the need arises."

Chloe tossed back her head and laughed. "You, with a gun? You're a city slicker. You probably don't even know how to handle one. Chances are, you'd end up shooting off your own foot."

"Being from a city, as you put it, doesn't preclude one's knowledge or ability with firearms, Chloe."

"You know how to shoot a gun?"

"I've handled weapons before. Many times." Mostly while hunting pheasant in the highlands of Scotland, but Payne didn't think she needed to know that. The weekends he'd spent with some of England's foremost idle rich were a thing of his past, and he would prefer not to dwell on that time of his life. Those days were long gone, and he had new, more exciting horizons ahead of him.

"Have you ever shot anybody?" she asked as they reached her horse.

"Not intentionally, no."

"Prescott has," she said. "And he did shoot him intentionally. Fact is, he killed the man."

Chloe's matter-of-fact response left Payne speechless for a moment. She wasn't teasing him this time, or trying to intimidate him with the raucous ways of the West; she was serious. Dead serious, by the sound of it. "Why did he kill him?"

"He was trying to steal Prescott's horse."

This explanation seemed to make sense. Stories about horse thieves and how American Westerners treated them had been circulated around London since the first man had gone out West. The miscreants had either been hanged from the nearest tree or, as in this case, shot on sight. Even Payne could understand why a horse thief would need to be dealt with in such a hasty, barbaric manner. In such a harsh land as this, where the closest town could sometimes be fifty miles away, the possession of a horse could mean life or death—life if you had one, death if you didn't. But to think that his own brother had actually killed a man. . . .

"They were about a hundred miles from here," Chloe said, "out in west Texas, the middle of nowhere. No water, no shelter for miles around, and a bad storm was brewing. The other man's horse had stepped in a prairie dog hole, broken his leg, and had to be shot. When he tried to steal Prescott's horse— the way Prescott tells it—they got into a fight, and the man drew on him and missed. Then Prescott got ahold of his gun and shot the man dead in his tracks."

"That's self-defense, Chloe, not murder."

Her eyebrows arched in surprise. "I never said anything about murder."

"No, but with all your talk about shootouts at high noon, you more or less implied it."

She mounted her horse in one easy movement, gathering the reins in her ungloved hand. "All I'm implying, Payne, is that if you're going to carry a gun—if you're even thinking about it—you'd better know how to use it."

With that, she pulled the reins, turning the horse with an audible clicking sound of her tongue, and rode off down the street.

A thousand conflicting thoughts and impressions raced through his head as Payne watched her until she disappeared around a corner. He stood there a moment longer and then turned to collect his own horse, which was tied to a hitching post down the street. The only conclusion he could reach was that Chloe was one incredible lady.

No, not lady, exactly, he amended. One incredible young woman. She didn't have the sophistication or the mendacity of the so-called ladies he had encountered in the past, who spent much of their time plotting little schemes and dramas to give meaning to their rich, boring lives. Chloe was different. Though he hadn't known her long, he could already tell that she was totally guileless and completely honest. She said what she thought and felt and behaved the same way.

If that were the case, he wondered, then why had she warned him about wearing a revolver? Could it possibly mean that she cared for him?

No, she didn't care yet. But she would.

Smiling, Payne mounted his horse and rode after her.

7

Chloe had never felt so frustrated in her life. She and Prescott were due to be married in less than three weeks, they still had hundreds of things to do before their wedding day, and he had suddenly announced at breakfast that morning that he was going to go to Dallas for a week or two. Just like that, out of the blue. One minute it had been, "Please pass the gravy, Aunt Em," and the next, "Oh, by the way, I'm going to Dallas this morning." When she and Aunt Emmaline had asked him why the need for such a prolonged trip, he had said, "Business," stubbornly refusing to elaborate.

To make matters worse—and it infuriated Chloe to even admit such a thing—she was actually beginning to get used to having Payne underfoot. Moreover, she was beginning to like him. She wasn't the only one, either; Aunt Emmaline gushed and giggled like a schoolgirl whenever Payne complimented her cooking or told her how pretty she looked in a new dress.

And while he was still as unfamiliar with the day-to-day workings of the ranch as Chloe would be if suddenly thrust into Queen Victoria's court, even the ranch hands had taken a shine to him. They no longer called him "that London dandy," but "Mr. Payne." They didn't balk or snicker when he asked them to show him how they used their ropes to lasso a calf for branding. They even warned him about the dangers of saddle-breaking the wild bronco they'd caught out on the range. Payne had heeded their warnings—but only after he had tried his hand at bronco-breaking and landed on his backside in the middle of the muddy corral.

His behavior toward Chloe still caused her distress, though. He was always showing up when she least expected him, and in the oddest of places. He appeared once at the church social that Prescott hadn't been able to attend because he'd had to work on the ranch books, and again outside the dry goods store in town a few days ago, offering to carry her parcels. If she didn't know better, she would swear that he had followed her on both occasions with the express purpose of being seen in public with her. Did he intend to cause gossip? Lordy, she hoped not.

What bothered Chloe most was that Payne still acted far too familiar with her, especially when they were alone. She had lost count of the times he had all but cornered her, leaning close, his breath fanning her cheek as he spoke to her in that deep, velvety voice of his. Though his words sounded innocent enough on the surface, his intimate manner embarrassed her and made her feel funny inside. Much funnier inside than Prescott had ever made her feel.

"Are you going to see me off?"

The sound of Prescott's voice beside her startled her. She had been sitting on the front porch swing, lost in thought as she rocked back and forth, staring blindly out at the overabundance of spring flowers in the garden. She looked up and studied her handsome bridegroom-to-be. He seemed uncomfortable and out of place in his dark blue traveling suit, as uncomfortable and out of place as Payne had looked the day the wild bronco threw him.

"Or are you going to sit there and sulk 'til I get back?"

"I'm not sulking," she said, taking exception to his brisk tone of voice.

"Sure looks to me like you're sulking."

"Well, I'm not."

"Then are you going to wish me well like a good girl, or what?"

"If I knew why it was so all-fired important for you to take off for Dallas like this, I'd be happy to wish you well. But since you won't tell me, I'll—" She broke off and inhaled a deep breath. Acting petulant, she knew, would not make Prescott change his mind. If anything, it might make him more determined to go. "I'll wish you well anyway. Have a safe trip, Prescott."

With his familiar boyish grin on his face, he bent toward her and planted a kiss on her forehead. "That's my girl."

Before he could move away, a sudden, indefinable urge made Chloe lift her head. She wound her hand around Prescott's neck, her fingers combing through the thick hair at his nape, and brought his head down to hers. Her lips captured his, lingering there to taste the blended flavors of coffee and tobacco so unique to Prescott.

At that moment, Payne came around the corner of the front porch. He was on his way to the stable to collect a horse for a morning ride, but the sight of his brother and Chloe wrapped in such a close embrace brought him up short. He stepped back, letting his back hug the wall, his gloved hands balling into fists as he experienced a powerful surge of . . . what? Jealousy? Anger? Perhaps a little of both.

Payne rationalized that he had every reason to feel jealous. Prescott had everything he'd ever wanted—a home, the security of a family, and the respect of his peers. These were all things Payne had been denied, even as a child. Prescott also had the love of a good woman, a decent woman, one who would stand by his side no matter what the circumstances. One to whom Payne felt oddly attracted.

But why should he feel angry? His plan was going well—very well, in fact. Within a matter of weeks, he would set the final part of his scheme into motion, drive the final nail into the coffin of the Triple T, and rid himself once and for all of the bad memory left to him by his uncaring father. Then he would finally be even with his so-called family.

When all was said and done, he would take his earnings from Wyngate with a clear conscience and get on with his life, while the rest of them could . . . Well, they could do whatever the hell they wished. Their welfare was of no concern to him. Why should it be? They had never been concerned about his welfare, not once in all of his thirty years of existence.

Chancing a quick peek around the corner of the house, Payne saw Prescott straighten, his kiss with Chloe obviously ended.

When Prescott didn't respond to her kiss, a

strange uneasiness filled Chloe. She felt confused by the emotions she had wanted so desperately to feel but didn't. The expression on Prescott's face told her he didn't feel those emotions, either. Only a trace of humor filled his gaze, not passion. Well, maybe they weren't supposed to feel passion, or overwhelming desire, or whatever it was people in love usually felt, she thought. Maybe they were above such base feelings.

Then again, maybe they weren't. Perhaps all they needed was the right kind of inspiration, the kind she knew he had experienced with countless other women, countless other times. He had garnered a reputation of sorts around town, and though he had tried to keep it hidden from her, she had heard about it. Oh, how she had heard, from Ivy, Daisy, and Rose, and most of her other so-called friends.

"Want me to bring you back something pretty from Dallas?" he asked.

His casual question brought her up short. What was she thinking? She wasn't the one who needed inspiring; she was about as inspired as a woman on the verge of marriage could get. Prescott, on the other hand, needed to realize that she wasn't a child who would be satisfied with just "something pretty from Dallas;" that she wanted more—much more from him.

"Yes," she said, leaning back in the swing and striking what she hoped was a seductive pose. "I'd like a lacy nightgown. For our wedding night. Something in silk will do. Get the color you like best."

A flush slowly crawled up Prescott's neck, and his grin vanished. "You ought not be talking like that. A young lady your age—why, it ain't fitting."

"Fitting! Goodness gracious, Prescott, we're going

to be married. Husband and wife. How do you think husbands and wives talk to each other?"

"Not that way, that's for dang sure."

"Yes, they do. How do you suppose they get together and make babies?"

Prescott jammed his hat on his head with one hand as he bent down to hoist up his valise with the other. "I'll be back in a week or two. Sooner if all goes well. You behave while I'm gone."

"*You* behave," she said as he stormed down the front steps. Now angered by his high-and-mighty attitude, she leaped out of the swing and marched to the porch railing. "You hear me, Prescott Trefarrow? While you're up there in Dallas, you behave yourself. We're getting married just as soon as you get back here."

He grumbled something that she couldn't understand and rode away.

"Damn that man!" She stomped back to the swing and sat down with such force that the ceiling joists from which it hung loudly groaned. "Damn him, damn him, damn him!"

"A lovers' quarrel, so close to the wedding day?"

Chloe's head swung around. Payne leaned against the far corner of the porch, his arms and ankles crossed as he clicked his tongue and slowly shook his head.

"That doesn't sound good to me," he said. "Not good at all. Trouble definitely seems to be afoot in paradise."

How dare he eavesdrop on her private conversation with Prescott! She realized that her earlier thoughts of Payne had been totally false. She wasn't beginning to like him at all. In fact, at the moment, she almost hated the very sight of him. "Mind your own business, Payne," she said.

"I was minding it," he said, crossing the porch, "until I heard you and Prescott. It's not easy to ignore something that's going on right beneath your very nose. What's the matter? Didn't he like your little come-hither ploy?"

"Come-hither?"

"Your flirtation, your coquettish act," he explained as he sat down beside her, draping his arm across the back of the seat. "The rather heavy-handed assertion of your feminine wiles."

Chloe folded her arms and glowered out at the front yard. "I don't know what that man likes or doesn't like. At the moment, I swear, I don't particularly care, either."

"Yes, you do."

"Ha!"

"Chloe, if you didn't care, you wouldn't be in such a royal snit."

"Well, I've got a right to be in a royal snit, don't you think? He's got no cause to act all high and mighty when all I did was— Well, I was just trying to—oh, I don't know—be like a loving fiancée ought to be, I guess. Dadgummit, Payne, we're getting married in a few weeks. We're going to spend the rest of our lives together. He could at least try to act like a husband and not my big brother. Why, do you know that he . . ."

As Chloe continued to vent her frustrations, apprising Payne of his brother's faults, both past and present, a realization slowly came to him. Though she didn't know it, she had hit on the problem. Even Payne could see that Prescott didn't think of her as a loving bride-to-be, one to desire and lust after. Prescott simply saw her as his little sister.

Payne could easily understand why his brother saw her that way. According to what Aunt Emmaline had told him about them, Prescott had known Chloe all of her life. He had held her as an infant, watched her grow up, and no doubt even dried her tears when she had skinned her knee as a little girl. The death of her parents and her subsequent move to the Triple T must have strengthened their bond. Payne could see how Prescott would have been there to comfort Chloe, to help ease her painful loss. He hadn't been the only one, of course, but the twelve-year gap between their ages made him closer to her than anyone else at the ranch. Aunt Emmaline and his father, Garrett, had already been into their middle years, while Prescott hadn't been much more than a child himself, though he would have been close to the age of twenty at the time.

No, Prescott and Chloe's wasn't a relationship like countless other young lovers, and Payne seriously doubted that it ever would be.

He suddenly felt a powerful rush at having reached such an obvious conclusion. His mind began to race with thoughts, ideas, and possibilities. When he first saw Chloe at her engagement party, he had thought only to ingratiate himself in her life, befriend her, make himself indispensable, perhaps even turn her against Prescott if the need arose. And he had succeeded, up to a point. He could already tell that she had softened toward him, that she was beginning to trust him a little more each day. Otherwise she wouldn't be opening up to him now, telling him her innermost thoughts and feelings about her beloved Prescott.

But why stop at this vaguely flirtatious friendship? Why not take it one step further?

It would be a heady game, he decided, a very heady game indeed. With his arm still stretched across the back of the swing, he casually placed a hand on her shoulder, his fingers and thumb rubbing the shallow indentation of her collarbone in a gesture of tender consolation. Instead of turning her against his brother, he could just as easily turn his brother against her.

Much later that afternoon, Prescott stepped off the train and onto the platform at Dallas's bustling Union Depot. City folks, he thought with a disdainful sniff. They were always in such an all-fired hurry. You just couldn't trust folks who wouldn't slow down long enough to give you the time of day, let alone a polite nod.

With his battered valise held more closely to him, he started across the platform to the terminal building. Just as he was in sight of the doorway, a familiar figure caught his attention. Prescott knew he had seen the man before, but he couldn't remember where. It must have been in Waco, since he hadn't been to Dallas in well over a year.

Standing a few feet away, minding his own business as he waited for the train to Waco to start boarding, Chauncey Blodgett thought of the bottle of rum he had hidden away in his coat pocket. He couldn't wait to have himself another taste of it. Finding good rum in this godforsaken country had been almost impossible. The local natives liked their foul-tasting bourbon better. And if not bourbon, even worse, their rotgut rye. A good name, rotgut rye, for that's surely what it did—rot out the guts and make you crazy. But not his soul-soothing rum. It went down too smoothly, tasted too sweet, made you feel too pleasant to be harmful.

Blodgett turned to look around the platform. Suddenly his thoughts of the bottle in his pocket vanished as his stomach twisted into knots. The Cap'n's brother was looking right at him!

He pivoted sharply on his scuffed heels and scurried behind a large group of the train's departing passengers. No one was supposed to know he was here. If that blighter Prescott caught up with him and started asking questions, the Cap'n would be in an awful spot. Blodgett knew only too well of his own loose tongue. Pour a drink or two down his throat, and he'd tell everything he knew to anyone who asked. He could never let that happen; he owed the Cap'n too much to risk betraying him. After all, hadn't Payne saved his life back in that filthy alley in London?

Urged onward by fear, Blodgett darted behind a large wagon full of bags and valises that was parked near the edge of the platform.

Prescott frowned as the little man disappeared from view, but he went on about his business, making his way through the crowded terminal to the bustling street outside. He'd probably been mistaken, anyway. A lot of folks looked like other folks; that man could have been nothing but a stranger. Or maybe his overworked imagination was playing tricks on him.

"Need a ride, mister?"

Prescott eyed the driver and carriage with uncertainty. He really couldn't afford to hire a carriage. He had only enough money in his pocket to pay for a few nights in a good hotel and buy himself a few meals, maybe even visit one of Dallas's better sporting houses if he was in the mood. Still, if he didn't spend some money, or at least make an attempt to prove to the influential bankers of Dallas that he was a successful businessman worthy of their time and attention, he might not get the loans he needed.

"Yeah," he said, tossing his valise to the driver. "You know of a good hotel around here?"

"Sure. I know all of 'em."

"Then I'll leave the choice to your discretion." Prescott settled himself in the carriage seat and smiled. "Discretion." He liked that word. It sounded kind of distinguished, like something Payne might say.

"You gonna be in town long?"

"As long as it takes . . . my good man." Prescott had to stop himself from laughing at his audacity. Lordy, he was sounding more like his brother by the minute. Give him enough time, and he supposed he might even develop a sissified accent like Payne's.

No, not sissified, he amended, feeling a slight twinge of guilt for thinking such a thing about his brother. No Trefarrow had ever been a sissy, not even the womenfolk. Payne was cultured. Yeah, that was it. Cultured and refined.

Now if he could only come up with some of his brother's culture and refinement and display it for the bankers he would be meeting soon, all would be well.

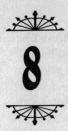

8

Life at the ranch went on as usual, even without Prescott to oversee the details. The hands rounded up strays and brought them back to the main herd, cleaned out the stalls regularly, and fed and groomed the horses.

But while an easy daily routine seemed to pervade down at the bunkhouse and the stables, a noticeable tension developed inside the homestead. It seemed that every time Chloe turned around, Payne was nearby, watching her, offering to help. His constant nearness began to take its toll.

"He's like a puppy dog, Aunt Em," she said one afternoon as she sat at the kitchen table, peeling potatoes for dinner. "A gangly puppy with big feet."

"That boy's feet aren't big," Emmaline said. "At least, they're no bigger than Prescott's."

"You know what I mean, Aunt Em."

"Maybe he's just lonely for his brother. They were getting on real well before Prescott had to leave."

"If Payne misses Prescott so much, why doesn't he go into town and find himself a new friend?" And leave me alone, Chloe thought. The looks he gave her were becoming disconcerting.

"Payne's a bit too old for a playmate, don't you think?"

With a sigh, Chloe picked up another potato. "I guess."

Emmaline watched the way Chloe attacked, rather than peeled, the potatoes. If she didn't start paying more attention to what she was doing, they'd end up with nothing but boiled peelings for supper. "Something bothering you, child?"

"Maybe." Hearing the wistful tone of her voice, she wrenched her thoughts off of Payne and back to the discussion at hand. "Maybe Payne's not the only one who's lonely for Prescott."

"You, lonely for— Ha!"

"It's not funny. I am marrying the man, you know. Doesn't that give me a right to miss him as much as Payne does?"

"The only thing you miss are the fights you and Prescott have regularly."

"Aunt Em, we don't fight."

"Well then, squabble. I swear, you two are like that old cat and dog we used to have. Always at each other, raising the other's dander. I'm amazed the two of you ever stayed calm long enough to find out you liked each other, let alone were in love."

"I think we were always in love. It just took Prescott a little longer to realize it than it did me, that's all."

"Maybe," Emmaline said quietly.

Taking her tone for one of disbelief, Chloe felt a

need to defend herself. "Prescott does love me, you know."

"I never said he didn't. I know he loves you."

"So what do you mean by 'maybe'?"

Emmaline realized she couldn't keep it to herself any longer. She turned down the fire beneath the skillet of sizzling chicken and sat down at the table beside Chloe. "I've known Prescott most of his life, since Garrett brought him home from England. I've known you all of yours, since the day I helped your mama deliver you. Next to my own three grown daughters and my eleven grandchildren, the two of you are the most precious people in my life. Lord have mercy, I was more pleased than I had a right to be when you two told me you had decided to get married. At first, that is. But when I had some time to think about it, to think about what you were fixing to do, I couldn't help but get a little worried."

"Worried?"

"Yes. For one thing, you two are too dadgum much alike."

"Aunt Em, we're as different as night and day."

"In some ways you are, but in others . . ." Emmaline's voice trailed off, and she shook her head. "It's not good for a couple to have so much in common. There's got to be a little difference to keep the attraction alive."

"We're attracted to each other." At least, Chloe knew she was attracted to Prescott. She could only guess how he felt about her. There were times when she was almost convinced that he still thought of her as an annoying little girl, one to be tolerated more than cherished and desired.

Emmaline placed a flour-covered hand over

Chloe's. "You know he's had other women, don't you?"

Heat rushed to Chloe's face. "Yes, I know. But once we're married, that's all going to be ancient history. He'll have me to come home to every night. He won't *need* to go see those floozies at Carrigan's."

"And if he should go see them, what then? Men will be men, you know. They like to let on that they're strong, but they're weak in a lot of ways, weaker than us women."

The thought of Prescott going to another woman for intimate consolation made Chloe stop and think. She knew that as a bride-to-be, and a woman in love, she should feel hurt and jealous by the notion, but in truth, she could feel nothing. The idea didn't even make her angry.

"Well, he might do it once," she said, "but I'll make sure he won't ever do it a second time. If I have to, I'll clobber him with a skillet and knock some sense into him."

Emmaline studied her a moment and then rose to her feet. "Maybe I'm wrong. Maybe you two are suited to each other after all. Lord knows you're both stubborn and hard-headed enough."

Chloe could live with a stubborn and hardheaded man, but could she live with an unfaithful one? Did Prescott have it in him to even want to be faithful? Aunt Em was right about one thing: he did have a mile-wide weak streak where some women were concerned, and even Chloe wasn't so naive as to try to deny that. But he was also a man of honor, one who lived by a stringent set of ethics that had been drummed into him by his father. And Garrett had been one of the most honorable men that she had ever known.

Though she tried to push it to the furthermost recesses of her mind, the question of Prescott's future fidelity still plagued her as she prepared for bed later that night. In the dim glow of her dressing table lamp, she eyed her reflection in the mirror. Did she possess the necessary qualities it would take to keep a man like Prescott faithful to her for more than a few weeks or months after they were married? She wasn't sure.

Although she considered herself somewhat attractive—not a raving beauty, perhaps, but not ugly either—Chloe knew that looks weren't everything. Nevertheless, she had to admit that they did play some importance, and all in all, her looks weren't so bad.

She had thick blond hair of an even color that hung in loose curls down to her waist; clear, dark blue eyes; a smooth complexion that was pale most of the year and tended to freckle only in the height of summer.

And while she supposed her figure was all right, it wasn't exactly overly endowed. Some might call her slender, and at one time, Prescott had called her skinny. But that was all right with her. Who wanted to look like a voluptuous hourglass anyway?

No, her appearance was not a problem. Her major liability, she knew, was her naivete. She didn't come close to having the worldly knowledge that Carrigan's floozies had, mainly because she didn't have their experience. Why, she hardly knew how to kiss a man. Prescott had all but told her as much the morning he'd left for Dallas.

But what was she supposed to do to acquire that kind of knowledge? She doubted she could find a set of detailed instructions or a pattern in a book. What should she do? Go out and find a man, a stranger who would take pity on her and—?

Overwhelmed by a sudden rush of embarrassment at the unfinished thought, Chloe quickly doused the lamp and crawled into bed. Goodness gracious, what was she thinking? She could no more approach a total stranger for that sort of tutelage than she could fly. She was a lady, and she would behave as one, no matter what.

Still the idea wouldn't go away. And the longer it lingered, the more she thought about it, about being with a man, having him kiss her, touch her in such a way that it made her lose control of all her senses, the more uneasy she grew. She tossed and turned in her bed, unable to fall asleep.

Deciding that a drink of water would help put her at ease, she quietly let herself out of her room. On tiptoe she headed down the hall to the kitchen at the back of the house, hearing the comforting sound of Aunt Em's snores as she passed her room. How nice to be able to sleep the slumber of the innocent, Chloe thought, then realized that she had just labeled herself as one who wasn't innocent. Well, maybe the old saying held some merit after all—there was no rest for the wicked. But did merely having wicked thoughts make one truly wicked at heart?

In the kitchen, she pumped a glass full of water and downed it in a few gulps. A second glass soon followed the first.

Still filled with the restlessness that had driven her from her bed, she wandered out onto the back porch and sat down in the old rocking chair Aunt Em kept near the door. A breeze blew out of the north, cooling her heated flesh and bringing her some relief. It was still only late spring, and already the nights were warm enough for one to sleep without covers. Summer would soon bring days so hot that one could barely breathe and nights so unsettling that—

"Couldn't sleep either, eh?"

Chloe flinched and almost leaped out of the rocker at the unexpected sound of the deep voice close by. When she recognized Payne's familiar silhouette at the corner of the porch she felt some of the fear leave her.

"You nearly scared me to death," she said, pressing a shaky hand to her still pounding heart. "I didn't know you were out here. Why aren't you in bed, sound asleep like Aunt Em?"

"I tried, but as it appears to be with you, sleep is an elusive commodity tonight." Tossing aside the cigar he had been smoking, he pushed himself away from the corner railing and approached her. "Tell me, are the nights in Texas often as warm as this one?"

Chloe smiled. "No. Some are warmer. Lots warmer."

Payne's groan made her stifle a laugh. Coming from England, he probably considered tonight a scorcher. Was there a surprise in store for him!

"Come August and September, when it really gets hot," she said, "you'll probably wish you were back home in London. I don't imagine it gets as warm there as it does here, London being so far up north and all."

"No, it doesn't. But I'll adapt."

He sounded very definite, she thought, as though getting used to a new climate would be as easy for him as breaking in a new pair of boots. "Then you're staying on?"

"Of course. Why would I leave?"

"Oh, I don't know. I just thought that you'd—" She broke off, uncertain how to end her remark. In truth, she didn't know Payne well enough to assume anything about his plans. What he did with his life was his business, not hers.

"You wouldn't be trying to get rid of me, would you, Chloe?"

"Certainly not. You're Prescott's brother, his family. You've got as much right to be here as he does."

"That's true," Payne said, drawing closer to her side.

"Just because you don't know anything about ranching, it doesn't mean you don't have it in you to learn."

"That's true, too."

He knelt down beside her, making her acutely aware of her state of dress, or rather her lack of it. She wanted to wrap her arms around herself and hide her thin nightgown from his gaze, but she fought down the urge. Surely he couldn't see anything in the dark. "There is a lot to learn, you know."

"I imagine there is."

"And not just about cows and steers and bulls and horses, either." His nearness was making her ramble like a nervous schoolgirl, but for the life of her, she couldn't stop the words from rushing out of her. "There's the weather to contend with and all its ramifications. You've got to know which pasture has the most water and the greenest grass, and which has been grazed the least. The one thing you can't afford to do is let your herd over-graze a pasture. That's courting nothing but disaster."

"Yes, courting nothing but disaster," Payne said, running a finger up her slender arm.

Chloe flinched at his touch. "What are you doing?"

"Just making certain you're not getting too cold. I couldn't live with myself if you caught a chill."

"I'm all right. I'm not cold."

"I know," he said huskily, his hand encircling her upper arm, his fingers casually brushing against the side of her firm breast. "You're very warm. Very soft, too. Like the finest satin."

Suddenly her mouth went dry. She was finding it very difficult to breathe normally, as her rapid heartbeat seemed to constrict her airway. "Payne, please don't."

"Don't what?" he asked, letting his hand trail down her arm to caress the slender outline of her fingers.

"You know—what you're doing."

"What am I doing, Chloe?"

"I don't know, but I wish you'd stop it."

"You don't like it when a man touches you?"

"No."

Payne clucked his tongue. "Poor Prescott."

"Prescott's not a man."

"He's not?"

"No. I mean, he's a man, but he's my fiancé, my future husband."

"So you like it when he touches you."

"I wouldn't be marrying him if I didn't."

"Does he touch you often?"

She hesitated a moment, knowing instinctively she couldn't tell Payne that Prescott almost never touched her because he respected her too much. Payne might think ill of his brother, might think him less of a man, just because he put her feelings before his own.

"Often enough," she finally replied, convinced it was a suitable response.

"I see. Then it's me you object to."

"I don't object to you," she said. "It's just that I don't like the way I feel when you touch me."

"Just how do I make you feel?"

She searched for the right word, wondering why she even felt compelled to answer him. "Itchy."

Chloe couldn't have surprised him any more if she had blatantly offered him the use of her body for the night. "Itchy," he repeated.

"I know it's not a ladylike way to feel, but—"

"Who says it isn't ladylike?"

"Miss Ponsonby."

"Who is Miss Ponsonby?"

"The headmistress of the finishing school I attended in Austin."

"And she told you that ladies weren't supposed to feel 'itchy' when they were touched by a man?"

"That's right."

Payne snorted. "Then I'm afraid Miss Ponsonby is one very misinformed woman. All ladies feel 'itchy' at one time or another in their lives."

"*All* of them?"

"All of them."

"Even the titled nobility in England?"

A low rumble began in the center of Payne's chest, coming out in a bubble of deep laughter. "Dear, dear Chloe, I could tell you stories that would leave a blush on your pretty face for the rest of your life. But I won't. For one thing, the night's far too short for me to begin delving into such a complicated explanation. For another, I'm not in the mood at the moment to disillusion you with such foul crudities. Suffice it to say that very few of the so-called ladies of England, whether they be either married or unmarried, behave like ladies behind closed doors. Bedroom doors, to be perfectly blunt."

Chloe swallowed. "You've known ladies like that?"

"Many of them."

She sank back in the rocking chair, surprised by his candor. "Lordy mercy, I don't believe it."

"Do you doubt that I would have knowledge of such things?" he asked, not caring that he sounded defensive. Granted, he wasn't titled nobility, but he had just as much right, when enticed, to crawl between a noblewoman's sheets as he did those of a common whore. And he had been enticed by both. Many times, many places, and all with the same satisfying conclusion.

"Well, no—you're a man," Chloe said. "It's expected of you to do things like that. But for a lady of the realm to—" She broke off, unable to verbalize her thoughts. "It's unseemly, that's all."

"It's not unseemly, Chloe. It's perfectly natural. And very understandable, too."

"A moment ago you said 'married or unmarried.'"

"That's right."

"Well, the ladies who are married—don't their husbands care? Don't they ever object when their wives have a—a dalliance behind their back?"

"Some care, some don't. As for objecting . . ." Payne shrugged. "You have to understand something, Chloe. For the most part, many men choose to turn a blind eye to their wives' extramarital activities. It's the polite thing to do, you see, the accepted thing to do. Above all things, one must not be the cause of a scandal. Besides, they can't really object to their wives' activities when they're being unfaithful themselves."

"With mistresses, you mean?"

Payne looked startled. "How do you know about such things?"

"I've read books," Chloe said with what she hoped was an informed, worldly tone.

"Then you must have learned from these books that most titled marriages are arranged."

"Yes, but I always understood that love came later."

"Chloe, my dear, listen very carefully. Joining estates and wealth are of the utmost importance when considering the union of two families. Love has very little to do with it. In England, love has very little to do with anything."

Chloe shook her head. "I can't believe it."

"Believe it. I know what I'm talking about."

"Oh, I don't doubt you. You're from England; you should know better than anyone what goes on there. It's just that I can't believe that the ladies in England are no better than those floozies at Carrigan's."

It was Payne's turn to be surprised. "You know about Carrigan's?"

"Know about it? Of course, I know about it. Everybody within fifty miles of Waco knows about Carrigan's floozies. We women just don't talk about them, that's all."

If she knew about the saloon girls at Carrigan's, there was a strong possibility she knew about Prescott's association with them. Though Payne wanted to explore that vein further, he knew that now was not the time to do so. Somehow, their conversation about infidelities among England's nobility had supplanted the earlier erotic mood he had managed to create. He had to get that mood back and try to intensify it to such a fever pitch that Chloe would turn to putty in his hands.

"With the obvious exception, they're really not much different from you, you know."

Chloe inhaled sharply. "Why, I'm nothing at all like those—those tainted women."

"Don't be offended. I said 'with the obvious exception.' Even a blind man can see you're decent, honorable, and quite undeniably a virgin."

Still insulted at the comparison, Chloe forgot to be offended by Payne's candor. "Then that makes me nothing like them, because they sure as shooting aren't any of those things."

"No, but you're as giving as they are, as kind, as sweet . . ." He let his hand cover hers, his face moving closer and closer to her parted lips. "Chloe. Sweet, sweet Chloe."

Despite her lack of experience, she realized what Payne was about to do. Deep down she wanted him to kiss her, but she couldn't let herself succumb to his charm. If she did, she would be no better than one of Carrigan's floozies.

"I'm tired. I think I'll go to bed." She leaped to her feet so suddenly that Payne lost his balance and would have ended on his backside had he not stretched out a hand to brace his fall. " 'Night," she said. "See you in the morning."

Watching her retreat like a frightened rabbit, Payne shook his head in dismay. He'd been so close, so damn close, and she'd slipped right through his fingers. Next time, he wouldn't disrupt the mood with talk of titled ladies with wandering eyes. He would take advantage of the situation as swiftly and efficiently as he could.

9

"Nasty weather this morning, isn't it?"
Prescott pulled off his hat and slapped it against his leg, splattering raindrops across his host's highly polished foyer.

He had been invited to have breakfast with one of his father's oldest, most trusted friends, Abner Harris. Had it not been for his chance encounter with the man the day after his arrival in Dallas, he'd still be wandering around, trying to make contact with the local bankers. But with Mr. Harris putting in a good word for him, he'd managed to line up meetings with the presidents of two of the largest banks in town, which were known for handing out big loans.

"As my pappy always said, 'Be thankful for the rain, it's good for the crops, and don't you forget it.'" Abner Harris chuckled as he took Prescott's hat and hung it on the rack next to the front door. "'Course, that was before we left Missouri and moved down here to Texas. After we'd been here a while, then the rain was good for the livestock, not the crops. Ranching's a might different from farming."

"Don't I know it. The only crop Papa would allow to grow on the Triple T was corn. Aunt Emmaline had a vegetable garden out back of the house, of course, but corn was the only other thing we grew. When the harvest came in, Papa would pick out a dozen or so of his prize steers and fatten them up on it. Feed 'em right out of his hand, almost."

"Yeah, I remember," Abner said, gesturing for Prescott to enter the dining room ahead of him. "Best beef I ever tasted came off of your ranch, son. Too bad you're having so much trouble. It'd be a damn shame if you lost it."

"I don't intend to let that happen, Mr. Harris. That spread's been in my family for over fifty years. I'm not about to let the likes of that shifty bastard Wyngate get control of it, not without a fight."

Harris grumbled in sympathy for him, then called out, "Rosalita! We're ready for breakfast now."

A moment later, a door in the corner of the dining room swung open and a dark-haired woman poked her head through the opening. She gave a sullen nod and disappeared, letting the door continue to swing behind her. Prescott got a good look inside the adjoining room, where glasses, pitchers, plates, and serving pieces were stacked neatly on shelves. In a big, fancy house like Harris's, it could only be the butler's pantry, he concluded.

"She's mad this morning," Harris said. "I don't know at what or who, but I 'spect it's something I said or done. You be sure and tell her this breakfast is the best one you ever ate, even if it ain't, you hear? Best damn cook in the whole state of Texas, Rosalita is, and I'd hate like hell to lose her, but when she gets mad, you gotta watch out. She's liable to put hot chili peppers in your biscuits. She's done it before."

"I like hot chili peppers," Prescott said, taking a seat at the long dining room table.

"I do too, but not in my biscuits."

Rosalita came through the swinging doors, bearing a huge tray laden with food. When she had finished laying out platters of ham, bacon, and steak, bowls of gravy and eggs, and a big plate piled high with steaming biscuits and fresh rolls, she muttered something to Harris in her native tongue and stalked out of the room.

"Yeah, just like I thought," Harris said, red-faced. "It's something I done. Lord knows what it was, but I'll have to figure out something to make it up to her. Probably end up with more of her relatives around the house."

Prescott waited until they were almost finished with the meal before he decided to broach the subject he'd come to discuss. It wasn't good to start talking business when the stomach was empty. "You find out anything about Wyngate?"

"Found out lots," Harris said, sawing into a thick slab of steak and aiming the fork at his mouth. "Don't figure you'll be liking it much, though."

"Damn him! I knew it. I knew all along he was behind all the shenanigans."

Harris chewed his bite methodically then swallowed it. "Don't go damning the man yet, son. He may be guilty of a lot of things, but buying up all your bank loans ain't one of them. Someone else is behind them shenanigans."

"You're sure?"

"As sure as I can ever be about a thing like that. Fact is, Wyngate's fit to be tied. Everybody in town has known all along how he's had his eye on your place, known how he'd sell his own mama to own it, if she wasn't already dead. Hell, not too long ago, all the man could do was brag about how he'd be taking over the Triple T just any day. Then a few weeks back, he wouldn't say nothing about it. We'd ask him how much headway he was making, of course, but he'd just clam up, not say a word. Acted as though your spread didn't mean anything to him anymore. But all the time he was denying interest in it, you could see this real mad look on his face, like someone else had beat him to the punch."

"Then if Wyngate's not behind it, who bought up all my loans?"

"Well, Woodley—that's my agent—asked around for me. Mentioned one man's name, but I swear I never heard of him before. Alls I know is he's some foreigner with a lot of money to throw around."

"A foreigner?"

"Yep. Someone, the way I figure it, who's got it in mind to own himself a large chunk of Texas. Your chunk, it appears."

"What name did Woodley mention?"

"Blodgett. Chauncey Blodgett."

Prescott frowned. "What the hell kind of name is that?"

"British. At least that's what Yates said. He's the head teller down at Mittelkopf's bank in Waco, the one Woodley got all this from."

Prescott knew Yates, but he was surprised the man would give out such information to a virtual stranger. He had thought that all bank transactions were confidential and not open to general gossip.

"Anyhow," Harris continued, "Yates told Woodley that when he heard Blodgett talking, he knew right off he was British. Not upper-class with all them fancy vowels and such, but lower class. Cockney, I think is what Woodley said. I can't say about Yates, of course, but I know for a fact that Woodley wouldn't know a Cockney accent if he stumbled on one. That boy's never been out of the state of Texas in his whole life."

"No, but Yates would know," Prescott said. "He's from England."

"I'll be damned."

Prescott nodded as he spread butter and jelly on a biscuit. "I got it straight from the man himself."

"You don't say."

"Well, hell, Waco's not near as big as Dallas. Folks run into each other all the time. My first time to meet Yates outside of the bank—my only time, as a matter of fact—was right after he went to work for Mittelkopf. We got to talking, and before I knew it, he'd told me most of his life story. Not that he had much to tell, mind you. At the time, I wasn't really interested in hearing what he had to say, but for some reason, it stuck. I guess 'cause my grandpappy was from England and all."

"Ya don't say. Small world, ain't it?" Harris said.

Prescott suddenly realized he was missing something, something important. It was a small world. He felt instinctively that there was a connection between this Blodgett character and—of course! The little man he'd seen at Union Terminal was the same one he'd seen in Waco weeks earlier. Prescott and Payne had been leaving Henry Johnson's office after the reading of their father's will when he glanced across the street and saw the man standing there, watching them. Though the man hadn't said or done anything to make himself too obvious, Prescott had seen the slight nod of his head in their direction a moment before he'd scurried off down the street the same way he'd done just the other day at the train terminal. He remembered looking at Payne, thinking that his brother might know the stranger and offer some kind of explanation, but Payne had acted as though he hadn't seen him at all.

He couldn't be certain, of course, but Prescott was willing to bet that the little man was Blodgett. More than that, he had a strong hunch that his brother knew him.

That didn't make sense, though. If Payne knew Blodgett, why would he keep their association a secret? Why hadn't he introduced them that day in Waco, or brought him out to the ranch to meet the family?

Harris paid no attention to Prescott's silent musings as he lathered butter on a biscuit, liberally topped it with jelly, and popped it into his mouth.

The answer to his own question finally registered in Prescott's befuddled brain. Payne had paid off the Triple T's loans himself, using Blodgett to—

"Ahhhh!"

Harris's shriek of pain put an end to Prescott's thoughts. Prescott's head snapped up in time for him to see the businessman leap to his feet, grab a cup of coffee, take a sip, and then toss the cup aside. Harris then lunged for a pitcher of water, turning it up to his mouth and drinking it as quickly as he could, either unaware or not caring that more of it splashed down the front his suit than went down his throat.

"What in God's name . . ." Prescott pushed away from the table and started toward Harris, concerned that he was having some kind of strange physical attack. "Are you all right?"

Harris shook his head rapidly, his face as red as his now bulging, bloodshot eyes. "More water," he gasped. "Get me more water!"

Prescott didn't hesitate. He hurried through the butler's pantry and into the kitchen, where Rosalita immediately handed him a large, full pitcher and gave him a beatific smile. He wondered about the smile, of course, but didn't take the time to ask. Instead, he rushed back into the dining room and shoved the pitcher into Harris's hands.

At last, when the pitcher was empty and Harris looked considerably more at ease, Prescott ventured to inquire what had happened.

"That woman," Harris said. "That damned, infernal woman."

"Rosalita?" Prescott all but whispered, well aware that the cook was just two rooms away, close enough to hear every word Harris said.

"Who else would put hot chili pepper salsa in my quince jelly? She's out to kill me. I tell you, that woman is out to kill me."

"No, I am not," the cook said as she came into the room. "If I wanted to kill you, I would do it with a gun or a knife."

"Or keep dosing my meals with those peppers from hell," Harris said. "They may be slower, but they're just as effective. I'll be dead either way."

"I no want you dead, I only want to get your attention."

"My God, woman, all you have to do is talk to me. You talk to me and I'll listen, I swear I will."

As the cook began rattling away in her native tongue like a Gatlin gun, Prescott decided that it was time for him to make a quiet exit. He had no desire to listen to a domestic squabble between Harris and his cook. Besides, he had other things to do, like celebrate the fact that his long-lost brother had found it in his heart to bail the family ranch out of debt. For surely that's what

Payne had done, Prescott decided. All that talk about
not having any money or land back in England had been
nothing but a ploy to keep it a secret. Whatever Payne's
reasons were for keeping Prescott in the dark, he'd still
come to the rescue, and just in the nick of time.

After donning his rain slicker and hat, Prescott let
himself out of the house. Despite the heavy downpour, he smiled, wondering when Payne was going to
give him the good news.

Then the answer came to him. At the wedding, of
course. That would be the best time. He could imagine how the scene would unfold: He and Chloe would
be standing at the altar, and Payne would come up
and put the loan papers in his hand—papers with the
words PAID IN FULL written boldly across them.

What a guy, Prescott thought, skipping down the
front steps like a man with a new lease on life. Without a doubt, his brother was one terrific guy. He'd
have to come up with a suitable way of repaying him,
of thanking Payne for his thoughtful efforts. He
didn't yet know what that would be, but he was sure
that in time he could come up with something.

Without any more worries to occupy his thoughts,
Prescott decided he deserved to enjoy the rest of his stay
in Dallas. And what better way to enjoy himself than
visit a particular sporting house on the east side of town,
where he knew from past experience that the girls were
friendly and the whiskey never stopped flowing.

As he reached the corner, a fleeting image of
Chloe came to mind, but he immediately dismissed it.
He wasn't married to her yet, and until they exchanged
vows before a preacher, he could see no reason why
he should curb his amusements.

10

"*It's crazy to go out* on a day like this, child," Emmaline said. "Why, the sky looks like it's going to open up any minute."

Chloe shoved a bottle of strong lye-soap cleaning solution into her saddlebag, next to an assortment of clean rags and polishing cloths. "If I ride fast, it'll only take me a few minutes to get to the house," she said as she closed the flap and fastened it. "Besides, even if I do get a little rained on, it's not going to hurt me. Not Whicker, either, for that matter. The fact is, that horse could stand a good bath."

"But what about when you get there? What if it's raining so hard you can't get back home again?"

"Then I'll just stay until it clears up. I'll be all right, Aunt Em. The last time I was there, I made sure I left a big stack of wood near the back door. If it turns cold—which I doubt—I'll just start a fire."

"What about food? You've got to eat. Lord knows, you barely touched your breakfast this morning."

Chloe patted the other pouch of her saddlebag.

"I've got two sandwiches, some pie from last night, and a jar of tea in here. And if this isn't enough, there are some provisions in the kitchen pantry that I had left there from the last time I went to the house. It's nothing fancy, but I won't go hungry for at least a day or two."

"I think it's crazy, you going over to that deserted house all by yourself. What if—"

"I'm taking a rifle with me," Chloe said, anticipating Emmaline's next objection. "There's not a rattler or two-legged snake alive who would dare come near me. I'll shoot them right between the eyes if they do."

"A lot of good that's going to do you if you run out of shells."

"I won't. I've got enough to hold off a small army of bandits until help arrives."

Emmaline watched Chloe slip on her long white riding coat and stuff her blond curls under her hat. "Well, I still don't know . . ."

"Admit it, Aunt Em," Chloe said, crossing to the woman to give her a hug. "You just don't want me going, that's all. You don't like the idea of being left to ramble around this big old place all by yourself. Not even for a few hours."

"I know the notion may seem silly to you, but it's not to me. Besides, it don't seem right, you going off while Prescott's not here."

"You forgot about Payne."

"That's not the same, and you know it."

"Still, he'll be here with you 'til I get back."

"No, he won't. He's not even here now." Under her breath, Emmaline added, "Talk about mad dogs and Englishmen, and it's not even a sunny day."

"What do you mean?"

"Oh, he took off this morning."

A faint blush crept over Chloe's already rosy cheeks. "He took off? Where'd he go?"

"With the hands, he said. Though the Lord above only knows what he intends doing with them. He may know how to ride a horse, but he can't be of any help to the men. That boy don't know beans about rounding up strays. Most likely, they'll end up bringing him home, slung across his horse with his leg broke."

Astonishment slowly supplanted Chloe's sense of unease. The notion of Payne showing any interest at all in the day-to-day operation of the ranch aroused her suspicions. He'd never volunteered himself before. What could be the sudden appeal?

"He's out with the hands?" she echoed.

"That's right."

"Rounding up strays?"

"I know, I know. I couldn't believe my ears at first, either. But that's what he told me when he took off this morning. 'I'm going to watch them and see how it's done. Perhaps even try my hand at wrestling a dogie.'"

Emmaline's feeble attempt at imitating Payne's English accent made Chloe smile. "Wrestling dogies, huh? I'd like to see him do that." Unable to keep a straight face any longer, Chloe burst out laughing.

"You mind your manners, young lady." Emmaline flung a cup towel in Chloe's direction, though she found herself smiling, too. "Try to give that boy some credit, would you? I know he's different from us and all, but at least he's willing to try to learn. That's more than you can say for some big city folks who come out here, thinking they already know it all."

To argue with Emmaline would be useless, Chloe

knew. Instead, she simply hugged the woman, grabbed her saddlebags, and headed for the back door. "I'll see you later today. Before suppertime, if I get the house straightened."

"You be careful, you hear?"

"I will."

"And mind the rain!" Emmaline shouted as the door slammed behind Chloe.

A jagged bolt of lightning flashed across the sky, illuminating the clouds high above. What had begun as a gloomy, drizzly morning had slowly grown darker, and now the day was as dark as night. Payne felt the hairs on the back of his neck stand on end. He didn't have to be a native of the region to know that a severe storm had arrived, and that he was caught in the middle of it.

Another brilliant flash of lightning brightened the sky, this time striking a tree about a hundred yards from the one under which Payne and his horse had taken refuge. He flinched as the entire top of the neighboring tree exploded, bursting into flames. His horse shifting uneasily beneath him, Payne watched in fascination as the once-sturdy tree trunk split in two.

It was time to leave this hellish place, he decided, digging his heels into the animal's ribs. But as he rode out from under the tree, he realized he had no idea where he was on the ranch, or in what direction the house lay. Where could he run to for shelter? He only knew instinctively that he was much too far from the house to risk riding there.

With nothing between him and home but miles of

rolling hills and considerably more targets for lightning, Payne hunched low over his mount's neck and rode across the pasture. He bypassed one clump of trees and skirted around the next. His horse struggled up each of the muddy hills they encountered, only to slide down on the other side. At one point, they crossed a winding creek that had swollen out of its banks and now flowed over large rocks slippery with mud and uprooted grass.

After what seemed like an eternity, with the horse panting and wheezing with exertion beneath him, Payne spied a cottage in a grove of trees just up ahead. The absence of light in the windows led him to assume that it was unoccupied at present. He would have thought it was even abandoned, were it not for the neat rows of flowers surrounding the house.

A second, smaller structure, no better than an open air lean-to behind the cottage, caught his eye, and he rode toward it. As a horseman of long-standing, he would see to the horse first before he sought asylum within the cottage. He couldn't very well leave the poor animal out in this hellish upheaval to fend for itself. Granted it wasn't much of a shelter, but it would suffice until the storm ended.

Once inside, he leaped off the horse, tied the reins to a sturdy-looking board, and then dashed back out into the pounding rain. When he reached the porch, the accumulation of mud on his boots caused him to slip on the wide planks, and he had to grab the porch railing to steady himself. It would be just his luck to escape being struck by lightning only to fall and break his neck within inches of safety.

As if to confirm Payne's thoughts, the nearly black sky suddenly brightened, followed by a loud clap of thunder that shook the very boards on which he stood. He didn't pause to knock but wrenched open the front door and entered the cottage.

Chloe's shriek of surprise at his unexpected entrance startled Payne so much that he slammed the door behind him and fell back against it, his heart racing with a combination of exhaustion and fear. She was the last person he had expected to find in this secluded hideaway. But now that he had stumbled upon her . . .

Slowly, as his initial alarm began to subside, another emotion took its place. Her clothes, as wet as his own, clung provocatively over her body. In the meager light from the fire she had managed to start, he could see the tips of her breasts pronounced beneath her thin blouse. The long, blond hair that hung in dripping tendrils around her face did little to hide the look in her eyes, or her glowing skin, or her moist, inviting lips.

Similar thoughts raced through Chloe's head at the sight of Payne standing at the door, his broad chest heaving as he gulped for air. In the dim light, she thought he looked almost demonic, with his wet hair in disarray, his green eyes wide and piercing, his soaked clothes hugging his taut, muscular body.

A part of her wanted to scream out at him, to tell him to go away and leave her alone, but the words died in her throat.

Electricity filled the small room. Neither could move. Neither could speak. Both could only feel the current growing stronger between them.

Time seemed to stand still.

Then another flash of lightning brightened the sky

outside. Another clap of thunder reverberated throughout the cottage. Pellets of hail began to beat down on the roof.

Suddenly, they both moved toward each other.

Like a drowning man grasping for a lifeline, Payne reached for Chloe and hauled her close to him. His hands explored and caressed every inch of her body as his lips descended and captured hers.

She could do nothing more than give herself to the sensations he ignited. The surges of pleasure from his touch and his kiss erased all reason, all notions of propriety. She could no longer control herself. She only knew that what they were about to do was right, was necessary. Her mind and her body, it seemed, were no longer her own.

Their hands tore at their wet, uncooperative clothing. Buttons snapped off, skittering in different directions across the bare wood floor. Layers of garments were peeled off—shirts, a thin blouse, a lacy camisole, and hasty fingers tackled fastenings on skirt and trousers.

At long last, bare flesh touched bare flesh. As Chloe wove her slender fingers through Payne's thick damp hair, she felt his muscles grow taut beneath his skin. He muttered something unintelligible as his breath and his wet tongue trailed a line of kisses down the graceful curve of her neck, to her dainty shoulder, down her arm, and then over to her full breast, which he tasted and teased until he heard a pleased moan from Chloe.

As the storm outside raged on, it vied for intensity with the storm that ran rampant inside the cottage.

When their weak limbs would no longer support them, Payne and Chloe fell to the floor, their long arms and legs tangling, rubbing, both unable to feel enough of each other as every nerve ending came alive with a million sensations. Desire coursed through their veins, and passion throbbed in their hearts, driving them closer and closer to the inevitable.

Just when Chloe thought she could stand no more, her throaty moans growing into whimpers of need, Payne straightened his arms and held himself mere inches above her.

"Look at me," he said huskily.

She did, and saw in his glazed eyes a desire that matched her own.

"No, look at me."

The quick dip of his chin indicated where he wanted her to look. Obeying, she let her gaze slide down the length of his body, until she finally became aware of their nudity and how wantonly her legs were wrapped around him.

"You can stop me now," Payne said.

"Stop you?"

"Just say you don't want this, say that you don't want me, and I'll stop."

Not want it? Not want him? Tell him to stop? She studied his face and saw the sincerity in his eyes as well as the unspoken plea to keep silent. How could she tell him to stop when she wanted, needed him so? How could she tell him she didn't want him when, at the moment, she wanted him more than she wanted life itself?

In answer, she wound her arm around his neck and pulled his head down to hers. As their lips joined, his tongue exploring her sweetness, she slid her other arm between them, her fingers finding and curling around his own. With a gentle squeeze of reassurance, she helped to guide him into her.

The piercing pain that suddenly shot through her

made her stiffen and gasp in surprise. Then, as his warmth slowly filled her, she felt the pain begin to subside, and an indescribable pleasure soon overpowered her.

Instinct told her that she should do more than just lay placidly beneath him, and Chloe met each of Payne's thrusts with one of her own. The thrill she experienced as they came together, then pulled apart, then came together again grew with such rapid intensity that she lost the ability to think rationally. She could only feel, enjoy, and take pleasure in his nearness.

While heat built gradually inside of Chloe, it raged almost out of control in Payne. With every ounce of his being, he tried to restrain his need to let go until he was certain that Chloe was ready. But the longer they made love, the more aware he became that something more than a simple act of intercourse was taking place, something so intangible that he was at a loss to give it a name. He only knew that seducing and making love to this woman beneath him was unlike anything he'd ever done before, because she was unlike anyone he had ever known before. He couldn't stop loving her now if his life depended on it.

As if from a great distance, Payne vaguely heard her tiny whimpers evolve into loud, breathy sighs. He increased his thrusts, knowing that the time was at hand. And none too soon, for his strength of will had all but reached the breaking point, and he couldn't maintain it much longer.

When he felt her body grow suddenly still beneath him, heard her small cry of ecstasy, he let himself go. In an instant, waves of pleasure washed through him, one after the other, the results rushing out of him and into her.

Time stood still for a moment as they both floated in the warm, cloud-like world of complete and utter satiation that only lovers know, both reluctant to leave it and return to cruel reality.

But reality did return, of course, slowly and inevitably.

Payne tightened his hold on Chloe and gently rolled onto his back, making certain that she rolled with him. It came as a surprise to him that he couldn't seem to let go of her, that he needed her to stay close to him. He'd never before felt this way about a woman after making love.

With all the women he'd known in the past, once his appetites had been appeased he'd been happy to roll off and go to sleep or get dressed and go away. But the thought of leaving Chloe now, just walking away from her and never looking back, disturbed him. Even worse, it filled him with a mounting sense of dread.

One part of him wanted to laugh at the very idea that he, of all people, could be having such thoughts. But another part of him wanted to berate himself for even thinking of putting a mere woman ahead of his plans, his goals. He had to wonder just who had done the seducing—he or Chloe—because he felt as caught in her innocent feminine snare as a helpless animal in a greedy hunter's trap.

Love. The sudden realization registered with a blinding clarity that hit him hard in the center of his chest. He was in love with Chloe.

Such thoughts played no part of Chloe's musings. Though she felt comforted by Payne's presence, his nearness, she felt embarrassed by it, too. She couldn't deny what she had done, and with whom she had done it, no matter how hard she tried, but it was wrong. It should have been Prescott, not his brother, who had taken her virginity and introduced her to that realm of passion. It should have been, but it wasn't.

Her fate as a fallen woman was all but sealed, and there could be no turning back. She had done it with Payne, and she couldn't undo it. But what should she do next? Simply act as though nothing had happened? Try to go on as she had done before? Could she possibly keep such a secret?

Though Payne couldn't read her thoughts, he had a strong hunch what was going through her mind. How could he not? The way she rolled onto her side in a tight ball told him as much. She had been a virgin, physically as well as emotionally, and she undoubtedly felt ashamed for what she had done with someone other than her intended, guilty for having betrayed her fiancé so close to their wedding, and embarrassed for lying naked in the arms of a virtual stranger. Poor thing, she was so young and vulnerable. He knew he had an obligation to ease her conscience.

"Are you all right?" he asked.

Chloe didn't answer him immediately. She didn't know what to say, or even how to say it. She'd never been in this position before. Surely people didn't just chit-chat casually after making love. The idea of conversing with Payne seemed an impossible task for her to undertake at the moment.

"Chloe? Are you all right?"

She moved her head in an almost imperceptible nod.

"Are you sure?"

"Yes, I'm fine."

Wanting only to reassure her, to let her know that

their act had meant something much more to him than physical release, Payne drew her closer, his hand circling her waist and tightening until her back was pressed close to his chest. He buried his face in the curve of her neck and planted a trail of kisses around to her jaw. "You're more than just fine, my darling. You're wonderful. The most precious thing I've ever known in my life."

A small whimper of regret emitted from Chloe's throat as she brushed his arm aside. She jumped to her feet and began to stumble around the room in search of her discarded clothes.

"I have to go," she said.

"Go?" Realizing that the moment was lost, Payne stood up too. "Darling, there's a storm outside. You can't leave now."

"I have to go. Aunt Em's probably worried sick."

"Wouldn't you rather have her worried than grieving? Good God, Chloe, don't you know you could be struck by lightning if you try to go out there?"

"That's a chance I'll have to take. I can't stay here."

A sudden recollection occurred to Payne, and he leaped at the opportunity. "You can't go. Unless you go with me, and I'm not ready to leave."

She pulled her damp camisole over her head and stared at him. "What do you mean?"

"You don't have a horse to ride."

"Yes, I do. I put him in the shed behind the house when I first got here."

"Perhaps you did, but he's not there now. The only horse in that shed is mine. Yours—"

"Must have run off," she finished for him. "That coward. It never fails. Let it thunder and lightning the least little bit, and Whicker spooks like a rabbit every time. I thought I had him tied up securely."

"In that shed? It's hardly a sound structure. Why, most of the boards are so loose, a gentle tug will pull one off. My guess is that's what your Whicker did."

"Yeah, mine, too." She shook her head and stepped into her riding skirt, fumbling with the fastening at the waist. "I've got to fix it before we come here."

"We?"

"Yeah, Prescott and—" She broke off, knowing now that she and Prescott, the man she had thought she loved and hoped to marry, might never be.

Payne sensed what she was thinking and crossed the room to take her in his arms. "We'll tell him. No. I'll tell him. After all, in this situation it is my duty."

"Tell him what?"

"That you and I are lovers, of course. That we intend to be married as soon as possible."

Shock forced Chloe out of his arms. "You'd tell him that?"

"Why not? We are lovers, aren't we?"

"But—but I can't marry you! I'm engaged to Prescott."

"Not for much longer. As soon as he returns from Dallas, I'll find an opportune moment when we're alone, and—"

"And you'll do no such thing." She thrust her arms into her blouse and began pulling on her boots. "How can I break off my engagement to him? I gave him my word, and a long time ago. Why, his family raised me practically my whole life."

"People end engagements all the time."

"Not around here they don't. Our word is our bond. It always has been and always will be. Once a

Texas lady makes a commitment she sticks to it, come hell or high water."

"You mean to tell me that you'd go ahead and marry my brother for the sole purpose of keeping up appearances?"

"No. It's more than that. Much more. I'm committed to him, don't you understand?"

"And what about me? What about us? Good God, Chloe, we're lovers now. You can't pretend that it never happened."

"No, but I can try to forget it," she said, jamming her hat down on her head.

She started for the door, but Payne grabbed her arm and stopped her. "There's one thing you can't forget."

"What?"

"You and I just made love."

"Don't you think I know that?" She wrenched her arm free and reached for the doorknob.

"What happens when two people make love, Chloe? It may not happen all the time, but it does sometimes."

"I don't know what you're talking about."

"I'm talking about the possibility that I may have just given you a child—my child." He saw the shock register on her face, but he didn't relent. He'd come too far, and he had too much to lose, to back off now. "If I have, you'll never be able to forget what we've done. Never. You'll remember it as your pretty belly swells, and each time you look at the child after it's born. Maybe no one would be able to tell, since Prescott and I look so much alike. But you would know. Would you let him believe that it's his baby?"

"I—I—"

"Think about it, Chloe," he said, backing away from her. "Think long and hard. Are you the kind of woman who would stoop to such vile duplicity, just for the sake of appearances? It's been done before—you certainly wouldn't be the first. But could you live with yourself knowing that you had cheated, and lied to both Prescott and me? And to our child?"

She stared at him, speechless.

"Still, if you need more incentive to tell the truth, here's another thing you might want to consider. A woman who tries to foist off her bastard child on her husband can create an even bigger scandal than simply breaking her engagement to marry her fiancé's brother."

With that, he turned away from her and began to pick up his own clothes.

11

A few days later, Chloe stood on the front porch with Aunt Emmaline and Payne, watching Prescott ride toward the house. Dear God, she couldn't be pregnant.

If she were, her life would be ruined, her reputation in shambles. Prescott wouldn't just throw her out of the house, he'd throw her out of his life as well. Aunt Em would be heartbroken and disgusted by the sight of her. And the people in town . . . Well, they'd have a merry old time gossiping about her, the one lady above reproach who had succumbed to temptation.

She knew of only one person who would be pleased at the prospect, and that was Payne. From the moment they had returned to the house together after the storm, he'd been very solicitous and protective of her. He'd explained to Aunt Em how Whicker had run off, leaving her stranded at the house, where he'd found her, and how they had waited out the storm together. Since then, she hadn't been able to make a move without him being there. He'd held out her chair for her at mealtimes and always asked how she was feeling when he knew Aunt Em couldn't hear. But worse than that, he watched her every movement like a hawk, for fear, she supposed, that she might do something that would harm his would-be child.

She glanced over Emmaline's head and saw the determined look in his eye now. Damn the man. He probably expected her belly to blow up like a balloon at any moment, to prove to everyone what a virile beast he was, and that she was nothing more than a wanton slut.

Oh, God, what should she do? Dare she tell Prescott?

Maybe she should tell him what had happened, that she and Payne had been overcome by the heat of the moment and had lost their senses. With it all out in the open, he could then make the decision. If he was a gentleman, he would forgive her. And if he wasn't a gentleman? If he didn't forgive her?

Well then, damn him to hell, too, she thought, angered and frustrated with the possibility. If Prescott couldn't see how badly she felt for the mistake she'd made, if he persisted in being his usual stubborn, narrow-minded self, then she would remind him of all of his past transgressions, and he could just go to blazes—and take his brother along with him on the journey.

A sense of smug satisfaction filled Payne as he waited for his brother to dismount and join the welcoming party on the porch. There was no way he could lose, because he had it all planned down to the last detail. He would try the direct approach first. He would wait until he had Prescott's undivided attention, then he would explain to him how he loved Chloe and wanted to marry her. If that didn't work, then he would resort to utilizing his alternate plan. Of course, that one would require a bit more strategy, but either way, he would succeed in the end.

"You have a nice trip?" Emmaline asked as Prescott climbed the porch steps, his battered valise in one hand, his hat in the other.

"It was okay, I guess. Got a loan."

"You did? That's wonderful, Prescott."

"It's not a very big one. But if we're careful, it should tide us over for a couple more months. How did everything go here?"

"Just fine." Payne stepped forward and took his brother's valise from him. "Nothing too far out of the ordinary happened while you were away." He glanced over at Chloe and noted that she continued to hold herself back from the others. Her look of embarrassment held a trace of defiance. This couldn't be easy on her, he thought, feeling regret well up in his soul because he knew her discomfort was his fault.

"It's good to hear that," Prescott said, wiping a hand across his face. When he looked down at the palm, he grimaced at the dark streaks on it. "Lord, I must be covered head to foot in coal dust. We had the windows opened all the way home because it was so hot. Riding trains may be the quickest way to get places these days, but I swear, they're the dirtiest, too."

"Want a bath before supper?" Chloe asked, finally coming forward.

"I'd better, if it ain't too much trouble. Don't want y'all making me eat alone on the porch 'cause I'm so dirty."

"No trouble at all. I'll go start heating up some water." She started to turn and enter the house, but after one step, she stopped, turned back, and gave Prescott a welcoming peck on the cheek. She felt like a hypocrite doing it, but no matter what Payne had said or thought, she had to keep up appearances for Aunt Em's sake.

Payne never had the opportunity to confess his and Chloe's intimate encounter to his brother that night, as Prescott went to bed immediately after supper, pleading exhaustion. Chloe didn't have the chance to confront Prescott the next morning, either. He had to see to too many chores around the ranch, and her "bits of gossip," as he called it, would just have to wait. But as the days passed, they both found it more and more difficult to confront Prescott, until the point where, if they told him, he might be angry that they hadn't told him sooner.

Before Chloe knew it, her wedding day had dawned, and she still hadn't confessed anything to Prescott. The tension had eased somewhat, though, because Payne had taken off for parts unknown a few days before, promising his brother and Aunt Em that he would return in time to see the bride march down the aisle.

If only Payne would just stay away, everything would be so much better, Chloe thought as she stood at the open vestry window, staring at the dark clouds rolling in from the south. Her life would be far less confusing and far less difficult if he would.

She felt an ominous ache begin to pound right behind her eyes. These thoughts were far too unpleasant for a bride to be having on her wedding day. She should be happy and glowing, not sullen and gloomy like the darkening sky outside. She had seen her reflection in the dressing table mirror that morning, noting the dark circles beneath her eyes and how her mouth turned down rather than up at the corners. She had a nagging feeling that something was going to go wrong, that something unforeseen would happen and her wedding to Prescott wouldn't take place.

The notion caused the pain in her head to grow more pronounced. As if to compound her mounting discomfort, the others in the vestry with her began chattering more loudly, their high-pitched giggles grating on Chloe's nerves. More than anything at the moment, she needed some peace and quiet.

The Campbell sisters, her friends since childhood, were resplendent in matching gowns of yellow taffeta. They stood in one corner, gossiping and giggling merrily with each other, as they always did when they weren't bickering over petty matters. Aunt Em sat off by herself in another corner, tears streaming down her plump cheeks and falling into her lacy handkerchief.

If those four weren't cause enough for a throbbing head, the ring bearer and flower girl were. Aunt Em's youngest daughter and son-in-law had arrived from San Saba that morning with their little son and daughter, and the children hadn't stopped fighting once. Trevor persisted in irritating his sister, Eliza, by pushing her, calling her names, and making her whine so shrilly that the sound alone threatened to shatter glass.

Chloe's arms stiffened at her sides, and her jaw

clenched in frustration. Enough was enough, she couldn't take any more.

"Aunt Em!" she said in an uncommonly loud voice that pierced through the din.

Everyone immediately fell silent, and Aunt Em's head snapped up.

"Aunt Em," she began again in a somewhat softer tone, "would y'all mind leaving me alone . . . for just a while?"

"What for, Chloe?" Ivy Campbell asked.

"Yes, dear, what for?" Aunt Em echoed, rising to her feet.

"I'm getting married in less than an hour," she said.

"Yes, we know," another sister said.

"Well, if it's all the same to you, I'd like a moment alone to—" She needed to think of an excuse to get them out of the room. Then the solution came to her. "To pray. I'd like to say my prayers in private, if y'all don't mind." She fluttered her lashes over her eyes, not wanting them to see the hypocrisy she knew was evident in her gaze.

"Such a dear, sweet girl," Aunt Em said. She lifted a hand and brought it to rest against Chloe's cheek. "Of course we'll leave you alone to say your prayers. Come along, girls, let's leave Chloe in peace. Trevor! Get off your sister and stop wallowing around on that floor like a heathen. Look what you've done to Eliza's pretty dress. Good gracious alive, what's your mother going to do with the two of you? She spent a fortune on those clothes, and now you two have all but ruined them. This is a church, not a hog pen. You two ought not behave. . . ." The remainder of Aunt Em's admonishments became muffled as she closed the vestry door behind them.

Chloe expelled a long, relieved breath. Silence.

Blessed, peaceful silence. Oh, for this day, for this extremely trying occasion just to be over and done with. She didn't know how she would survive the next few hours—the ceremony and the reception afterwards at the Triple T.

Aunt Em's recently vacated chair beckoned, and she crossed to it, turning it so that her back faced to the window. Making certain beforehand that her beautiful gown would not be wrinkled, she sat down and began to massage her throbbing temples. Somehow, before the wedding began, she had to tell Prescott what had happened, what she and Payne had done. If she didn't, she could only imagine what his reaction would be when he discovered that night, their wedding night, that she wasn't a virgin. Naturally, he would be furious, and justifiably so. For that reason alone, she couldn't keep the truth from him. To do so would be as great a sin as what she and Payne had done.

But had it been a sin? Almost every Sunday, Reverend Campbell preached against fornication and other sins of the flesh, but how could something so wonderful and so pleasurable be sinful? Surely God wouldn't have made it feel so good if He had intended it to be a sin.

One thing was certain, though: At the time, she hadn't been able to stop herself. She had behaved with such uncommon wantonness, such total abandon when she gave herself eagerly to Payne, a man to whom she seemed unable to deny anything. Neither morality nor modesty had been a factor when she had lain naked in his arms, allowing him to bathe every inch of her body with his passionate kisses and take her to such heights of pleasure.

Warmth flowed through her veins at the beautiful recollection, but it was soon replaced with the cold truth of reality. What she had done was wrong. If it had been right, she wouldn't now be suffering pangs of guilt for what she had done to Prescott. Poor, hard-working, innocent Prescott, he—

The long piece of cloth that appeared in front of Chloe's eyes brought her troubled thoughts to an abrupt end. Suddenly it covered her mouth and was quickly tied behind her head, muffling her sharp gasp of surprise.

An immediate urge to know her assailant made her turn sharply in her chair. She caught the briefest glimpse of a man's lean thigh covered by black trousers, and then her sight was blinded when a burlap bag was pulled down over her head. Apprehension finally overtook her surprise as the perpetrator's large hands hauled her roughly out of the chair and bound her wrists behind her back. An instinct born of fear made her scream, but hardly a sound came through the gag, certainly not enough to be heard in the vestry.

"Easy, lady. Easy," an alien voice grated near her ear. "You and me's fixing to go for a little ride."

Chloe shook her head vigorously, even as she felt his broad shoulder press into her stomach and the floor disappear out from under her feet. A strong hand anchored her knees as she kicked furiously. But even that small protest ended when his free hand came down hard across her backside.

"Behave yourself," the man said, "or you'll get worse."

Then he hauled her out the window, Chloe realized as a gust of air blew up the skirt of her wedding dress and chilled her bottom. Heaven only knew what sort of outrageous spectacle she now presented with her petticoats and frilly drawers exposed. But her moment of embarrassment soon gave way to a surge of anger. How dare this man—no, this animal—treat her in such an ungentlemanly manner!

Surely, there would be a witness to this horrendous act. There had to be, because she had invited half of Waco to the wedding. Once they saw she was being abducted, they could run and tell Prescott. This callous, uncouth barbarian would have hell to pay then.

But Chloe's hopes for a quick rescue began to waver as her abductor carefully deposited her on a plush cushion in a conveyance of some sort.

"You'd best brace yourself, lady," he growled as he planted her feet far apart on the floor. "This here ride might get a bit rough."

A scant second later, the door closed, leaving Chloe surrounded by silence. Her already flagging spirits sank to their lowest depths as her enclosure lurched into motion. Heaven help her, she wasn't going to be rescued from the unknown miscreant after all, at least not in time for her own wedding.

"When I grow up, I'm going to be a rancher, just like my daddy," Trevor said, looking up at the stern-looking Reverend Campbell who towered over him.

As his bald dome reflected the muted light that shone through the church's one and only stained-glass window, a semblance of a smile appeared on the preacher's thin-lipped mouth. "Ranching's an honorable profession, son, and don't ever let anybody tell you any differently."

Trevor nodded solemnly. "I know. My daddy says

it's a hell of a sight more respectable than being a damn sod-buster."

Reverend Campbell's lips pursed even more tightly, and his face turned a bright shade of pink. "Your father said those exact words to you, did he?"

Again, Trevor nodded. " 'Course, I don't rightly know what a sod-buster is, but Daddy says it's not as good as being a rancher, and my daddy never lies."

"Young man, your father might mean well, but he—" The reverend broke off when he saw Emmaline coming toward them.

"There you are, you little rascal." She gave her grandson a warning look before turning an apologetic expression on the preacher. "Do try and overlook his bad manners, Reverend Campbell."

"It's not his manners I object to, Mrs. McCardie. It's his language. I've never before heard such foul words come out of a mouth as small as his."

"Fowl?" Trevor piped up. "Oh, we don't ranch chickens. We ranch cows and horses. My daddy says that only a damn sod-buster would ranch—"

"That's quite enough, Trevor." Emmaline grabbed the boy by the collar of his shirt and turned him around. "Go to the back of the church where you belong and wait there with your sister. Don't you dare budge, either. Chloe should be ready any minute now."

"That's good to hear," Reverend Campbell muttered as Emmaline pushed her grandson, making him march alone up the aisle.

It certainly was, Prescott thought. He stood near the pulpit, shifting uneasily as he ran a finger inside the tight collar of his stiff new shirt. Had he known what today would be like, he would have insisted that

Chloe elope with him. All this fuss and bother over a little wedding ceremony! A preacher said a few words over you, and you were married; it was that simple. You didn't need half the town to watch the event take place.

The sooner they got this show started, the sooner it would be over. "Aunt Em? What seems to be holding up Chloe?"

"Yes, my thoughts exactly," Reverend Campbell said. "The congregation appears to be getting a little restless. I hope she's not having second thoughts."

"Of course she's not," Aunt Em said.

"Well, I have heard one or two make that speculation," the reverend said.

"Who would say such a thing?" Emmaline asked, irritated at the notion.

"Oh, no one in particular. It was just gossip I overheard."

"Well, you've heard wrong. Chloe is not having second thoughts." Turning to Prescott, she added, "She's not. She's in the vestry right now, saying her prayers, that's all." Then, to the reverend she said, "You do approve of praying, don't you, preacher?"

Reverend Campbell took exception to the bite in her tone. "Most assuredly, Mrs. McCardie. However, I've always said that a wife's first duty is to her husband. But if Chloe doesn't hurry along, she may find herself without one to be dutiful to!"

"All right, if you insist, I'll go fetch her. I may interrupt her private moment with our Almighty, but I will fetch her." She turned on her heel and marched up the aisle, muttering, "Pompous old windbag," under her breath.

Moments later, a loud scream ripped through the

sanctuary, bringing an end to all muffled conversation. Every head turned toward the scream's source, and they saw Emmaline come staggering down the aisle, a gloved hand clutching her heart.

Prescott rushed to his aunt's side. "God in heaven, Aunt Em. What's the matter?"

"She's gone, Prescott! Chloe's done run off!"

12

Blodgett stood behind the broad trunk of an ancient Texas live oak across the road from the church, his bloodshot eyes growing round with amazement as fifty or more people seemed to explode in one body out through the church's arched doorway. Then, still huddled together, with the women squawking like a gaggle of geese, they hurried down the path to the gate and began looking up and down the road, as if trying to see something or someone Blodgett already knew wasn't there.

Cap'n hadn't been far off the mark about this one, Blodgett thought. He'd said that lot would be upset, and they were, now they knew their wench was gone. But with them behaving so skittish and all, Blodgett knew he couldn't show his face until they'd settled down quite a bit. Though when that would be, he couldn't say. By the looks of them, he'd wager it wasn't going to be any time soon.

From his hiding place, he heard bits and pieces of the raucous contention. Men warned those women who were wailing and waving their hands to cease their caterwaulings. Other blokes just shook their heads in dismay, while some speculated on where the bride could have run off to. One plump lady in particular wept so loudly about her "poor, poor darling Chloe," that the Cap'n's brother had to wrap his arms about her and let her sob into his shirt.

Brave chap, the Cap'n's brother, taking it upon himself to comfort a distressed woman, Blodgett thought. The last time he'd tried to comfort a woman, she took it all wrong and had tried to talk him into marrying her. And when he'd refused, she'd started swearing all kinds of nasty, horrible things . . . like drawing and quartering him, skinning him alive, even gelding him. Lucky for him the local sheriff had happened along about that time. Of course, getting himself locked up in jail for a fortnight hadn't been lucky at all, but he'd been a far sight better off there than marrying that blowsy old tart.

Thinking of tarts, Blodgett noticed a trio of young women in the crowd who didn't seem to be as upset as all the others. In fact, from what he could see of them, they looked almost pleased, their faces taking on a satisfied smirk that wenches often got when they thought they'd gotten a man in their clutches. And if Blodgett wasn't mistaken, he'd swear the man they had their eyes on was the poor bugger who'd just narrowly escaped the matrimonial noose—the Cap'n's brother.

He scratched his grizzled chin with a dirty finger and wondered just how much longer he should stay hidden. Through the leafy boughs overhead, he caught a glimpse of the gray sky and shuddered. He didn't like rain, didn't like it at all. It got a body all wet, and likely as not, it made him smell worse than he did when he was dry. A few more minutes, he told himself. He'd wait a few more minutes before presenting himself to the wedding party. Then he'd tell them all he'd seen—that is, what Cap'n had said to tell them he'd seen.

"I wonder where Chloe could be?" Ivy asked as she fanned her flushed face. "She was so looking forward to today."

"Yes, she was," Rose agreed with a nod.

Daisy frowned at her sisters. "She seemed a trifle disturbed to me."

"Oh, do be quiet, you silly child," Ivy said. "You don't know the first thing about what goes on in a bride's mind on the day of her wedding."

"Oh, and you do?" Daisy challenged.

"Hush up, girls," their mother, Mrs. Campbell said quietly. "Don't start bickering now. It's not fitting. Can't you see how it's upsetting poor Emmaline? Not to mention poor Prescott."

Ivy leaned toward Rose and whispered in a very loud voice, "Do you suppose—oh, I hate to even think of such a thing, let alone ask it. But do you suppose someone could have abducted her?"

Prescott whirled around as a unified gasp of shock rose up from the assemblage of women. "Abducted!" he said. "But who would want to kidnap her? Why?"

"Why, for money, of course," Ivy said.

"Or to add her to a white slavery harem," Daisy said quietly with a strange gleam in her eyes.

"Money?" Prescott shook his head. "If Chloe was abducted, and the reason was for money, they'll soon learn that they've got the wrong girl. Chloe doesn't have any money."

"She's got the Rocking B," Rose insisted. "That's worth something."

"Only if someone's offering to buy it," Prescott said. "And they're not. Hell, it ain't even for sale. She's keeping it, and it'll be joined with the Triple—"

"Oooo!" a feminine voice suddenly shrieked. "What is that awful smell?"

As the odor grew stronger in the prevailing breeze, all heads turned in the direction of its source. Not unlike the Red Sea under Moses' command, the group divided in half to make a wide path for the stranger who appeared in their midst.

"Couldn't help hearing what you lot were talking about," Blodgett said, sauntering toward Prescott, keenly aware of the man's suspicious look.

"Who the devil are you?" Prescott asked, standing his ground as he tried not to reel from the man's foul stench.

"Blodgett's me name. Chauncey Blodgett."

"I've seen you before, haven't I? In Dallas, and here in Waco."

"You could have," Blodgett said, nodding his head. "I get around some."

"All the way from England, I'll bet."

"Aye, and you'd win that wager, you would."

Prescott could tolerate no more of the man's interference or his presence. "Can't you see we're busy here? Say what's on your mind, and then go away."

"I just wanted to offer you me services, is all."

"Services?" Prescott gave him a look that clearly reflected his skepticism. The last person he would want to employ was a man like Blodgett.

Undaunted, Blodgett proceeded to explain. "Y'see, I was coming down this very road here, not more than fifteen minutes ago, just minding me own business, thinking what a nice day it would be if these blooming clouds hadn't a-come up so sudden like they done. And when I seen this church here, sitting all peaceful like with all these nice rigs and horses around it, I thought to myself that there was a funeral a-going on. Well, that's what a church is for, isn't it? Funerals?

"So, I stop—to pay me respects to the dearly departed, you might say. And that's when I seen her."

"Her?" Prescott said.

"Aye. Well, I knew right off that it wasn't no funeral you lot were having, but a wedding. I tell you, gov, it ain't every day you gets to see a wench come crawling out of a window when there's a door so handy."

"You saw a wench—er, a young woman crawling out of the window?" Prescott asked, his attention now fully caught. "Which window?"

"Why, that'un over there." Blodgett pointed a grimy finger at the open vestry window. "A right comely wench she was, too. Her skirts was a-blowing in the breeze, showing off a right goodly portion of her—"

"Jesus Christ, man, out with it!" Prescott growled. "What happened? She came out of the window and . . ."

"And I figured she were taking herself off into them woods there. Just for a minute or two, you know, to heed nature's call. But was I shocked when she took off down that road like the hounds of hell was after her. Fairly flew, she did."

"Chloe wasn't abducted," Emmaline all but screamed at Prescott. "She ran away!"

Speculation, first quiet murmurs and then loud voices, erupted among the town's matrons.

"I had a very odd feeling that she wasn't quite herself today," Ivy declared to anyone who would listen. As it happened, everyone did.

"Yes, I did, too," Rose said with a firm nod of her head.

"And me," echoed Daisy.

"We were the last ones with her, you know," Ivy said with a feigned sigh of regret, as if Chloe had passed on to her greater glory, instead of merely running away. "She never would say what was wrong with her, but I knew something was. I could tell. Forgive me, Prescott, but I got the feeling she was having . . . well, second thoughts."

"She was?" Rose asked, but after a jab of Ivy's elbow in her ribs she repeated with more conviction, "Er, she was! Yes, yes, she was obviously having second thoughts."

"And who could blame her?" Ivy said with a slight sniff. "You haven't been exactly the most attentive of fiancés, Prescott, running off to Dallas like you did just days before the wedding."

"Doing heaven knows what with only heaven knows who while you were there," Daisy added. "Chloe's heard all those nasty rumors about you and your proclivities toward loose women."

The bridegroom without a bride eyed the three chattering Campbells but made no comment. Instead, he began to pace back and forth at the churchyard gate, trying to gather together his scattered wits.

"Yes, your proclivities," Ivy said. "I'm surprised

she ever agreed to marry you in the first place."

A hushed gasp rose from the women, while most of the men groaned with impatience. Emmaline's sobs grew all the more louder.

Separated from the throng by a few feet, Eliza frowned at her brother. "Who are they talking about, Trevor?"

"Cousin Prescott, I think," he said. "Now hush up. I want to hear what they're saying."

"Don't tell me to hush up, you bully!" Eliza said, punching Trevor's arm with her small fist.

"I'll tell you to hush up any time I like, and if you hit me again, I'll give you a bloody nose." To prove his superiority over his little sister, Trevor gave her a forceful shove that sent her sprawling backward onto a mound of dirt.

Stunned for only a moment, Eliza's face soon contorted in fury. She leaped back to her feet and pushed him as hard as her tiny frame would allow.

No one in the wedding party paid the slightest bit of attention to the childish fracas taking place nearby. All of them, even the men, were too enthralled with the present gossip of Prescott's past transgressions. When the subject of Carrigan's floozies was mentioned, Emmaline did the only thing she could think of to end it. She issued a loud wail and suddenly collapsed against the man standing nearest to her. Though he staggered somewhat under her weight, he managed to carry her back into the church.

"I've heard enough of this bellyrot!" Prescott started the moment he knew his aunt was safely out of hearing range. "I'm not the scoundrel you make me out to be, and Chloe isn't dim-witted or weak in the head! If anything, she's just confused. And if you think I'm going to stand here and listen to all of you speak of her with such callous disregard, you're crazy. I'm going to go find her!"

Without pausing to express his gratitude to Blodgett— or to inquire into the man's relationship with his brother, which still intrigued him, though he couldn't think about it now—Prescott hopped over the low picket fence that surrounded the churchyard. He quickly covered the distance to his carriage, leaped up to the perch, and with a flick of the reins and a loud shout, he sent the horses into motion just as a loud clap of thunder rumbled overhead.

"That boy's got the right idea," Mayor Whaylon said. "It's the first sensible thing I've heard said here all day."

Following the mayor's lead, all the men began to agree.

"Where do you suppose she ran off to?" one asked.

"Well, she can't have gotten far," replied another.

"What do you say we stop all this jawing and give old Prescott a hand," said still another. "He's going to need some help looking for her."

"No, no," said Mayor Whaylon. "At a time like this, it's best that he's alone, if and when he finds her. A high-strung girl like Chloe is bound to need a good talking to."

All agreed, and the wedding party began to disperse in an orderly manner. But order became a rarity when a bolt of lightning suddenly flashed across the sky, quickly followed by fat drops of rain that threatened to drench the congregation. Some of the more nervous horses reared up on their hind legs, and excited husbands and fathers hurried their womenfolk, dressed in their Sunday best, into wagons, buckboards, and carriages.

Only when the last wagon had finally rolled out of sight, and the last rider had flung himself across a horse, did Blodgett release a low chuckle.

"Now that wasn't as hard as I thought it'd be," he said with a smug smile. Patting a hand against his hip, he heard the comforting clink of coins in his pocket—coins that Cap'n had given him. "No, not hard at all."

But his pleasure vanished when he felt a drop of rain fall on his cheek. Muttering a vile imprecation, he began to run toward the nearest shelter of his choice, knowing he would have to be fleet of foot to reach the saloon before he got too wet.

As the precipitation grew into a steady downpour, the once dusty road produced pools of muddy water. Small birds perched high upon leafy limbs hid their heads beneath their wings for protection. Squirrels scampered up tree trunks to their warm, dry nests. A furry yellow cat, baring a tasty field mouse between her teeth, darted into a hole beneath the church floor. With all of nature's routines delayed while the heavens replenished the earth, only the pleasant sound of rainfall could be heard.

A slamming door shattered the damp serenity. Still wearing his long, flowing robe, Reverend Campbell raced across the sodden churchyard. On a slick patch of grass, he slid to a stop within inches of Emmaline's still wrestling, now mud-covered grandchildren. An unholy oath passed his lips as he separated the urchins. He gave Eliza a sound whack across her little bottom, latched onto young Trevor's ear, and marched the two of them off into the church.

* * *

Lightning flashed and thunder exploded outside the speeding carriage. Every nerve and every muscle in Chloe's rigidly held body screamed out in silent agony. She had experienced fear before, but never under conditions such as these.

The carriage negotiated a sharp curve in the road. Incapacitated by her bound hands, she could only give a muffled yelp of alarm as she felt herself being thrown into the corner. Before she could recover from that particular jostling, another sharp turn in the opposite direction pitched her onto the floor.

For a time, she simply lay there, letting her body roll back and forth, hitting first one seat and then the other. Then tears of frustration began to burn her eyes, and after frustration came much-warranted anger. She would not be reduced to behaving like a limbless reptile. She was a human being, a lady! And ladies didn't roll around on the floor of carriages; they sat properly in seats.

Determination giving her wisdom as well as strength, she began to sway with the movement of the coach instead of trying to fight it. It took great effort, and quite a few bruises to accomplish the act, but she eventually succeeded in throwing the upper half of her body onto the seat.

Before tackling the next obstacle—that of getting her hips to where her shoulders were now—she paused for a time to catch her breath. But just as she moved again, the coach swerved around another sharp curve. Not wishing to lose the tenuous position she'd worked so hard to gain, she stiffened her legs, and her heart sank as she heard and felt the heel of her shoe rip the hem of her beautiful wedding gown.

Rage instantly swept through her, clouding all

thoughts but one. The moment she got out of this vehicle, she was going to give her captor and tormentor a dose of his own foul medicine. But she would not stop at simply tying him up, flinging him around, and tearing his clothes. She would extend the treatment to something far more painful. A good swift kick to the groin ought to do it, she decided. The man had to be a brute to treat her in such a horrid manner—a callous, savage, greedy brute who had obviously abducted her for only one reason.

Her abductor, damn his black heart to hell, had a rude awakening in store for him when he made his ransom demand. Aside from her ownership of the Rocking B, what money she had was tied up safely and securely in a trust, and it wouldn't be released to her until she either turned twenty-one or got married. She had over three years to wait for the former, and his abduction of her had now put a stop to the latter ever taking place.

When she thought of marriage, Prescott's face emerged clearly in her mind's eye. She had come so close to being his wife, despite all of her misgivings and her awful sin against him. Her eyes closed tightly to hold back tears of regret.

Oh, Prescott, wherever you are now, please come and free me from this living nightmare. I'll give you all my love and devotion, and never, ever, will I be tempted again. I swear it!

13

From the church in Waco, Prescott drove straight to the ranch, bringing the carriage to a sudden halt just inside the stables. A moment after the wheels stopped turning, he leaped down from the driver's perch and landed in a haystack, mere inches from where Julio, a ranch hand, lay kissing the foreman's daughter. His unexpected arrival naturally startled the lovermakers, but Prescott didn't seem to care.

"Fasten your britches, Julio, and saddle up Chieftan!" he yelled. "Margaret will have to wait."

With uncommon agility for one with so thick a waist, Julio untangled himself from the young woman and stood up to face Prescott. "Chieftan, Señor Prescott?"

"Yeah, and be quick about it!" Prescott's gaze traveled from the supine girl's long, shapely limbs up to her familiar face, where he found a warm, inviting smile. He shot her a halfhearted scowl and then left for the house. Margaret was a nice girl, and Julio a hardworking ranch hand, but he would be a dead man if her father ever found out about them.

Some moments after Prescott arrived at the ranch, Emmaline, her daughter, son-in-law, and two mud-caked grandchildren pulled to a stop in front of the house. Emmaline climbed down from the wagon and stormed inside as if she'd never experienced a fainting spell at the church.

"Prescott!" She unpinned her best hat, peeled off her gloves, and tossed them in the general direction of the hat rack near the front door.

"I'm back here," he called out.

She stalked down the hall to his room, pushed open the door, and found him in the act of changing clothes.

"I'm going to tell you one thing," she said, slamming the door behind her. "When you find her—*if* you find her—you be good to her, you hear? If I hear tell of you so much as raising your voice to that girl, I'll tear your hide off with a hickory switch, you understand?"

"I'm not going to touch her. I just want to bring her back home where she belongs."

"And then what?"

"What do you mean?"

"Are you deaf, or just plain stupid? I mean, what are you going to do once you get her home? Are you going to marry her and treat her like a wife should be treated, or are you going to ignore her the way you've been doing?"

"I don't ignore Chloe."

"The hell you don't! You haven't said more than two words to that girl since you got back from Dallas. I don't know what went on there, and I don't want to know, even though I've got a pretty good idea. But if you're going to be her husband, you're going to have to learn to talk to her. And you'll have to start treating her like a wife, not—"

"You've said that already,"

"*Not* a little sister," Emmaline finished. "Good Lord Almighty, even Payne treats her better than you, and he hasn't known her nearly as long as you have."

"Speaking of my brother," Prescott said, "just where the hell is he?"

"That's what I'd like to know." Emmaline planted her fists on her hips. "Did you do something or say something to that poor boy to upset him, make him feel like we didn't want him around here?"

"Why would I do something like that? He's my brother!"

Emmaline felt some of her steam evaporate. "It seems kind of odd, don't you think? He said he'd be back in time for the wedding, and I haven't seen hide nor hair of him for nigh on to three days."

"Well, that ain't my fault," Prescott said, shoving his feet into a pair of well-worn boots. "Payne's a grown man. He can take care of himself. Right now I've got a runaway bride to find."

"I'm not so sure she ran away," Emmaline said, sinking down onto the foot of Prescott's bed.

"That man Blodgett—"

"I know, I heard what that dirty little weasel had to say, but something about it just doesn't ring true."

"Like what?"

"I don't know. It's just a feeling I've got. He was there. Why?"

"There's nothing strange in that, Aunt Em. After all, it was a public road."

"I know, but he just sort of popped up out of the

blue. At a very convenient time, don't you think?"

"Yeah, now that you mention it, his showing up like that was pretty convenient, wasn't it?" In fact, Blodgett's sudden appearance in front of the church had been just one more in a long series of unexplained coincidences. Maybe they weren't coincidences at all. "He knows Payne, you know."

"Payne? Our Payne knows a man like that?"

Prescott nodded. "The day Payne and I went into town to hear the reading of Papa's will, I saw him standing across the street. I got the feeling Blodgett was waiting for us to come out of Henry Johnson's office. But the moment we reached the foot of the stairs, he took off down the street."

"What did Payne have to say about him?"

"Nothing. He didn't even let on like he knew him."

"Maybe he didn't."

"Oh, Payne knew him, all right," Prescott said with a thoroughly convinced nod. "The way he acted, I could tell they weren't total strangers. He dismissed him too easily."

"Well, both of them are English, and England isn't that big of a country."

"There's more to it than that, though. I saw Blodgett again when I went to Dallas."

"What was he doing there?" Emmaline asked.

"Beats me. As far as I could tell, he was trying to hide. From me, most likely. I'd just stepped off the train, and he took one look at me and suddenly disappeared. The next time I saw him was just a while ago, at the church."

Tiny hairs stood up on the back of Emmaline's neck. "Like I said, his being there today and knowing so much was awfully convenient."

"You don't think that Payne would . . . " Prescott let his voice trail off, unable and somewhat unwilling to voice the thought running through his head.

"That Payne would what? Help a filthy scoundrel like that abduct Chloe?"

"Yeah. She wouldn't run off, Aunt Em. I know her. She wouldn't do something stupid like that."

"She might, if she thought she had a good reason."

"What good reason could she have? You know what a stickler she is for doing the proper thing. Lord, if they didn't teach her much else at that finishing school, they certainly taught her propriety."

Emmaline shrugged. "Maybe those overstuffed magpies, the Campbell sisters, weren't too far off the mark. Maybe Chloe did have second thoughts."

"About marrying me? That's a bunch of hogwash, and you know it. Why, she's been after me since she was thirteen years old, just about the same time she discovered there was a difference between men and women. And she was never shy about letting her feelings about me be known, either. Let me tell you, it was embarrassing as hell, having a kid that young traipsing after you all over town, looking at you all moon-eyed."

"If it bothered you so much, you should have discouraged her and made her think differently."

"How the devil was I supposed to do that? She had her mind set on having me, and there was no changing it. You know how stubborn she can be."

"It's not all her fault. You let her think that way, Prescott. That's what upsets me. You let her chase you and look all moon-eyed at you, and you didn't do a thing about it."

"That's right, I never did. But I'll tell you something else. Even though I had plenty of opportunities,

I never touched her. Not once." He rose and moved to put on his rain garb. "And if anybody says I did, they're a damn liar."

"Settle down. I know you didn't touch her. Why, you hardly ever kissed that girl, yet you were still going to make her your wife."

"That's 'cause I respected her."

Emmaline watched Prescott don his oil-skin poncho. "Respecting is one thing, but the question is, did you ever love her?"

" 'Course I loved her. I wouldn't have asked her to marry me if I hadn't."

But did he love Chloe as a man loves his wife, his soul-mate? Emmaline wondered. Or did he love her as a sister, a person to be protected and tolerated rather than truly desired? As Prescott stomped out of the room and left the house, she decided sadly that it probably was the latter.

After many long hours of riding in the pouring rain, Prescott's determination began to ebb. He felt as miserable as the waning light of day looked, his spirits as sodden and heavy as his clothes. Every path he had taken and every road he'd traveled showed no sign whatsoever of Chloe.

Beneath the dripping leaves of a massive cottonwood tree, he reined in his horse and gazed down at the muddy earth. An invading army, let alone a solitary woman on foot, could have preceded him along this road, and no one would ever be able to tell it. The heavy rains had washed away all traces of previous travelers.

"Damn!" he swore, gazing up at the gray sky. Where the hell was she?

Prescott realized how futile it would be for him to continue searching for his missing bride. He had to go home and get some rest and something to eat, but he would start out fresh first thing in the morning.

Night descended in full as Prescott made his way home. On the way to the ranch, however, he made a slight detour, taking the right-hand fork in the road toward Waco instead of turning left toward the Triple T. More than food or the comfort of his bed at the moment, he needed a drink. A good stiff shot of Carrigan's rotgut rye would surely ease his disappointment.

Better enjoy this while you can, a voice in the back of his head told him as he approached the saloon. He knew that as soon as he found Chloe, brought her back home, and married her, his nights of drinking, gambling, and carousing with the girls at Carrigan's would be a thing of the past, something he could look back on fondly in his later years but probably never experience again.

After tying his horse to the hitching post, he headed for Carrigan's double swinging doors. Even before he entered the boisterous saloon, tobacco smoke began to sting his eyes, and odors of whiskey, human sweat, and cheap perfume assailed his nostrils. High-pitched giggles from Carrigan's girls mixed with the deeper, huskier growls belonging to the patrons.

An uncommon reticence took hold of Prescott, and he paused for a moment at the saloon entrance. If things had gone differently today and Chloe hadn't run off, he would be smelling a sweeter, less-cloying fragrance, hearing a softer, gentler voice, doing his rightful husbandly duty by his bride instead of considering slaking his lust with one of Carrigan's girls.

Depression hit him quickly and unexpectedly. He

should be home, consoling Aunt Em, damn it, not consorting with loose women. He started to walk away but stopped mid-stride when a familiar voice rising above the din caught his attention.

"I owe the Cap'n me life, I do. Why, if it hadn't been for him, I'd be locked up good and tight in that London prison he sprung me from. And all because some old tart swore I stoled her fancy earbobs. I got no use for earbobs. And they weren't all that fancy, either."

"You said Trefarrow did this for you?" asked one of the men sitting at the table with Blodgett.

"Aye, Cap'n Payne Trefarrow. 'Course, he ain't really no cap'n, but I calls him that just the same. Shows I got respect for him, don't you know."

His mind suddenly bombarded with a multitude of questions, Prescott was unaware of how he pushed open the swinging doors and entered the saloon. Once inside, he quickly found Blodgett sitting at a table with a group of men, with three stacks of coins in front of him.

"Trefarrow!"

Hearing Henry Johnson call out his name, Prescott snapped out of his daze. He gathered his scattered wits and managed to face the men, most of whom he counted as his friends.

"You don't look so good, man," Johnson said.

"Yeah, well, I've felt better," Prescott said.

"I heard about what happened today. Hell, we all did. Damn shame something like that had to happen to a good man like you. Damn shame. Well, don't just stand there. Pull up a chair and have a seat. Myra, honey! Bring us over a bottle of Carrigan's finest. Just put it on my bill."

The saloon girl, standing at the bar, flashed Prescott a smile then turned to fill Johnson's order.

Heaven help him, the whole damn town knew that Chloe had stranded him at the altar. Would he ever be able to live down the shame?

Myra brought over the fresh bottle of whiskey and a glass for Prescott. Johnson poured him a stiff shot, and before he could set the bottle down, Blodgett shoved his glass across the table.

"If you wouldn't mind, gov, I still feels a bit parched."

Johnson cast the Englishman a somewhat skeptical look and then reluctantly filled his glass.

"Here's to luck," Blodgett said, raising his glass. "May the lady be kind to all of us."

Prescott watched as the foul-smelling man downed the shot in one long gulp and wiped his mouth with the back of his hand. Only then did Blodgett notice Prescott's scrutiny.

"What you looking at me like that for?"

"I'm curious," Prescott said. "Just what were you doing at the church this morning?"

"At the church? I—I dunno what you mean."

"Why were you there?"

"Just minding me own business, taking meself a walk, is all," Blodgett said, then grinned. "Enjoying the sights of your fair country, I was."

"Really, that's all?"

"Aye."

Prescott shook his head. "I don't think so."

"'Ere now, you calling me a liar?"

"No, just doubting your word."

Johnson and the others at the table shifted uneasily in their chairs, but Prescott ignored them.

"It seems kind of strange to me," he continued, "that a man like you would come to the United States all the way from England only to end up in a backwater place like Waco, Texas. Unless you had some kind of business to tend to."

"Aye!" Blodgett said, jumping on the lead Prescott had thrown him. "That's why I'm 'ere, all right. Business. You know, you're a very astute man, Mr. Trefarrow. Might interest you to know that I consider meself astute as well."

"I thought as much," Prescott said with a sneer that was noticeable only to those at the table who weren't half drunk. "What kind of business?"

"Er, what kind?"

"Yes, what kind?"

"Oh, nothing important. Just a few paltry money matters is all."

Prescott eyed the stacks of silver dollars on the table in front of Blodgett. "That money doesn't look very paltry to me. If I had to guess, I'd say it was close to a hundred dollars or more. A hundred dollars around these parts is a lot."

"Aye, it's a lot in England, too. But I earned it. I didn't steal it or nothing."

"The question is, who did you earn it from?"

Blodgett blustered a moment, stalling for time until an answer came to him. "Why, from the man I worked for, that's who."

"And who would that be?"

"Who would who be?"

"The man you're working for. What's his name?"

"Er, I doubt you'd be knowing it."

"I might. I know lots of folks. 'Specially if they're from around these parts."

"Well, that's just it, Mr. Trefarrow. He's not. From 'round here, that is."

"Then he's foreign?"

Blodgett grinned drunkenly. "To you, maybe, but not to me. 'E's as English as I am."

"Oh, your boss is English?"

"Aye! A fine, upstanding Englishman."

"Well, you've got me there," Prescott said. "The only Englishman I know is my brother, Payne."

"Ah," Blodgett said, nodding.

"You call him Cap'n, don't you?"

"Aye."

" 'Cause he's your boss?"

"Aye, that he— No! Cap'n's not me boss. What makes you think that?"

"He gave all this money to you, didn't he?"

Blodgett frowned, too confused and drunk to think straight. "Aye, but we're just chums. Good chums, you know?"

"So, you don't work for him?"

"No! I've done things for him, but I wouldn't call it work. I'd say they're more like favors actually."

"And he's paid you for doing these favors for him."

"Aye! Very gen'rous, 'e is."

"With whose money?"

"What d'you mean, 'whose money?' 'Is, of course."

"No, it couldn't be," Prescott said. "He told me he didn't have any."

Blodgett snorted, giving the men at the table a telling wink. "Not yet, 'e don't, but 'e will in time. 'E's a smart lad, Cap'n is. Very smart."

"Smart enough to find himself a wealthy patron, or employer?"

"Aye."

Prescott picked up Blodgett's coins and let them drop back into their stack. "Is that who he got all this money from, the man he's working for?"

"Aye, 'e's like me, earned every penny of it honestly from that bloke."

"What bloke?"

Blodgett hesitated, his breathing becoming more erratic as the seconds ticked past. "I—I don't think I ought to be answering that."

Suddenly tired of playing guessing games, Prescott's face contorted with rage. He reached across the table and grabbed Blodgett by the grimy lapels of his coat. "What bloke, damn you?"

"Th—the one in that other place."

"What place?"

"I don't know. It's a big place. A city, north of here."

"Dallas?"

"Aye! That's it. Dallas."

Dallas? Prescott was growing more and more confused with the answers Blodgett was giving him. Had Payne been to Dallas? Before or after he'd arrived in Waco?

"What's his name?" he asked, releasing Blodgett so suddenly that the man fell back in his chair.

Blodgett grabbed the bottle and refilled his glass. "Which one?"

"The one in Dallas. What's his name?"

Blodgett gulped and shook his head. "I—I don't remember. Me mind's not so good these days. When I was younger, now, I could recall all sorts of details."

"What does he look like?"

"Why, he looks just like you. You're twins, aren't you?"

"Not Payne. The man in Dallas. What did he look like?"

"Why, I don't know. I never seen—"

"Now that's a lie," Prescott said, lurching toward Blodgett again, his expression full of wrath. "I saw you in Dallas myself just a few days ago. What's more, you saw me. That's why you ran off like a scared rat, wasn't it?" He picked up a handful of Blodgett's coins and held them tightly in his fist under Blodgett's nose. "You'd been to see the man who gave you this."

Blodgett's red face turned even redder. "I—I might have done."

"There's no might about it. That's what happened, isn't it? The man in Dallas gave you this money to give to my brother."

"No, this lot's mine, I tell you. It's my share."

"Your share."

"Aye!"

"Then there was more than this?"

Again, Blodgett hesitated. "Aye. The Cap'n got the biggest portion. He needed it, he did, or he would've give me more. He's a good man, the Cap'n is."

"So my brother gave this to you out of the goodness of his heart, is that what you're saying?"

"No! I told you before, I earned it."

"That's right. You did favors for him."

"Aye, favors."

"What kind?"

Now too drunk and too frightened of Prescott to think before speaking, Blodgett sputtered, "Honest favors, like buying up all them bank loans and taking 'em to that bloke up in Dallas. I didn't steal me money from Cap'n or nobody. I come by it honest-like, I tell you."

Bank loans, Prescott thought, the answers coming to him with painful clarity. Payne hadn't paid off the Triple T's outstanding bank loans as a wedding present to him and Chloe—he'd bought them for some man in Dallas. A sinking feeling settled in the pit of his stomach. He dreaded having to voice the thought that currently plagued his mind, but he knew to get the whole truth out of Blodgett he would have to do so.

"Wyngate's the bloke who paid Payne to buy up my bank loans," he said.

"Aye, that's right."

"Sam Wyngate."

"Aye. I'll swear to it on the Bible if you like."

As Prescott sank back in his chair, Blodgett bypassed the use of his glass, choosing instead to drink straight from the bottle of whiskey.

He had lost the ranch. The knowledge ate at Prescott's gut. All the fighting, the scrounging, the begging he'd done to keep the Triple T had been nothing but a waste of time, effort, and worry. He had lost it to Wyngate, after all. And Payne—his long-lost, so-called loving brother—had helped aid his downfall.

Filled with a new determination and an unquenchable thirst for revenge, Prescott sat forward again. "Where is he?"

"Where's who?" Blodgett asked, his slurred speech clearly indicating that he was on the verge of passing into that heavenly oblivion drinkers strove to reach. "Wyngate? Why, he's in—"

"Not Wyngate, you asinine old drunk. My brother. Where's my brother?"

"Off with his newest wench, I reckon." A belch erupted from Blodgett's throat and nearly sent Prescott and the others reeling. "Cap'n always did have an eye for the ladies. And they for him." His mouth contorted into a leering grin. "I've yet to see one who could resist him. Ladies and tarts alike all yield to the Cap'n eventually. 'Course the one today did put up more of a struggle than the others ever did."

Prescott had thought his spirits were as low as they could go, but at this they sank even lower. He had a strong, sick feeling that he knew the identity of his brother's latest conquest. "So, Chloe put up a fight, did she?"

"Aye, kicked like a mule, she did, when he carried her out of that church window. But he managed her all right."

"Where'd he take her?"

"Dunno exactly."

Though Johnson and the others at the table looked as stunned as Prescott felt, they still had enough presence of mind to move out of the way when Prescott again lurched across the table and grabbed Blodgett by the lapels. "Take a guess," he growled. "And you'd better make it a good one."

"H—he said the name of the place. I never heard it before, I swear."

"Dallas?"

"No, no. He wouldn't take her there."

"Fort Worth?"

"No."

"Austin?"

Blodgett shook his head.

"San Antonio?"

"Aye, San Antonio! That's the place."

14

Many hours, many miles, and many changes of horses later, Chloe found herself lying very still on the cold wood floor of the carriage. Her apprehension had reached an insurmountable state. Except for the loud pounding of her heart, she could hear no sound. The carriage had come to a stop.

A horse whickered nearby as she felt the conveyance tilt to one side. She envisioned her detestable abductor leaping down from the driver's perch and heard the splash his feet made when he landed in a puddle.

"Take care of the horses first," she heard him say gruffly. "They've had a mighty rough ride for one night."

"And your fancy coach here?" asked a much younger voice.

"I don't rightly care what you do with it. Sell it if you want. I ain't gonna need it no more."

"Whatever you say, mister."

"How about the room? Is it ready yet?"

"Oh, yes, sir! Done up just like you wanted. Only one little window facing the back roof, and just the one door into the room."

Dearest heaven, he was planning to imprison her in a tiny, virtually windowless cell.

"Good. Now you'd best get them horses on into the barn," said her abductor.

A moment of silence preceded the loud jangling of harnesses. The splashing of hooves had almost faded into silence when the carriage door suddenly swung open, letting in a gust of cool fresh air.

Chloe didn't move a muscle. She couldn't, frozen with fear as she was. She could only pray again for quick, divine intervention.

"You okay, lady?" her abductor asked, almost making her believe that he was concerned. But when his warm hand came to rest on her shoulder, she flinched at his touch.

"Easy," he said in a gruffer tone. "Another short ride, then it'll all be over."

Once again, Chloe felt herself hoisted over his broad shoulder, the outside air chilling her exposed limbs as he hauled her out of the carriage. She could only imagine what he intended to do with her now. He'd already abused her emotionally by stealing her from Prescott and the people she loved, and he had abused her physically by subjecting her to such rough treatment that it would take days, perhaps weeks, to recover. What other cruelties could he possibly inflict on her? Surely he wouldn't force himself on her. Alarmed at this thought, she began to sob.

"Listen up, and listen good, lady," he warned. "You stop that whining this minute, or I'll make you sorrier than you've ever been in your life. You hear me?"

She had, and though it proved a difficult under-taking, Chloe somehow managed to heed his warn-ing. A moment passed, and when she heard voices that seemed to grow louder as they drew closer to them, she realized why he had insisted that she be quiet. Obviously, he was taking her into some kind of crowded place. Was it a boarding house or hotel?

A second notion suddenly occurred to her. Surely he wasn't going to imprison her in a sporting house full of floozies and profligate lechers. Her reputation was in enough of a shambles as it was, and now she was going to be trapped in a bordello.

Upon entry into the establishment, a welcoming warmth began to banish her outer chill. She felt a fleeting moment of hope when she heard voices and laughter and the sound of an upright piano nearby. Thank heaven. Maybe one of the patrons of the place would take notice of her unorthodox means of arrival and raise an alarm.

But as before, her hopes of being rescued were quickly dashed as the laughter and music began to fade. Wooden boards creaked under her abductor's weight, and Chloe soon realized he was carrying her up a tall flight of stairs. At the top, he proceeded for a short distance, made a sharp turn, and then stopped.

Her heart raced faster than ever at the squeaky sound of a bolt sliding home, and her mounting fear culminated in a scream as she felt herself being thrown into the air. But the scream abruptly became a grunt when she landed on a soft feather mattress. Her hour of reckoning, God save her, had arrived.

Though she was certain he would now begin to treat her to all kinds of vile, unspeakable brutalities, he surprised her by turning her over and cutting the ropes from her wrists, his fingers tenderly caressing and manipulating her stiffened flesh so that the blood flow would return to her fingers. Then his feathery touch stroked the exposed curve of her shoulder, pulling up the torn sleeve of her wedding gown.

What kind of kidnapper was he? Without question, he was loathsome and despicable, but she had to admit, and reluctantly so, that his actions just now showed that he bore a small amount of consideration for her as well.

An urgent need to look at her abductor forced her to turn over. She sat upright in bed and for a long breathless moment, she waited for him to order her in that gruff voice of his to remain still. But when no objection came, she wrenched the hood off her head, flung it aside, and clawed at the gag that he had wrapped around her mouth.

Despite the darkness of the room, Chloe easily found the shadowy form at the end of the bed. Standing with his back to her, he pulled off his shirt, presenting her with a sight that made her tremble. Muscles rippled across his shoulders and down his arms, convincing her that he bore more than enough strength to snap her in two if he should choose to do so. And then her fear fled in the face of embarrassment when he bent at the waist and pushed down his britches, giving her an unimpeded view of his bare buttocks.

Stricken with panic, Chloe reached out a hand and groped blindly for something she could use as a weapon. She wasn't about to let this rapist attack her without a good fight first. But finding no such weapon, and realizing she had no other recourse but to await his next move, she drew her knees up close to her chest and wrapped her arms tightly around them.

Outside, the clouds opened up, allowing a tiny stream of moonlight to come through the small window high on the wall. The beam of light, though dim, shone on his bare hip, illuminating a small birthmark.

For some inexplicable reason, Chloe felt her fear begin to dissipate. She had seen a birthmark like that before, she was sure of it.

Then her kidnaper moved, turning around slowly to face her. Instinct forced her gaze to travel up his lean torso, past the thick mat of hair on his chest, and on to the sharp angle of his chin, now covered by more than a few days' growth of hair.

Her heart all but stopped beating. In the shock of recognition, a mounting rage erased all her doubts, all her fears, all traces of concern that she might have had for her safety.

"You son of a bitch," she said quietly through clenched teeth. "You low-down, rotten, stinking son of a bitch!"

"Ladies shouldn't use language like that, Chloe," he said, finding a match in his coat pocket and lighting a lamp.

"Right now, Payne Trefarrow, I feel less like a lady than I've ever felt in my life. What the hell do you think you're doing?"

He thought for a moment. "Taking what's rightfully mine?"

"Yours? I'm not yours, rightfully or otherwise."

"But you are. You became mine the day you gave yourself to me."

"You're crazy."

"Mad, perhaps, for you, but not crazy." He moved then, toward the bed, toward her.

She backed up, springing to her knees like a cat ready for a fight. "Don't even think about it," she said as the mattress sank under his weight.

"I don't have to think about it, my love. I can remember it so vividly that I feel it." He leaned toward her, his intentions clearly written on his face.

"You touch me, Payne Trefarrow, and so help me I'll—"

"Melt away in my arms?" he interrupted softly, his lips mere inches away from hers. "Glow like a thousand candles? Shimmer like the finest satin from Paris?" He expelled a husky growl. "Burn me to a cinder with your passion, Chloe. I love you."

"You can't."

"But I do. I love you so much, I'm willing to risk everything for you. That's why I've abducted you. After the love, the passion we shared, I knew I couldn't let you marry my brother. You're mine, not his."

Though his words sent a surge of joy through her, she maintained her stance of defiance. "You shouldn't have done it, Payne. You shouldn't have done this."

"I had to. Neither of us could tell Prescott. We tried—in our own halfhearted fashion—but he was far too busy to listen to either of us. So I decided to take matters into my own hands."

"But to kidnap me . . ."

"Listen to me, Chloe. If you had married my brother, you would have committed an even bigger sin than I've committed by stealing you from him. It would have been a lie, don't you see? Your marriage to him would have been a lie."

He was right, of course, and she couldn't deny it. But as sound as Payne's reasoning might be, he had driven a wedge between him and his brother that would last a lifetime. "Was it worth it, though?"

"Oh, yes. You're worth everything to me."

"But poor Prescott. You've stolen your own brother's happiness!"

"My brother's a strong man. He can handle it."

"Maybe he can. I'm not so sure I can, though. You've done more than interrupt my wedding. You've branded me an adulteress."

"Only for a while. Once we're married, Chloe, you'll have your good name back again."

The idea surprised her. "Married?"

Payne nodded. "And it will still be Trefarrow." Then his hand encircled her throat, and his fingers sifted through her thick, loosened hair. His mouth descended to hers and silenced, if only for a moment, whatever objections she might have made.

The initial touch of his lips banished what remained of her feeble protests. The feel of his tongue sliding across hers unlocked a wealth of precious memories that she had tried to forget, filling her with a familiar sweetness. And when his free hand moved up her waist to capture the fullness of her breast, she once again became, without question, his.

At what moment she helped him remove and discard her tattered wedding gown, her torn petticoats, her shoes and stockings, Chloe couldn't say. It was enough for her to know that the paltry garments no longer hindered her flesh from experiencing the warmth of his. But all too soon, even that pleasure began to pall, when a hunger borne of nearly three weeks of deprivation began to rage within her. As on that day in her childhood home, she was helpless to suppress it but strove all the more for assuagement. She would think about her conduct later. At the moment, she only wanted Payne and the pleasure he could bring her.

As they lay locked in passion, he silently extolled his admiration of her like a connoisseur handling a fragile, priceless rarity. Not one inch of her body did he leave untouched, or unexplored. Where his hands led, his lips followed—to her belly, where they caressed the soft velvet-like skin; to her breasts, where they teased and tasted her hardened nipples; to her thighs, where they brought further excitement to the quivering flesh.

Chloe's tiny whimpers echoed in the room as tremors of pleasure began to ripple through her. The more intense the tremors grew, the louder her whimpers became. Still, she held back, determined to hold on to the moment as long as possible so that she could share it with Payne.

Though her drowsy expression seemed to contradict his own tense excitement, the sight of it thrilled him nonetheless. He experienced an even greater thrill when her sleepy orbs opened wide as he entered her, his lips claiming hers to stifle her loud outcry.

Though he moved slowly at first, with each parry and thrust he soon gained in momentum. The motions carried Chloe higher and higher until she clung to the very edge of the abyss of fulfillment. Then she leaped into the deep, bottomless chasm as convulsions wracked her body.

Within moments, he once again carried her to that peak. Then he took her there yet again. When he could hold himself back no longer, he finally found his own blessed release. The lonely days and nights he'd spent remembering their first encounter, dreaming of finding that special peace and contentment with her yet again, had finally come to an end.

A long time passed before he found the strength to move. He looked down into Chloe's serenely sleeping face and felt a determination so strong that it frightened him. She was his, by God, and no other man but him would ever have her!

15

Prescott left Waco before the crack of dawn, riding like a man possessed. When he reached Salado by late midmorning, he stopped long enough to eat something and change horses, leaving Chieftan at a reputable-looking stable and promising to return and collect him on his way back home. From Salado, he headed for Austin.

When he arrived there by early evening, he dropped off his horse at a stable. Surely by morning his mount would be rested enough for another long ride, he thought. Now if he could only say the same about himself.

"There's a right nice little place down the road," the boy handling his horse told him as he started out of the stable in search of accommodations for the night. "Beds are real clean, and the food's good, too."

Prescott gave a momentary thought to staying in a hotel. He'd been to Austin many times before and knew that the nearest one lay over a quarter of a mile away. At the moment, the last thing he felt like doing was walking that distance, or worse still, getting back on a horse and riding there. He didn't want to see another four-legged creature until morning.

"Good food, you say?"

"Yep, and plenty of it. You get your money's worth at the Baldridge place. Lucy—I mean, Mrs. Lucille Baldridge is one little lady who can sure cook up a storm when the mood strikes her."

"I hope she's in a cooking mood tonight," Prescott said, "'cause I'm hungry enough to eat a bear."

"No sir, no bear," the boy said. "Don't suppose she'd even know how to cook one. See, this is Thursday. Every Thursday she makes chicken and dumplings."

"That'll do." His taste buds already salivating, Prescott got directions from the boy, hoisted his heavy saddle over one shoulder, and headed down the street to the Baldridge place.

Less than five minutes later, he climbed the tall flight of steps of a tree-shaded, two-story white-frame house surrounded by beds of colorful flowers in full bloom. The woman who answered his knock looked no more than twenty-five or -six, certainly no older than thirty. She stood about five feet tall and possessed an ample bosom that belied her small stature. He thought the broad smile etched on her apple-cheeked face would welcome any weary traveler.

"May I help you?" she asked, her blue eyes twinkling.

Prescott lowered his saddle to the porch and swept off his hat, knocking it against his leg to dislodge some of the dust he'd accumulated during his long journey. "The boy down at the stables said you rented rooms for the night."

"We sure do. You want one?"

"If you have one to spare, I'll be more than happy to take it."

"I've got more than one. Come on in." She held the door open wide for him and let him walk past her. "You had supper yet?"

"No, ma'am, but I hear tell you make the best chicken and dumplings in the whole state of Texas." Flattering a woman's cooking skills, Prescott knew from experience, was the one sure-fire way of getting her to offer a hungry man a second helping. Maybe even a third helping if he laid it on good and thick.

Lucille Baldridge giggled. "That Josh! I swear, I don't know what I'm going to do with that boy. He brags to everybody he meets about my cooking."

Inside the house, Prescott detected the fragrant aroma of freshly baked bread and something else containing vanilla. Dessert perhaps? He sure hoped so. "Smells to me like Josh was doing more than just bragging; he was telling the truth."

"Why don't you just leave your things right here in the front hall for now and go get yourself washed up. You can take them up to your room after you've eaten."

Watching Prescott attentively as he deposited his saddle and saddlebags on the floor, she couldn't help but admire the way his broad shoulders moved beneath his shirt. He was a fine figure of a man, she thought as he straightened and smiled at her. Oh, yes, very fine indeed.

"It's this way," she said, preceding him down the hall toward the back of the house. "Mr. Baldridge, my hus—that is, my late-husband, God rest his soul, fixed me up a little bathing room right next to the kitchen. It makes it right handy for my guests who like the water good and hot in their tubs."

"You're a widow?"

"Mmm-hmm."

What a shame, Prescott thought, and what a waste.

"He was going to put in one of them fancy new flush toilets for me," she said, "but that cursed mule of his had to go and kick him in the head, and he up and died. My husband, I mean. I ended up selling that cursed mule."

"How long ago was that?"

They had reached the kitchen, and she opened a door to show Prescott the adjoining room, cozily furnished with a big claw-footed tub, a small dresser, and a chair. "Why, only a few months ago," she said with a sniffle. "I've been in mourning ever since."

"I'm real sorry, Mrs. Baldridge. I didn't mean to dredge up painful memories for you."

"Oh, don't you fret none. I'm all right. Really, I am. Now you just get washed up, and I'll have your supper waiting out here for you good and hot when you're finished." She started to close the door, but stopped and looked back at Prescott. "I hope you don't mind eating here in the kitchen. Er, my other boarder, Mr. Tilsett? Well, he ate some time ago."

"The kitchen will suit me just fine. Eating in fancy dining rooms always makes me uncomfortable anyhow. I feel like I have to watch my table manners."

She smiled at his attempt to put her at ease and fluttered her lashes as she closed the door.

Washing off some of the dirt and dust he'd accumulated made Prescott feel much better, but feasting on the three helpings of Lucille Baldridge's chicken and dumplings, followed by a big bowl of her tasty peach cobbler, nearly did him in.

"Want some more?" she asked, standing by his shoulder with a steaming roasting pan of the succulent dessert.

"I couldn't eat another bite if my life depended on it. Josh was right, Mrs. Baldridge—you sure know how to cook."

"You're too kind, Mr. Trefarrow. There's lots better cooks in Austin than me."

"Not much better, I'll wager." He pushed away from the table and started to stand up.

"You feel like having another cup of coffee?"

"No, thank you, ma'am. It's delicious and all, but if it's all the same to you, I'll just wait and have it in the morning. I'm so tired, I'd probably fall asleep before you got my cup filled."

"I understand. You look like you've come a long way today."

"Not that long," he said. "Just Waco, is all."

"I've got distant cousins in Waco. Well, they're not my cousins. They're my hus—I mean, my late-husband's, but I like to think of them as my family, too. But enough about them. You're 'bout ready to drop. Why don't you just go settle yourself down for the night?"

"Which room's mine?"

She hesitated a moment, then gave him a sly smile. "It'll be upstairs," she said, her high voice descending to an almost husky purr, "the last door on your right. And don't you worry none about making a lot of noise. You know, snoring, or talking in your sleep . . . or anything else. Mr. Tilsett has a room downstairs. Poor man's been kind of sickly here of late. The doc's got him taking laudanum at bedtime, so he sleeps real sound."

With a tired nod, Prescott went back through the

hall to collect his belongings and then he trudged up the stairs. The last door on the right proved to lie at a greater distance from the other doors along the narrow corridor, but he thought nothing of it. And he was too tired to notice that his room was furnished so cozily and looked so feminine and lived in. With a weary groan, he stripped down to his bare skin, turned back the covers, and crawled into bed.

No sooner had his head hit the pillow than he fell into a deep sleep, his thoughts conjuring up his favorite dream-mate. As before, she seemed to float in mid-air, her long dark hair blowing away from her beautiful face in a breeze that he could almost feel. But unlike all the other times, when she had held open her arms in a beckoning gesture and her wide black eyes invited him to come closer, this time she appeared alarmed. She moved her head slowly from side to side as her moist lips mouthed the words, "No, no." When Prescott tried to close the distance between them, she moved farther away, a look of extreme disappointment crossing her features, her beckoning arms falling to her sides.

Strange, he thought, rolling over onto his side. She had never done that before.

Some time later, as he snored softly in dreamless slumber, he felt an arm reach across his body, and a tiny hand encircle his half-erect manhood.

"Poor baby," a feminine voice cooed in his ear, her fingers caressing his flesh, bringing it fully to life.

"Chloe?" he whispered sleepily, knowing he should chastise her boldness but finding too much pleasure in her touch to voice an objection.

"No, sugar, but if you want to call me Chloe, you go right ahead. I don't mind none."

Fully awake now, Prescott recognized the voice. "Mrs. Baldridge?"

"Not tonight. For you, I'm Lucy."

He rolled over onto his back. "Lucy, you shouldn't—"

"But I have to." Before he could stop her, she tossed the covers aside, threw her arms around him, and climbed on top of him. "I've been without a man for so long, and you're so nice and seem so accommodating, and—oh, my!"

Prescott had time for but one thought, one hope, that Chloe wouldn't find out about his innocent indiscretion. Then all reason vanished from his thoughts. He flung his arms out wide and let the good widow have her way with him.

Still wrapped in warm, sleepy afterglow, a faint smile curved the outer corners of Chloe's lips. A soft purr vibrated deep in her throat as she rolled over in bed. One pale arm stretched out to touch her lover, but it encountered a cold empty space.

Payne's absence caused her such an intense pain of loss that she came wide awake and bolted upright in bed. Surely he hadn't left her, deserted her so cruelly after what they had just done?

"Easy, Chloe," he said, his deep voice soft, yet commanding, from a dark corner. "What's the matter, did you have a bad dream?"

Relieved to know he hadn't abandoned her, she pressed a hand to her pounding heart and expelled a sigh of relief. "No. I just thought you might have . . ."

"Gone without telling you? No, I'm still here, if

that's what you were worried about. I just woke up myself a moment ago."

He emerged from his shadowy hiding place and stood silhouetted against the small amount of early morning light that poured through the high window. Unabashedly, Chloe drank in the sight of his masculine beauty. She knew she should feel outraged by his audacity, or at the very least ashamed. But for the life of her, she couldn't find either of those emotions within her. Even Adonis would pale in comparison to Payne.

He approached the bed slowly and took her hands in his.

"I'm yours, Chloe. Body and soul. I could never leave you. You've bewitched me completely."

Hearing the pain in his voice, she peered up into his face, and her heart swelled when she saw the anguish in his eyes. At that moment, she knew that truth had come before pride.

She lay back, resting her head on a pillow, and held out her arms. "You've bewitched me as well. Come love me, Payne. Love me and never let me go."

16

"Tell me something," Chloe said.

"I'll tell you anything, my love."

"What's it like to live in London?" She lay wrapped in Payne's arms, unaware of the time of day, or even of the day itself. "I imagine it's a fascinating place."

"Fascinating?" Payne would never have ascribed that word to England's greatest city, but he supposed that, to Chloe, who had never been there, it would hold a certain fascination. "Yes, it's fascinating, all right."

She heard the underlying cynicism in his voice and felt a certain element of withdrawal on his part. "You didn't like living there?"

"Not particularly, but I had no choice. It's where I made my living."

"Gambling, right? Prescott said you were a professional gambler."

"Yes. Among other things."

Rather than appease her, his evasion only increased

her curiosity. "What else did you do?"

"Stop asking so many questions, Chloe. Close your eyes and go to sleep."

"I can't. I'm not sleepy. I want to know, Payne. I want to know everything about you."

"No, you don't. You might think you do, but you don't."

"If I didn't, I wouldn't have said so. What's the matter, are you afraid of revealing your checkered past to me? Do you think I'll be so shocked that I'll try to run away? I can't very well do that; you've bolted the door and hidden the key."

"Chloe, my past is just that—my past. It's not a part of me or my life anymore. It's ancient history."

"But very interesting history, I'll bet."

"Some of it was, some of it wasn't. Mostly it was—" he searched for the right word "—sordid. Something I'd rather forget."

"Come now, it couldn't have been that bad. You're a gentleman, for heaven's sake. Even I know that English gentlemen don't live sordid lives."

"You do if you're not considered a gentleman by those who think of themselves as your betters."

"Who? Oh, you mean the royalty and titled nobility, people like that?"

"And upper-class merchants and middle-class money-lenders and just about half the population who can speak the Queen's English."

"You speak the Queen's English."

"That doesn't make me a gentleman, though. It only makes me acceptable to a few. A very precious few. And they're the ones who count."

The way he talked, in the present tense instead of the past, Chloe knew he was hiding something.

Something so deep within him that the merest thought of it filled him with pain. She could hear it in his voice.

"Who would the precious few be?" she asked.

"What do you mean?"

"Who counted? Whose approval meant so much to you that you haven't been able to forget?"

"The list is too long, my dearest. Much too long."

"I've got time. And I'm all ears."

Payne inhaled deeply, wondering if he should—or even if he could—open up to her and tell her about his life. But as he exhaled, he found the choice had been made for him. The words, and the pain, simply poured out of him.

"There's my father, for one. My loving papa. Loving, hell. The bastard deserted me and my mother when I was little better than a newborn. He took Prescott, but he left us to be cared for by Mama's so-called concerned family. If the truth were known, they didn't care a whit about us. Mama especially. She had disgraced them, you see. They thought it unforgivable that she had married beneath her station in life."

"Hold on a minute. Did I hear you right? They didn't think Uncle Garrett was good enough for her?"

"Yes, so her family thought."

"Why, I've never heard of such a thing. Your daddy was a pillar of the community. People all across the state didn't just know him and like him, a lot of them looked up to him."

"Obviously he didn't have that sort of influence on certain individuals in England. Neither did I. I was nothing more than a whelp to be tolerated. Mama loved me, though. Up until the very end when she died, she was the only one who showed me any kind of affection."

"How old were you?"

"Six. Almost seven."

"How did she die?"

"I'm not sure. Her brothers, my uncles, would never tell me. I was too young, they said; I wouldn't understand. I only know that she got sick, took to her bed, and never got up from it again. One night I kissed her good-night, and the next morning she was gone from this earth."

Chloe knew firsthand about a loss such as his at so young an age. She had experienced the death of her own parents when she was only eight. "It must have been very painful for you, losing her so young."

"Yes, it was. I grieved for her, in my own childish way. Funny, looking back on it now, I suppose I became something of a rebellious little brat. But I only behaved like one to combat the loss of her. I just didn't understand. Papa had left me, then Mama left me. I had no one."

"Not even your uncles, your aunts, your cousins?"

"God, no. My uncles were straight-laced, scripture-spouting fanatics who had only one thought in mind: money. Making it, scrounging for it, hoarding every penny they got their greedy hands on. Everything they did was proper and above reproach, mind you, but they were as miserly a threesome as you'd ever want to meet. Their wives weren't any different, either. Though I have to admit, they did try to console me in their own fashion. And my cousins—well, the less said about them the better. They made my life hell. Absolute hell."

He took a deep breath and continued. "And then

there was school. Until Mama died, I lived at home and had a tutor. He was a stern but kind old man who looked sort of like a little white mouse. He's the one who insisted I learn to speak the Queen's English, like every well-brought-up young gentleman should. But once Mama was gone, my uncles saw no need in having the extra mouth to feed, and his services were promptly terminated."

"But surely you made friends at school, didn't you?"

Payne slowly shook his head. "I didn't stay long enough. I ran away. From all three of them."

"Three schools? And you were only six years old?"

"No, by the time I was sent away to the first school, I was about nine. Perhaps ten. Actually, the other boys weren't so bad. It was the teachers I couldn't tolerate. They all seemed to have a penchant for caning unruly lads, and I was probably the unruliest lad of the lot. Like I said before, I was something of a rebellious brat. Even at the age of twelve. That's when I ran away the last time."

"Your uncles found you and brought you home, of course."

"Not bloody likely," he said with a wry chuckle. "I didn't give them the chance to find me. Besides, I'd had enough of *home,* as you call it. I borrowed some money from some of my classmates, stole the rest, and I caught the first train to London."

Twelve years old, alone on the streets of London. Chloe found it unthinkable. "My God, Payne, how did you live?"

"Rather badly, at first," he said. "I remember going for days without food. Then one day I got so hungry I stole a cold pork pie from a vendor's cart. That's when I discovered I had a knack for thievery and started using my very nimble fingers. I picked pockets for a while, snitched the odd purse or two off a lady . . . anything to put food in my belly."

"And a roof over your head," Chloe said suspecting that the worst was yet to come.

"The roof came later. My first bed was a rubbish heap. A big steaming rubbish heap full of scraps from the lowest dregs of London's inhabitants. Then I happened upon a deserted crate and that became my home. I used rags for blankets to keep warm on cold winter nights."

She had heard enough; she didn't want to hear any more. She wanted to stuff her fingers in her ears and beg him to stop. But she couldn't. She knew that Payne needed to get these sad, painful memories off his chest, to let them out into the open so he could banish them forever.

"The day I turned fourteen, my life changed. For the better, as it happened. I had grown very tall, and despite my sporadic, often unhealthy, eating habits, I had filled out rather nicely. A very manly physique, for one still so young, I was often told. You see, that day, the very day I turned fourteen, I met the fair Annabelle. She was thirty-eight but pretended she was only twenty-five. I suspect to delude her clientele." He smiled wistfully. "I tried to steal her purse, but her fingers were quicker than mine. She grabbed my wrist and clung to me like a vise. I thought she was going to call for a bobby—a London policeman—and turn me over to him, but she didn't.

"I remember how she looked at me. It was like she could see something underneath the dirt and grime. She asked me my name, and when I told her it was

Master Payne Trefarrow, she smiled. The fair Annabelle often smiled that same smile when she encountered something or someone she thought was particularly exciting. The next thing I knew, she was whisking me into a carriage and driving me to her little house right outside Mayfair. Mayfair's one of the nicer parts of London, where a lot of the swells live.

"From the moment I entered her house—er, her establishment, really—my life became much easier. You see, she had a salon, of sorts, a place where people from all walks of life could come in the evenings and discuss art and politics and, of course, the latest titillating gossip from court. But that part of my education came later.

"The earliest part was very hard, not just on me, but I suspect on Annabelle as well. I don't suppose I'd had a real bath in months, and she took it upon herself to make me presentable. She quite literally had to clean me up to make me look human, rather than the filth-ridden guttersnipe I was."

He shuddered involuntarily, recalling that time in his life. "I've never had a more hellish scrubbing. It took three tubs of hot water to clean off my accumulation of grime. But afterwards, once I was clean enough to pass her scrupulous inspection, she bought me expensive clothes that fit, gave me a soft clean bed to sleep in, and fed me until I thought I'd burst. I never wanted for food again, nor love and attention. Annabelle was—and still is, actually—a lady well worth remembering with fond affection. She became the mother I needed so badly."

Tears of sympathy trickled silently down Chloe's cheeks. Payne, the man she loved, had been so lonely, so unloved as a child, she couldn't help but feel the agony he'd gone through. But all of that was now ancient history, thanks to a charitable woman of possibly questionable virtue, who had taken him under her wing and cared for him in a way that even his own family had denied him.

"The part that I still find hard to accept was how ambivalent Annabelle's clientele was of me. As I said, they were important people from all walks of life—noted artists and politicians, tilted nobility. Even a royal or two visited her salon. They watched me grow from a boy into a young man, and most of them considered me nothing more than Annabelle's well-behaved little servant boy. They could speak of equal rights for the lower classes in one breath and then order me to polish their boots in the next.

"Although I hated the constant hypocrisy, mine as well as theirs, Annabelle made certain that I behaved and spoke like a gentleman at all times. And on a few occasions, I got to converse with them on an educated level, because by then I had all but taught myself what I needed to know. I conducted myself properly when in their presence, but I was never quite good enough to be introduced into their tight little circle of upper-class snobs.

"That's what they are, you know," he said with a slow shake of his head. "Snobs. Filthy rich people who believe they're better than anyone else because they've got money and titles and vast estates. The noble peerage. Noble, hell. They let you look at them from the outside of their protected lives, let you dream of being one of them, then when you ask for the smallest crumb of acceptance, they shut the door in your face without a qualm."

And they break your heart, Chloe thought. In spite

of all the hardships he had faced, despite all of his protests to the contrary, Payne still wanted to be a part of that closed inner circle of people. He wanted to be treated not as an outsider, merely to be used and tossed aside when the newness faded, but as one of their equals. Which he was, to her way of thinking.

Not knowing what to say to him to ease his pain, she quietly gathered him into her arms and kissed his forehead, his eyes, the bridge of his nose, and then his lips.

"I love you, Payne Trefarrow." Her words came on the softest of whispers.

But he heard them. "God, please don't say that if you don't mean it, Chloe."

She took his face in her hands and looked him straight in the eye. "I never say anything I don't mean. I love you."

He seemed to crumble, his face twisting in silent agony as tears welled up in his dark green eyes.

"I love you," she said again. "I love you, I love you, I love you."

And then Payne buried his face in her chest and began to weep uncontrollably.

17

    Prescott got up the next morning feeling as if he'd had very little rest the night before. In fact, he hadn't. The young widow, Mrs. Baldridge, proved to be as exhausting as those long, arduous miles he'd traveled between Waco and Austin.

"Good morning, Mr. Trefarrow," she said happily as he entered the dining room.

" 'Morning, Mrs. Baldridge."

"How about a nice thick juicy steak and a setting of eggs for breakfast?"

Though the steak and eggs did sound appetizing, Prescott wasn't sure he could do justice by the woman's cooking. He'd done that the night before, and the three helpings he'd had of her chicken and dumplings still weighed heavily in his stomach.

"Maybe just a cup of coffee," he said.

"Just coffee? Why, I'd have thought that a man of your stature would need a lot more than one cup of coffee to start off his day. You need something more substantial to keep you going 'til noontime."

"If all he wants is coffee, Lucille, then all he wants is coffee," came a voice from the adjoining kitchen doorway. "Don't force the man to eat. Hell, the less he puts in his belly, the more we'll have for ourselves."

For reasons Prescott couldn't explain, he had a sudden sinking feeling in his stomach when the owner of the voice appeared—a feeling that had nothing to do with his chicken-and-dumpling-laden stomach. The man was well into middle age, quite sturdy looking despite the pallor of his skin, and he walked with the aid of crutches, a pair of stiff splints supporting his right leg.

"'Morning," Prescott said, praying that the man was Mrs. Baldridge's other boarder, Mr. Tilsett. "You must be—"

Lucille quickly interrupted. "My mister."

Prescott's sinking feeling quickly evolved into a sense of full-fledged doom. "Your mister?"

"My husband, Mr. Baldridge," she said, her back turned to the man in question so that only Prescott could see her apologetic expression.

"Your husband?" he mouthed.

Lucille offered him a look of halfhearted shame, but the twinkle in her big eyes belied the token expression.

Dear God, Prescott thought, she had played him for a fool. Played him like a well-tuned instrument the night before, too, and all the while her husband had been sleeping under the very same roof. There never had been another boarder.

Slowly backing up toward the hall-tree where his dusty hat hung on a peg, he took a shot in the dark, hoping his assumption proved correct. "Mrs. Baldridge told me about your leg."

"Yeah, what about it?" Mr. Baldridge said.

"It was a mule, I understand."

"*Was* is right." Mr. Baldridge grunted as he sank down into a chair, the furniture groaning under his weight. "Son of a bitch won't be kicking nobody else. I shot the damn critter dead in his tracks. Broke my leg in two places, but I still managed to get three rounds into him before I passed out."

Prescott swallowed hard and reached out blindly for his hat. "Well, I—I, er, hope you get to feeling better."

"Mr. Trefarrow," Lucille said, following him into the front hall, "aren't you going to stay for breakfast?"

"I'd better be on my way, ma'am. Thanks for the use of your bed and all."

"Did you pay up yet?" Mr. Baldridge called out. "We don't give no free handouts here at the Baldridge house. Hell, we'd be out of business in no time if we did that."

"It's all right, Malcolm, honey," Lucille said, her head turned slightly, but her eyes locked hungrily on Prescott. "He paid up last night. Real generous, he was, too." Then, in a quieter voice, "You take care of yourself. And y'all come back soon, y'hear?"

With his saddle in one hand, saddlebags in the other, and his hat firmly planted on his head, Prescott fled through the front door.

Never again, he told himself as he rode out of town a few minutes later. Never again would he be taken in by a pretty face and a pair of sparkling eyes. He didn't have time to fight off women. He had a fiancée to find and a twin brother to beat the living daylights out of.

*   *   *

"Payne, we can't stay here in this room forever," Chloe said. "We've got to go back home to Waco some time."

"I know, but not right now," Payne said. He sat, leaning back in a chair, his feet propped up on the end of the bed, looking for all the world like a man thoroughly contented with his lot in life. "It's too soon."

"Too soon?"

"That's right."

"We've been here for three whole days, Payne."

"I know. I can count the days off of a calendar as well as you can."

"Well then, couldn't we at least go outside and walk around a little bit, stretch our legs?" Get some fresh air, she thought. "This is a nice room and all, and the food they bring us is okay, but I'm getting kind of tired of looking at the same four walls. Heavens above, we don't even have a decent window to look out of, just that dinky little old hidy-hole up next to the ceiling."

"The view isn't much," he said.

Knowing that reason wouldn't help her win the argument, she went back to her first tactic—begging. "Please, when can we go?"

"I don't know."

"Tomorrow, next week? Next month?"

"When I feel the time is right."

"And when will that be?"

He looked at her then, smiling as he lowered his chair's two front legs back to the floor. "When you marry me, of course."

"We've been through all this before. I can't marry you."

"You can't marry Prescott, either. Not now. Not after what we've done."

"I know, but I can't even think of marrying you until I've confronted your brother. He has a right to know what we've done, how we feel about each other. To do anything else would be, well, it just wouldn't be right."

"Not 'fitting,' isn't that what you mean?" he snorted. "I wonder if I'll ever get used to your quaint colloquialisms and not think them amusing."

His tone of voice irritated her. "Well, it wouldn't be fitting, dadgummit! I'm his fiancée."

"And my lover."

She waved her left hand in front of his face. "I'm still wearing the engagement ring he gave me, for heaven's sake."

"That can be remedied easily enough. Just slip it off, and I'll buy you a ring to put in its place. One with a much bigger stone, I might add."

"No, you don't understand. The ring itself, or the size of the stone, has nothing to do with it, really. It's the prin—"

"Principle of the thing. Yes, I know, you've said that before." Too many times, he thought.

"Well, it's the truth." She heaved a sigh of frustration. "I love you, Payne. I've told you that a dozen times. But I can't marry you until I've made a clean break with Prescott. He has a stake in this too, you know. This isn't just between you and me."

"What are you saying? That if he refuses to let you end the engagement, you'll go ahead and marry him? That's utterly ridiculous, Chloe, and you know it.

Once he finds out that we're lovers in every sense of the word, he won't want to have a thing to do with you, much less still consider making you his wife. Give the man some credit, please. He does have his pride, you know."

There was no reasoning with Payne, absolutely no reasoning at all. He was as stubborn and hardheaded and single-minded as Prescott.

"You two sure fit the bill," she muttered. "Honest to goodness, save me from identical twins."

"What was that?"

"Nothing."

"You really shouldn't talk to yourself, Chloe. It's a sign of mental instability."

"Well, if I'm mentally unstable, Payne Trefarrow, it's only because you've made me that way. I was as sane a person as you'd ever hope to find before you came into my life, but knowing you has driven me mad."

He locked his hands behind his head, leaned back in the chair again, and smiled. A few more days, he thought. Just a few more days of confinement with him and she would eagerly dispense with her loyalty to Prescott, throw propriety to the wind, and marry him. And then he would have it all, everything he'd always wanted: a wife, a home, and, in time, a family.

She came to him again in his sleep, looking sad and disappointed and not at all welcoming. Prescott tried calling out to her, wanting her to stay. He heard himself ask what was wrong, why she was no longer friendly. But all she did was mouth "No, no," and shake her head.

And then the wisps of fog that she seemed to float in suddenly vanished, and he got his first clear view of her body. He'd never seen a figure like hers before. She had all the features that he liked best, but had never found on only one woman. Long legs, well-rounded hips, and a nipped-in waist. Higher up, her breasts, though small, were large enough, he was sure, to fill his hands.

Consumed by his dream, Prescott rolled over. He opened his mouth and lunged for her moist, inviting mouth. But instead he got a mouthful of hay for his efforts.

He gagged a moment then spat out the fodder. Lord Almighty, what he wouldn't give for a real bed, with real sheets, and a soft feather mattress to sleep on. Since the incident in Austin with Mrs. Baldridge, he had made a point of avoiding all boardinghouses, hotels, and inns. He just couldn't afford to take any more chances. That left only sleeping outdoors under the stars on the hard ground, or like last night, when he thought it would rain, trespassing into someone's barn and finding shelter in their loft.

"Wake up," a soft voice ordered him.

Already half awake, thanks to the mouthful of hay, Prescott managed to open one eye.

"Just what are you doing in my hayloft?"

His inquisitor, he discovered, was a young woman about Chloe's age, or perhaps a little older. One could only describe her as sturdy. Her figure was extremely well-endowed, not unlike Lucy Baldridge's, except this girl's body was much taller than Lucy's— a good six feet, by Prescott's estimation—and she wore not a dress and apron but a tight pair of men's Levi's and a faded workshirt that clung to her uncorseted upper torso like a fine leather glove.

The erotic dream he'd been having came flooding back. He found he could barely speak.

"Well," he finally said, "I was trying to sleep."

"In my barn?" Her big brown eyes scanned his prone body slowly.

"Well, last night, I didn't know it was your barn. I'm sorry."

Despite her size, she dropped gracefully to her knees in his bed of hay. "No need to be sorry. I'm sure it was an honest mistake."

"That's right nice of you." Lord, but she had big teeth. And her mouth looked big enough to encircle an entire cob of corn. "What's your name?"

"Lucinda. But you can call me Lucy."

"Lucy?" Oh God, not another one.

"Mmm-hmm. What's your name?"

"Er, Trefarrow." A strong feeling of impending doom stopped him from giving her his full name.

She stretched out on the hay beside him and let one of her large, sturdy fingers trail a path up his arm. "That's a funny name. Where are y'all from?"

"Wa—" Prescott broke off abruptly, deciding that a small lie wouldn't hurt. "Waxahachie."

"That's up Dallas way, ain't it?"

"Sure is."

"You're a mighty long ways from home, Trefarrow. What y'all doing 'round these parts?"

"Just seeing the country."

"You never seen San Antone before?"

"Heard lots about it," he said evasively, wondering how he could possibly extract himself from this situation without hurting the poor girl's feelings. She wasn't what he would consider a raving beauty. In fact, she wasn't even very pretty. But there was something about her that drew him, made him want to be kind, thoughtful. And that something, he strongly suspected, was the size of her chest. "Don't have hills nearly as big as you've gotten back home."

"Waxahachie, right?"

He nodded and leaped right ahead, needing to ask her the most important question of all. "Are you married?"

"Me?" She laughed, somewhat wistfully. "No, I ain't, Trefarrow, I'm an old-maid spinster."

"Aw now, Lucy, you're still way too young to be old."

"Not that young," she said. "Twenty-six."

"That's not so old."

"Old enough. Not many men left around these parts willing to marry a woman my age. They like 'em young. Young and kinda foolish, if you ask me." She snuggled a bit closer. "How old are you?"

"Thirty," he said.

She smiled shyly. "You married?"

He gave a fleeting thought to Chloe, his runaway, or kidnapped, bride-to-be. Now was not the time to tell poor, plain Lucy the truth. "No, I'm not married, either."

"A good-looking man like you still on the loose?" She shook her head. "That's a shame, Trefarrow. A sad, doggone shame. The ladies up around Waxahachie must be plumb loco or something."

"Naw, just particular, Lucy. Just very particular."

He knew then what was going to happen, that poor old plain, sturdy Lucy was going to get what she seemed to be asking him for, and he wasn't up to fighting it. Why should he? Poor plain spinsters needed some loving just like jilted fiancés did.

"So, that's what it's all about," Lucy said afterwards, her plain face glowing like a young girl's, her massive chest, now bare to Prescott's gaze and questing fingers, heaving like twin, pink-crested mountain peaks.

"That's what it's all about, all right," he said, feeling drained but very satisfied. Lord, but she had been sweet, he thought. One of the sweetest he'd ever known. Innovative, too, for one with no experience.

"You think maybe you got me with child?"

His questing fingers suddenly stilled. "What?"

"That's how babies are made, ain't it?"

"Well, yes, but—"

"You figure you give me one?"

Prescott withdrew, both emotionally and physically, from the supine woman. "I hardly think so, Lucy."

"How come? I got your seed in me."

"Yes, I know, but—"

"And I'm as fertile as they come. Leastways, I think I'm fertile. My ma sure was, and Pa says I take after her. Birthed ten young'uns, she did, 'fore she up and took sick and died on us all."

"Ten?" He felt the blood drain from his face.

"Uh-huh. Five boys and five girls."

"And you're the oldest, right?" He prayed that she was. Younger brothers and sisters wouldn't be a threat to his well-being.

"The oldest girl, yeah. Got four brothers older than me. Older and bigger, and lots meaner, Pa always says."

Four older brothers and a father who was still alive? Heaven help him, Prescott thought as he groped for his pants.

"Where are they now, Lucy?"

"The little'uns are yonder in the house."

"And the older ones and your father?"

"Well, most likely, they're on their way in from the fields. They been up working since before daybreak. It's almost time for breakfast, so they should be in any—hey, where are you going, Trefarrow?"

"I hate to run this way, Lucy, but I've got to be on my way." He'd already pulled on his pants and boots and slipped his arms into his shirt. He would have to wait and fasten his clothes later, when he was on the road. If he lived that long.

"Ain't no need for you to be in such an all-fired hurry now. Why don't you stay a while and meet my family?"

He threw his leg over the top of the ladder and started down. "I wish I could, Lucy. I really wish I could. I'm sure they're delightful people. But the thing is, I've got important business waiting in San Antonio."

"But San Antone ain't that far from here," she said, crawling on her knees to the edge of the hayloft, her breasts hanging over the side. "Less than an hour's ride is all."

Prescott saddled his horse in record time. "Well, you know what they say, 'Business waits for no man.'" And his primary business at the moment was staying in one piece. He had a feeling that if he waited too long, and her brothers and father got hold of him, he would be in serious jeopardy.

"You gonna be riding back this way?" Lucinda called out as he led his horse out of the barn.

"You never know," he said, and with a wave of his hand, mounted his horse and rode off.

"What a strange fella," she said, slowly pulling on her pants. Nice and friendly, but downright peculiar.

"Lucinda! You up there, girl?"

The masculine voice calling from below alarmed her. "Yes, Pa. I'm coming right down." Lordy, lordy! Was she in trouble now? It was a good thing Trefarrow had decided to leave when he did, else they'd both be in hot water.

"Who was that come a-tearing out of here a minute ago? I ain't never seen him 'afore."

"Nobody you know, Pa. He was just some fella, asking directions."

"What was that last thing you said?"

"I said—"

"Aw, hell!" Lucinda's father growled. "Robert Earl, shinny on up to the hayloft and see what your little sister's up to. Mumbling to herself that a-way, she don't sound right. Something's wrong."

"But, Pa, she said the man was just—"

"And I said shinny on up that ladder. Don't you sass me, boy."

"Yes, sir."

Robert Earl, Lucinda's oldest brother, obeyed his father without another word. He hoisted his six-foot-six-inch, two-hundred-eighty-pound frame up the ladder, the rungs groaning under his weight. When he reached the top, puffing and wheezing, he froze at a sight of his little sister trying to cover up her not-so-little charms. Hay clung to her tousled hair and a pink flush of embarrassment stained her cheeks. Robert Earl didn't have to be a mental giant to figure out what had happened.

"Pa!" he yelled. "She's done been raped."

"What?"

"I said Lucinda's done gone and got herself deflowered."

Robert Earl's booming voice echoed throughout the barn, finally catching the attention of his hard-of-hearing father.

"The hell you say, boy! Get back down here. Lucinda!"

"I'm coming, Pa."

"Is Robert Earl telling the truth? Have you been deflowered?"

As dressed as she was ever going to be, Lucinda shamefully followed her brother down the ladder. When she reached the dirt floor of the barn, her trembling hands holding her gaping shirt together, she kept her head lowered.

"Speak up, girl. Is that what happened?"

Lucinda could only nod.

"Th-that fella that was high-tailin' it outa here—was he the one?"

Again, she nodded.

The old man's nostrils flared as a dark color suffused his face. He lifted his tightly clenched fist to the heavens. 'If thine eye smighteth thee, pluck it out!' Boys, saddle up the horses and load your shotguns. We're gonna catch ourselves a despoiler of innocent virginity!"

Prescott had ridden less than a mile from Lucinda and her barn when he had a feeling he should be riding faster. Though he hadn't encountered anyone during his hasty departure, he knew well enough to heed his instincts. As he kicked his horse in the ribs to spur him on, he took a glance back over his shoulder to see if anyone followed him. Though he saw no horses or riders, he did see a small cloud of dust near the barn's entrance.

Heaven help him, he thought. They were on his trail. Well, if nothing else, he had learned a valuable lesson this day—under no circumstances could he trust a woman named Lucy, no matter what her age or size. He just hoped he lived long enough to make use of the knowledge in the future.

18

"All right," Chloe said, "I know better than to ask you to take me back home to Waco, but can we at least get out of this room for a while? I'm about to go crazy in here, Payne. Absolutely crazy, do you hear me?"

"You want to go out looking like that?" he asked, referring to her near naked state. She was wearing nothing more than her petticoat and camisole.

"It won't take me a minute to put on my wedding dress." She looked at the mound of ripped and wrinkled satin and lace that was lying in the corner. "What's left of it, that is."

"No, I can't have you wandering around in public in that rag."

"Well, what else am I supposed to wear? It's all I've got. Unless you were considerate enough to pack some of my things before you kidnapped me."

"No, unfortunately, I didn't. I barely had enough time to make the few arrangements I made."

"Then what will I do for clothes?"

"There's only one thing we can do," he said. "I'll just have to go out and buy you something."

Chloe wanted to go out and choose her own clothes, but she kept silent. To argue with him, she knew, would be a waste of time. "Nothing too flashy or gaudy. Just something plain, but tasteful."

"Don't get your heart set on a Worth original, my sweet. We're in a section of San Antonio that doesn't cater to that particular class of clientele. You'll be lucky if I can find you a skirt and shirtwaist."

"That'll be fine. And while you're gone, I'll have myself a nice hot bath."

Payne gave her the wicked smile that she had come to know and love.

"You wouldn't want to wait until I return, would you?" he asked. "We could share the bath."

"We've shared enough as it is, don't you think? Besides, I'm used to taking baths alone."

"Whatever you say, dearest." He dropped a kiss on her forehead. "We'll have time for baths and other things in the years to come."

After he left the room, she listened for him to lock the door behind him as he'd done the few times he'd left her alone. But this time she heard no such sound. Thank heavens, she thought. He was finally beginning to trust her. About time, and with good reason, too. After all that they had shared, and after all the love they had professed for each other, the notion of running away from him now held no appeal to her. True, she still wanted to go back home to Waco—and the sooner the better—but she wanted more to be with Payne. In fact, she never wanted to be apart from him.

* * *

Less than five minutes after Payne left the saloon and sauntered down the street in search of a dress-maker or dry goods store, Prescott entered it. He'd been within sight of the outskirts of San Antonio when his horse suddenly threw a shoe. Rather than ride on into the center of town and risk laming his horse, he had stopped at the first livery stable he encountered. As luck would have it, a nearby saloon caught his eye. What better place to hide, he thought. Surely Lucinda's brothers and father wouldn't think of looking for him there; they would probably be more inclined to head for the middle of town.

Once inside the small establishment, which was nearly deserted at this early hour, Prescott didn't waste any time. He approached the bartender and ordered a stiff shot of whiskey. The man eyed him curiously, thinking he recognized Prescott but reluctant to say anything.

"I need a room," Prescott said. "You know of a place close by where I can get one?"

"The boss tells me we got an empty one upstairs. I don't 'spect it's very fancy, if fancy's what you're looking for. Probably all it's got is just a bed and a chair, but I 'magine it's clean. The boss is real particular 'bout things being clean around here, so you don't go be making a big mess now, y'hear?"

"Wouldn't dream of it. How much?" Prescott dug into his pocket for some money, laying out an appro-priate amount to cover the cost of the room the bartender quoted him and the price of his drink.

"It's the one at the front," the bartender said.

A view overlooking the street, Prescott realized, would give him the advantage of seeing and recogniz-ing anyone who came into the saloon before they could see and recognize him. The disadvantage, however, would come at night, when he was asleep. Anyone could climb onto the overhanging porch roof and enter his room through the window, catch him unawares, and beat the daylights out of him before he had a chance to defend himself. He would just have to pray that the latter never happened.

He turned and started to leave but then stopped and looked back at the bartender. "Y'all serve meals here?"

The man nodded. "Just like the sign out front says, mister, 'Good Eats and Drinks.'"

"Then send something up to my room later, would you?"

"We don't have no menu, or nothing. You have to eat what old Manuel is in the mood to cook."

"That's fine. I don't care what it is, just make sure there's plenty of it."

"You want some coffee or whiskey to drink with your meal?"

Prescott deliberated a moment before he reached a decision. "Coffee. A whole pot. And make it strong." Whiskey, he knew, would only make him drunk and eventually put him to sleep. Now more than ever, he needed to stay alert.

As he climbed the stairs, he noticed that only the lower half of the flight could be seen from a small corner of the saloon, the one nearest the swinging doors. Be grateful for small favors, he told himself. If necessary, he could sneak down the stairs and observe the patrons without making his presence known. That might keep him one step ahead of Lucinda's irate family.

He reached the top of the stairs and turned down

the narrow corridor, bypassing a door where he caught the muffled sounds of splashing water. As the bartender had said, his room lay at the front of the building and was sparsely furnished. He dropped his saddle and saddlebags just inside the door, closed it, and turned the key in the lock for good measure.

Next came an inspection of the room's view. The bartender hadn't been too far off the mark about that, either. When he stood at the window and peeked out through a small opening in the plain cotton curtains, he could see a good distance in both directions—all the way from the livery stable at one end of the street to the busy intersection of shops and an occasional house or two at the other. The only blind spot was directly beneath him, where the saloon's small overhanging roof totally obliterated his view.

Accepting the room's one major flaw, Prescott turned away from the window. The bed looked comfortable enough. He sat down on the side and bounced for a moment to test how much or how little it squeaked. He eased his feet out of his boots and, with a sigh of relief, stretched out on the bed, his arms folded beneath his head. All in all, it wasn't a bad place. It wasn't home, of course, but then no place really was.

Payne returned from his shopping expedition to find Chloe pulling on her tattered petticoat and camisole. He felt a stab of regret at not having the money to buy her the sorts of clothes she deserved. She should be wearing silks, satins, and velvets, the finest fabrics that Paris had to offer, not cottons and simple homespuns.

"You'd best take those off and toss them into the rubbish heap along with your dress," he said, putting the paper-and-twine-wrapped parcels down on the bed.

"I'd like to, but I can't. These particular unmentionables are the only ones I've got. Unless you bought something for me to replace them."

He gestured to the parcels. "That's all I could find. Have a look at them and tell me what you think. If they're the wrong size, or they're not to your liking, I'm sorry; they'll just have to do."

As Chloe imagined, Payne had thought only of her outer appearance, and not that she might have a dilemma with a lack of spare undergarments. But as she opened the packages, she couldn't help but admire his taste. He had purchased a full, brightly colored skirt that she'd often seen Mexican women wear, and a snowy-white *camisa* with short puffy sleeves and a scooping, ruffled neckline.

"They're lovely, Payne."

"Then you approve?"

"Oh, very much." She crossed to him and kissed his cheek. "Thank you."

"I'll see that you have some new"—he cleared his throat in mock embarrassment—"unmentionables, as you called them, the next time I go out."

"Buying unmentionables that fit properly isn't as easy as buying a skirt and blouse. So I hope when that time comes around, you'll let me go with you."

He sat down on the end of the bed and watched her pull on her new clothes. "So, did you miss me?"

"A little bit," she conceded with an impish smile.

"Well, I suppose your missing me a little is better than your not missing me at all." He reached into his pocket and pulled out a slender cigar, which he lit with a match that he extracted from a small box he kept in his other pocket. "Did anything happen while I was gone?"

"Such as what?"

"Such as anyone disturbing you or trying to come into the room while you were bathing."

She shook her head, her long, golden mane swinging loosely about her nearly bare shoulders. "No, nothing like that. I think we have a new neighbor, though. He just arrived."

"He?"

"I'm just assuming it's a man. I sort of doubt it's a woman, but if it is, then she has a very heavy gait and wears spurs on her boots. I heard him, or her, pass by the door and go to the other room at the end of the hall."

"How long ago was that?"

"Oh, just a few minutes after you left. Why?"

"No reason, really. I just like knowing who's staying in such close proximity to us, that's all."

Payne decided to ask the bartender about the saloon's latest guest when he took Chloe downstairs for supper. Naturally, he would be subtle about it and not rouse Chloe's suspicions. He didn't want her to suspect that he was deliberately prolonging their stay in San Antonio until Prescott found them.

It had been a very nice plan, he thought, abducting Chloe right from under his brother's nose and leaving a clear trail so obvious that even a blind fool could follow it. Of course, his brother was hardly a fool. Somewhat foolish, perhaps, for letting a wonderful girl like Chloe slip through his fingers, but certainly no fool. And not a man who took embarrassment easily, either, Payne decided. Right now, Prescott was probably scouring the countryside, trying to find her.

With that thought came another, which filled Payne with shame. In his own odd way, his brother had loved Chloe, but Prescott's love could never come close to matching the way Payne felt about her. Prescott not only needed but deserved this slap in the face, this rude awakening. Just as he needed to know the truth about their father. And Payne would be the one to tell him . . . in time.

Another stab of shame and regret overwhelmed the first. In the beginning his main goal had been to assist in the collapse of all that his father had considered most important. Witnessing his brother's humiliation had been more of an added bonus. Now he wasn't so sure about the latter.

In the past few months, since his arrival in Texas, he had come to know his twin brother fairly well. Oddly enough, he had learned to like and respect the man. Though unsophisticated and driven, for the most part, by his baser urges, Prescott was very hardworking and took a lot of pride in his home, his land, his heritage.

Heritage—*that's* where his problem lay. If he chose to help Prescott protect his heritage, he would end up protecting their father's as well. To do that would be to condone Garrett's behavior—his desertion, and total disregard he'd shown for Payne and his mother.

Payne knew he could never do that. His hunger for vengeance wouldn't let him. Garrett and everyone associated with him now and in the years to come would have to pay for what Payne and his mother had suffered. He would hate Garrett Trefarrow and all that he stood for until the day he, Payne Trefarrow, departed this earth.

"I'm ready if you are."

Chloe's soft voice pulled Payne out of his tormented reverie.

"How do I look?" she asked.

He studied her for a moment, giving himself time to put aside his angry thoughts. Finally he rose to his feet. "Very much like a beautiful, blond señorita."

"*Muchas gracias, señor,*" she said with a demure curtsy.

"Is there such a thing as a blond señorita?"

"I don't know, and at the moment I don't care," she said. "Come on. I'm starved. I wonder what they're serving for supper."

"Probably the same thing they've served every night since we got here—beans, cornbread, and tamales."

"Well, whatever they've cooked, I intend to eat my fair share. I'm starved."

As Chloe and Payne started for the door, Prescott began snoring, sound asleep in his room. At the same moment, four riders reined to a stop in front of the saloon and dismounted.

"Why we stopping here?" asked the youngest. "The middle of town's only a short ride away."

Robert Earl took off his hat and shook his head. "Didn't you see that horse in the corral back yonder, the one with the white blaze betwixt his eyes?"

"Yeah."

"Trefarrow's horse had a white blaze there too. I got me a good look at it as he came a-riding out of our barn this morning."

"So?" said the second oldest. "Lots of horses got white blazes. That don't mean that'un's his."

"We'll just see 'bout that," Robert Earl said.

"We'll go in here and ask around, see if anybody knows who owns that horse. And if we find him, I get first crack at him, understand?"

"We gonna kill him?" the youngest asked.

"Yeah, good and slow," Robert Earl said with a menacing snarl.

"But if we kill him," said the third brother, "who's gonna marry Lucinda, make an honest woman of her?"

"Yeah," said the second. "Pa just said bring him back home. He didn't say nothing a-tall 'bout killing nobody."

Robert Earl stopped in mid-stride, one booted foot on the wooden porch, the other still planted in the dusty street. "On second thought," he said, "maybe we won't kill him. Maybe we'll just hurt him real bad, make him sorry he was ever born."

The three brothers nodded in approval, liking Robert Earl's new plan better than his old one, and they mounted the porch and entered through the saloon's swinging doors. Due to the angle of the setting sun outside, it took a moment for their vision to adjust to the dimness of the room. Once they grew accustomed to the dark, smoky interior, they began to scour the premises.

The bartender looked up from the glass he'd been wiping and saw the four massive men standing just inside the pair of swinging doors.

"You gents look like you're kinda thirsty," he said. "How 'bout some beer? It's good and cold."

The youngest grinned and took one step toward the bar, but Robert Earl clamped a beefy hand on his shoulder and pulled him back. "Thank you kindly, sir, but we ain't here to drink."

"You boys see the sign out front?" the bartender asked. "This here's a saloon. Got some food, and it ain't bad, but most what we do in here is drink."

"We're looking for somebody," the second oldest said.

"Oh?"

"A fella named—" Robert Earl broke off to look at one of his brothers, his voice dropping to a whisper. "What'd Sis call him? Trefallow? Trefarrow?"

"Trefarrow," his brother said.

"Trefarrow," Robert Earl announced loudly. "You got anybody here by that name?"

"Nobody here that I know," said the bartender. "'Course now, we got paying guests staying upstairs—only two of them—but I got no idea what moniker they go by."

"I just heard my name," Payne said, reaching the midway point on the flight of stairs. "I'm Trefarrow. Who wants me?"

"That's him!" Excited, the youngest brother pointed an accusing finger up at Payne. "I seen him just afore he rode off."

"Yeah, I seen him, too," said the second brother. "He's the one, all right."

Robert Earl took one look at Payne, then shot a glance at Chloe. His mouth twisted into a snarl. "You got a lot of nerve, Trefarrow."

"I beg your pardon?" Instinctively feeling that trouble was afoot, Payne put himself in front of Chloe, shielding her with his body. "Do I know you?"

"No, but you know our little sister real good," said the third brother.

"Yeah, remember Lucinda?" asked the youngest. "The one you deflowered this morning in our—"

Robert Earl silenced the boy by shoving him aside and stepping in front of him, advancing toward the foot of the stairs. "He knows what he done to her, Calvin Lee. Don't you, Trefarrow? What the hell kinda name is that, anyway?"

"Payne, who are these men?" Chloe asked.

"Never mind," he said. "I'll handle them. You go on back to the room and stay there."

"Now, ain't that just like a lily-livered coward?" Robert Earl said. "Can't face us like a man. Has to go and hide behind his floozie's skirts."

Chloe took exception to this. "I'll have you know I am not a floozie! I'm a—"

"I said, get back to the room. Now!" Payne gave her a hard shove that would have sent her staggering up the stairs had she not thrown out a hand and regained her balance.

When Payne turned back around, Robert Earl reached up and, grabbing him by the shoulders, pulled him down to the bottom of the steps. "You got a lot to answer for, Trefarrow."

"Now, gentlemen," Payne said, "I'm sure if we could only sit down and discuss the matter sensibly, calmly, like civilized human beings, we could straighten out this grave misunderstanding in no time."

"He sure does talk funny, don't he?" the youngest asked. "Kinda like one of them sissy-boys from back East."

"Sissy-boys don't do what he done to our little sister, Calvin Lee," Robert Earl said. "And by the time we get through with him, he ain't gonna be doing it to nobody else, neither."

"What, exactly, am I supposed to have done to—"

Robert Earl's fist hit Payne squarely in the jaw, painfully interrupting his question. A second blow to the jaw quickly followed the first.

"I'm next," said the second brother.

"And I'm after you," said the youngest.

"Wait your turn, Calvin Lee," said the third.

Chloe watched in horror as one brother after the other passed Payne between them, punching him hard in the face.

"Somebody do something!" she screamed. But one glance at the saloon's patrons told her that they were useless. They had deserted their tables and places at the bar and were moving to the far side of the room, well out of the way of the fracas. No one seemed to care.

Knowing she had to do something, and quickly, before the four men killed or maimed Payne she turned on her heel and ran back up the stairs, down the hall to the second room. She didn't bother to knock, but burst in.

Roused from his sound sleep by the loud noises from downstairs, Prescott was sitting on the edge of his bed, watching the door. When he saw the key fall out of the ineffective lock and clatter to the floor, he took only a moment to mutter a curse before he leaped off the bed and headed for the window, intending to make a quick getaway.

"Help me, please!"

The familiar voice stopped him in mid-stride.

"Please, you've got to do something. They're down there beating him—" Chloe broke off, when she recognized the dark figure silhouetted in front of the curtain. "Prescott!"

"Chloe?" He turned in time to catch her as she threw herself into his arms.

"Oh, God, Prescott! Thank heaven you're here. They're killing him."

"Who?"

"Payne, your brother! They're killing him. You've got to stop them."

"Wait a minute now. How many of them are there?"

"Four."

Only four? So, Lucinda's family hadn't come after him *en masse,* he realized—probably just her father and three oldest brothers. Or, if not the oldest, then the biggest and meanest of the bunch. Prescott probably stood a pretty good chance of getting away from the saloon, if they could keep themselves distracted long enough by beating the stuffings out of Payne. He could get a horse, or steal one, and—

"Come on, they're killing him!" Chloe urged, pulling his arm impatiently.

"No, they're not." Prescott refused to budge. "They're just teaching him a lesson is all."

"A lesson? But he didn't do anything."

Prescott laughed and extracted himself from her grasp. "You'd be surprised by what my brother's been up to."

"Well, he certainly didn't do what they're accusing him of. He didn't deflower their little sister. He couldn't have. He was with me this morning, and all last night, too, and the night before that, and the night before that, and—"

"What are you saying?" Prescott stared at her in disbelief.

"What do you think I'm saying?" she countered. She felt better now that the truth was out.

"You slept with him? You slept with my brother, Payne?"

Chloe squared her shoulders. "Yes. I guess you may as well know, he and I are lovers. Something, I realize now, that you and I never were."

"He—he put his hands on you?" Prescott felt a powerful surge of outrage at the notion. "You let him put his— That son of a bitch! I'll kill him." He took two steps toward the door, then he stopped, suddenly remembering who was downstairs waiting for him, whom he needed to avoid at all cost. "No, on second thought, I'll let them kill him for me."

The disjointed bits and pieces of information began to take shape in Chloe's thoughts. "They called him Trefarrow," she said. "They knew his name. Two of them even seemed to recognize him." Her eyes narrowed as realization dawned. "Because he looks exactly like you."

"Me?" Prescott said, feigning innocence.

"You're the one who deflowered their little sister. Don't bother to deny it, because I know you are. You have to be the one, 'cause it sure wasn't Payne."

"Sister? What sister?"

She punched his arm with all the strength she could muster. "Stop it, Prescott. Your pretense isn't working. I know what went on. I've always known, since the very beginning. You and your weakness for women . . . Carrigan's floozies especially. Well, it makes me sick. How could you do such a thing?"

"It's not what you think, Chloe. Honest, it's not."

"Oh, really? Then what is it? Or rather, *how* was it? Was she that good? Was she so irresistible that it was worth getting your own brother beaten to a pulp?"

"No! If you really want to know, she was kind of plain."

"Then you did do it! Damn you!" She punched him again, and again, as hard as she could.

"Cut it out, Chloe. I only did it 'cause I was worried about you."

"What? You made love to another woman out of concern for me? That's the biggest lie I've ever heard."

Prescott had to climb over the bed to dodge the next swing she aimed at him. "It's the truth. I didn't know what I was doing. I was asleep in her hayloft, thinking, dreaming about you. When I woke up, she was standing over me, and . . . well, it just sorta happened. I didn't mean for it to."

Chloe lunged for him and landed on her stomach in the middle of the bed. She quickly rolled over, planted her feet on the floor, and grabbed the water pitcher from the nightstand. "Lies!" she said, shaking the pitcher at him. "It's all lies, Prescott. If you were dreaming at all, you sure as hell weren't dreaming about me. One of your other women, maybe, but not me!"

"Wh—what other women?"

"Carrigan's floozies!" she yelled. "And any other female in a skirt! Anyone but me. That's the way it's always been with you—you, you *whoremonger.*"

"Now, now, Chloe."

"I've been such an idiot. I thought I loved you. It seems that all my life, I've only thought of two things: marrying you and having your children. I even went to my aunt's boring finishing school to become the lady I thought you wanted me to be. But look what good it did me. You never loved me, never."

"Yes, I did. I mean, I do. I've always loved you."

"No, you don't. If you loved me, you wouldn't have gone to all those other women. Be truthful for once in your life, Prescott. How many have there been? Ten, twenty? A thousand?"

"Oh, come on, Chloe. I haven't had that many women. No man could have that many."

"No, but then you're not a man, are you?"

"I damn sure am!"

"Then act like one, dammit! Stop hiding in here like a coward and go down there and help your brother."

"Why the hell should I?"

Chloe stared him squarely in the eyes. "Because he's your brother. And because I love him," she said simply. "I'm going to marry him, Prescott. He's asked me, and I'm going to do it."

The discovery that Chloe had slept with his brother had done more than surprise him; it had infuriated him. But hearing her confession of love for his brother and her intentions to marry him stunned Prescott— so much, in fact, that he failed to move fast enough when she swung the big water pitcher at his head.

As shards of porcelain rained about his shoulders, he crumpled to his knees, the room spinning about him.

"All right, you no-account, womanizing skunk." Chloe grabbed him by the shirt collar and hauled him to his feet. "If I have to drag you kicking and screaming every inch of the way, you're going downstairs, and you're going to help your brother out of this mess you've gotten him into. You got that?"

"Uh-huh."

"Good. Now let's go."

Though he towered over her by a good five inches and outweighed her by eighty pounds or more, Chloe managed to maneuver Prescott out of the room, down the hall, and down the stairs. When they reached the bottom and saw Payne rolling on the floor with one of the brothers, Prescott seemed to pull back a bit. But Chloe shoved him forward, right into the back of Robert Earl, who stood above the thrashing pair, shouting obscene encouragements at his brother.

Robert Earl turned and stared at the man who had bumped into him. "What the—"

Chloe shoved two fingers into her mouth and blew a loud, piercing whistle that captured everyone's attention—including Payne and the brother he was about to best.

"Stop this madness right now!" she said. "Can't you all see? You've got the wrong man."

Everyone gazed first at Prescott, then Payne, then back at Prescott again, unable to believe their eyes.

Payne took advantage of the momentary distraction and leaped to his feet. He lifted his opponent, holding him by his shirt-front, and punched him soundly in the face.

"Which one's which?" asked the second brother.

"Aw, hell, it don't matter," Calvin Lee muttered, stalking toward Prescott. "One's as good as the other. Lemme at him."

Chloe stepped back with a groan of frustration. Reasoning wasn't going to work with this bunch. Except for Prescott, who still seemed a little befuddled, every last one of them had blood in mind, and obviously nothing but blood would appease them. Well, if they wanted blood, she'd be happy to give it to them.

She spied an overturned chair and picked it up. Despite its considerable weight, she swung it at the biggest and meanest looking of the four brothers, breaking it over the back of his head. He staggered a moment, then turned around and looked at her.

"Ma'am, little ladies ought not—"

She cut him off in an instant by drawing back her foot then bringing it forward again quickly, placing the toe of her shoe into the most sensitive area of his anatomy.

Robert Earl blinked at her a moment, then his mouth opened to emit a high-pitched whine, and his face slowly contorted in agony as he crumpled to the floor, his hands grasping his crotch.

"All right, who's next?" she asked, pulling up the sleeves of her *camisa*.

Crouched behind the bar, the bartender spied a note pad and a pencil nub resting on a shelf. It was his first day on the job, and until a few minutes ago, he had thought he would enjoy it. It had sounded a lot more appealing than waiting on old ladies at the dry goods emporium.

He chanced a quick peek over the long wooden counter, then ducked back down again, jotting down all the damage he'd seen. Somebody was going to pay for this, and it damn sure wasn't going to be him.

What seemed like hours later, long after the last table had been broken and the last glass shattered, the owner of the saloon walked in. He took one look at the condition of his establishment and felt his heart constrict in his chest.

"What the hell happened?" he asked.

The bartender pointed to the heap of bodies laying in the middle of the floor. "Them four's the ones that started it," he said. "They came in here looking for somebody I ain't never heard of before and ended up picking a fight with one of the guests from upstairs."

"One of my paying guests?"

The bartender nodded.

"Where'd they go to? Back upstairs?"

"Naw, sir. They're gone. All three of them."

"Three? I only had two staying here when I left this morning."

"Another one showed up."

"And he left, too?"

"That's right. 'Course, he didn't do it under his own steam. The young lady had to haul both of the gents out to a wagon she had out front. Last I seen, she was driving off down the street with them."

"Without paying," the owner said, sinking down into the one lone chair that remained upright and intact. "They left without paying their bill, and they've destroyed my business."

"Naw, sir, now that's where you're wrong." The bartender stepped out from behind the counter and dropped a handful of silver dollars and several sheets of paper into the owner's hands. "She left this money. Said that that bunch there could pay for the rest."

The owner eyed the sheets of paper. "What's this?"

"A list of all the damages I figure they done. I may be off the mark by a couple of dollars, but it's as close as I could come under the circumstances." With that, the bartender tipped his hat and headed for the swinging doors.

"Wait a minute! Where are you going?"

"I quit. I'm going back to measuring ladies' yard goods down at the emporium. Bartending's way too wild a life for me."

19

"Let me see if I've got this straight," Emmaline said. She sat in her rocking chair on the back porch, a bowl of snap beans in her lap. "You've decided not to marry Prescott?"

From the moment Chloe had driven up early that morning with a badly bruised and battered Payne and Prescott groaning in the wagon's bed, the day had been quite wearing on the nerves. Two of the ranch hands had carried the wounded pair inside, then she and Chloe had put them to bed and dressed their "battle scars," as Chloe called them. Emmaline wondered what kind of "battle" the boys had been in. It looked to her like they had fought a pack of ferocious bears, but she chose not to ask. Sometimes, she realized, not knowing the why of a matter was a whole lot easier to handle than knowing. Besides, she would find out eventually. Chloe had never been the kind of girl to keep secrets, even ones so obvious.

"No, I'm not marrying him, Aunt Em."

"Why not?"

Chloe sat down on the top step and stared out at the setting sun. " 'Cause I'm in love with Payne, and I'm going to marry him," she said.

"The boy kidnaps you, carts you off to heaven knows where, you're both gone for days without a word, and just when I'm at my wits' end, out of the blue you all show up here. And now you say you're in love with him?"

"It didn't happen quite like that, but I suppose it's close enough."

Emmaline shook her head in confusion. Young people today were far too flighty for her. "What about Prescott?"

"He understands."

Understanding didn't mean that Prescott approved, Emmaline thought, but maybe Prescott's approval wasn't needed in a situation like this. "Are you sure about that?"

"No, I'm not. But if he doesn't understand, it's his own fault, Aunt Em. I can't be held accountable for his happiness. I've got to think of my own. And I'm not about to spend the rest of my life with a man who doesn't love or respect me the way a wife should be loved and respected."

Emmaline sighed and nodded her gray head. "All I can say is, it sure took you two long enough to come to your senses."

"You knew? The whole time Prescott and I were planning the wedding, our future, you knew we didn't really love each other?"

"Oh, you two love each other all right. You just don't love each other in the right way, that's all."

"Well, Payne and I do love each other in the right way." They had loved each other, quite often, in every way imaginable, as a matter of fact. Chloe had a feeling that a few of the ways in which they had made love might be considered immoral, perhaps even illegal, by some people. Now that they were back at the Triple T, however, their lovemaking would probably become almost nonexistent until they were legally man and wife. They couldn't risk shocking Aunt Em or causing any more talk than was already being bandied around town.

"We're getting married, too," she added, "when we feel the time is appropriate."

Emmaline eyed Chloe for a long moment and then chuckled and shook her head. "All I can say is, you'd better make it soon."

"What?" Chloe blushed, wondering if Aunt Em had read her thoughts.

"I said, you two had better get married pretty quick." She went back to snapping her beans. "The quicker the better, if Payne's anything like the rest of the Trefarrow men. And I have a feeling he's no exception."

"Aunt Emmaline!"

"Oh, don't look so shocked, child. Men are men, and God help us, women are women. Anticipating the marriage vows seems to be a time-honored tradition in this family. Well, maybe not a tradition, exactly, but just about everyone's done it."

"Everyone?"

"Everyone," Emmaline said emphatically, leaving little doubt in Chloe's mind as to what she meant. "Young people in love who have their hearts set on getting married shouldn't be expected to wait until their wedding night to enjoy the pleasures of matrimony. Oh, I know a few of them do, but the ones who don't aren't really sinning. They're just . . . well, jumping the gun a bit is all."

Chloe swallowed hard. "Would you think any less of me if I told you that Payne and I—" She broke off with a groan, unable to finish.

"Got a head start on acting like man and wife? Land sakes, no, child. You're two fine healthy children with normal healthy urges."

"Healthy?" Chloe said, thinking of Payne lying in bed, his body swollen and bruised. "Well, one of us is."

"Don't you go worrying your sweet little head about him now. He'll get better. Just let him heal up some, and he'll be back to his old self in no time. Prescott, too."

"Prescott can go straight to blazes for all I care. He's the reason Payne's so busted up and all."

Emmaline stopped her rocking and bean-snapping again. "My Lord! He and Prescott did that to each other?"

"No, no. It was those four brothers that did it to both of them."

"What four brothers?"

Chloe didn't hear the question. "At least, I think they were brothers. If not brothers, then they were close cousins. I'm sure they were all related in some way, 'cause they looked so much alike. I swear, Aunt Em, they were the biggest, ugliest, hairiest men you've ever seen."

"And they just started a fight with Payne and Prescott for no good reason?"

"Oh, they had a good reason, all right. The best one ever, if you ask me. Only thing is, Payne was the one who got the beating that Prescott rightfully deserved. And wouldn't you just know it would be over some woman. Not just any woman, either. Their sister."

"The four brothers' sister?"

Chloe nodded. "Prescott was at it again."

"That boy!" Emmaline picked up a bean and snapped it soundly in two. "One of these days, Prescott's going to come across a woman who won't fall at his feet when he flashes her one of his charming smiles. And when that day comes, she's going to turn him inside out and upside down, and he's not going to know what hit him. Mark my words, child. Just mark my words."

"One of these days, maybe," Chloe said, "but not now. Chances are, he hasn't met that woman yet. I doubt she even exists."

"Oh, she exists, all right. Somewhere in this world is a lady who matches Prescott when it comes to his stubbornness and willpower."

"That's just the problem, Aunt Em. Where women are concerned, Prescott has no willpower. He likes them in all shapes and sizes and ages." She rose to her feet and headed for the back door. "I'm going to go check on Payne."

"Good. If he's awake, tell him that supper'll be ready in about a half an hour. You'd best tell Prescott, too. I've cooked enough to feed an army. They'd both better have hearty appetites."

"I'll tell Payne," Chloe said with a smile, "but as for Prescott, well, I wouldn't mind if he starved to death."

Chloe left the kitchen and went down the hall to Payne's room. She approached the door quietly on the off chance that he might still be asleep. The trip home from San Antonio had been a long one, and quite tiring for a man in his battered condition. He had weathered it well, however, not making a sound, even when she'd been unable to avoid the scores of large holes in the road.

Prescott, on the other hand, had not been as stoic as his brother. Each time one of the wagon wheels dipped into a rut, he had groaned loudly and sworn at her. At one point, he had even threatened to strangle her if she didn't drive more carefully. She, of course, had countered his threats with a few of her own, such as turning the wagon around and taking him back to San Antonio, where the four brothers could dole out the punishment that Prescott so justly deserved.

All thoughts of Prescott vanished as she opened Payne's door and found both his bed and the room empty. Where the devil could he have gone?

Then a sound further down the hall, near her own room, caught her attention. Obviously Payne had awakened and gone looking for her. What a sweet man.

She tiptoed toward the sound, planning to surprise him. They still had a half hour left until suppertime, and with Aunt Em and Prescott otherwise occupied, she and Payne might be able to squeeze in a little hugging and kissing. If they were very quiet about it, maybe they could even—

The sight of Garrett's partially opened bedroom door interrupted her pleasant train of thought. Payne hadn't gone looking for her after all. Or, if he had, he'd made a wrong turn.

She pushed the door open wider and found him standing in the middle of the room, surveying his father's things—the few belongings that Emmaline hadn't been able to part with.

Payne looked up at Chloe, the bruises around his eyes and jaw looking darker and severe against the pallor of his skin.

"Why didn't anyone tell me?"

"Tell you what?" she asked.

"About this." The sweep of his arm encompassed the room and its sparse furnishings.

"What's there to tell? It's your father's room."

"And that? Was that his, too?" He crossed to the wheelchair that sat forlornly in the corner and grabbed it with both hands and held on to it for support.

"Yes."

Payne released a shaken breath. "My God! He was an invalid?"

Chloe hesitated. Didn't he know? Hadn't anyone told him? "I suppose to an outsider, he might be called an invalid. But I never thought of him that way. To me, he was just Uncle Garrett. Always full of life. Full of vim and vinegar, as Aunt Em would say. Even up until the day he died."

Feeling sick to his stomach, Payne sank down on the edge of the bed. "What was wrong with him? Did he get thrown from a horse? Was he gored by some rampaging bull? What?"

"No, he got shot."

"Shot? Somebody tried to kill him?"

"Yes, as a matter of fact, someone did. But I understand that's what happened during the war. He tried to kill the enemy, and the enemy tried to kill him."

"What war, Chloe?"

"Our war," she said. "The War Between the States."

"Jesus, that ended over twenty-five years ago. Are

you telling me that my father spent the last twenty-five years of his life confined to that chair?"

"No, of course not. Uncle Garrett was too vital a man to let himself be confined by anything. This was his ranch, his land. Next to Prescott, I suppose it was his life. Nothing happened around here that he didn't see to personally."

"Are you saying that he had somebody drive him around the ranch in a wagon?" The thought made Payne even sicker inside.

"No, he rode a horse. He had a special saddle made."

"That's impossible. Special saddle or not, no paralyzed man can sit a horse."

"But Uncle Garrett wasn't paralyzed, Payne. Whatever made you think he was?"

"You did. You told me he was an invalid."

"No, you called him that. I didn't."

"Then what the hell was wrong with him? You said he was shot."

"He was."

"Goddammit, Chloe, I'm tired of your evasiveness. What was wrong with my father?"

Chloe's head snapped back as if he'd slapped her. "He had no legs."

"What?"

She watched in horror as all the remaining color drained from Payne's face, leaving him a ghostly shade of gray. She could even see the tiny beads of sweat appear on his upper lip.

"He lost them in the war," she said. "The way I understand it, some Yankee soldier shot him, and the doctors—well, they didn't take very good care of him. I don't suppose they had the time or the necessary equipment to remove the bullets from his legs, so they just sawed them off at the—"

"Jesus Christ!" Payne clamped a hand over his mouth and ran from the room.

Wanting to comfort him, Chloe started to follow. But just as she passed Prescott's room, he stumbled out into the hall and blocked her path.

"What the hell's going on out here?" he asked. "Somebody stampede the horses out of the corral?"

She shoved him against the wall. "Why didn't you tell him about your father? *His* father?"

"Who, Payne?"

"Yes, you idiot—Payne."

"Tell him what?"

"Oh, you make me sick, Prescott Trefarrow. You've never thought of anyone but yourself. He didn't know!"

"Know what, dammit?"

"That Uncle Garrett had no legs."

Prescott's face took on an expression of bewilderment, one that she was seeing with greater frequency of late. Not only was the man a callous-hearted womanizing brute, he was about as dumb as a post.

"No one ever told him," she said. "Not you, not Aunt Em. Not me, either. I thought he knew."

"That makes two of us."

"No, three of us." Emmaline emerged out of the kitchen doorway, wiping her hands on a cup towel. "That poor boy must be suffering something fierce."

"Where is he?" Chloe stepped away from Prescott, but once again she was stopped—this time by Emmaline.

"You just leave him alone, child."

"But he needs to—"

"Be by himself," Emmaline insisted. "For the time being, anyway. He's all right. He's out in the yard, retching his guts out. I imagine the last thing he wants or needs at the moment is some woman standing over him, trying to make him feel better."

"She's right," Prescott said. "Just leave him alone, Chloe. He'll come around when he's got it out of his system."

"Y'all just don't understand, do you?" Chloe backed away from them. They couldn't possibly know or feel the agonizing turmoil that Payne was experiencing. But she could feel it as strongly as if it were her own.

"Understand what?" Emmaline asked. "That learning about Garrett has shocked him? Of course, I understand it. I'm not blind."

"No, he's more than just shocked, Aunt Em. Much more. He's never had anyone to hold him, to tell him that everything would be all right when it all seemed so hopeless. We've always had each other, but he's had no one."

"That's a damn lie," Prescott said. "He had our mother."

"Only until he was six years old," Chloe said. "That's when she died. And considering the kind of family she had, the way they brought her up, I can't help but wonder how much affection she gave Payne before she passed on." Seeing Prescott's look of disbelief, she added, "Payne told me all about her—how frail and sickly she always was, how she took to her bed one day and never got out of it again. He's needed love for so long, so very long."

It all came pouring out of Chloe then, everything that Payne had confided to her in the little room in

San Antonio, every last detail that she could recall—the sudden loss of his mother, his self-righteous, uncaring uncles and aunts, the loneliness and brutality that he had tried to endure when they sent him away to school, his life as a pickpocket on the streets of London, his encounter with the fair Annabelle, how she had changed his life forever . . .

When she finished, Chloe saw that Emmaline appeared to be on the verge of tears, and that Prescott looked almost as sick as Payne had just moments ago.

"Garrett didn't know," Emmaline said, her voice thick with emotion. "If he had known, I'm sure he would have done something. Sent for Payne, brought him home, here to the ranch—anything other than letting him suffer the way he did. He thought Victoria's brothers were raising him right, giving Payne what he needed. That's why he never—" She broke off and shook her head sadly, her apron coming up to cover her face and muffle her sobs.

"And I thought I'd had it bad, growing up without a mother," Prescott said.

"You had a mother," Chloe said. "We both had one."

"Me?" Emmaline asked.

"Yes, Aunt Em, you. You've been a mother to both of us. Without you, heaven only knows what Prescott and I would have become."

"Oh, hush up." Emmaline sniffed and wiped her eyes, trying to hold back the tears that still threatened. "I only did what I thought was right. Two young'uns needed raising, and I raised them. It's just a crying shame that Garrett's in-laws didn't do the same with Payne."

"Well, he may not have had anyone before," Chloe said, "but he certainly does now. And I'm going to go tell him, make him see that he's not alone in this, like he's been alone in everything else."

"No, I'll go," Emmaline said. "Lord knows what he's thought of his daddy all these years, but he needs to know a few things about Garrett. I've got a feeling he'll take it a lot better if it comes from me."

Leaving Chloe and Prescott in the hallway, Emmaline walked back through the kitchen and out the back door. He was standing where she had seen him minutes earlier, leaning against a tree in the back yard, his head hanging, his cheeks still pale.

Payne straightened when he saw her approach. "I've been such a fool, Aunt Em. Such a damnable, laughable fool."

"You've been no such thing, child."

"Oh, if you only knew," he said.

"In the name of God, how were you to know about your mother and father, what drove them apart, what kept them apart? You were only a baby at the time."

"What did drive them apart?"

Emmaline studied him a moment, wondering what answer she could give him that would sum it all up. Finally it came to her. "It was pride."

"Whose pride? My father's or mother's?"

"Both. Neither one of them was very deprived of that particular deadly sin. They had it in great abundance. Mainly, though, I suppose most of the fault lies with your mother's family. I'll believe until they put me in my grave that if it hadn't been for them, there wouldn't have been any trouble between Garrett and Victoria. Garrett used to say that your mother's family was so full of pride, all of them looked like they were about to pop. To my way of thinking, though, pride doesn't mean a whole lot if it hurts the family. And in this case, it did. The pride of your mother's family is what drove her and Garrett apart.

"They didn't like Garrett, you see," Emmaline said. "Oh, they were polite enough to him, at first. I guess they felt they had to be, considering our family and all."

"Our family?"

"Yeah, we've got cousins—very distant cousins, I might add, who have some kind of infernal title. Duke, viscount, something like that. It may have meant a lot at one time, but it doesn't mean much now. They're all dirt poor from what I understand. But that's why Garrett was in England in the first place, visiting family and seeing how they ranched over there. Only, I don't suppose they call it ranching, do they?"

"No, but go on."

"Anyway, that's where he met your mother—at some fancy-dress ball or something, at some moldy old manor house. He met her family, too. And they soon let him know that, titled relatives or not, they didn't much care for him. For one thing, he was a rancher, and I guess they thought ranchers were no better than simple sheepherders or peasant farmers. Always hip-deep in mud and manure and not one of their class."

"So?"

"They were merchants," she said. "Every dad-blame one of them from the old man right down to the youngest son, according to Garrett. Very wealthy, very proper, middle-class British merchants. Which, I suppose, is the other reason they never cottoned to your daddy. He was an American, a red-blooded Texan, with not enough true English blood running in his veins to suit them, and they had this notion that no one but an Englishman of their class was good enough for their Victoria."

"So they married over these objections?"

"Yes, Garrett and your mother fell in love anyway. They got married, and about ten months later, you and Prescott came along." She laughed. "I remember the first letter I got from your daddy, telling me about you two boys. He was so proud, all he did was boast and brag—how much alike you were, how little you both were, but what big appetites and how much spunk you had.

"He had such high hopes, such big plans for you boys. He couldn't wait to bring all of you back here to the ranch. He wanted everyone in Waco to meet his wife and his identical twin sons. You two were going to be the first of a dynasty, he said.

"Just before all of you were due to set sail, you and Victoria came down with something. In the long run, it really didn't amount to a hill of beans, just a mild fever was all, but it was enough to keep you from making the voyage. Garrett wanted to stay until both of you were better, but—" Emmaline broke off abruptly, her voice thickening with emotion. "But he got word that our father was dying. He had to come home, he was needed here. And I assure you, if he hadn't been needed, I wouldn't have sent for him. But I was here alone, just me and my three little girls. My husband had been dead a good while by then, so I had no one but the hands to count on. I needed Garrett. Papa needed him."

"So that's when he left us."

"He left you and your mother behind with her family, and he and Prescott came home alone. He wanted Papa to see at least one of you before he died."

She looked off in the distance and took a deep breath. "They got here two days after we buried Papa. He never got to see either one of you."

Clearing her throat, she continued. "After a few days, Garrett started writing letters, making arrangements. He had it all planned, right down to the last detail. As soon as you and your mother were well enough to travel, you were to sail over from England. He even bought tickets on the fanciest steamship he could find sailing out of London. He thought Victoria's family would be accommodating, help out a little, get the two of you situated. Why wouldn't he think that? Their letters, what few of them they wrote, never indicated otherwise. But as you can probably guess, they were anything but helpful. The minute Garrett was out of sight, they stepped in and convinced your mother that she'd be better off staying on in England. Maybe even turned her against your father, for all I know.

"Well, months passed, and Garrett had had enough. He was going after you two. Going to catch the first ship back to England, he said, and bring you both here, where you belonged. He wasn't about to let her family interfere or keep his family apart any longer, but—"

"But what?"

Emmaline sighed. "He caught the ship, well enough."

"But I take it he never made it to England?"

"Not by a long shot. By that time, you see, war had

broken out, and Union ships had blockaded all the sea lanes. Garrett had no choice but to turn around and come back home.

"I tell you, he was so mad, there was absolutely no living with him. We had hands quitting left and right, he got so ornery. I learned real quick just to stay out of his way.

"Then one day, he came home and told me he'd up and joined the army. The next thing I knew, he'd gone off to fight the damn Yankees. I guess he figured *they* were the ones keeping him away from his wife and son."

"And he lost both of his legs in battle," Payne said, now painfully aware of his parents' turbulent history.

"Yeah, that he did," Emmaline said. "When he came home with nothing but a pair of stumps for legs, he was running a high fever. He was sick for days, but when the fever finally broke, he told me that Victoria's family had won. He couldn't go to her and ask her to be his wife, when he was only half a man and could never again be a husband to her. His pride, you see, wouldn't let him.

"That damn pride again. It kept a young man and young woman who loved each other an ocean apart, and it separated two brothers who have turned out to be little better than strangers. It's not worth it, Payne. Having that much pride just isn't worth the heartbreak and destruction."

She wrapped her arms around him and held him close. "I know it hurts to find out about your daddy so late and all, but you had to know."

"I'm glad you told me, Aunt Em. You've answered a lot of questions that I've had for a long time." But as comforting as those answers were, Payne realized, they only made his present situation all the more worse.

"My brother Garrett was a good man, a decent man, and I won't have you thinking unkindly of him because he wasn't a father to you the way he should have been. He did his best by both you boys. At least, he did the best he could for you under the circumstances. He didn't know what Victoria's family was doing to you, or to her. He thought they were taking care of both of you. He never knew she died, either. The last contact he had with her was when we got word that she had divorced him. Desertion, the paper said."

"She divorced him?" With a chuckle, Payne shook his head. "I was always told that he divorced her."

"Is that what your mother's family told you?"

"Yes."

The strong obscenity Emmaline muttered beneath her breath surprised even Payne. "Those people have a lot to answer for," she said. "If not in this life, then certainly in the next. Damn their souls."

"When you consider all the circumstances," Payne said, "I'm as much to blame as they are."

"How's that?"

"I believed everything they told me."

"You're not the guilty party. Heavens above, you were just a child at the time. Children believe anything and everything they're told, until they're old enough to find out differently for themselves."

"Still, I should have written . . . Father." Saying the word felt so strange, Payne thought, so alien. "I should have tried to contact him in some way."

"From what Chloe tells me, you had your hands full just keeping body and soul together. Folks do what they have to do, whether others feel what they do is honorable or not. You're no different. The only thing you're guilty of that I can see is stealing Chloe out from under Prescott's nose, and that's not much of a crime in my book. If nothing else, it woke the boy up, made him realize that he can't have everything he wants. Besides, those two weren't in love with each other anyway. At least, not the way a young couple ought to be in love."

"Try telling Prescott that," Payne said. Since their rather hasty departure from the saloon in San Antonio, his brother hadn't said more than a half-dozen words to him—and those only when absolutely necessary.

"I have told him," Emmaline said. "Just give him some time. Once his cursed Trefarrow pride has had a chance to heal, he'll come around." She lifted a hand and pressed it gently to Payne's cheek. "If I haven't told you before, I'll tell you now. It's good to have you home, son. You belong here. Don't ever think of going anywhere." Standing on tiptoe, she kissed the place on his face where her hand had been. Then she turned and headed back into the house, leaving Payne alone with his guilty thoughts.

He had to agree with Emmaline on one point—having too much pride could be destructive for a man. But it could be even more destructive to continue harboring a need for revenge—revenge that Payne now knew was groundless, unfounded, and totally unnecessary. To avenge his mother's disgrace by destroying his father's memory would be the biggest sin of all. His father hadn't been the cruel, uncaring bastard he had always believed, but an innocent man who had tried but failed to keep his family united.

Dear Lord, Payne thought as a horrible notion suddenly occurred to him. He had to stop it. Somehow, he had to stop the chain of events that he'd helped set into motion. He only prayed that he still had time to get word to Wyngate and stop the destruction of everything Garrett Trefarrow had stood for.

With his attention focused solely on finding Blodgett, Payne turned and ran as fast as his feet would carry him to the stable.

20

Payne paced the parlor like a caged lion, his strides taking him from one side of the room to the other and back again. Each time he passed the front windows, he peered out through the curtains and saw the same scene. Chickens scoured the yard for tasty tidbits, clucking to one another in a calming tone. Higher up, birds flitted from treetop to treetop, rustling the branches. All in all, everything looked normal—too normal, to his way of thinking.

He knew he shouldn't be anticipating trouble. To anticipate it would only bring it down about his head. He should be grateful that everything was going so smoothly. In the three weeks since he returned from San Antonio with Chloe and Prescott, he'd had no word or sign of Wyngate, from Blodgett, either. Obviously Blodgett had gotten to the man and told him the deal was off. At least, Payne prayed that he had.

"You keep that up, you're going to wear a hole in that rug," Prescott said as he sauntered into the room. "And when you do, Aunt Em's going to tan your hide and have it hanging on the barn door so's everyone can see."

"It's my wedding day," Payne said. "I'm allowed to be nervous, aren't I?"

"Not that nervous. Anybody looking at you would think you were a man waiting to take his last walk to the gallows, not a groom about to trek down the aisle." Prescott dropped into a chair and stretched his long legs out in front of him. " 'Sides, there ain't nothing for you to be nervous about. You're getting what you want, aren't you?"

"If you mean Chloe, then yes, I am getting *who* I want, not what."

Prescott chuckled and shook his head. "For the life of me, I can't figure what she sees in you."

A half-dozen retorts formed in Payne's mind, but he dismissed them all. Prescott didn't need to hear the differences between the two brothers spelled out to him; he knew them already. Their similarity ended with their identical looks. They were as opposite as night and day, as black and white.

"She loves me, Prescott. What's more, I love her."

Love was such a paltry word for what he truly felt for Chloe. The truth of the matter was that he didn't think he would want to live if he had to live without her.

"You saying I didn't love her?" Prescott asked.

"I'm saying that your love for her was questionable, very questionable."

"Bullshit. Love is love, and I loved Chloe."

"Obviously not enough to stay away from other women," Payne said. "A perfect example is the way you behaved with the sister of those four Neanderthals who tried to kill us and nearly succeeded. I, at least, have been faithful to Chloe."

" 'Have been' ain't quite the same as will be, little brother," Prescott said with a sneer. "Wait 'til you've been married for a spell and your feet start to itching. Itching so bad that not even the wife can scratch 'em. We'll see then just who's the most faithful."

Payne moved away from the window with a smile on his face. "For your information, Chloe is more than adequately equipped to scratch any itches that I might experience either in the near future or the far distant one."

"You don't say."

"Oh, but I do say. If you'd taken the time to treat her like a woman who loved you, you would have found that out for yourself. But then, if you had done that, she wouldn't have turned to me for solace, would she?"

Prescott's eyes narrowed as his forehead wrinkled with a scowl. "You asking to get your nose busted again? Is that what this little lecture of yours is all about? 'Cause if it is—"

"My broken nose is fine just the way it is, thank you. And this little lecture of mine, as you put it, is my way of saying that you had your chance, now I've got mine, so you can just leave Chloe and me alone."

"Oh, I'll leave her alone, all right." Prescott rose to his feet. He crossed the room to stand directly before Payne, nose to nose. "But I'll tell you one thing—if I ever hear of you being mean to her, mistreating her in any way, so help me God, I'll make you rue the day you were ever born."

"Why would I ever want to mistreat Chloe? Have you already forgotten that I love her?"

"Yeah, well, I love her too, and don't you forget it."

"Not as much as I do, apparently. You've never been faithful to her."

"I may not have loved her in the same way you do, but I still love her. At least I had the decency to keep my pants buttoned at all times. Yours fell down around your ankles so often, I'm surprised you didn't fall and break a leg."

"Boys, boys!" Emmaline started as she came into the parlor. "What in heaven's name is going on in here? I could hear the two of you all the way back to the kitchen. Are you trying to pick a fight with each other?"

"No, not a fight," Payne said. "We were just having a friendly discussion is all."

"Discussion my ass," Prescott said.

"Prescott Trefarrow!"

"Well, I'm sorry, Aunt Em, but he started it."

"I did no such thing," Payne protested. "You started it."

"The hell I did! All I did was come in here and find you pacing up and down like the nervous bridegroom you are. Only thing I could think of was that you were getting a bad case of cold feet."

"I assure you, my feet are anything but cold."

"It didn't look like it to me."

"Stop this right now!" Emmaline said. "I'm ashamed of both of you, behaving this way, like two little kids. Well, you're not kids anymore; you're grown men. Chloe's in her room getting ready, Payne. You ought to be doing the same."

"I am ready, Aunt Em."

"Not with that growth of beard on your face. Go shave it off."

"I'm trying to let it grow."

"You can start growing it again after you're married," she said. "No bride wants to kiss a groom whose face feels like coarse wool. It'll scratch her all up."

Prescott chuckled.

"And you," she said, turning on him.

"Me?"

"If you think I'm going to let you go to the church wearing that old suit, you've got another think coming. Why, the seat's so shiny I can see my face in it. Get to your room and put on your new one."

"My new suit?" he asked. "The one I had made for Chloe's and my wedding?"

"That's the one."

"But I'm saving that for a special occasion."

"Would your funeral be special enough? 'Cause that's where you'll be wearing it if you don't mind me. Now both of you—*march!*"

Forcing a scowl to her face and planting her fists on her hips, Emmaline tapped her toe as Payne and Prescott left the parlor. The moment they were out of sight, however, her arms dropped to her sides and a smile curled the corners of her lips. It was about time they fought. Since their return from San Antonio, they'd been far too polite and civilized toward each other. Too steady a diet of that had made her wonder if they would ever behave like a family, bickering and arguing and airing their grievances from time to time. Bickering oftentimes kept families close, and up until now, Payne and Prescott hadn't said one harsh word to each other, even though Payne deserved a good tongue lashing by Prescott for his scandalous behavior with Chloe. But all that was in the past. They were finally beginning to behave like brothers—*real* brothers who cared enough about each other to argue childishly.

That fact alone assured her that everything would be all right, that she could rest easy.

Recalling the pot of water she still had boiling on the stove, Emmaline left the parlor and started to go through the front hallway, where sunlight and a cool breeze poured in through the opened door to the kitchen. Just then, she caught sight of a stranger climbing the porch steps. Though the angle of his hat obscured his face, she thought she recognized his build. Even his slight limp looked familiar. Was it somebody from town, coming to pay his respects to the soon-to-be bride and groom?

"Good morning," she said, "what can I—" Abruptly, her smile faded as the man looked up and swept off his hat, giving her an unimpeded view of his face. The silver-streaked black hair, the bushy mustache above his full lower lip, and the aquiline nose told her instantly who he was.

"Morning, Mrs. McCardie."

"Mr. Wyngate," she said coldly. "What do you want?"

Chloe stood in front of her full-length mirror and studied her reflection. Though her dress wasn't nearly as fancy as the one she had worn on her first wedding day, she thought it just as beautiful. Mrs. Buchholtz, the dressmaker, had found a simple, unadorned white taffeta gown in her size. They had added a slight train to the skirt, taken some of Mrs. Buchholtz's new Belgian lace to trim the hem, bodice, and sleeves, and had transformed the plain dress into a fashionable wedding gown.

Smoothing down the rustling fabric over her hips

as she turned to view her profile, she knew that Payne would be pleased with her efforts. But she had to wonder if he would be pleased about the other. Her hand came up to caress her still-flat belly, and a feeling of warm satisfaction washed over her.

Though she didn't yet show it, and the doctor hadn't yet confirmed her suspicions, she knew beyond a shadow of a doubt that she carried Payne's child. His son, she hoped. A man like Payne needed sons, at first. Of course, she hoped that their daughters would come later.

As loud voices nearby wrenched her out of her fanciful musings, she wondered who was arguing. She opened her bedroom door to listen more closely, and the voices grew louder, Prescott's rising above the others.

"I don't believe it," Chloe heard her former fiancé say. "My brother's a goddamn Judas!"

Dread crawled up Chloe's spine when she realized that Prescott was repeating her words, that he was telling Payne of her first assumption of him. She had to stop him. She knew that Prescott's pride had been wounded by her behavior with his brother, but he had no right to vent all of his anger on Payne. She deserved her share as well.

She slipped her feet into her shoes and hurried out of the room. As she drew closer to the parlor, she heard another voice, one that she had thought never to hear again.

"He's a businessman, Trefarrow, not a Judas," Wyngate said. "Shortly after I found him in London, I made him a legitimate business offer. And like the intelligent man he is, he accepted it."

"He had no right," Prescott said. "No right at all,

you hear? The Triple T isn't his to sell. It's mine."

"Not according to your late father's will," Wyngate said, reaching into his coat pocket and producing a pair of legal-looking documents. "Let's see. It says here that Garrett left the ranch to both of you, equally. Equally means that it's as much your brother's to sell as it is yours. Care to see the will for yourself?"

"I've seen it," Prescott said, his voice raised so loud that it rumbled throughout the room. "Hell, I was there with Papa when he had the lawyer draw it up. But that still don't change the fact that I'm not selling."

"Neither am I," Payne said. "I tried to stop this from happening, Wyngate. Didn't you get my message? Didn't Blodgett tell you I'd changed my mind, that the deal we made is no longer suitable?"

"Oh, he told me, all right," Wyngate said. "I just assumed that you were in need of more financial backing to entice the Bliss—"

"I don't want any more of your money, thank you," Payne quickly interrupted, guilty heat flaring within him.

Wyngate shrugged. "Well, whether you need more money or not is not the real issue here. I've got a big problem. We all do, come to think of it."

"Yeah, you," Prescott said. "You're the problem. You don't know how to take no for an answer. You never did."

To refute Prescott's opinion of him, Wyngate knew, would only encourage him more and make the situation all the more uncomfortable, so he simply ignored him. "You see, I've invested a lot of time and capital in this venture. Too much, in fact, to simply walk away and forget about it."

"I can't do anything about the time," Payne said, "but I'll see to it personally that you get your money back. Every penny of it."

"It's not the money I'm really concerned about," Wyngate said. "Granted it is a great deal, but I can absorb the loss if necessary. It's the land I'm thinking about. It's mine."

Prescott took a step forward, his face flushed with rage. "The hell it is. The Triple T is Trefarrow land, Wyngate. It has been for fifty years, and it will be for the next hundred and fifty, if I have to lay down my life for it."

"I hate to disillusion you, Prescott, but you're wrong," Wyngate said. "Before your grandfather laid claim to it, every acre of the Triple T belonged to my family."

"Now that is a lie, sir." Emmaline, who had been sitting quietly in a chair as the argument raged, suddenly slammed her fist down upon the arm of the chair. "We Trefarrows were the first to settle here. We took this land, poured our hearts and souls, our very lives, into it. We've even got our dead buried on it. But it was all worth it to make it what it is today."

"I'll admit your family has taken very good care of it, Mrs. McCardie," Wyngate said. "I have no dispute with that. You're exceptional caretakers. But that's all you Trefarrows are—caretakers. You weren't the first ones here. Not by any means. My grandfather was."

"Your grandfather?"

"My grandfather. He and more than a dozen other settlers were close associates of Moses Austin. They came to this part of Texas and settled it long before your father ever left England or fought alongside General Houston at San Jacinto."

"Moses Austin and his bunch are ancient history, Wyngate," Prescott said. "You know as well as I do that all those land grants and claims were nullified by Santa Anna, back sixty-odd years ago."

"It still doesn't change the fact this land did, and still does, belong to my family. I've got all the necessary documents to prove it."

"Those documents of yours are nothing but worthless pieces of paper," Prescott said. "There ain't a court in this state that'll uphold your claim. Good God, they're older than the state of Texas itself, given to your granddaddy by a Mexican government that don't even exist anymore."

"Are you willing to risk everything you've got to reassure yourself of that?" Wyngate asked. "Is that what you want me to do, take this matter to court and let a judge decide who is the rightful owner? Because, rest assured, if I have to take it that far, I will."

"Why haven't you done so before now?" Payne asked.

Wyngate chuckled wryly. "Contrary to what you and your aunt and brother might think, I'm a fair man."

Both Emmaline and Prescott snorted but Wyngate ignored them. "Time and time again," he said, "I tried showing my documents to Garrett, hoping he would listen. When that tactic didn't work, I made him what I thought was a reasonable offer for this place. After all, he and Camden, his father, did work hard to make this a profitable ranch. But Garrett only laughed in my face and ordered me to leave."

"Which I'm fixing to do," Prescott said. "I'm getting damn sick and tired of listening to all this bullshit of yours, Wyngate."

"Watch your language," Emmaline said.

"Language, hell, Aunt Em. It is bullshit, and Wyngate knows it. He knows he hasn't got a leg to stand on. We've got the upper hand here. He's just trying to show us what a big man he is. Hell, up until a few years ago, Wyngate here wasn't no better than the rest of us, just trying to scrape out a living to hold body and soul together. Then he came into money somehow—most likely by illegal means, if you ask me—and he gets this idea in his head that he wants back what he thinks is rightfully his. Well, it ain't his. It hasn't been for a good long time. The Triple T is ours, and it's going to stay ours."

Wyngate shook his head as he laid aside Garrett's will and revealed the small stack of papers that he had hidden beneath it. "That's where you're wrong again, Trefarrow."

A heavy feeling settled in the pit of Prescott's stomach. He knew what those papers represented. How could he not know when he'd signed so many of them in the past? They were bank-loan agreements, giving him money when he'd needed it at a time when he'd considered being in debt as natural to a rancher as breathing. Even from a distance, and looking at the papers upside down, he could see the signature scrawled across the bottom of the pages. The signature was his.

Payne stepped forward. "You don't have to do this, Wyngate. I told you I'll give your money back to you. I just need a little time."

"Sorry, Payne, but your time has run out," Wyngate said. "These are legal, binding notes, proving that I'm now the owner of the Triple T. If you don't believe me, then by all means take them to your lawyer and have him verify it." He stood as if to leave, eyeing Prescott and Emmaline. "I've tried my dead-level best to be civil about this, hoping that you'd be reasonable people. But, as in the past, civility just hasn't worked. You've left me with no other alternative. I'm sorry, but you've got thirty days to pack up all of your belongings and get off my property."

He took one step toward the door and then stopped. "By the way, Payne," he added, "I'll be taking over the Bliss girl's land as soon as you marry her. That was our agreement, if you'll recall. I supplied you and Blodgett with all the necessary funds to cover your travel expenses from England and purchase your brother's loans. The additional Bliss acreage is quite an unexpected bonus, a nice piece of property. I've had my agents survey it."

Stunned by Wyngate's last revelation, Prescott and Emmaline could only stare at him as he walked out of the parlor. Then their eyes slowly moved to Payne, who stood beside the window with his back to them.

Out in the hall, Wyngate caught sight of Chloe, leaning weakly against the wall. "Congratulations, my dear," he said, crossing to her so that he could kiss her cold hand. "You make a very lovely bride."

"How much?" she asked, her voice hoarse with a combination of anger, pain, and disappointment.

Payne heard her and turned sharply. Before his brother or aunt could move, he headed for the hallway.

"How much what, Miss Bliss?" Wyngate asked.

"How much do we all owe you?"

Wyngate chuckled. "It's like I told Trefarrow and Mrs. McCardie—I'm not interested in the money. I've got more than plenty of that. All I want is the land."

"Like everything else in this life, it's got a price, hasn't it?"

Wyngate seemed surprised at her astuteness. "Of course it does. But I doubt that you, a mere girl of what—eighteen?—could comprehend the value of a property such as yours and the Triple T."

"Tell me how much, Mr. Wyngate."

He studied her a moment, wondering where this pointless conversation would lead. "Roughly, the two properties are worth, oh, two hundred, two hundred fifty thousand. Why, the water rights alone—"

"And the total of Prescott's loans?" she interrupted.

"His loans?" Though he presented an outward expression of mild surprise, inside Wyngate was anything but surprised. He now knew in what direction Chloe's train of thought was heading. Astute was too mild a word for this lady. Shrewd was a much better one.

"Roughly," she said.

"Thirty thousand."

"And the total amount that you gave to Payne and Blodgett?"

"At this point it's close to three thousand."

Chloe smiled. "Mr. Wyngate, that only adds up to thirty-three thousand dollars. Yet you expect us to just up and leave our ranches, our homes, that are worth over two hundred thousand dollars?"

"Business, Miss Bliss, is—"

"Business," she finished. "I know, I've heard that saying all my life. But this isn't business. What you're talking about is highway robbery. You're a thief, Mr. Wyngate."

"Now wait just a minute."

"No, you wait. You may wear nice clothes and act

like a proper gentleman and all, but you're still nothing but a common thief."

"Trefarrow!" Wyngate bellowed, an angry tinge creeping up his neck. "This woman of yours is—"

"Not finished yet." Chloe didn't have to turn around to know that Prescott and Aunt Em were standing behind her, listening to every word being spoken. "You and I are discussing business. Don't involve Prescott in this."

"I discuss business with no woman."

"You will with me . . . if you want your money back."

"I'll tell you the same thing I've told Trefarrow and Mrs. McCardie, Miss Bliss. It's not the money I'm concerned about. It's the land. I want the Triple T."

"Obviously you're not going to get it. Because we're not interested in selling it to you. Now I know that you're holding the notes on this ranch, and I'll be more than happy to give you what you've got coming to you. After that, you—"

"*You'll* give me the money?" Wyngate tossed back his head and laughed. "My dear, you're as dirt poor as the Trefarrows. No, what am I saying? That's far too generous. Considering that for the past ten years or more you've been living off their charity, you're probably poorer."

"Am I?"

"I'm not a fool, Miss Bliss. Of course you are."

"Don't be so sure."

Chloe's confident tone drew a look of impatience from Wyngate. "You have money?"

"Yes, I have money."

"Not enough, I'll wager."

"Oh, more than enough, Mr. Wyngate. If you

doubt my word, feel free to contact my uncle's lawyer."

"Your uncle?"

"Actually, my late uncle. My mother's younger brother. He died a few years ago." She paused for half a heartbeat, then added, "In Denver."

"Denver? Denver, Colorado?"

Chloe nodded. "He was a businessman, too. But unlike you, he got his hands dirty doing honest labor. He didn't go around stealing homes from decent, hardworking people. Simply put, Mr. Wyngate, he dug holes in deep dark mines."

"Silver." Wyngate all but whispered the word.

"That's right. His wasn't the richest vein of ore ever discovered. Just the second richest. And because he never married and had children, he left everything he owned to me. I inherit the bulk of his estate the moment I marry or turn twenty-five."

"So you're—"

"Let's just say that I'm comfortably well off," Chloe said. "Rich is such a vulgar word, don't you think?"

She waited for him to respond, but when he didn't, she took his arm and ushered him to the front door. "I'll send a telegram to my uncle's lawyer today, the moment I'm legally married to Payne. He'll see to it that you're sent a check for the amount that you've got coming to you. Not a penny more, not a penny less, Mr. Wyngate, so don't be expecting a bonus. And as soon as you receive it, I would like a letter of confirmation from you. On second thought, better make it a telegram; it'll be much quicker. And then I don't ever want to hear from you or see you again. I'm sure the same thing goes for Aunt Em and Prescott and Payne. Is that understood?"

"Quite clearly, Miss Bliss."

"Then if there's nothing more, I believe our business is concluded. Good day, Mr. Wyngate."

He slowly donned his hat. His expression was unreadable. "Good day, and good-bye, Miss Bliss."

21

Chloe watched Wyngate descend the porch steps, mount his horse, and ride away. When he was finally out of sight, she turned around. Aunt Em and Prescott stood just outside the parlor doorway, but she saw no sign of Payne. She had hoped that he would be there with his aunt and brother, wearing the same look of surprise that Prescott wore. But he wasn't, and his absence only heightened her feeling of loss, of having been used.

"Damnation, girl," Prescott said. "If I'd known you had money, I'd've married you years ago."

Emmaline jabbed an elbow into Prescott's rib. "Shut your mouth, you ungrateful whelp."

"Ungrateful?"

"Yes, ungrateful. Chloe's just saved our homes from that fancy-dressed snake in the grass. You ought not be talking to her that a-way."

"It's all right, Aunt Em," Chloe said.

"No, it's not. It's wrong. He's wrong and should be ashamed of himself."

"I'm not offended. Especially not by anything Prescott has to say. I know that he's just being himself—crude and thoughtless."

Prescott let her opinion of his character slide by without comment. "How come you never told me you had money?"

"Because I didn't have any."

"You mean, all that stuff that you just told Wyngate was nothing but a lot of bunk?"

"No," Chloe said, "it was the truth. What I just said to you was the truth, too. I don't have any money. Right now, at this very moment, I have less than twenty dollars to my name. However, as soon as I marry Payne, I'll inherit my uncle's estate. I won't be rich then, either, but like I told Wyngate, I will be comfortably well off."

A look of skepticism flashed across Prescott's green eyes. "About this uncle of yours . . ."

"What about him?"

"How come you never told me about him?"

Chloe shrugged. "Maybe you just didn't listen. For your information, I've talked about him often."

"Not to me, you didn't."

"Yes, to you, Prescott." Heaving a sigh of frustration, she shook her head. "Oh, what's the use? Nothing I've ever said to you has been important enough for you to stop what you were doing and listen to me. You've been too busy the last ten years, trying your darnedest to avoid me. To you, I was nothing but a pest. Until a few months ago when *you* decided it was time to settle down and take a wife, you couldn't even spare me the time of day, much less listen to what I had to say about my family. Even when you asked me to marry you, you only heard what you wanted to hear."

"Hell, girl, I've had this ranch to run. It don't take care of itself, you know."

"That's no excuse," Emmaline said. "I've had things to do, too, but I still found the time to listen to her."

"*You* knew?"

"From the very beginning," Emmaline said. "I was the one who went to Denver with Chloe when her uncle died, remember? We even stayed an extra day so that her uncle's lawyer could read the will."

Prescott sank onto the bench beneath the hatrack. "No, I don't remember."

"It was only five years ago, Prescott," Chloe said.

"A lot's happened in the last five years," he said. "How am I supposed to keep track of the comings and goings of a thirteen-year-old girl?" He raked both hands through his hair. "Did Papa know?"

"Of course."

"Damnation!" He looked at Emmaline. "Papa knew, you knew, of course, Chloe knew. Everyone but me. You never said a word, Aunt Em. All this time, all the sleepless nights I've spent worrying over how I was going to find the money to keep the ranch running, you never said one word."

"There wasn't anything for me to say," Emmaline said. "It wasn't my inheritance. It was Chloe's. It was her place to tell you or not tell you. Frankly, if you ask me, I think she did the wise thing by keeping her mouth shut."

"Thank you, Aunt Em," Chloe said, stepping away from the front door and heading for the parlor.

"Yeah, that's right," Prescott said, "side with Chloe. She's been the answer to the Triple T's problems all along, but for God's sake, don't ever let old Prescott know. No, keep him in the dark. He doesn't deserve to know. He doesn't deserve a good night's sleep, either. Hell, he might even do something really shameful, like ask her for a loan."

"Oh, hush up," Emmaline said. "Quit your whining. There's no way she could've loaned you the money, and you know it. The will states she had to be twenty-five or married, whichever came first, and she was only thirteen. Besides, you would have made her life more miserable than you already have."

"Now hold on a dadblame minute. I haven't made her life miserable. Far from it. Hell, I was going to marry her, wasn't I?"

"For all the wrong reasons," Emmaline countered.

Chloe turned a deaf ear onto the remainder of their argument. Prescott and Aunt Em would just have to work out their differences on their own. She had a much more pressing matter to tend to at the moment. The matter being Payne, of course.

She found him standing at the window, his back to the parlor. One part of her wanted to give in to the emotion that tugged at her, to drop to the floor and weep the buckets of disappointed tears that threatened. However, the stronger part of her wouldn't let that happen. Now more than ever she knew she had to be strong and resolute.

"Are you ready?" she asked him.

Payne turned, and even from a distance she could see that he had been moved by what she had done for the family. A few hours ago, before Wyngate's untimely arrival, before she knew of Payne's nefarious association with the man, she might have been touched by the amount of pride and love now reflected in Payne's gaze. But now she hardened herself against any emotion he might be feeling.

"You've got to know, Chloe. I never intended for any of this to happen. Not this way."

He hadn't intended it? What a consummate liar he was, Chloe thought. To set out to totally destroy everything for which his father and brother had worked so hard to maintain had been his plan all along. She could see that now. And, to give him credit, he had almost succeeded. As far as she was concerned, she didn't even want to think what his intentions had been. The merest thought of it filled her with a sickening dread.

"It doesn't matter now," she said, keeping her voice calm.

"Yes, it does. Don't you see, I— Oh, hell, how do I begin?" He took one step toward her and stopped. "I never had anything. No home, no family, nothing. I never knew I could be drawn into people's lives, become a part of them, the way I've become a part of yours and Aunt Em's and Prescott's. And then to do what I tried to do, ruin everything you've worked for, all your hopes and dreams, and yet have you love me so unconditionally in return . . . No one's ever done that for me before, Chloe. No one. Until I met you, everything, everyone, came with a price."

Steeling herself against the pain and rage that threatened to become uncontrollable within her, Chloe cleared her throat. "We have a wedding to go to, Payne. Remember?"

"Yes, our wedding." Relieved, he chuckled and began to close the distance between them, intending to take her in his arms and hold her close. He wanted to do more, much more, but he didn't dare with his aunt and brother in such close proximity. "I find it hard to believe, after all that's happened here today, that you still want to marry me."

As he reached out for her, she managed to elude his touch by brushing past him and going toward the spot at the window he had just vacated. Still want to marry him? Lord above, if she had any real choice in the matter, she would send him packing right on the spot. But she knew she couldn't. She had to marry him to inherit the money she needed to save the Triple T.

"You've saved us all, you know," he said. "If no one's bothered to thank you yet, and I suspect my brother hasn't, then I will. You have my eternal gratitude, Chloe."

"Your thanks aren't necessary." Nor were they needed, or even wanted. "Prescott's, either. To be honest, I did it more for my own benefit than for anyone else's."

"But your generosity—"

"Was really nothing more than plain old selfishness." She turned then and looked him squarely in the eye. "You see, I needed a home, someplace to raise my baby. Now if you don't mind, I'd rather we dropped this subject altogether and get on with the business at hand."

"Wait a minute." Payne grabbed her arm as she started past him. "Did you say 'baby?'"

She hated having to look at him, hated having to gaze into his eyes, but the need to see how he felt about the news of his impending fatherhood was far greater than her present dislike of him. What she saw in his deep green depths could only be described as surprise, joy, and elation.

"A baby?" he asked again. "You're going to have *our* baby?"

"Yes, Payne, ours."

"Oh, God, Chloe. . . ."

Again, he moved to take her in his arms. This time, instead of avoiding him, she let him hold her. But she could tolerate it for only a moment. Standing close to him, breathing in the scent of him, his hair tonic and soap, she knew a moment of revulsion so strong that she felt her stomach churn.

"We really don't have time for this, Payne," she said, pulling out of the embrace. "If we're not at the church by noon sharp, Reverend Campbell might take it into his head that we've run off again. That's the last thing we need to happen. We've already given Ivy, Rose, and Daisy enough to gossip about for years to come, don't you think?"

Payne thought her somewhat elusive behavior a bit odd, but he decided it would be wiser at the moment not to question it. She was carrying his child, she still wanted to marry him, and his life, his future, had never looked brighter, so who was he to argue? Thank goodness she seemed to understand or at least forgive him for nearly taking the Triple T away.

When they arrived at the church a half hour later, Chloe and Prescott in one buggy, Aunt Em and Payne in the other, a crowd of well-wishers greeted them at the churchyard gate. Chloe held her head erect as she climbed out of the buggy. She even managed to smile at a few of the guests as she walked past them.

As they had previously arranged with Reverend Campbell, Payne ushered Aunt Em down the aisle first, seating her in the front pew, then taking his place at the foot of the altar. At that point the organist heralded the bride's presence by playing the opening strains of the wedding march. Though tempted to walk down the aisle on her own, Chloe reluctantly slipped her hand through the crook of Prescott's arm and took the first of many hesitant steps. The closer she drew to her final destination at Payne's side, the heavier guilt weighed on her heart. She had to be the biggest hypocrite ever born. Not only was she wearing white, when she no longer had the right to wear the traditional color of virginity, but she would be repeating sacred vows that she had absolutely no intention of keeping.

Thankfully, the ceremony went by quickly, almost in a blur, it seemed to her. She stood beside Payne, letting him hold her hand as they listened to Reverend Campbell then said the words he directed them to say. She didn't flinch when her handsome groom slipped the plain gold wedding band onto the third finger of her left hand, nor did she let her own hand tremble when she placed his wedding ring on his finger. Only when Payne lifted her veil and placed a loving kiss on her lips did her control began to crumble.

Accompanied by the organist, the two marched back down the aisle and out of the church. Sunshine poured down on them from the cloudless sky above. The strong scent of roses wafted through the air. A small flock of birds flew by overhead. Anyone with a clear conscience would believe that their union had just been blessed by the Almighty Himself. But Chloe, who had no clear conscience, knew differently.

As they reached their buggy, she suddenly wrenched her arm free of Payne's grasp when he started to help her up into the seat. "I can take care of myself, thank you," she said.

The coldness in her voice, and the iciness in her

stare, hit Payne so hard that he could only blink at her in confusion. "What?"

"I said, I can take care of myself. You've done your duty. I don't need you any longer."

"Chloe, what the devil are you talking about?"

Although painfully aware that almost everyone could hear her, she knew she couldn't stop now that she had started. "I've gotten what I wanted, what I needed—your name for our child, and the inheritance for the Triple T. Now would you please go away and leave me alone."

As the shock of her words registered, so did the gawking stares of all the onlookers. "You can't mean that," Payne said in a hushed voice.

"Oh, but I can, I do. I mean every word. If I could have avoided this wedding, believe me, I would have. I wish to God I'd never met you, Payne Trefarrow. You almost ruined your brother and Aunt Em's lives. You came very close to ruining mine. I did the only thing I could do, I married you, now get the hell out of my life."

"Chloe, I—"

She wanted to stop, but couldn't. The floodgates had broken and her rage poured forth. "How dare you think that you've got the right to give away the Triple T and the Rocking B to someone so vile and loathsome as Sam Wyngate? How dare you?"

An audible gasp rose up from the surrounding crowd.

Looking embarrassed and very contrite, Payne tried to ignore the gasp. "I'm sorry, Chloe, but you more than anyone should know the reasons behind my actions. I wanted revenge for what I thought my father had done to me and to my mother. I thought it was my right, my duty to seek retribution. I had no idea then that I was wrong. Honest to God, I didn't."

"Well, you were."

"I know that now. And you know it, too. Can't we at least try to put all that behind us and get on with our lives?"

"That's exactly what I intend to do. Get on with my life. As far as your life is concerned . . ." She managed an unconcerned shrug. "I don't care what you do. You can go straight to hell, and with my blessing."

"But what about the child? Our child."

Another gasp rose up from the wedding party, and it was Chloe's turn to be embarrassed. But instead of blushing and looking apologetic, she only lifted her head and smiled. "You'll never know, will you?"

"What do you mean?"

"I mean that I'd rather die than let you come near our son. Or daughter. And so help me God, if you do try to come near either of us, I'll have you shot on sight. From this moment on, Payne Trefarrow, you no longer exist in my life."

She turned, intending to climb into the buggy, but he reached out a hand and stopped her.

"You can't do this, Chloe. Not after all that we've been through."

"I have no other choice."

"But you said you loved me."

The tears she had managed to hold back began to well up in her eyes. "I did love you. I loved you more than I've ever loved anything or anyone in my life."

"Then don't do this to us."

"There is no us. Not any longer. It hurts now, but I'll get over it. And rest assured, when I do, I'll be over you."

With that, she wrenched her arm free and climbed into the buggy. Gathering up the reins, she gave a flick of her wrists and sent the horse into motion. The buggy rounded the curve in the road and disappeared out of sight, and she never looked back.

22

"*Boy, I'll tell you,*" Prescott said. "When that little lady gets a bee in her bonnet, it's a doozie, ain't it?"

The brothers lay beside each other, hidden from view by a waist-high stand of dying Johnson grass. Prescott, on his back, had his arms folded beneath his head as he stared up into the sunny, late-autumn sky. Payne, on his belly, had his ear tuned to what Prescott was saying, but his gaze was focused on the figure captured in his spyglass.

He'd used the spyglass a lot of late, watching Chloe with such regularity, keeping track of her every movement, that he knew her daily routines by heart. Yesterday, Sunday, she'd puttered around in her garden a bit. But today, Monday, she'd done her wash in the morning and was now hanging clothes on the clothesline beside the house—her house. In the four months since their wedding, she hadn't been back to the Triple T once, not even to pay a visit to Aunt Em. Those four months had seen a major

change in Payne's life, and in his relationship with
Prescott as well. But that span of time had made an
even bigger difference in the size of Chloe's stomach.

"She's got more than a bee in her bonnet," Payne
said, snapping the spyglass shut and turning over
onto his back. "If I didn't know better, I'd say she
was carrying a full-grown Shetland pony in her belly.
I wonder if she's having twins."

"Twins? Don't you know nothing? A twin can't
have twins."

"Are you sure about that?"

"No. It's just something I've always heard."

"Well, you might try telling that to Chloe."

Prescott guffawed. "And get a load of buckshot in
me for talking to her? No, thank you. I'm pretty partial
to having my ass in the condition it's in."

They lay there for a moment longer, silently, just
enjoying each other's companionship. Once Prescott
had forgiven him for trying to give the Triple T away
to Wyngate, hardly a day went by that one didn't
learn something new about the other and find mutual
gratification in the effort. They worked side by side,
talking constantly and quite often laughing. Payne
shared some of his adventures with Prescott, while
Prescott all but bragged about his. Getting to know
his brother made Payne finally feel like an accepted
member of the family.

He marveled at how his luck had been both good
and bad at the same time. The good part was that
Prescott had managed to put the past behind him.
The bad part was that Chloe still refused to have anything to do with him. On the few occasions he'd
accidentally met her in town, she'd openly snubbed
him by ignoring anything he said to her, even his very

presence. Of course, she treated Prescott the same way, but Payne considered Chloe's relationship with his brother, or the lack thereof, none of his concern. He had enough problems of his own just trying to figure out a way to penetrate the thick barrier in which she had insulated herself.

"You think she'll ever forgive us for what we done?" Prescott asked him.

"It doesn't look like it," Payne said, somewhat amazed that his brother seemed able to read his thoughts.

"Aunt Em said that the last time she went over to see Chloe, to make sure she was doing okay, she asked about us."

The news came as such a surprise to Payne that he sat upright and stared at Prescott. "She did?"

"Now, don't go getting all excited. According to Aunt Em, Chloe keeps a loaded shotgun by the front door, and I got a feeling she wouldn't mind using it on you. Besides, she didn't ask about us directly. She more or less hinted, in a roundabout way, at having an interest in what you and me were doing."

"What does she think we're doing? Having bacchanalian orgies every night right under Aunt Em's nose? Not bloody likely."

"I don't know about no bacchanalian orgies," Prescott said, "but I 'spect she thinks we might be getting drunk and fooling around with other women a lot."

"That's your problem, not mine. And for your information, a bacchanalian orgy *is* getting drunk and fooling around with women."

"Then why didn't you say so instead of giving it some fancy name I've never heard of before?"

"Look, just add 'bacchanalian orgy' to your growing vocabulary and tell me what she wanted to know about us."

"It's like I said, she didn't ask anything directly. She just wanted to know how everybody at the ranch was doing."

"Everybody, meaning you and me?"

"Everybody, *including* you and me. There's a difference. She more or less lumped us in with all the others."

"Yes, I guess you're right." Suddenly bored with the conversation, Payne rose to his feet and started for his horse, which was tied next to Prescott's beneath a nearby tree. "You know something? I'm growing very tired of all this."

"All what?"

"On spying on my own wife just so that I can be sure she and the baby are getting on all right."

"If it bothers you so much, stop spying on her. You want to know anything about her, ask Aunt Em. She'll keep you up to snuff on Chloe's condition."

"You don't understand. It's more than just her condition I'm worried about. We're married, for God's sake. I'm her husband; she's my wife. We can't go on like this for much longer."

"You mean, *you* can't go on for much longer." Prescott grinned. "I know a bad case of itchy feet when I see it."

"Well, if my feet are itching, Chloe's the only one I want scratching them."

Without warning, a loud blast shattered the peacefulness of the moment. The branch directly above Payne broke off the main trunk of the tree and came very close to hitting him on the head. He quickly dropped to his belly and hugged the ground.

"Get off my property!" Chloe yelled from some distance away. "Both of you!"

"Good Lord Almighty, Payne, she's shooting at us."

"Loaded shotgun by the front door, eh? Seems to me she's brought it with her."

"I never had a woman try to blow my head off before."

"There's always a first time for everything."

Despite the rapid beating of his heart, Prescott chanced a peek through the dry blades of Johnson grass near his head. He saw Chloe standing at the edge of the porch, aiming the muzzle of a shotgun in their direction. At the top of his lungs, he yelled out, "Dammit, Chloe! Put that away before you kill somebody. It's just me and Payne out here."

"I know perfectly well who's out there," she called back. "Why do you think I didn't hit you? I told you both never to show your ugly, conniving faces around here or I'd shoot 'em off, didn't I? Well, I meant what I said. Now both of you get your mangy carcasses off my property, or the next time I might not miss."

"We're leaving! We're leaving!" Raising his hands in a gesture of surrender, Payne moved into view. Slowly, he began to inch toward his horse in a backward gait. "See? We're on our way."

"Good! And don't ever come back!"

Some time later, as they left the Rocking B and rode onto Triple T land, Payne said, "Surely, there's got to be some way of healing this breach between us."

"I sure ain't no expert on women, but if I were you, I wouldn't try the direct approach with her,"

Prescott said. "Not unless you're wearing a full suit of body armor. That's one little lady who means business. She said she don't want to have nothing to do with either one of us, and I, for one, intend to take her at her word."

"Were she anyone else, I would as well. But I can't. She's my wife, and I love her. And at the rate we're going, I'll be a grandfather before she ever lets me near her again."

They rode a short distance more, both deep in thought.

"Neutral ground," Prescott suddenly said.

"What?"

"I said, neutral ground."

"What's that got to do with anything?"

"Well, I was just thinking. If you could figure out a way to get Chloe on neutral ground, you might have a chance of getting through to her. Just a slim chance, you understand. But hell, a slim chance is better than no chance at all."

"What sort of neutral ground would you suggest?"

"Oh, I don't know. You need to find someplace where she'll be sure to mind her manners. Someplace where she wouldn't dare tote her shotgun to. Someplace like church, for instance."

"I've tried church," Payne said. "She stopped going because of me."

"Yeah, that's right, she did, didn't she? Aunt Em says she's not even going into town anymore. Probably afraid she'll run into you. Either that, or she's tired of the gossip." Taking the lead, Prescott turned his horse onto a well-trodden path. "One thing's for sure. You don't stand a chance while she's in that house. She's got it fixed up like a damn fort. You've got to get her away from it someway or somehow."

"I could try kidnapping her again."

Prescott considered the idea for a moment, then shook his head. "Nah. Kidnapping might have worked once, but it won't work a second time. Not with Chloe. Besides, she's probably expecting you to do something that stupid."

A short distance more, and the house came into sight.

"You know what you need to do?" Prescott asked.

"Other than finding a way to talk to my wife so she'll forgive me?"

"Yeah, other than that."

"What?"

"You need to get away for a spell."

"Away?"

"That's right. I don't mean take a long trip back to England or nothing, just someplace close by. Like Austin, maybe." As soon as the words left his mouth, Prescott cringed. "No, on second thought, you don't want to go there. You might run into Lucille Baldridge, she'd mistake you for me, and you'd be in an even bigger fix than you are now."

"If Austin is out of the question, I don't think it would be wise for you to suggest San Antonio. Considering how hastily we had to leave it, I don't think we made a very good impression with the village folk."

"Well, wherever you decide to go, plan to stay gone for a week. Two at the most. Long enough to get your mind off the problems you've got here. Maybe once she realizes you're gone she'll begin to miss you. Hey, I know! How about Dallas? We've got a friend or two up there that'd be happy to show you around."

"When you say 'friends' . . ."

"Yeah?"

"Are you speaking of Wyngate?"

"Good God, no! I wasn't even thinking about him. I'm talking about Abner Harris."

Payne mulled the name over in his mind. "I've never met the man," he said.

"I know you haven't. But now would be the perfect time to meet him. Yeah, go up to Dallas, let Abner show you around, get yourself introduced to some of his cronies, make a few business contacts."

"For what purpose? Not to get another bank loan, I hope. We still haven't paid off the sizable one you got months ago. One we couldn't afford, I might add."

"Not back then, perhaps, but our prospects are looking brighter now. A whole lot brighter."

"How's that?"

"Well, if all goes well, come next spring, we'll be able to pay it off in full."

"At the risk of repeating myself, how's that?"

"Hell, man, you've seen the herd."

"Yes, I have," Payne said. "I've seen it every day, but what's that got to do with anything?"

"Noticed how its grown?"

"Now that you mention it, yes."

"This past summer's been a good one. Just about every cow we own will be calving come springtime. We sell off some of the mamas and a few good baby bulls, we'll be back in high cotton. You tell that to them bankers and financiers up in Dallas, you'll impress them right out of their diamond-studded shirts."

"I don't know." Payne was still reluctant to leave Waco and Chloe for any length of time.

"Think about it. Getting away, letting your head clear will do you a world of good. Trust me. I know what I'm talking about."

23

Payne stared morosely out of his rain-drizzled hotel room window down at the street below. Dallas looked nothing like London. The buildings were newer, the streets wider, the pedestrians' clothes nothing at all like the styles fashionable Londoners wore. But the weather was almost identical—cold, very wet, and quite dreary.

He blew out his breath slowly and watched the vapor form on the windowpane, obliterating his view of the street. "'Do you a world of good to get away,' he said. Ha! 'Trust me,' he said. Miserable lying bastard."

Payne had been in town for over a week—eight full days, to be exact—and still all he could think about was Chloe. Every waking hour, she filled his thoughts. At night, she crept into his dreams, making him wake up in a cold sweat. He would never be able to forget her. Never.

The only good thing to come from this trip had been his meeting Abner Harris. The man was a veritable walking contradiction. On the one hand, he talked and acted like the most illiterate hayseed ever born. Yet at the same time, he dressed like a gentleman and conducted business with some of the wealthiest, most highly educated men of the day. It wasn't at all unusual for Harris to receive daily wire dispatches from the financial districts in New York City, or Boston, or even the latest political news from Washington, D.C.

A strange people, these Texans, Payne thought. A strange country, too. The longer he stayed in America and got to know it, the stranger it became to him, and the more he grew to love it. For reasons he couldn't explain, he was certain it had gotten into his blood, just as it had gotten into his father's blood. He could see now why Garrett and Prescott had worked and fought so hard to maintain control of the Triple T. To lose the ranch would be like losing a part of their soul.

The same way losing Chloe had taken part of his soul.

He turned away from the window. Why did his thoughts always have to come back to her? Why couldn't he take Prescott's advice and get his mind off her for a while?

Because, he realized as he heard a knock at the door, she possessed a part of his heart. And until he got her back into his life again, he could never be whole.

He opened the door, expecting to find a bellboy. Since his arrival in Dallas, invitations to local society gatherings and functions had been sent to him with aching regularity by the town's more class-conscious matrons, who seemed to take great joy in having an

Englishman in their midst. The invitations were always delivered by a uniformed bellboy with a silver tray.

But this time a short, rotund, balding stranger with a neatly trimmed white beard and mustache looked up at him, taking in the sight of Payne's half-unbuttoned, collarless shirt and wrinkled trousers. A fellow Englishman? he wondered, even before the man spoke.

"Er, Payne Richard George Trefarrow?" the man asked, his clipped upper-class accent not only surprising Payne, but confirming his hastily formed assumption as well.

"Yes."

The man bowed slowly, almost regally, at the waist and then, just as slowly, straightened again. "Milord."

Milord?

"Might I come in and have a word with you for a moment?"

"Are you certain you've got the right man?"

"If you are Payne Richard George Trefarrow, son of the late Garrett William Charles Trefarrow, then yes, I'm very happy to say I have the right man."

"You can't have."

He smiled. "Ah, but I do." Then he heaved a sigh of relief and added, "Finally."

"But I'm no lord."

"If you would only allow me to come into your room, I will be more than happy to explain."

"I wish you would, Mr.—er," Payne said as he stepped aside and let the man enter.

"Wilberforce. Sir Henry Wilberforce."

Startled was too mild a feeling for what Payne felt. He couldn't believe that a representative of Her Majesty, Queen Victoria, was actually standing beside him in his hotel room, informing him that he now had the right to be called "milord."

"*Sir* Henry?" he asked.

"Yes. I was knighted by her majesty almost twenty years ago. Twenty years in which I have faithfully, and at times with great difficulty, served her and the realm, locating missing heirs to near-extinct titles. I've been to America many times, but this is the first occasion I've ever had to travel as far as Texas." Looking somewhat uneasy, he leaned toward Payne and in a soft voice, asked, "Do they really have gun battles in the center of the streets here as the dime novels say they do?"

Taken aback by the man's question, Payne told him the first thing that crossed his mind. "Only at high noon, and if you're wearing a black hat. Otherwise you're very safe."

"And the savages?"

"Savages?"

"Yes, the red Indians."

"I've never seen one wearing a black hat, so I assume you're safe there, too."

Sir Henry relaxed. "That's comforting to know. Quite comforting, in fact. On the train journey from Chicago, I kept expecting a war party to attack us at any moment. Very unnerving, I must say."

"I'm sure it was," Payne said. "Now, about this lord business . . ."

"Yes, yes, we must tend to the more important matters at hand, mustn't we? The discussion of your native savages and gunslashers will just have to wait, I suppose."

"Gunslingers," Payne said.

"Beg your pardon?"

"They're called gunslingers, not gunslashers."

"Ah, quite right. Gunslingers. I'll have to remember that. Must be correct in our usage of colloquialisms, mustn't we? Especially when around the local populace. And a quite colorful populace it is at that, I must say."

"Sir Henry," Payne said, more anxious to hear about his newfound title than the man's newfound opinions of Texans.

"Ah, yes, the matter of your 'lord business,' as you put it."

With a chuckle, Sir Henry untied the large envelope he had been carrying and produced a sheaf of documents that, to Payne, appeared to be written on parchment and lambskin. It was the real thing, he thought, finally realizing that Sir Henry Wilberforce was authentic too, and not just some figment of his Chloe-deprived imagination.

"Your earldom," Sir Henry began, "is a very old and honorable one. It dates back to the mid-seventeenth century, when King Charles the Second reclaimed the throne from Oliver Cromwell's Puritan Protectorate. You see, your Cornish ancestor, Giles Trefarrow, was a loyal supporter of the king and his cause. And in gratitude for his unwavering loyalty, King Charles bestowed upon him the title of the first Earl of St. Keverne and gave him lands to govern in that region of Cornwall."

Earldom? The high ranking was so astounding to Payne that he stopped listening to Sir Henry's oratory on the Trefarrow family history. He was an earl? All the time he had lived in London, scraping about for food and shelter, he had been an earl? It was absolutely unbelievable.

" . . . until the sixth earl, and that's when things began to change."

"I beg your pardon?" Payne said, dragging his attention back to Sir Henry's dissertation. "I'm afraid I didn't catch that last bit."

"I said, the line of succession went unbroken until after the demise of the sixth earl, and that's when things began to change. The sixth earl would be your—let me see . . ." Sir Henry leaned over to study his documents through the wire-framed spectacles perched on the end of his nose. "Ah, yes, here it is. Your great-great grandfather. At that time, the second son inherited the title, because the first son had died of 'an unknown malady,' it says here." Peering up at Payne, Sir Henry's pale blue eyes twinkled. "In situations such as these, 'an unknown malady' almost always means the pox."

"Smallpox?"

"No, no, no. French pox." In a whisper, Sir Henry added, "Venereal disease."

"Ah."

"Yes, ah. Nasty business, the French pox. I, er, don't suppose you've ever . . ."

"No, never," Payne said with great conviction.

"Good, good. Now then, after the demise of the seventh earl, your great-grandfather, the eighth earl, inherited the title. That's where all the complications began. You see, your great-grandfather had four sons and five daughters."

"*Nine* children?" Payne said.

"Yes, nine. Six children, I can understand, but nine is quite unthinkable. Extraordinary, too, considering he only had the one wife. And then the oldest son and heir, the ninth earl, married on four separate occasions."

"Four wives?"

Sir Henry nodded solemnly. "Four, and he outlived each one of them. A sad state that, because none of them ever produced anything but daughters. And naturally, females cannot inherit titles."

"Naturally," Payne said.

"Quite right. The eighth earl's second son, as is customary, went into the service of the Queen. Served as a member of the Royal Scots Fusiliers, I understand." Consulting his documents again, he added, "Yes, it says here that he had gained the rank of captain when he died in battle, without issue, in the Crimea."

"And the third son?"

"Why, the Church, of course."

"Yes, of course," Payne said.

"He never married."

"Never?"

"No, never." Sir Henry cleared his throat uneasily. "At the time of his passing, there was a rumor going about the area that he had—how shall I put it?—developed a fondness for a certain young rector in the neighboring parish."

"I see," Payne said, clearly understanding Sir Henry's unspoken message.

"Er, you aren't—"

"No, I'm not. As a matter of fact, I'm married, and my wife is expecting our first child shortly after the first of the year."

"Oh, how delightful! My heartiest felicitations to both you and your wife."

"Thank you."

"And speaking of Lady Trefarrow—will I have the honor of meeting her shortly?"

"No, I'm afraid not. She's at home in Waco."

"Waco?"

"That's a town just south of here. The Triple T is located a few miles outside of town."

Sir Henry looked thoroughly confused. "The Triple T?"

"The family ranch."

"Ah, yes, that's right. I was informed by those who have known of your family's whereabouts that your grandfather, Camden Trefarrow, had become a cattle breeder after he left England."

"He did more than just breed them. Thanks to his hard work, the Triple T is responsible for raising some of the finest longhorns in the state of Texas."

"Longhorns?"

"Neutered bulls with very wide horns."

"Yes, of course." Sir Henry cleared his throat to cover his added confusion. "I suppose it's your late grandfather, Camden, whom you have to thank for your good fortune."

"How's that?"

"Well, naturally, if he hadn't sired your father, and your father hadn't sired you, then you wouldn't be inheriting the title and estates today. The title of the tenth earl of St. Keverne would have been bestowed on the next in line. And my task of locating him would have been much more difficult."

"The next in line? But I thought you said that my grandfather's oldest brother only had daughters."

"He did, he did. However, there was a second son born to—let me see . . ." Sir Henry studied his documents again, murmuring and shaking his head until he found the passage for which he was searching. "Yes, here it is. The fifth had two sons, the first, who later became the sixth earl, your great-great-great grandfather, and the second son, who served in the military. That son later married and had two sons, who had one son, who had two—"

"That's all right, Sir Henry," Payne said. "I think I understand the point you're trying to make."

"Do you? Oh, I'm so glad. To be honest, there are times when I find it quite difficult to keep track of all these noble offspring. Finding you so easily, I must say, was a stroke of nothing but pure luck."

"Just how did you find me?"

"Well, as I always do in these situations, I began with the various parish records. Must have a legal marriage before one is even considered as an heir. You'd be amazed at all the number of—how shall I put it?—*by-blows* that are issued to the nobility. Makes my task devilishly hard. But I hasten to assure you that the legality of your birth is not in question. I've all the necessary documents to prove that you are the rightful heir."

"You managed to locate my grandfather's marriage documents?"

"Of course."

"But I thought that he married my grandmother here in Texas, not in England."

"No, no. I have it all right here." Sir Henry tapped a finger on his documents. "He married your grand-mother in the village church in St. Keverne. Just a stone's throw from Castle Raven's Lair."

"*Castle* Raven's Lair?"

Sir Henry nodded. "Your estate."

"I have a castle?" Payne felt a sudden need to sit down, and promptly did so on the side of his bed.

"Well, it's not a very big one, you understand. Only thirty or forty rooms, I would guess. Nothing at all like Windsor, but it's a castle nonetheless. Quite old, too, from what I've seen of it. And in rather bad need of repairs, if you don't mind my saying so, milord. Alas, there is no actual money connected to the position, as some of your more careless forbears seem to have squired it all away."

"A castle," Payne murmured, feeling a noticeable constriction in his chest as Sir Henry continued to ramble on about the family history. At the moment, he had a little more than twenty dollars and change in his pocket, yet he now owned a castle. One with thirty or forty rooms. One in need of repair.

His financial status be damned, he thought. He had a title, by God. He was an earl, a ranking member of England's ruling class. A member of the nobility. He would finally be one of the select few who had so callously mistreated him in his youth, had kept him on the outside until it suited their baser needs to let him only into the outer fringes of their elite circles. More than that, he could flaunt his new position in front of his mother's family, who hadn't thought his father good enough for their daughter. He could make them rue the day that they had ever spurned his father, turned his mother against him. He could use his position to—

To what? Payne wondered, suddenly realizing in what direction his thoughts were headed. To exact revenge for the miserable life of loneliness his father had led? His father was dead and so was his mother. His original plan to get revenge for his mother's suffering had led him nowhere, except into the arms of his brother and the legacy of his father's equal suffering.

As he thought more on the matter, he realized that seeking revenge would be a waste of time and effort. He couldn't go back and change the way he had led his life, and he couldn't undo all the damage he'd done—to Chloe, to his brother, to those he had encountered through the years. Furthermore, he had no need for the title of tenth earl, or the estate that went with it. And he certainly had no need for a castle that, by the sound of it, was falling into ruin.

But he did have a need for Chloe. A great, consuming need for her. Accepting the title, he thought, might be a way of getting her back. After all, she had always wanted to be a lady; she'd told him often enough during their delightful seclusion in San Antonio. Now she could be one, in every sense of the word.

Payne didn't want the title. He had no use for it, or the responsibilities that went along with it. But he would accept it. He would accept anything, be anything, do anything, to bring Chloe back into his life. The question was, would Chloe accept him?

Suddenly, the germ of an idea began to form in his mind. It was a long shot, he knew, but one he had to try.

"Sir Henry," he said, rising to his feet. "I'm not sure if it's customary in this sort of situation, but I'd like to make a public announcement."

"A public announcement?"

"Yes, a gathering of some sort. Very formal, I think. I'd like for everyone to know that I'm now the tenth earl."

"I don't suppose that sort of thing is too out of the ordinary. Not here, at least. Americans, I'm told, are quite keen for those with titles."

"Good. I insist that you be present as well. Just to make it look official."

"Well, I hadn't planned to stay on. But since I've already found you here in Dallas, and I no longer have to travel all the way to that Waco place, I suppose I could find the time to linger on a few extra days."

"How about a few extra weeks?" Payne asked.

"Weeks, milord?"

"Maybe not that long. You see, I'm not quite sure how long it will take me to make all the arrangements. I want it to be a special occasion. Something lavish." Something that would be sure to impress Chloe.

"Ah, a gala?"

"Exactly. A gala."

"Will milord be having champagne?"

"If Dallas has any, Sir Henry, I promise I'll have it."

Sir Henry beamed. "It sounds delightful, milord. Haven't been invited to a gala celebration in years."

"Then you'll stay?"

"Wouldn't miss it for the world."

"Good, good. And maybe, if it's not too much to ask, you could help me with a few of the plans. Advise me who to invite, what food, if any, I should serve—that sort of thing. This is all very new to me, you understand."

"Of course, of course. Milord should understand that I've never been much of a social creature. Spent most of my time poring over musty old ledgers and documents. But I do know champagne."

"Then you're just the man I need."

24

"Who the devil can that be?" Emmaline peeked through the curtain, having heard the sound of an approaching horse as she passed by the window. She watched a stranger pull to a stop and dismount in front of Chloe's house.

"Who is it, Aunt Em?"

"I have no idea. I've never seen the man before."

Now well into her seventh month of pregnancy, Chloe put aside the delicate baby shawl she had been knitting and hauled herself up and out of her rocking chair. Resting both hands on the small of her back, she ambled over to the window and peered out. "I've never seen him before, either. I wonder what he wants?"

"I bet I know," Emmaline said with a groan. "He's probably that Bible salesman."

"What Bible salesman?"

"Oh, the one Reverend Campbell was talking about in church last Sunday. He said a man would be around to see us all about a register for preserving our family heritage. Heritage, my foot. They're just wanting more money. You know, it never fails. Come Christmas or Easter, there's always somebody coming around, trying to sell something. This time it's a Bible salesman."

Chloe dropped the curtain. "I don't know about you, but I don't need a Bible. I've already got one."

"Want me to tell him to go away?"

"Yes, I do," Chloe said, then sighed. "But you'd better not. It's cold and rainy out today. The poor man's probably in need of a hot cup of coffee and a warm fire."

"Then I'll invite him in," Emmaline said as a knock sounded at the door.

"Just don't buy a Bible from him."

"Why would I do that? I don't need one, either."

As Emmaline opened the door, letting in a gust of damp, chilly air, Chloe started to sink back down into the rocking chair. But she stopped when she heard her name mentioned.

"Mrs. Payne Trefarrow?" the stranger asked.

"No, sir, I'm not," Emmaline said.

"I'm sorry. I understood that this was the home of Mrs. Trefarrow."

"Oh, you've got the right house, just the wrong lady."

"Is Mrs. Trefarrow at home?"

"She might be," Emmaline said. "Then again, she might not. What do you want with her?"

"I've been sent to deliver a message to her."

"Who's it from?" Chloe asked, holding her shawl more tightly around her as she approached the door.

"I wouldn't know about that, ma'am," the stranger said. "All I was told was to see that Mrs. Payne Trefarrow got this personally, and that I wasn't to let nobody else but her accept it."

"Well, I never," Emmaline said, indignant at the man's explanation.

"I mean no offense, ma'am," the stranger said. "Honest, I don't. Fact is, I find this whole business kind of strange myself. All I done with the others was just leave them with whoever came to the door first. This one's different, extra special, I guess. And this being my job, I do what I'm told. So, is Mrs. Trefarrow home?"

"It's all right, Aunt Em," Chloe said. "Yes, I'm home. I'm Mrs. Trefarrow."

Looking considerably relieved, the stranger reached inside his oilskin rain slicker and produced an envelope. He handed it to Chloe and then tipped his hat to her and Emmaline. As he turned and started to head back out into the cold, drizzly rain, Chloe called out to him.

"Wait a minute. Wouldn't you like to come inside for a minute? Maybe have a cup of coffee and dry out a bit?"

"That's a mighty tempting offer, ma'am, but I better not. See, I got just two more of these things to deliver, then I can head on back up to Dallas."

Chloe's eyes widened. "You're from Dallas?"

"Yes, ma'am."

"And this"—she turned the envelope over, but saw only her name—"this letter was sent to me from someone there?"

"I guess it was. I don't rightly know for sure. See, I just work for a messenger service in Dallas. We hand deliver letters and parcels to folks all the time. Never had to come all the way to Waco before, but I 'spect there's a first time for everything, ain't there. Well, good day to you both."

"I've never heard of such a thing," Emmaline said as Chloe closed the door. "Hand delivering a letter all the way from Dallas to a person. Land sakes, what will this world come to next?"

"I don't think this is a regular letter, Aunt Em." Chloe carefully studied the envelope, noting the rich feel of the heavy parchment paper and the elaborate way in which her name had been inscribed on the front.

"Well, what is it then, if it's not a letter?"

"If I didn't know better, I'd swear it was an invitation. A very formal invitation."

"A formal invitation to what? Nobody we know up in Dallas is getting married, and if they were, I don't think they'd be inviting us. Nobody's died lately either, that I know of. Besides, they wouldn't be sending you an invitation to the funeral in a solid white envelope. There'd be black on it somewhere. Silliest thing I ever heard."

For reasons she couldn't explain, Chloe's heart began to race with anticipation as she slid her finger under the flap and broke the wax seal. Inside she found a neatly folded card and removed it. Slowly opening it, she began to read. As she scanned the fancy calligraphic printing, her eyes grew round in amazement.

"Oh, my heavens!" she said.

"What is it?"

"I don't believe this."

"Believe what?"

"It says here that I'm invited to a reception in Dallas. A royal reception, by the sound of it."

"Royal?" Emmaline crossed to her side and peeked over her shoulder to read the note.

"I guess they're royalty," Chloe said. "It's the Earl and Countess of St. Keverne who wish my presence in two weeks."

"No, that's out of the question. You can't go all the way to Dallas in your condition. Not two weeks from now. You can't go *anywhere* 'til after that baby's born."

"Aunt Em, I can't *not* go. I've never been invited to something like this before. It's a royal reception. I might not ever be invited again. So if I don't go now—"

"Hold on," Emmaline said with a frown. "Did that thing say the Earl and Countess of St. Keverne?"

"Uh-huh."

Emmaline giggled in surprise. "My Lord! I think that's our kinfolk."

Kinfolk? Chloe wondered. "You're related to the Earl and Countess of St. Keverne? Royalty?"

"Not just me. All of us Trefarrows. That includes you, too, now that you're married to Payne. And they're not really royalty. Just earls and countesses is all."

"That's royalty in my book."

"No, no. As I recollect, it's only kings and queens and princes and princesses who are the real royals. And maybe dukes and duchesses and viscounts and— Oh, hell, none of that really matters much. And when you come right down to it, the St. Kevernes, royalty or not, are still nothing but kinfolk."

"And they're relatives of yours. I don't believe it."

"Ours. They're relatives of ours. You're part of the family now, too."

"Whatever," Chloe said, offhandedly as another thought suddenly struck her. "I wonder what I should wear. Better yet, what have I got that'll still fit me? Lordy mercy, Aunt Em, this invitation couldn't have come at a worse time. I'm almost as big as a horse."

"Oh, for pity's sake, child, you're as big as you're supposed to be. And that's nowhere near the size of a horse, I promise you. Believe me, I've seen larger women than you in my time."

"That may be true, but I still don't have anything suitable to wear."

"Well, if you've got your heart set on going to meet these folks, then have yourself something made. I'm sure Verlene Buchholtz can whip you up a dress in two weeks' time."

"Yes, of course, Mrs. Buchholtz."

"She can probably make you something in less time than that, if I know Verlene. That woman's an absolute genius with a needle and thread."

"You're right. I'll go see her first thing in the morning."

Emmaline stiffened sharply and glared at Chloe. "You'll do no such thing."

"But if I don't go see her, how—"

"I'll send one of the boys into town early tomorrow to bring her out here to you, that's how. In your condition, the less gallivanting around you do, the better off you and that baby will be. You need to save your strength for that long train ride up to Dallas. If you really are fixing to go."

Excitement glittered in Chloe's deep blue eyes. "Come to think of it, one dress may not be enough. I may need two or three. Maybe more than that."

"What in heaven's name for? You're only going to be there a day or two."

"That's just it. The longer I'm there, the more social functions I can attend. You never know, Lady Trefarrow might decide to invite me to have high tea with her."

"High tea? Mercy me, I haven't heard that expression since Mama was alive. She was English, you know. Just like Papa."

"Is it true that the English always have their high teas at precisely four in the afternoon?"

"I guess the more proper ones do," Emmaline said. "We never did when I was growing up. We'd just have supper at five or six, whenever Papa came walking through the door and was ready to eat."

"That settles it, then. I won't take any chances. I'll need one or two simple daytime dresses for high tea. And then, of course, I'll need something fancy to wear for nighttime."

"If I were you, I wouldn't get anything too fancy," Emmaline said. "Something simple, without a whole lot of ruffles. And no corset or bustle, either. Either one will suffocate that baby you're carrying."

"A ball gown, maybe?"

"A ball gown!"

"Sure. Lord and Lady Trefarrow might be planning on having a dance of some kind."

"Lordy, lordy, lordy," Emmaline said, shaking her head. "Have you lost your mind, child? In your condition, dancing is the last thing you need to be thinking about."

"I'm not. Why, if somebody asked me to dance, I'd be absolutely mortified."

"Worse than that, you'd drop that baby right in

the middle of the dance floor. Talk about a shocking scandal. . . . Folks in Dallas would be talking about it for years to come."

"Aunt Em, I said I wasn't going to dance. I just want to be properly dressed, that's all."

"Well, to make sure that you're not tempted by some young handsome buck with mischief in mind, I'd better go with you."

"Oh, would you? That would be delightful."

"I'm not so sure." Seeing Chloe's inquisitive look, Emmaline added, "The more I think about it, the more I have to wonder just why these long-lost relatives of ours have suddenly decided to come pay us a visit now."

"Maybe they felt it was time to renew family ties."

"Ha! They could have done that at any time during the past thirty years. That's how long it's been since we last saw or heard from any of them. And even then, it was only through letters. If Papa hadn't decided to send Garrett over to England, and if Garrett hadn't needed a place to stay, we wouldn't have heard from those people at all."

"Still," Chloe said, "family is family."

"You might be right," Emmaline said. "But if you ask me, I think they're here because of money. They need it, and they think we've got it."

"Oh, surely not."

"You don't know this bunch like I do, child. Back before the war, when Garrett went to visit, the lot of them were as poor as church mice. Barely had two pennies to rub together."

"But they're titled."

"A title doesn't mean a hill of beans. It's just a fancy name that some long-dead king or queen gave some ancestor of ours for doing something they consider noteworthy. It's money in your pocket that counts." Emmaline picked up the invitation that Chloe had set aside and studied it. "Earl and Countess St. Keverne. Hmmph! The one thing I detest is somebody coming around, looking for a handout."

"That's a terrible thing to assume," Chloe said. "How can you be so sure they're here to borrow money from us?"

"I'm not sure about anything. It's just a strong feeling I've got. And I'll tell you something else. My feelings have never let me down before. 'Course, with this bunch, you never can tell. For all I know, their lot in life could have changed for the better." But Emmaline seriously doubted it. She had never known a Trefarrow to have more than a few dollars in his or her pocket at one time. Plenty of debts, yes, enough to break an elephant's back. But never any money.

25

Chloe tightened her hold on the strap that hung near the carriage door as the vehicle turned the corner. She tried to stay seated upright, to keep her gown relatively unwrinkled, but it seemed almost impossible. Each time the carriage turned or swerved, she slid halfway across the seat.

Regaining her former position, she placed a hand on her belly and heaved a sigh of relief. Would this trip ever end?

"You're not getting queasy again, are you?" Emmaline asked.

"A little, but I'll get over it."

"I knew taking that filthy train up here was a mistake. We should have stayed at home like I wanted in the first place. Lord knows, it's a wonder you haven't gone into labor by now."

"I'm fine, Aunt Em. Really, I am, so stop worrying. I'm not going to go into labor because of a silly train ride. Which, I might add, was two days ago. I'm just a little anxious is all."

"Anxious about what?"

"About getting to the hotel in one piece and giving a good first impression when I meet my new in-laws."

"In-laws, hmmph! You don't need to meet that bunch of leeches."

"Aunt Em! Now you promised you'd be nice."

"And nice I'll be. Until they bring up the subject of borrowing money from us—money that we haven't got. Then I'll tell them how the cow ate the cabbage. Send 'em all packing back to England where they belong."

Chloe had an urge to scold Emmaline, inform her that Lord and Lady Trefarrow should be treated with dignity and respect, even if they had come to Texas to borrow money. But she knew anything she might say would fall on deaf ears. Aunt Em already had her mind made up, and nothing she could say would change her preconceived opinions of the St. Kevernes. Instead, she decided to take a different approach.

"I think it was very thoughtful of them to send us all invitations."

"That's another thing, now that you mention it," Emmaline said. "How come your invitation was hand delivered, and Prescott's and mine was just given to whoever answered the door?"

"I don't know, Aunt Em."

"Sounds a bit fishy, if you ask me."

"Prescott didn't seem to think so."

"How would you know what Prescott thought? You haven't seen or talked to that boy since you up and married Payne."

"I know, but I've heard."

"From whom?"

"Well, Mrs. Buchholtz, for one."

"I doubt that. Verlene's not a gossip. Who else has been talking about Prescott?"

Chloe sighed, knowing she would have to reveal her sources. "Ivy, Rose, and Daisy Campbell."

"The three worst gossips in the whole state of Texas, to my way of thinking. And, of course, you believed every word they said."

"Why shouldn't I believe them?"

"Because any one of those girls would give her eye teeth to be Mrs. Prescott Trefarrow, that's why."

"What's that got to do with them saying good things about him?"

"Everything. Now that you've made it abundantly clear to everyone that you're no longer a part of his life, in any way, shape, or form, they can't say enough good things about him to you."

"Are you saying they're trying to make me jealous?"

"No, I'm saying that they know you're no longer an obstacle between them and Prescott. They talk about him behind his back, say all sorts of nice things about him, hoping that you'll run and tell him everything they said. Hoping, I might add, that he'll be so flattered he'll start paying attention to them. Well, one of them, anyway. The next thing you know, she'll announce she's in the family way, and Prescott will be roped, hog-tied, and branded."

"That's ridiculous."

"Well, that's the Campbell sisters for you. Ridiculous to the very end. Ridiculous, predatory, marriage-minded females, the lot of them."

Chloe couldn't believe what she was hearing. "Good gracious, Aunt Em, the last time Prescott set foot on my property, I took a shot at him. I would have hit him, too, if I'd thought it would do some good. But a load of buckshot isn't going to make him change his evil ways, and I know it. Furthermore, the Campbell sisters know I know it. Talk to Prescott? That's the last thing I feel like doing."

"What about tonight?"

"What about it?"

"If he gets to town on time, he's going to be at the reception. Are you going to completely ignore him in front of those leeches? You do that, and they'll know for sure that all isn't right in the Texas branch of the family."

"If Prescott does show up, which I seriously doubt, and if I do see him, I might acknowledge his presence. But that's all I'll do. You won't catch me carrying on a lengthy conversation with him just for the sake of civility. And for the last time, Aunt Em, the St. Kevernes are not leeches."

"What about Payne?"

The mention of her husband brought an abrupt halt to Chloe's train of thought. "What about him?"

"Will you speak to him tonight?"

Chloe thought about it a moment, weighing the pros and cons. More than anything, she wanted to behave like the lady she tried so hard to be, and leave her newfound English relations with a positive, lasting, impression. Letting them discover that she and her husband had serious marital problems would be a serious breach of social etiquette. Any sort of domestic strife was meant to be kept strictly private, discussed and settled only behind closed doors, not in public. The problem was, the door that stood between her and Payne was three feet thick and a mile wide, and everyone knew it.

"I suppose I'll have to speak to him, won't I?" she said at last. "If he has the nerve to show his face at the reception, that is."

"Oh, he'll be there."

"How do you know?"

"Because, child, you'll be there."

Their sudden arrival at the hotel put an end to any further questions Chloe might have posed to Emmaline. As she slowly climbed out of the carriage, Chloe had the distinct feeling that Aunt Em knew a lot more about Payne and his activities than she had revealed to her so far. In the five months that she had been separated from Payne, living alone at the Rocking B, waiting for the birth of her child, Aunt Em had come to visit her often. On each occasion, she had imparted little tidbits of news about Payne, which Chloe had heard, of course, but chosen to ignore. In the last two weeks, Aunt Em's monologues had centered mainly on the arrival of the "leeches." And each time Aunt Em mentioned them, Chloe had thought she detected a certain bit of mischief in her tone. Chloe had ignored that, too, until now.

Something, she decided, was definitely afoot.

Once inside the warm foyer of the hotel, Chloe pushed back the hood of her wool cape and loosened the silk frog fastening at the throat. As she climbed the short flight of steps to the lobby level, she thought about removing the heavy garment entirely but decided against it. It would be wise to hide her advanced condition for as long as possible.

"Do you see anybody here that you know?" she asked as Emmaline came up beside her.

"No, nary a soul," Emmaline said, glancing around

the high-ceilinged lobby with its polished hardwood paneled walls and marble floors.

"Gracious, I hope we're not the first ones to arrive. It's the more accepted fashion to be just a few minutes late."

"The invitation said seven o'clock, child. That clock over there says that it's now ten past. Is that fashionable enough for you?"

"I hope so," Chloe said. The last thing she felt like doing was getting back in a wretched cab and riding around for a while longer. Her gown was wrinkled enough already.

"Is that?— Yes, I think it is."

"Who?"

"The man standing over there by the big potted palm tree. See him?"

"The short bald one?"

"Yes. That's Garrett's friend, Abner Harris. He came out to the ranch once."

"I don't recall ever meeting him."

"You wouldn't. You were at school in Austin at the time."

Harris spotted the two women standing near the lobby's wood rail banister and smiled as he recognized the older one. Making his apologies to the man and woman with whom he'd been conversing, he turned and advanced toward Chloe and Emmaline.

"Mrs. McCardie, how nice to see you again," he said, taking her gloved hand and pressing it warmly.

"Nice to see you again, too, Mr. Harris," Emmaline said.

"Call me Abner, please."

"Thank you. I don't believe you've ever met my niece, Chloe, have you? She's Payne's wife."

"No, I've never had the honor," he said, his brown eyes twinkling with an odd sort of humor. "However, I have heard a good deal about you. Both from your husband and his brother."

At his reference to Payne and Prescott, Chloe had to force a smile to her lips. "It's a pleasure to meet you, Mr. Harris. Have Lord and Lady Trefarrow arrived yet?"

"I do believe they have," he said with a slight laugh. "Are you anxious to meet them?"

Chloe took a deep breath and nervously released it. "Anxious, yes. I've never meet titled nobility before."

"Then you've a treat in store, young lady. They're right this way, in the ballroom."

Harris offered one of his arms to Chloe and the other to Emmaline, and they set off across the lobby to the open double doors at the far end of the room.

"I have to tell you, the arrival of the Earl and Countess of St. Keverne have caused this town quite a stir," Harris said, as a formally garbed man at the ballroom's entrance helped Chloe off with her cape. He took Emmaline's cloak as well, and carefully laid them both aside with a mound of others. "Haven't seen this much hubbub since the war ended."

"Have you met them?" Chloe asked.

"Well, let's just say that I know the Earl a little better than I know the Countess. But from what I've seen of her, I'm almost certain she's a very nice young lady."

"They're young folks, then, are they?" Emmaline asked.

Chloe, gazing inside at the ballroom, didn't see the humor that flashed across Emmaline's eyes. Never in her life had she seen so many glittering crystal chandeliers or so many formally dressed men and women in one place. There had to be close to a hundred or more people present.

"The Countess is young, yes," Harris said.

"And the Earl?" Chloe asked. "Is he young too?"

"Mmm, I'd say he's around thirty or so. Ready to meet them?"

Feeling her heart race in anticipation, Chloe stared imploringly at Emmaline. "Do I look all right?"

"Child, you look beautiful," Emmaline said.

Chloe ran her gloved hands down the sides of her triple-tiered ivory silk gown, starting at the high-fitting empire waistline and ending at the hem of the second tier. Then, nervously, she touched the single strand of pearls that rested at her throat. Unlike many of the other women present, who wore gowns that exposed a good bit of bosom, Chloe's bodice was demurely covered with a sheer lace the same color as her gown.

"There's not too many wrinkles on the back of my dress?" she asked. "That wretched carriage driver drove us here so recklessly that I—"

"You have no more wrinkles on you than any of the others I see here," Emmaline said. "You look just fine. Now relax. Enjoy yourself."

"I can't relax, Aunt Em. Not until I'm sure I've made a good impression on the Countess."

"You'll do that, right enough," Harris said. "Fact is, I think the Countess will be suitably surprised."

Harris offered her his elbow again, and Chloe took it, letting him lead her into the ballroom. To her immense relief, no one seemed to pay much attention to her arrival, just an occasional glance and a nod was all. As they passed chattering groups of guests,

Abner Harris smiled and nodded at a select few, informing Chloe in a hushed voice that the tall, robust man was the mayor, and the man with whom he conversed was Attorney General from Austin.

And then, as the crowd grew thinner, she saw Payne. He stood at the far end of the room, beside a small man who wore a row of medals on his evening coat. She studied her estranged husband longingly, wishing with all her heart that she could deny the tumult of emotions that raced through her, wishing that Payne didn't look so handsome in his formal evening attire. She wished even more that she could stop loving him, thinking about him, remembering how they had been, when in fact, she loved him even more now than she had before.

Tearing her eyes away from Payne, Chloe looked at his companion. The Earl? she wondered. No, he couldn't be Lord Trefarrow. Abner Harris had told her that Lord Trefarrow was thirty or so. This man was a good deal older—fifty or sixty, at the very least. Maybe the man was merely one of the Earl's cohorts, associates, or whatever a nobleman's aides were called.

Deep in conversation with Sir Henry, Payne felt a sudden surge of awareness, as though someone were watching him. He turned and saw who that someone was: Chloe. And she looked even more lovely than she had the last time he'd seen her. Her complexion was radiant, her eyes sparkled, her moist lips . . .

No, better not think about her lips, Payne told himself. He'd thought about them too often here of late, dreaming of kissing them again, of hearing them utter words of love to him. Better to keep his mind on the business at hand and relegate his fantasies of her to the back of his mind, where they belonged.

"Sir Henry, I'd like you to meet my wife, Chloe Patience Bliss Trefarrow. Chloe, Sir Henry Wilberforce."

Chloe extended her hand to the elderly gentleman. "Sir Henry," she said, "how nice to meet you."

Sir Henry took her fingers and bowed his head over them. "Oh, the pleasure is all mine, I assure you, milady."

"You're too kind. Are the Earl and—" Chloe broke off abruptly. "Milady?"

Payne reached out and extracted her hand from Sir Henry's. "If I may steal my wife away for a moment, Sir Henry, there are a few things we need to discuss in private."

"You called me milady?" Too bewildered by what had just happened to protest, Chloe let Payne lead her off into a secluded corner, behind a potted palm. "He called me milády. Why in heaven's name did he do that?"

"Because, my dear, that's how he's been trained to address a countess."

"I know, but I'm not—"

"Yes, you are."

"Payne, I'm no—" Suddenly, her heart began to race, and her breathing grew shallow as the impact of his revelation hit her. "Me?"

"That's right. You." Payne's hold on her tightened. "Chloe, are you all right? You're beginning to look very pale."

"I—I think I might need to sit down for a while."

"Are you going to faint?"

"I'm not sure yet. I might."

"I'll get you a chair." Payne searched the crowd,

and seeing a waiter looking in his direction, he beckoned the young man.

"And some water," Chloe said. "For some reason, I'm suddenly very thirsty. I'm really the Countess of St. Keverne?"

"You really are, my darling."

The waiter arrived and Payne ordered him to find Chloe a chair.

"But then," she said, "that must make you . . ."

"The Earl of St. Keverne."

"But how? When?"

"'When' is the easy part. I found out about three weeks ago. The 'how' is . . . well, let's just say that it's a very long story."

As her shock began to fade, Chloe felt her strength return. Not wishing to call too much attention to herself, she slowly pulled her arm out of Payne's grasp and stared at him. "Tell me. I've got time."

"Are you sure you feel like hearing the whole story? You still look rather pale."

"I'll be just fine. Now start talking. Is this some kind of elaborate scheme you've concocted to humiliate me again?"

Though her stinging accusation pierced Payne's heart, he managed to ignore the pain. She had every right to mistrust him, to question anything that he might have to say. "It's no scheme, Chloe. It's the truth."

"It can't be. You're no earl, and I'm darn sure no countess."

"Yes," he said, "you are. You've been a countess from the moment you married me."

"Why didn't you say anything?"

"How could I? I didn't know that I was an earl until just a few weeks ago. That's when Sir Henry found me and gave me the good news." He released a mirthless chuckle. "'Good news.' What an inappropriate term. Personally, I find this whole situation an unwanted and unnecessary encumbrance."

"Aunt Em said y'all were related to nobility. Is that how you got the title?"

Payne nodded. "The last earl died without male issue. Just daughters, no sons. No legitimate sons, that is. From all that Sir Henry's told me about our illustrious family, there are quite a number of illegitimate Trefarrows roaming the Cornish countryside. It seems as though Prescott has come by his wandering eye quite naturally. And speaking of my brother— where the devil is he?"

"I don't know, and I don't care," Chloe said. "Get on with your story. How did Sir Henry find you?"

"He searched through the family records, came up with my name, and traced me here to Texas."

"That simple?"

"To hear Sir Henry tell it, although it didn't sound at all simple to me. He searched for well over a year, as a matter of fact. If Sir Henry had found me sooner, before I ever fell in league with that bastard Wyngate and left England . . ." He looked down at Chloe and studied her closely. "Well, needless to say, if that had happened, you and I would have never met."

"And some other woman would now be the Countess of St. Keverne."

Payne shrugged. "A year ago, there was no one woman in my life. But there is one now. You, Chloe. You're my wife. My Lady Trefarrow. Does the title frighten you?"

"I honestly can't say what it does to me, Payne. I'm still too shocked to feel anything."

"Look at it this way—now's your chance."

"My chance?"

"Yes. Don't you remember? When we were locked away together in that little room in San Antonio, sharing our secrets and desires, you told me how much you wanted to be a lady. Well, now's your chance to be one in the fullest sense of the word. Lady Trefarrow, the Countess of St. Keverne."

Instead of feeling overjoyed, Payne's words filled Chloe with a blend of fear and extreme trepidation. Being a lady, she realized, wasn't quite the same as being a Lady. The latter held a wealth of responsibilities—responsibilities she wasn't sure she could handle. She would always have to be on her guard, like now, making sure that she said the right thing, did the right thing, walked and talked the right way. And she would have to live with her husband, instead of shooting at him when he approached her house.

Suddenly another thought struck her, and she stared directly into Payne's eyes. He was Lord Trefarrow, a rank, a position that she knew he didn't want. With the kind of childhood he'd had and the kind of life he'd been forced to lead until recently, he despised anything and anyone even remotely connected to the English peerage and upper class. Yet he seemed willing enough to put aside his long-held aversions, to give up the new life he'd begun in America and go back to the society that had spurned and mistreated him so cruelly. Why?

Obviously, because he loved her. He loved her so much that he wanted her to have the one thing for which she had always yearned, dreamed of being.

A newer, stronger love for Payne began to bloom in the depths of Chloe's heart. It erased all the bitter anguish, the hurt, the torment that she had endured these last lonely months. That he could give up everything for her told her just how much he truly loved her.

"Chloe?"

"You mean Lady Trefarrow, huh?"

"If that's what you want."

"I've had some time to think about it, and frankly, I'm not so sure I do."

Payne stepped back, stunned by her announcement. "What?"

"I said, I'm not so sure I want to be that kind of lady. A lady, yes, but not a *Lady*. Do I really look like a countess?"

To Payne, she looked like a queen, an empress. More than that, even—the most beautiful woman in the world.

"Besides," Chloe said, "what kind of life would our child have in England? He's a Texan, Payne, not an Englishman."

"Our child." Payne gazed down at her rounded belly and stretched out a hand. At the very moment he touched her, he felt a fluttering movement and then a kick. The surprise of it made him laugh. "He's a strong one, isn't he?"

"Very," Chloe said, gazing deeply into his face and loving the feel of his hand on her.

"Does he do that often?"

"Often enough to keep me awake at night. I swear, I don't think I'll be able to stand it until he comes in February. I haven't had a good night's sleep in months."

Payne tore his gaze away from her midsection and looked into her eyes, seeing her loneliness but also her love. "Chloe," he said, wrapping her in his arms. "I've missed you so much."

"I've missed you, too."

"Then let me come back. I love you."

Without thinking of the consequences or of her past distrust of him, but thinking only of how much she wanted to be with him for the rest of her life, Chloe lifted her arms and wound them around Payne's neck. "Oh, God, I love you, too."

"I was such an idiot. Can you ever forgive me for what I did? For what I tried to do?"

"Forgive you?" she said, making her hold on him even tighter. "I don't know. I'm kind of stubborn. It might take a while. Like forty or fifty years, maybe."

"That long?"

She pulled back so that he could see her nod.

"Oh, what the hell," he said. "For forty or fifty years, I suppose I could try to be good."

And then he lowered his head and kissed her, and all the lonely nights and days and weeks and months they'd spent apart vanished into the realm of oblivion.

26

    Moments after Prescott's train arrived at Union Depot, he stepped out of the terminal and hailed a carriage. Giving the driver directions to the hotel, he climbed inside and settled back for the ride. Family, he thought as he took off his hat and let his head fall back against the high, plush seat. If it weren't for family, he'd be back at the ranch right now, in his own bed. He'd put in a full day's work, starting before dawn that morning, and he was nowhere near finished. A hundred or so head of strays still needed rounding up so they wouldn't freeze to death when the bad spell of cold weather hit. He had fences to mend and the bunkhouse roof to patch. Ranch hands could get right testy when they woke up with rain and sleet falling on them. But when family came visiting—especially family he'd never seen or heard from before—work would just have to wait.

    He only hoped that Aunt Em wouldn't be too upset with him for not getting all gussied up for the new kinfolks. He'd barely had time to ride into Waco to catch the two o'clock train. And even then, he'd almost missed it. Only when he'd climbed on board and taken his seat had he realized that he'd left the bag with his Sunday best back in his room at the ranch.

"Family," he muttered as his eyes slowly closed.

Within a matter of seconds, he fell into a deep sleep that only extreme physical weariness could bring. His mind and body now totally relaxed, his dream mate came floating into his thoughts. Instead of being surrounded by a misty haze, her image was clearer this time, her face more beautiful than he'd ever seen it before, almost a perfect oval.

Carefully inspecting each of her features, starting with her waist-length dark flowing hair, her long porcelain smooth neck, her high cheekbones, he saw that her eyes weren't really black at all, as he had thought, but a clear dark gray, her lips a luscious inviting pink. And when she opened her arms out wide, silently beckoning to him to come take his pleasure, he noted the fullness of her breasts and their rose crested tips.

"Hey, mister, wake up!"

Rudely roused from what promised to be a very erotic slumber, Prescott bolted upright. Almost hitting his head on the roof of the carriage, he whipped his head around in confusion, studying the interior with wide fright-filled eyes. For the life of him, he couldn't recall where he was or why he was there.

"Here we are."

"Where?" Prescott asked, hearing as well as feeling the rapid beating of his heart.

"At the hotel."

"Hotel?"

"Yeah, the one you told me to bring you to. What's the matter? Change your mind, want to go someplace else?"

Suddenly it all came flooding back. Family. Aunt Em, Chloe, Payne, and the folks he was supposed to meet. Yes, the hotel. Now he knew where he was.

"Well, do you?" the carriage driver asked.

"No, I'm where I ought to be." He climbed down out of the carriage and huddled deeper into the folds of his sheepskin-lined coat, hoping to ward off the bitterly cold wind blowing out of the north. "I'm just a little groggy is all. I must've dropped off for a minute."

The driver chuckled. "It was longer'n that, mister. It took me a good twenty minutes to get here."

"Twenty, huh? It seemed like only a minute to me."

"You gonna be all right?"

"Yeah, I'll be fine, thank you." Slipping the driver a suitable gratuity, Prescott turned and entered the hotel. Family, he thought as he reached into his coat pocket and extracted his crumpled invitation. What a man had to do for the sake of his family.

Inside the lobby, he was stopped cold in his tracks by the unexpected sight of Chauncey Blodgett standing across the lobby. The slimy little weasel looked entirely different from the last time Prescott had seen him—drunk, frightened, and loose-tongued at Carrigan's Saloon. Instead of dirty, wrinkled clothes, more than a week's worth of beard, and untold layers of body grime, Blodgett now appeared spotlessly clean. He wore a neatly pressed black suit, white shirt, and polished shoes. He'd shaved his face, cut, washed, and slicked down his thinning brown hair. Seeing him grin and nod at a passing stranger, Prescott realized that the man had even cleaned his teeth.

Well, Prescott told himself as he made his way toward Blodgett, at least the vermin had put some use to the ill-gotten gains from his alliance with Wyngate.

When Blodgett saw Prescott advancing toward him, he had a sudden urge to turn and run. But he stopped himself from retreating like a coward, remembering that he had nothing to be afraid of now. The Cap'n's brother looked like he wanted to take his head off and stuff it down his neck, but his lordship, the Earl, would see to it that that didn't happen. No, best to face the man and set him straight about a few things—things that would no doubt surprise him.

"Mr. Prescott," Blodgett said. "Good seeing you this evening."

"It's a shame I can't say the same to you," Prescott snarled. "What the hell are you doing here, looking to cause more trouble?"

"Just the opposite, sir. Me and trouble have seen the last of each other, thanks to the benevolent generosity of his lordship, the Earl." There, Blodgett thought, get it out in the open, let young Trefarrow know up front that he wasn't dealing with the old Chauncey Blodgett. The old Chauncey hadn't had the ruling class on his side. "I'm on the straight and narrow now, I am."

"You?" Prescott snorted in disbelief.

"Aye. Not even drinking anymore. Oh, maybe the odd glass of sherry or port now and then, when me duties demand it, you understand, but nothing stronger." He arched his back and tugged at his embroidered vest. "I'm a new man."

Prescott rather doubted that, but at least Blodgett looked cleaner. Leaning forward and taking a sniff, he even had to admit that Blodgett smelled cleaner as well. "So, you're working for the Earl now, instead of Wyngate, huh?"

"Beggin' your pardon, Mr. Prescott, but I never did actually work for that Wyngate bloke. Your brother, the Cap'n, yes, but never Wyngate."

"Mmm." Prescott nodded slowly. "Does the Earl know of your past weaknesses?"

"My drinking, you mean? Of course. He knows all about me."

"What about your underhanded double-dealings with my brother, your aiding and abetting the abduction of my fiancée? Have you told him about that?"

"As I said before, Mr. Prescott, his lordship knows everything."

Prescott studied Blodgett with a skeptical eye for a moment longer, and then he slowly shook his head. "Trusting the likes of you, the Earl must be even loonier than I figured. Must be all that inbreeding I hear they do over there in England."

"Pardon my saying so, Mr. Prescott, but his lordship isn't loony at all. He's one of the kindest, sanest men I know."

"That ain't saying much," Prescott mumbled. "So, will you going back with him when he leaves?"

"Aye, his lordship's already paid for me passage." Again, Blodgett puffed out his chest and tugged at his vest. "I'm his very own personal valet, you see."

"Heaven help the man," Prescott said, shaking his head as he turned and walked away.

* * *

Chloe's lips had never felt so soft or tasted so sweet, Payne thought as he let his tongue delve further into the recess of her mouth. And her body, though well advanced in pregnancy, had never felt more exciting. Full and lush and earthy—it tempted him beyond belief.

"A-hmm!"

At the intrusive sound, reality came crashing down on Payne. Two more minutes alone, undisturbed, and he knew that he would have been sorely enticed to disgrace both himself and Chloe behind the tree. He had missed her more than even he had realized.

Social mores and conventions being what they were, however, he managed to dampen his ardor and draw back from his wife. Keeping one arm wrapped firmly around Chloe's waist to hold her close to his side, he stared into the face of his aunt. Emmaline looked quite pleased with her discovery.

"Everything all right with you two?" she asked, her eyes twinkling.

A deep blush arose in Chloe's face. To avoid Emmaline's probing scrutiny, she hid her face in the front of Payne's starched white shirt.

"Everything is just fine, Aunt Em," Payne said. "As a matter of fact, it couldn't be better."

"That's good to hear. 'Bout time you two patched up your differences. I just wish I could say the same for your Sir Henry. The poor man's out here about to have an apoplectic fit. You two just upped and disappeared, and he couldn't find you anywhere. 'Course, I sort of figured what was going on when I spied the hem of Chloe's skirt sticking out from behind this tree. Silliest thing I ever heard, putting trees inside a house. Everybody knows they grow best outside."

"It's a palm, Aunt Em," Payne said, taking Chloe's hand and leading her back into the main section of the ballroom. "Put a tropical plant like this outside in this weather, and it wouldn't last overnight."

Payne's botanical lesson seemed not to interest Emmaline as much as the glow on Chloe's face. "Trees be damned. Are you two finally over and done with your silly quarreling? That is what that kiss was all about, I hope."

"Yes, it was," Chloe said, and nuzzled Payne's broad chest.

"Good," Emmaline said. " 'Cause it'd be difficult to explain why Lord and Lady Trefarrow don't even live under the same roof. 'Course now, y'all wouldn't be the first lord and lady to pretend to be happy while you went about living your own lives, but—"

"You knew?" Chloe asked, her eyes full of amazement.

"About his title? Of course I knew. Payne wrote me a letter and told me all about it right after we got those invitations."

"But why didn't you ever say anything?"

"Payne made me promise to keep it a secret, that's why," Emmaline said.

"And I thank you for doing so," Payne said. "You should have seen her face just now when I told her."

"Surprised, was she?"

"That's putting it mildly."

Emmaline sighed. "The face I'm wanting to see is your brother's. If he ever decides to show up, that is."

Having finally spotted them through the throng of guests, a flustered Sir Henry hurried toward them. "I do hate to intrude, milord, milady," he said breathlessly, "but your guests seem a bit anxious to meet you. So much so that a few of them are even speculating that this is all nothing but a hoax."

"It's all right, Sir Henry," Payne said. "Lady Trefarrow and I have had our brief reunion. Why don't you go ahead and introduce us now?"

"Introduce us?" Concerned about her appearance as well as her condition, Chloe crossed her arms across her swollen belly. "Oh, my heavens! Why do we have to be introduced? Wouldn't it be better if we just mingled a little, said hello to a few people, and then left?"

"No, no, milady, that's completely out of the question," Sir Henry said. "This entire gathering was organized for the specific purpose of announcing your new status to the pillars of Dallas society. Why, his lordship has even invited important political dignitaries from your own state capital. Once an event like this has been planned and all the guests have arrived, it would be tantamount to social disaster to call it off. I must insist that you go through with it."

"Rest assured, Sir Henry, we will," Payne said. "Now go ahead and make your announcement. We'll be right behind you."

Certain that Lord Trefarrow would keep his word, Sir Henry turned and headed toward a small raised platform at the end of the room.

Feeling more nervous than she'd ever felt before, Chloe held Payne's arm in a death grip as she slowly walked beside him into the crowd's view. All of her life she had wanted to be a lady, and now that the time had finally arrived, she wished she were any-where else but here. Sir Henry had said "social disaster." Well, she would be a social *disgrace* if she couldn't remember the right thing to say or the right thing to do. Even worse was the fact of showing herself in public in her present condition.

"Ladies and gentlemen, may I have your attention," Sir Henry all but bellowed at the top of his lungs. All conversation slowly began to die as heads turned in his direction. "It is with the greatest pride and honor that I now present to you . . . the Tenth Earl of St. Keverne . . . the oldest son and heir of the late Garrett Trefa—"

"The oldest?" Emmaline said, unaware she had interrupted Sir Henry. "Why, you're not the oldest, Payne."

His shock registered instantly. "I'm not?" Once again, he suddenly realized, he was being denied something that he thought by right was his. But in this instance, he couldn't find it within him to harbor any trace of remorse.

"Land sakes, no."

"Oh, my God," Chloe said, breathing a sigh of relief as she moved back a pace to stand beside Emmaline.

Sir Henry stopped his announcement and turned to stare at Emmaline with alarm written across his face. "He's not the first born son of Garrett Trefarrow?"

"No, he's not," Emmaline said. "Prescott is."

"Prescott's my twin brother," Payne told Sir Henry.

"His older brother," Emmaline added. "But not by more than ten or fifteen minutes. At least, I think that's what Garrett told me. It's been so long ago, he might have said you boys were twenty minutes apart. But the fact still remains, Prescott's the oldest."

The animation left Sir Henry's face, leaving him almost white as a sheet.

"I apologize profusely for the mistake, Sir Henry," Payne said. "I didn't know these latest facts about my birth until now. I always thought I was the oldest."

"I quite understand," Sir Henry said, beads of perspiration forming on his upper lip. "Mistakes are made all the time. It's a good thing we caught the error now instead of later. Just tell me one thing, if you would."

"If I can," Payne said.

"Where the devil is your older brother?"

After a moment of silence, the sound of spurs jangling on the hardwood floor caught everyone's attention. Heads quickly turned from Sir Henry to stare at the ballroom entrance and the man who appeared there.

Windblown, unshaven, and garbed in his sheepskin-lined coat, work clothes, and mud-covered boots, Prescott frowned at the crowd as he waved his crumpled invitation in the air. "Sure hate to bother you folks this a-way," he said, "but who the Sam Hill is Earl St. Keverne?"

Payne laughed and shook his head. "There, Sir Henry, is your new Lord Trefarrow."

"Him?" Sir Henry asked in shocked disbelief.

"Yes, him. My brother, Prescott. The oldest son and heir."

Sir Henry felt his knees begin to wobble and quickly sat down on the edge of the raised platform. "Oh—my—God!"

Payne lifted an arm high and directed Prescott to come toward him. "Ladies and gentlemen," he said loudly, "the Tenth Earl of St. Keverne. Prescott Trefarrow."

What began as a small smattering of applause soon erupted into a thunderous roar as Prescott made his way across the ballroom floor. Men he'd known for many years, and even total strangers, reached out and slapped him on the back. Grinning broadly, Abner Harris grabbed hold of his hand and gave it a hearty shake. A few of the more world-traveled women actually curtsied.

Standing off by himself in one corner, observing the sudden change of events, Chauncey Blodgett visibly paled. The Cap'n's brother was the new Earl? Not the Cap'n himself? Heaven help him! The new life he'd planned for himself back home in England now wouldn't be worth spit.

By the time Prescott reached his brother's side, it was difficult to say if he was more embarrassed or confused. "What the hell's going on here, Payne?"

"We're introducing the new Earl of St. Keverne to the fine citizens of Dallas," Payne said.

"And the Earl is our kin, right?"

"That's right," Emmaline said, grinning, more pleased with the outcome than either Payne or Chloe.

"Well, where the hell is he?"

"He's standing right here," Payne said. "Congratulations, Prescott. You're the new Earl."

It took a moment for the message to sink into Prescott's befuddled brain. "Me?" he said. "I'm the new earl?"

"That's what I said."

Prescott grinned. "This is some kind of joke, right?"

"No, it's no joke. I couldn't be more serious." Payne pulled Chloe to his side and held her close. "Nor could I be more delighted. I've got a strong feeling that you're going to make a wonderful earl."

"I'm not going to make a dadblame thing. You're crazy. I ain't no earl."

Suddenly Sir Henry shot to his feet. "Oh, yes you are," he said. "You're the Tenth Earl of St. Keverne. Now start acting like it."

"Just who the hell are you, mister?" Prescott demanded, not liking the looks or the effrontery of the man glaring at him.

"Sir Henry Wilberforce, at your service"—Sir Henry visibly grimaced—"*milord*. Thank goodness I've a staff for situations such as this."

"Situations such as what?" Prescott asked.

"Transforming you from the scruffy barbarian you are now into an impeccable member of the peerage."

"Now listen here, Sir whoever you are, ain't no staff or nobody else gonna be transforming me into anything."

"Oh, yes, we will. Even if it takes us the next ten years."

Three thousand miles away in the county of Cornwall, England, in a small house on the edge of a great crumbling estate, a young woman abruptly awoke from a troubled sleep. Bathed in sweat, her long dark hair hanging in damp tangles about her slender shoulders, her dark gray eyes widened with fright as she bolted upright in her bed.

No, not again, she thought. He had haunted her dreams all her life, but she had never seen him so clearly; his chiseled, unshaven face; his lust-filled, green eyes glaring at her; his full mouth leering. His large, muscular body seemed ready to pounce on her, wrap her in a cage-like hold, and squeeze the very breath out of her.

God in heaven protect her. Her demon was going to come into her life and destroy her.

Payne held Chloe as close as her burgeoning stomach would allow and twirled her slowly about the floor of the ballroom.

"He doesn't look very happy, does he?" she asked.

"Who?" Oblivious to everyone around them, Payne didn't want to take his eyes off of her for one brief moment. Given the opportunity, he could feast on her beauty for the rest of his life and still never have enough of her.

"Prescott."

Payne reluctantly glanced across the ballroom. Standing beside a chattering, gesturing Sir Henry, his head lowered and occasionally nodding, Prescott looked positively morose, as if he'd lost everything he'd ever held dear. But better him than me, Payne thought. "No, he doesn't."

"I don't think he's as pleased with the inheritance as you were."

"Me, pleased? What makes you think I was pleased?"

"Well, you were, weren't you?"

"Not at all. The only reason I agreed to accept the damn thing in the first place was because I thought it was something you'd want me to do."

"Me?"

"Yes, you. You're the one who's always had her heart set on being a lady in every sense of the word, aren't you? If the title had been mine, then you'd have been Lady Chloe Trefarrow." He savored the sound on his tongue. "It's rather elegant and befitting, don't you think?"

Chloe groaned. "No. It doesn't sound right. Lady

Chloe Trefarrow. It doesn't feel right, either. The thought of being titled, of being something I'm not, gives me the shivers. Being ordinary Mrs. Payne Trefarrow will suit me just fine. But what about you? You're not upset about having the title slip through your fingers, are you?"

"Not in the least," he said. "You, better than anyone, should know how I feel about English nobility."

"I believe you once called them all hypocrites. Isn't that right?"

"With the odd exception or two, yes."

"But will you be happy here in Texas?"

Returning his gaze to her, he felt his heart overflow with love. "As long as I have you beside me, my darling, I can be happy anywhere."

"On the ranch, chasing strays from sunup to sundown and branding calves?"

"Anywhere."

"Riding the countryside in all kinds of weather?"

"As cold or hot as it gets, I won't care. We Trefarrows are a very sturdy lot."

"Coming home covered in sweat and dirt?"

"I've always liked a nice hot bath," he said.

"But you're so used to a more—oh, I don't know—a more civilized way of life."

"I like adventure and excitement, too. The question is, will you be happy with me?"

As the sound of music faded in her ears and the other dancers dissolved into a thick mist of oblivion around them, Chloe didn't think twice about propriety or convention or what anyone would think. She cupped Payne's face in her gloved hands, slowly brought his head closer to hers, and kissed him with all the love she possessed. Where their lips led, their bodies followed, coming together and causing heat to sear through her veins and the baby, their baby, to kick in her stomach.

"Does that answer your question?" she asked when she pulled back a moment later, seeing the love and passion emblazoned in the depths of his green eyes.

"More than adequately, my darling. More than adequately."

And to prove his point, he drew her to him and kissed her again. Let people talk, he thought. Chloe was his, and she always would be.

COMING NEXT MONTH

RAIN LILY by Candace Camp
Maggie Whitcomb's life changed when her shell-shocked husband returned from the Civil War. She nursed him back to physical health, but his mind was shattered. Maggie's marriage vows were forever, but then she met Reid Prescott, a drifter who took refuge on her farm and captured her heart. A heartwarming story of impossible love from bestselling author Candace Camp.

CASTLES IN THE AIR by Christina Dodd
The long-awaited, powerful sequel to the award-winning *Candle in the Window*. Lady Juliana of Moncestus swore that she would never again be forced under a man's power. So when the king promised her in marriage to Raymond of Avrache, Juliana was determined to resist. But had she met her match?

RAVEN IN AMBER by Patricia Simpson
A haunting contemporary love story by the author of *Whisper of Midnight*. Camille Avery arrives at the Nakalt Indian Reservation to visit a friend, only to find her missing. With the aid of handsome Kit Makinna, Camille becomes immersed in Nakalt life and discovers the shocking secret behind her friend's disappearance.

RETURNING by Susan Bowden
A provocative story of love and lies. From the Bohemian '60s to the staid '90s, *Returning* is an emotional roller-coaster ride of a story about a woman whose past comes back to haunt her when she must confront the daughter she gave up for adoption.

JOURNEY HOME by Susan Kay Law
Winner of the 1992 Golden Heart Award. Feisty Jessamyn Johnston was the only woman on the 1853 California wagon train who didn't respond to the charms of Tony Winchester. But as they battled the dangers of their journey, they learned how to trust each other and how to love.

KENTUCKY THUNDER by Clara Wimberly
Amidst the tumult of the Civil War and the rigid confines of a Shaker village, a Southern belle fought her own battle against a dashing Yankee—and against herself as she fell in love with him.

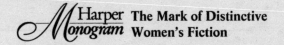

ANALISE

Analise Caldwell was the reigning belle of New Orleans. Disguised as a Confederate soldier, Union major Mark Schaeffer captured the Rebel beauty's heart as part of his mission. Stunned by his deception, Analise swore never to yield to the caresses of this Yankee spy...until he delivered an ultimatum.

ROSEWOOD

Millicent Hayes had lived all her life amid the lush woodland of Emmetsville, Texas. Bound by her duty to her crippled brother, the dark-haired innocent had never known desire...until a handsome stranger moved in next door.

BONDS OF LOVE

Katherine Devereaux was a willful, defiant beauty who had yet to meet her match in any man—until the winds of war swept the Union innocent into the arms of Confederate Captain Matthew Hampton.

LIGHT AND SHADOW

The day nobleman Jason Somerville broke into her rooms and swept her away to his ancestral estate, Carolyn Mabry began living a dangerous charade. Posing as her twin sister, Jason's wife, Carolyn thought she was helping her gentle twin. Instead she found herself drawn to the man she had so seductively deceived.

CRYSTAL HEART

A seductive beauty, Lady Lettice Kenton swore never to give her heart to any man—until she met the rugged American rebel Charles Murdock. Together on a ship bound for America, they shared a perfect passion, but danger awaited them on the shores of Boston Harbor.